Isabella was somehow even more beautiful than he remembered

And probably more treacherous, Marc reminded himself as he fought for control over his suddenly rampaging emotions and libido.

It had been six years since h

Six years since he'd held he

Six years since he'd kicke
his life.

And still he wanted her.

It came as something of a shock, considering he'd done his best not to think about her in the ensuing years. Sure, every once in a while something would come up and her face would flash through his mind. He'd be reminded of the scent, the taste, the feel of her. But through the years those instances had grown fewer and further between and his reaction to them—and her—had dimmed. Or so he'd thought.

All it had taken was a glimpse of her through the small window to throw him right back into the seething, tumultuous heat that had characterized so much of their relationship. At that moment, he hadn't cared about the future, or his family's company, which he had sacrificed so much for through the years. He hadn't cared about anything but getting to her…

* * *

Claimed
is part of the Diamond Tycoons duet—
Marc and Nic Durand are ruthless, sexy and powerful,
and only the women they love can tame them.

had seen her.

her, kissed her, made love to her.

walked her out of his apartment and

CLAIMED

BY
TRACY WOLFF

MILLS
BOON

Tracy Wolff collects books, English degrees and lipsticks, and has been known to forget where—and sometimes who—she is when immersed in a great novel. At six, she wrote her first short story—something with a rainbow and a prince—and at seven, she ventured into the wonderful world of girls' lit with her first Judy Blume novel. By ten, she'd read everything in the young-adult and classics sections of her local bookstore, so in desperation her mum started her on romance novels. And from the first page of the first book, Tracy knew she'd found her lifelong love. Tracy lives in Texas with her husband and three sons, where she pens romance novels and teaches writing at her local community college.

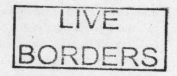

One

Isabella Moreno froze in the middle of her lecture—in the middle of a sentence, really—as the door in the back of her classroom opened and the president of the Gem Institute of America walked in. But it wasn't the presence of Harlan Peters that threw her off her game. She was a damn good professor and she knew it; a visit from her boss was no big deal. No, it was the tall, dark and silent man standing next to him that struck fear into her heart even as he sent shivers up and down her spine.

Don't forget gorgeous, she thought as she forced herself to continue her discussion of the cutting and polishing of off-shape sapphires. Her graduate students had begun turning to look at what had distracted her and it was only a matter of seconds before she would lose the attention of every female in the vicinity. Already, there were twitters and giggles coming from various corners of the room, and they didn't even know who the mystery man was yet.

Not that she did, either. Not really. Oh, she recognized him. It was hard to be in the gem industry for any length of time and not be able to identify Marc Durand, CEO of the second largest diamond exporter and jeweler in the country. His too-long black hair, bright blue eyes and fallen angel face were hard to miss…and even harder to ignore. But the look on that face, the glittering contempt in those distinctive eyes and the derisive twist of those full lips was not something she was used to seeing from him. They turned him into a stranger.

The Marc she knew—the Marc she'd once loved—had looked at her only with tenderness. With amusement. With love. At least until the end, when everything had fallen apart. But even then he'd shown some feelings. Rage, hurt, betrayal. It had nearly killed her to see those emotions on his face, and to know that she was responsible for them.

But the look on his face now—the derision, the scorn, the *ice*—turned him into someone new. Someone she didn't recognize; someone she certainly didn't want to know.

When they'd been together, their relationship had been characterized by heat, so much heat she'd often wondered how long it would take before she got burned. The answer, it turned out, had been six months, three weeks and four days, give or take a few hours.

Not that she'd been counting.

And not that she blamed him for how things had ended. How could she when the way things had gone down—the way the two of them had self-destructed—had been almost completely her fault?

Oh, he could have been kinder. She was the first to admit that tossing her onto the streets of New York City in the middle of the night, with nothing but the clothes on her back, was a hideous thing to do. But it wasn't as if she hadn't deserved it. Even now, there were nights she lay awake staring at the ceiling and wondering how she could have done what she had done. How she could have betrayed the man she'd loved so completely.

But that was the problem. She'd been caught between two men she loved, adored, would have done anything for, and because of that, she'd ruined everything. She'd known her father had stolen from him and though she'd tried to convince her dad to give the gems back, she hadn't told Marc who the thief was until it was nearly too late for him to salvage his business. And then she'd made the situation worse by begging Marc not to prosecute, and by admitting that when she'd sought him out at the gala where they'd first met she'd been planning to steal from him, too. Her plans had changed—her life had changed—once she'd spoken to him, once he'd looked at her with those crazy blue eyes of his, but—

Isabella shied away from the painful memories instinctively. Losing Marc in the middle of everything else had nearly brought her to her knees six years before. She'd be damned if seeing him again, after all this time, did the same thing. Especially here, in the middle of her first graduate seminar of the day.

Forcing her wandering mind back to the task at hand, she was mortified to realize every student in the class was looking between her and Marc. As was the college president. Despite the years that had passed, the connection between them was obvious, the tension a live wire that threatened to spark at any moment. Determined not to let that happen, and not to let the atmosphere in the room get any more awkward than it already was, Isabella forced herself back to her task.

The next part of her lecture was on the world's most famous sapphires and their locations. When she got to the part about the theft of the Robin's Egg Sapphire—one of the most expensive and sought after gems in the world—she did her best not to look at Marc.

But in the end, she couldn't help it. Her gaze was drawn to his, the magnetic force of his personality—his will—allowing her to do nothing else. She froze the second their eyes connected, the sardonic look he leveled at her as sharp as the finest hewn diamond. Marc knew what had happened to the Robin's Egg. He'd made it his business to know before he'd confronted her in their bedroom—his bedroom—that long-ago night.

"We're sorry to interrupt, Dr. Moreno," Harlan said from his spot in the back of the classroom. "I was just showing Mr. Durand around the campus. He's agreed to teach a miniseminar on diamond production starting in a few weeks and I wanted to give him the lay of the land. Please, carry on with your lecture. It's fascinating."

But it was too late for that. All around her, students murmured excitedly. Not that she blamed them. It wasn't every day that one of the world's largest producers and brokers of responsibly sourced diamonds agreed to speak to a bunch of first year graduate students. Still, she was the professor here. This was her lecture. She needed to regain control, if not for the class—which was only half-over—then because she refused to let Marc Durand have the upper hand for one second longer.

He'd taken everything from her. Or, to be completely honest, she'd given everything to him, only to have it all tossed back in her face. She'd deserved it then, and had paid for it royally. But that had been six years ago. Since then, she'd moved across the country and built an entirely new life for herself. She'd be damned if she let him come in here and screw that up for her, too.

Refusing to let Marc see just how much his presence

here messed with her mind, she continued on with her lecture. Eventually the students settled down again and Marc and Harlan slipped out a lot more unobtrusively than they'd entered.

If anyone asked her what she spoke about for the last twenty minutes of class, Isabella wouldn't have been able to tell them. Her mind was far away, wrapped up in a past she regretted bitterly but couldn't change and the man who had altered the entire course of her life. She must have covered pretty well, though, because the students didn't call her on anything. Then again, they'd all been so enamored of Marc Durand that they probably weren't focusing on what she had to say, anyway.

Finally, the interminable class drew to an end and she dismissed her students. It was her usual habit to hang out in the classroom for a few minutes to give the students an opportunity to ask questions or chat her up about whatever was on their minds. But today she didn't have it in her to stay there one second longer than absolutely necessary, not when her insides felt scraped raw and she was certain any wrong move would shatter the peace she had worked so hard to achieve. The peace she had finally found.

Scooping up her books, and the papers her students had turned in that day, Isabella made a beeline for the door. She was parked around back. If she could get to the side exit, she could be in her car and off campus in less than five minutes. Then it would be just her and the convertible, the infinite ocean to her left as she followed the winding, waterfront freeway home.

Except she never got to her car, never even made it to the side door she was so desperate to reach. Instead, a strong, calloused hand grabbed her elbow as she tried to hurry down the back hallway. Though she was facing the other direction, she didn't need to see him to know who had grabbed her. Her knees turned to gelatin at that first touch, her heart beating wildly out of control. There would be no escape then. No drive by the ocean. No chance to put her thoughts in order before this confrontation.

Not that she was surprised. From the moment she'd looked up and seen Marc in the back of her classroom, she'd known this was inevitable. She'd simply hoped to put it off a little, until she could think about him without losing her ability to breathe. Of course, she'd already had six years and hadn't been able to change that, so another couple of days probably wouldn't matter.

Besides, if he was going to destroy everything she'd tried to build for herself with her new name and new identity and new, law-abiding life—then she might as well find out right now. Worrying about it would only make her crazy.

Bracing herself, she put on her best poker face before slowly, slowly, turning to face him. And if her knees trembled as she did, it was nobody's business but her own.

She was somehow even more beautiful than he'd remembered. And probably more treacherous, Marc reminded himself as he fought for control over his suddenly rampaging emotions and libido.

It had been six years since he'd seen her.

Six years since he'd held her, kissed her, made love to her.

Six years since he'd kicked her out of his apartment and his life.

And still he wanted her.

It came as something of a shock, considering he'd done his best not to think about her in the ensuing years. Sure, every once in a while her face would flash through his mind. Something would remind him of the scent, the taste, the feel of her. But through the years those instances had grown fewer and farther between and his reaction to them—and to her—had dimmed. Or so he'd thought.

All it had taken was a glimpse of her gorgeous red hair, her warm brown eyes, from the small window embedded in the classroom door to throw him right back into the seething, tumultuous heat that had characterized so much of their relationship. He hadn't cared about the president of the college, hadn't cared about the future he had so carefully mapped out for Bijoux, the family company he had sacrificed so much for through the years. He hadn't cared about the workshop GIA had hired him to teach now that he had moved Bijoux's headquarters to the West Coast. To be honest, he hadn't cared about anything but getting into that classroom to see if his mind was playing tricks on him.

Six years ago he had kicked Isa Varin—now, apparently, Isabella Moreno—out of his life in the cruelest manner possible. He didn't regret making her leave—how could he when she'd betrayed him so completely?—but in the time since, he had regretted how he'd done it. When he'd come to his senses and sent his driver to find her and deliver her things, including her purse and cell phone and some money, she had vanished into thin air. He'd looked for her for years, simply to assuage his conscience and prove to himself that nothing untoward had happened to her that night, but he'd never found her.

Now he knew why. The very passionate, very beautiful, very bewitching Isa Varin had ceased to exist. In her place was this buttoned-down professor, her voice and face as cool and sharp as any diamond his mines had ever produced. Only the hair—that glorious, red hair—was the same. Isabella Moreno wore it in a tight braid down her back instead of in the wild curls favored by his Isa, but he would know the color anywhere.

Black cherries at midnight.

Wet garnets shining in the filtered light of a full moon.

And when her eyes had met his over the heads of her students, he'd felt a punch in his gut—in his groin—that couldn't be denied. Only Isa had ever made his body react so powerfully. So instantaneously.

He'd ditched the GIA president as soon as he could, then had rushed back to make sure he caught Isa before she could slip away. And still he'd almost missed her. Not that he was surprised. She did come from a long line of cat burglars, after all. He knew from experience that nine times out of ten, if she didn't want to be caught, she wouldn't be.

As he waited for her to speak, he couldn't help wondering what he was doing here. Why he'd caught up with her. What he wanted from her. Because the truth was, he didn't know. He knew only that seeing her, talking to her, was a compulsion he couldn't resist.

"Hello, Marc." She raised her face to his, her voice and countenance as composed as he had ever seen them. He felt a brief lick of something deep inside—a feeling that made him uncomfortable for the simple reason that he couldn't identify it. So he ignored it, concentrating instead on her as their gazes met in a clash of heat and memories.

One look into her eyes—dark, endless pools of melted chocolate—used to bring him to his knees. But those days were long gone. Her betrayal had destroyed any faith he might have had in her. He'd been weak once, had fallen for the innocence she could project with a look, a touch, a whisper. He wouldn't make that mistake again. He would satisfy his curiosity, find out why she was at GIA, and then he would walk away.

As he stared down at her, those same eyes were alive with so many emotions he couldn't begin to sort them all out. Her face could be as unemotional as she wanted it to be, her body as ice-cold as it had once been fiery-hot, but her eyes didn't lie. Isa was as disturbed by this chance meeting as he was.

The realization had something relaxing deep inside him and he felt the power shift sizzle in the air around them. She'd once had the upper hand in their relationship because he'd trusted her blindly, loved her so deeply that he had never conceived that she would one day betray him.

But those days were long gone. Isa could pretend to be the straitlaced, boring gem professor all she wanted. He knew the truth and he would never be stupid enough to let his guard down around her again.

"Hello, Isabella." He made certain his face showed only sardonic amusement. "Fancy meeting you here."

"Yes, well, I go where the jewels are."

"Don't I know it?" Deliberately he glanced at the wall across from them, where one of the most expensive opal necklaces ever created was displayed behind glass. "The president tells me you've been teaching here three years. Yet there've been no heists. You must be slipping."

Her eyes flashed furiously, but her voice was controlled when she answered, "I'm a member of the GIA faculty. Helping to ensure the safety of every gem on this campus falls in my job description."

"And we all know how seriously you take your job... and your loyalties."

The mask cracked and he got a glimpse of her fury before she shored her defenses back up. "Is there something you need, Marc?" She glanced pointedly at his hand, which was still wrapped tightly around her elbow.

"I thought we could catch up. For old times' sake."

"Yes, well, it turns out the old times weren't all that good. So, if you'll excuse me—" She started to wrest her elbow from his grasp, but he tightened his fingers. Despite the anger that ran through him like molten lava at her words, he wasn't ready to let her go just yet.

"I don't excuse you." He put a wealth of meaning behind those four words, and saw with satisfaction that she hadn't missed his point.

"I'm sorry to hear that. But I've got an appointment in half an hour. I don't want to be late."

"Yeah, I hear fences take exception to lateness."

This time the cool facade did more than crack. She shoved against his chest with one hand at the same time she wrenched her elbow from his grasp. "Six years ago I put up with all your vile insinuations and accusations because I felt like I deserved them. But that was a long time ago and I'm done now. I have a new life—"

"And a new name."

"Yes." She eyed him warily. "I needed distance."

"That's not the way I remember it." She'd chosen her father over him, even after the old man had stolen from him. It wasn't a slight Marc had any intention of forgetting.

"No surprise there."

The insult—in her words and her tone—had him narrowing his eyes. "What's that supposed to mean?"

"Exactly what it sounded like. I'm not big on subterfuge."

Though it made him sound like an arrogant ass, he couldn't help throwing her words back at her. "Again, that's not the way I remember it."

"Of course not." She straightened her spine and lifted her chin. "Then again, you've always been more about perception than truth. Right, Marc?"

He hadn't thought it was possible for him to get any angrier. Not when his stomach already churned with it, his jaw aching from how tightly he was clenching his teeth.

Then again, she'd always brought out strong emotions in him. At one time, they'd even been good emotions.

Those days were long gone, though, and he wouldn't let her drag him back there. The Marc who had loved Isa Varin had been a weak fool—something he'd sworn he'd never be again as he'd watched security escort her from his building.

"That seems an awful lot like the pot calling the kettle black, Isabella." He put added emphasis on her new name, could see by the darkening of her eyes that the irony wasn't lost on her.

"On that note, I think it's time for me to leave." She started to step around him, but he blocked her path. He didn't know what was driving him, only that he wasn't ready to watch her walk away from him again. Not when she looked so cool and collected and he felt…anything but. And not now that he'd finally found her.

"Running away?" he taunted. "Why am I not surprised? It does run in the family, after all."

For a second, hurt flashed in her eyes. But it was gone so fast he couldn't be sure he hadn't imagined it. And still, a little seed of guilt lingered. At least until she said, "Whatever you're doing here, whatever you think you're going to get, isn't going to happen. You need to get out of my way, Marc."

It was an ultimatum, for all that it was said in a polite tone. He'd never been one to respond well to such things. Still, her fire excited him, turned him on, as nothing had in six long years. His reaction pissed him off, but he'd be damned before he let her see that. Not when she was there, in front of him, when he'd been so certain he would never see her again. He wasn't ready to let her walk out of his life for another six years, not when he still had so many unanswered questions. And not when he still wanted her so badly that every muscle in his body ached with it.

So instead of doing what she asked, he lifted a brow and leaned casually against the cool, tile wall behind him. Then asked the question he knew would change everything. "Or what?"

Two

Isa stared at Marc in disbelief. Had he seriously just asked her that? As if they were kids playing a game of double dog dare and it was now her turn to up the ante? Too bad for him that she'd given up childish games the same night she'd walked forty city blocks through sleet and freezing rain without so much as a coat to shield her from the weather. She'd moved past that night, had made a new, better life for herself here under a name no one in the industry could trace to her father. There was no way she would let him mess all that up.

"I don't have time for this," she told him with an annoyed snarl. "And while I'd like to say it was nice seeing you again, we both know that I'd be lying. So—" she gave him a mock salute "—have a nice life."

Turning on her heel, she once again started down the empty hallway. This time she only made it a couple of steps before he wrapped one large, calloused hand around her wrist and tugged her to a stop.

"You don't actually think it's going to be that easy, do you?"

His rough fingers stroked the delicate skin at the inside of her wrist. It was a familiar caress, one he'd done so often in their months together that she'd felt his phantom stroking in that exact spot for months—years—after they'd broken up. Even now, with everything that had passed between them, with the power he held to ruin her life all over again, her traitorous heart beat uncontrollably fast at the light touch.

Furious with herself for being so easy—and at him for being so damn appealing—she yanked her arm from his grasp with more force than his gentle hold demanded. She ended up stumbling back a couple steps before she could catch herself, a reaction that just annoyed her more. Why was she constantly making a fool of herself in front of this man?

Infusing her voice with as much frigidness as she could muster, she forced herself to meet his gaze. "I don't know what you're talking about."

Those glorious eyes of his mocked her. "Still a good liar, I see." He reached out and ran a hand over her braid. "Nice to see some things haven't changed."

"I never lied to you."

"But you didn't tell me the truth, either. Even when doing so would have saved my company and me one hell of a lot of time, money and embarrassment."

Old guilt swamped her at his words. She tried to push it away, but it was too constant a companion for her to do anything more than invite it in like she always did. Still, she refused to take all the blame in this situation. Not when the tender man she used to know had vanished like so much smoke. "Yes, well, you seemed to have landed on your feet."

"As have you." He very deliberately glanced into the classroom she had just vacated. "A professor at the GIA, one of the world's leading experts on conflict-free diamonds. I have to admit, when you disappeared so completely, I thought you'd decided to follow in your father's footsteps."

Isa drew in a sharp breath, horrified that his words still had the ability to hurt her, even after all this time. "I'm not a thief." She'd meant the words to sound scornful, but her voice broke in the middle of the sentence.

His look darkened and for a second, just a second, she thought he would reach out to her. To touch her like he used to—with so much tenderness that she couldn't feel anything but cherished. Every nerve ending in her body tingled at the thought and despite his hurtful words—despite everything that had passed between them—she almost melted into him. She had to lock her knees, in fact, to keep from leaning on him as she had so many times before.

But then he cleared his throat and the spell was broken. All the bad memories poured into her, overwhelming the good from one breath to the next. Tears burned behind her eyes, but she refused to shed them. Refused to be so weak in front of him. Besides, she'd already cried all the tears over him she ever would. Their relationship was in the past and she was going to keep it there.

She stepped back and this time he didn't pursue her. He just watched her with a smirk on his face. She supposed that meant the next move was hers. So be it.

Taking a deep breath, she looked him square in the eyes and did the only thing she knew how to do at this point. She opened herself up and told him the truth. "Look, I know you want your pound of flesh, and God knows, you deserve it. I'm sorry, so, so sorry, for everything my father put you through. But he's gone now and there's nothing else I can do to make things right. Can you accept my heartfelt apology and then we can both move on? You teach your class, I'll teach mine. And the past can stay dead."

He didn't move, didn't so much as blink, but Isa swore she felt him recoil at her words. She waited nervously for him to say something, anything, but as the seconds ticked by and nothing was forthcoming, she grew more and more nervous. To be watched by Marc Durand was to be watched by a hungry predator, one whose teeth and claws, speed and intellect, gave him an advantage over every other species on the savannah. Or the beach, she admitted ruefully, looking out at the ocean through the windows at the end of the hall.

She shifted under his scrutiny, uncomfortably aware that the last time he'd spent this much time looking at her she'd been naked and begging for him to make love to her. And while sleeping with him was the farthest thing from her mind right now, her traitorous body still remembered all the pleasure he'd brought her. Pleasure she had never seen the likes of before or since.

Her nipples hardened at the thought and her cheeks burned in humiliation. He hated her, was disgusted by her very presence. She'd spent six years in a new life, trying to forget him. And still she couldn't help fantasizing about what it felt like to be in his arms. Marc was an incredible lover—passionate, unselfish, fun—and the months she'd spent with him had been the best of her life.

But they'd been followed by the worst, lowest months, she reminded herself bitterly. She needed to remember that. Just because her body was still attuned to him, still wanted him, didn't mean the rest of her did. Sexual chemistry had only gotten them so far, after all.

He still hadn't said anything and the sensually charged

silence between them grew more and more uncomfortable—at least on her part.

Isa squared her shoulders, cleared her throat and said, "I really am late. I need to go."

She hated that it sounded like she was asking his permission, but the connection that had sprung up between them was such that she wasn't sure she'd be able to walk away if he didn't do something to help her sever it.

"There's a cocktail party tonight," he said abruptly. "In the gem gallery."

Surprised by the bizarre change in subject, she nonetheless nodded. "Yes. It's the spring faculty mixer."

"Go with me."

Isa shook her head, certain she must have heard him wrong. Marc couldn't possibly have asked her to attend the faculty cocktail party as his date? Why would he? Unless he planned to humiliate her there in front of all her colleagues.

The Marc she used to know, the one she'd been hopelessly in love with, would never do anything like that. But she hadn't seen that man in six long years and this one—hard, angry, uncompromising—looked like he was capable of anything. She wanted no part of him, no matter what her pleasure-starved body said.

"I can't."

"Why not?" It was obvious he didn't like her answer.

"I already have a date." The words poured from her lips before she had a clue she was going to say them. And while they weren't a lie, they weren't strictly the truth, either. She and Gideon, another professor, had made plans to go together weeks ago. They were just friends, though, and she knew Gideon wouldn't mind if she canceled on him.

But she would mind. She could barely stand the fifteen-minute conversation she and Marc were having in the hall. She couldn't even imagine what would happen to her—or the new identity she'd worked so hard for—if she spent an entire evening in his company. If she gave in to the attraction that still flared between them. Besides, she might be insane enough to still be attracted to him, but her days of being his whipping girl were long over. She was nobody's masochist.

"Who is he?" The words grated out from between his clenched teeth.

"Gideon. No one you know. But maybe I'll see you there."

She forced a smile she was far from feeling. She even gave a little wave before she started down the corridor for the third time in the past twenty minutes. This time he let her go.

By the time she opened the side door and stepped into the early spring sunlight, she'd almost convinced herself she was happy about that fact.

"Who pissed in your cornflakes?" Nic demanded.

Marc looked up from his computer with a scowl. Per his usual modus operandi at Bijoux's new California headquarters, his little brother had barged unannounced into Marc's office. Normally Marc didn't mind, but right now, just hours after that conversation with Isa, dealing with Nic was the last thing he wanted to do. Not when his brother was unusually perceptive—not to mention his wicked and slightly strange sense of humor. It was a dangerous combination, one that usually required Marc to be on his toes if he had any hope of staying one step ahead. And today, he didn't have it in him to even try.

"I don't know what you're talking about."

"Sure you do. Look at your face."

"That's pretty much impossible considering there's no mirror in here."

"Why, oh why, did I get stuck with a brother with absolutely no imagination?" Nic demanded, looking upward as he did—as if he expected the universe to answer his question. Frankly, Marc thought Nic had a better chance of finding the answer written on the ceiling than waiting for divine intervention, but he didn't mention that. It would only give Nic more ammunition.

Instead, Marc answered the question. "So that you'd look like the fun brother."

"It was a rhetorical question. Besides, I don't have to look like the fun brother. I *am* the fun brother," Nic told him with a roll of his eyes. "But, fine. You can't see your face. I can. And let me tell you, you look like someone…" He paused as if searching for the perfect descriptor.

"Pissed in my cornflakes?"

"Exactly. So what's up? More trouble with De Beers?"

"No more than usual."

"The new mine?"

"Nope. I just heard back from Heath and things are going well. Despite it being brand-new, we should be turning a very tidy profit by the fall."

"See? Who says you can't make money *and* responsibly source diamonds?"

"Greedy bastards with no heart or social conscience?"

Nic snorted. "Again, it was a rhetorical question. But good answer, anyway."

"That's why I get paid the big bucks."

Marc turned back to his computer, tried to concentrate on the spreadsheet that was open on the screen. Normally, this stuff was like catnip to him, but today looking at the production values of the various mines was nothing but an annoyance. Especially when he couldn't stop thinking about Isa—and the mystery man who was escorting her to the cocktail party. Was he a friend? A boyfriend? A lover? The last thought had his hands curling into fists and his teeth clenching so tightly that he could almost feel the enamel being ground away.

"See, there!" Nic said. "That's the look I'm talking about."

"Again, can't see it."

"Again, I can, so tell me what's causing it. If we're not losing money and we're not yet in our annual power struggle with De Beers, then what the hell has you so freaked out?"

Marc glared at him, offended. "I don't get freaked out."

"Well, you sure aren't freaked in." Nic crossed to the bar in the corner, pulled a couple of sodas out of the fridge and tossed one Marc's way.

"What the hell does that even mean?"

"It means I'm going to keep bugging you until you tell me what's wrong, so you might as well spit it out. Otherwise, you'll never get back to that spreadsheet of yours."

"What makes you think I'm looking at a spreadsheet?"

"Face it. You're always looking at a spreadsheet." Nic settled back into one of the visitors' chairs and kicked his feet up onto Marc's desk. "Spill."

Marc pretended to focus on his computer screen, but Nic didn't get the hint. Or if he did, he totally ignored it. Silence stretched between them, broken only by Nic's occasional swallow and the low, clicking sounds that came from Marc's gritted teeth. Finally, in the hopes of saving himself a hefty dental bill, Marc did what his brother asked and spilled.

"I ran into Isa today."

Nic's feet hit the ground with a thud as he sat straight up. "Isa Varin?"

"Isabella Moreno now."

"She's married?" He whistled low and long. "No wonder you're in a foul mood."

"She's not married!" Marc snapped out. "But even if she was, it's no business of mine."

"Oh, certainly not," Nic mocked. "You've just spent the last six years dating every redhead you could find in a ridiculous attempt to replace her. But her marital status is none of your business."

"I've never—" He broke off midrant. He wanted to tell his brother that he was dead wrong, that Marc hadn't done anything of the sort. But as he thought back over the last few women he'd dated, Marc realized that Nic might have a point.

He'd never noticed before but all the women in his life *were* redheads. Tall, slender redheads with delicate bones and great smiles. Hell. Had he subconsciously been trying to find a replacement for Isa all these years? He'd never thought so, but the evidence was hard to ignore. Damn it.

"So, why the name change if she isn't married?"

He didn't know, but he was going to damn sure find out. Still, he told his brother what she'd told him. "She said she wanted to start over."

Nic made a sympathetic noise. "I bet."

He didn't like Nic's tone. "What's that supposed to mean?"

"What do you think it means? Things didn't exactly end well between you. I know when you kicked her out, it was what you felt you had to do."

"It was what I had to do! Do you really think there was another option?" Marc waved the question away before Nic could answer it—they'd been over this ground hundreds of times since that night. "Still. I've paid a hell of a lot of money to private investigators through the years.

You would think one of them would have turned up this name change."

"Not if she didn't do it legally."

"It'd have to be legal. She's employed under the name."

"Have you forgotten who her father is? With the kind of contacts he had, she could buy herself a whole new identity without breaking a sweat."

"Isa wouldn't do that." But even as the words left his mouth, Marc wasn't so sure. What his brother was saying made a lot of sense. After all, she'd lied before. Stolen before. How else could the daughter of a world famous jewel thief—a woman who had been a thief in her own right— end up teaching at the world headquarters of the Gemological Institute of America—even if she was one of the best in her field? Working there, she had access to some of the finest gems in the world—they rotated through the institute on loan on a pretty regular basis, after all.

And while she might not be a thief, her father's reputation would be more than enough to keep the doors at GIA firmly closed to her. Unless she had done exactly what his brother surmised. Because if she'd changed her name legally, there was no doubt that the detectives Marc had hired to look for her in those first couple of years would have caught it.

"So, how's she doing anyway?" Nic broke into Marc's musings. "Is she okay?"

"She's fine." Better than fine. She'd looked amazing— healthy, happy, glowing even. At least until she'd seen him. Then the light inside her had died.

"I'm glad. Despite the debacle with her father—and despite what happened between the two of you—I always liked her."

So had he. So much so that Marc had asked her to be his wife, despite his determination before he'd met her to never marry. It wasn't as if his parents had set such a great example for him and Nic in that department.

"So, did you ask her out?"

"Did I—? Are you kidding me? Aren't you the one who was just reminding me how badly things ended between us?"

"You were a bit of an ass, no getting around that. But Isa has a big heart. I bet she'll forgive you—"

"I'm not the one who needs forgiveness in this equation. She nearly ruined all our plans for Bijoux!"

"Her *father* nearly ruined all our plans, not her."

"She knew about everything."

"Yeah, but what was she supposed to say? 'By the way, honey, that diamond heist you're so worked up about? The one that might bankrupt your business? I think my daddy did it.'"

"That would have been nice. So that I didn't have to hear about it from the head of our security team."

"Cut her a break. She was twenty-one years old and probably scared to death."

Marc frowned at him. "You're pretty damn understanding all of a sudden. If I remember correctly, you were calling for her head when everything was going down."

"Her father's head," Nic corrected. "I thought he should fry for what he did, but you were the one who refused to press charges. And who pulled every string you could to get him out of trouble. Hell, you're still paying back favors from that whole debacle."

Nic was right. Marc was—and the favors were often uncomfortable ones. More than once, he'd wondered what the hell he'd been thinking. Why had he worked so hard to keep Isa's father out of prison after what the man had done? But then he'd seen her face in his mind's eye—pale, drawn, terrified—and known that he hadn't had a choice.

Getting up, Marc crossed to one of the two picture windows that formed the outside walls of his corner office. Beyond the glass, he had a gorgeous view of the Pacific Ocean as it crashed against the rocky shoreline. He studied it for long seconds, letting the roll of powerful waves calm some of the annoyance—and confusion—inside of him. Moving Bijoux's North American headquarters to San Diego six months ago was one of his smarter moves. He'd done it because of the proximity to the world headquarters of GIA, but access to the ocean was a very nice side benefit.

"He was a sick, old man. Salvatore was dead before the year was out, anyway. He didn't need to spend the last couple months of his life in a cell."

"You did that for Isa, and because underneath that crusty exterior you've actually got a soft heart—"

"Crusty? You make me sound like I'm ninety!"

"You said it, I didn't." Nic's smartphone alarm went off and he sprung to his feet. "I've got to go. There's a marketing meeting starting in five minutes that I want to sit in on."

"Everything going okay with the new campaign?" Marc asked. He was the CEO of Bijoux, the guy who handled all the business stuff—governmental contracts, mining, employees, distribution. But his brother was the creative genius in the family. He handled marketing, public relations and sales. Anything that had to do with Bijoux's public image. And he did it brilliantly, something Marc appreciated because it gave him time to concentrate on what he loved best—growing his family's gem company into the largest socially and environmentally responsible diamond company in the business.

"It's going great," Nic said dismissively. "I just like to

be at all the meetings to hear the ideas, see what's going around. Get a sense of the zeitgeist, I guess you could say."

"And they call me the control freak in the family?"

"Because you are. While I am merely conscientious." Nic crumpled up his empty soda can and shot it toward the recycle bin in the back corner of Marc's office. "Yeah, baby, nothing but net."

Marc bit his tongue to keep from telling Nic that there was no net. God forbid he get another lecture on not being the "fun" brother.

Nic made his way toward the exit, then stopped at the doorway and turned back to Marc.

"Seriously, bro. Fate's given you another chance with Isa. You should take it."

"I don't believe in fate. And I don't want another chance with her."

"You sure about that?"

"Positive." After everything that had gone down between them? The last thing he wanted was to give Isa another shot at screwing up his business...or his heart.

Did he want to sleep with her again? Hell, yeah. What man wouldn't? She was beautiful when she was aroused. Not to mention sexy as hell—especially when she screamed his name while she came. Being with her had been the best sex he'd ever had.

Then again, she'd always been more the type to make love than have sex. He'd loved that about her when they'd been together. Now, however, it was nothing but a pain in his ass—not to mention other, more notable parts of his anatomy. He didn't do the whole tenderness thing anymore.

"Well, then, forget about her," Nic told him practically. "The past is dead. You've both moved on. Keep it that way."

"I intend to."

And yet, Marc couldn't help thinking about Isa—
and about her date to the party that night. *Gideon.* Just
the name set his teeth on edge. What kind of name was
Gideon, anyway? Who the hell was he? And what the hell
did he want with Isa?

An image of her standing in front of her classroom
flashed through Marc's mind. Her eyes alight with the
thrill of talking about her favorite subject, her skin flushed
and glowing. Her miles of red hair locked down in that
ridiculous braid, her gorgeous body hidden, and yet revealed, by the tailored pants and turtleneck sweater she'd
been wearing.

When he'd known her, she'd been all warm, sweet passion—for life, for gems, for *him.* Now she was a contradic-
tion, a bunch of stopping-and-going that, combined, made
for an even more intriguing woman. One that he couldn't
help wanting despite his anger, and her betrayal.

No, Isa hadn't been eager to renew their acquaintance
that afternoon. But he'd seen the way she looked at him, the
way she swayed toward him when he touched her. Maybe
getting her into bed again wouldn't be nearly as challenging as it once had been. The thought made him smile. Because once he got her there, he would take her—over and
over and over again. Every way a man could take a woman.

He'd get her out of his system once and then, finally,
he'd be able to put her—and all their unfinished business—behind him once and for all.

Three

He was there. Marc. Though she hadn't run into him yet, Isa had felt him watching her from the moment she and Gideon had walked in the door of the faculty mixer. It had always been that way with them—she couldn't help but sense Marc whenever he was anywhere close to her.

"Can I get you a drink?" Gideon asked, his mouth inches from her ear. She knew he did it because it was hard to hear in the gallery—overlaying the soft music was the sound of a hundred voices, all vying to be heard—but still, feeling his warm breath so close to her cheek and neck unnerved her. Made her feel a little uncomfortable.

Which was stupid. Gideon was her friend and occasional movie/mixer date. It had been that way since they'd met three years before and never once had he given any indication that he wanted more. They were buddies, pals, each other's port in a storm. So why was she suddenly feeling so awkward around him?

A shiver ran down her spine, and with it came the answer to her question. Because Marc was there, watching her. And though she hadn't so much as caught a glimpse of him, she knew he wouldn't like the fact that Gideon was so close to her, his face next to hers, his hand resting softly at the center of her back.

As soon as the thought came, she beat it down. She and Marc had been over for six long years. He probably couldn't care less that she was here with Gideon—any more than she cared who he was with. Any feeling she had otherwise was probably just a leftover from when they had been together. Back then, Marc had been extremely possessive of her. But then, she'd felt the same way about him.

"Isabel?" Gideon's smooth voice dropped an octave as concern clouded his bright green eyes. "Are you all right? You've seemed off ever since I picked you up."

He was right. She had been off—and not just for the past half hour. She'd been feeling strange ever since her encounter with Marc in the hallway earlier that day. And now, knowing that he was here made her feel a million times more off-kilter.

To make up for it, she flashed Gideon a wide, warm smile. "I'm sorry. I've just been caught up in my thoughts. But I'll put them away for now, I promise."

He grinned back at her. "Careful with that smile, woman. It's a lethal weapon." His own grin faded. "You know, if you need anything you can count on me, right?"

"Of course. But I'm fine. I swear." She leaned into him, gave him a brief kiss on his cheek. "Though I am thirsty."

"Your usual?" he asked, steering her toward a group of colleagues that they were both friendly with.

"That would be perfect."

After depositing her among their friends, Gideon took off toward the bar. Isa tried to relax, to enjoy the ebb and flow of the quick-witted conversation she was usually right in the middle of. But she couldn't. Not when it felt as if Marc's eyes were boring holes right between her shoulder blades.

"So, how was the ballet you went to last week?" asked Maribel, one of the other professors at the GIA. "I'm so sad I had to miss it."

"Yes, well, I think an appointment with your obstetrician trumps an afternoon at the theater," Isa told her. "But the ballet was great. It was student written and performed, but you would have never known it. The San Diego Ballet Academy has a really good program."

"Well the next time one of those afternoons of student work comes along, I want in. Even if it means I have to get a babysitter." Mirabel softly rubbed her swollen tummy.

"How is the baby? And how are you feeling?"

"The baby's fine and I feel gigantic. I can't believe I have two more months of this to go."

"Hopefully it will go fast," her husband, Michael, told her as he gently rubbed her back.

She snorted in response. "Really? And you know this because you're carrying around a beach ball in your stomach?"

They all laughed, even Michael, and Isa felt the tension finally begin to drain from her shoulders. Yes, Marc was here but there was no reason they had to do anything more than exchange a polite hello. If that.

Gideon came back with her drink—a crisp, cold glass of Pinot Grigio—but before she could do more than smile her thanks at him, she heard the dean's voice right behind her. "Good evening, everyone. I'd like to introduce you to the newest guest lecturer on our faculty."

The man hadn't even said Marc's name before her stomach dropped to her toes. Because, really, who else would the dean be personally escorting around the cocktail party besides the CEO of the second largest diamond conglomerate in the world?

Her friends welcomed Marc easily, much to her dismay. Not that she could have expected any differently. They were a fabulous, friendly, nosy bunch of people and any new lecturer—especially one of Marc's stature—would be of interest to them.

He fit in well, of course. Remembered everyone's name on the first go round. Told a quick story with a punch line that had everyone roaring with laughter. Asked appropriate questions that gave everyone in the group a chance to show off a little.

In other words, Marc was in perfect social mode—the one he slipped into so easily when he was doing the party circuit and the one she'd never been able to perfect, no matter how hard she'd tried. When they'd been together, she'd wanted to be the fiancée he could be proud of. She had tried so hard to be as charming and at ease as Marc was in the various social situations he'd thrust her into. But the fact of the matter was, she was shy.

She loved talking to her students, loved talking to her friends. But making small talk with strangers? Struggling to come up with something to say that would hold people's attention—especially the people Marc introduced her to? Those situations had made her intensely uncomfortable to the point that she would have anxiety attacks hours before they went out.

She'd never told Marc, of course. Had never wanted him to feel ashamed of her or find her lacking. She'd loved him so much, had been so desperate to be Mrs. Marc Durand, that she would have done anything he asked of her. Had done anything, everything—except betray her father.

And that one decision, that one stand against Marc, had cost her everything.

Anger churned in her stomach, combined with the wine and nerves until she felt more than a little nauseous. Gideon noticed that something was wrong right away. He put an arm around her waist and pulled her against him.

"You okay?" he asked softly, his lips pressed against her ear so no one else could hear. He was one of the few people she'd ever trusted with her social anxiety. It was one of the reasons he insisted on being her escort to parties, and why he always made sure she was with friends before he left her side to get drinks or anything else.

"I need some air," she whispered back.

"The terrace is open. I'll take you."

"No, I'm fine." He'd been enjoying the conversation immensely—the talk of ballet had turned into a spirited discussion of San Diego's arts scene—and it wasn't fair to take him away from it. "Stay. I'll be back in a couple of minutes."

He frowned. "Are you sure?"

"Positive." She leaned into him a little more, gave him a quick hug. Then excused herself to use the ladies' room.

As conversations ebbed and flowed around her, Isa made her way to the wide-open doors at the end of the room. They let out onto the terrace that overlooked the ocean and as she got closer she could feel the sea breeze sweeping through the room. It was a little chilly, a little salty and exactly what she needed to help her get her head back on straight. And to forget about Marc and the painful past she had no hope of changing.

Slipping around the last group of people, she walked straight out to the darkest part of the terrace. Bracing her hands on the iron fence that closed it in, she closed her eyes and let herself breathe. In, out. In, out. In, out. Already, she felt calmer. More in control. She wondered how long she could stay out here before Gideon came looking for her.

She was gorgeous. Dressed in a simple purple sheath that stood out like a beacon amid the sea of black cocktail dresses, she was as sexy, as sensual, as he'd remembered. More so even, maturity lending a lushness to her face and figure that hadn't been there before.

It was a lushness that clown Gideon had noticed. One he'd taken every chance to brush against or touch or hold. Standing there, doing nothing, while that bastard had pawed Isa had been one of the hardest things Marc had ever done. Especially when he'd wanted nothing more than to smash his fist into the jerk's face.

Only the fact that Isa seemed to like Gideon's touch had stopped him, even as it had cranked his anger into a lethal place. One where the six years between now and when she'd been his had melted into nothing, like snow on the first warm spring day.

He watched her weave her way through the bodies, watched as she slipped out onto the terrace, finding a dark corner with only a little light to stand in.

Watched as she took a deep, shuddering breath. Then another and another.

Her beautiful breasts trembled against the deep V of her neckline and Marc's fingers itched—ached—with the need to touch her there. To hold the warm, firm weight of her in the palms of his hands while he kissed, licked, sucked her nipples until she orgasmed.

It had been one of his favorite things to do when she'd been his.

As he stood there, watching her, an image came to him. One of Gideon on his knees in front of her, pleasuring her the way Marc used to. Rage exploded within him, turned his voice harsh and tinted his vision with red. Or maybe that was green.

Within seconds he was next to her. "Who is this Gideon guy to you?" The question came out before he even knew he was going to ask it.

Isa's eyes flew open and she whirled to face him, one shaky hand pressed to her chest.

"I'm sorry. I didn't mean to startle you."

"What are you doing out here?"

"I followed you." He stepped forward, ran his fingers down the sweet softness of her cheek.

"Why?"

He ignored her question, focused instead on the sudden increase in her breathing. She was either nervous or aroused. Or maybe both. He wanted to revel in her reaction, probably would have, if he hadn't been struck by the sudden realization that her response might be for Gideon instead of him.

"Who is that guy to you?" he asked again.

"Gideon?"

He didn't like the way she said the guy's name, all soft and familiar. It pushed at him, made him snarly. And more determined than ever to have her in his bed again. "Yeah."

"He's my escort. And—and my friend."

Her voice broke as he slid his hand from her cheek to her jaw to the pulse that fluttered wildly at the base of her neck. "Is that all?"

She wet her lips with her tongue and he nearly groaned. It took every ounce of control he had not to lean forward and brush his own tongue against hers.

"Is what all?" She was breathless now, her chest rising and falling unevenly.

The knowledge that she wanted him, too, sent a shot of lust straight to his groin. He stepped closer, brushed her body with his even as he circled her neck with his thumb and fingers. It wasn't a threat or an attempt to intimidate. No, it was simply a gesture of the possessiveness ripping through him like a freight train, one he couldn't have stopped even if he'd wanted to.

And he didn't want to. Not when need for Isa was a fire in his blood, a haze in his mind.

He leaned forward until his lips were only an inch or so from hers. "Gideon. Is he just a friend? Or is he more?"

"G-Gideon?"

He liked the confusion in her voice, liked that she couldn't remember who he was talking about. "The guy who brought you here." Marc leaned closer still, brushed his lips over the corner of her mouth. "Are you with him?"

Isa shuddered, trembled, against him. "No."

The denial came out as a whisper, but it was good enough for him. More than good enough as her skin flushed and her nipples peaked against his chest.

"Good," he said, right before his mouth closed over hers.

Four

The kiss was as much about possession as it was about pleasure.

It had been six long years since he'd touched her, since he'd held her, since he'd licked his way across her full pink lips, but, in this moment, in his mind, she was still his.

At the first press of his mouth against hers, Isa's lips parted on a gasp. He took instant, ruthless advantage, thrusting his tongue into the deepest recesses of her mouth. Her hands came up to his chest and he thought, at first, that she was going to push him away. Just the idea upset him more than he wanted to admit. He prepared for it, for the torture that would be letting her go. But then her hands clung instead of pressed, tangled in his shirt and held him close. It was all the permission he needed.

He brought his hands to her face, cupped her jaw. Stroked his thumbs along her cut-glass cheekbones. And kissed her as if he'd been dying to kiss her for all these years.

He *plundered* her.

Sweeping his tongue along her own, stroking and circling, teasing and tasting, he coaxed her into opening a little wider, letting him in a little deeper. She did, and he swept in, taking more of her. Taking everything she was offering and demanding more.

He licked his way across her lips, down the inside of her cheeks, over the slick roughness of the top of her mouth. She moaned then, a soft, breathy sound that shot straight through him and made him harder than he'd been any time in the past six years. Harder than he'd been any time since he'd last held her in his arms.

With that thought in his mind and desire pounding through his gut, he tilted her head to gain better access. And then it was on.

Their tongues tangled, slipping, sliding, stroking their way over and around and under each other. He sucked her tongue into his mouth and relished the way her body arched, the way her hips bumped against his, the way her fingers clawed at him, scratching him through the thin silk of his dress shirt.

He used to love the little pricks of pain, and the knowledge that he would carry her marks for hours, sometimes days. It was a blow to find out he still felt that way. That he still wanted her brand on his body—and his brand on hers—as much as he ever had. Or it would be a blow, he figured, as soon as this kiss was over. For now, he couldn't think about it. Couldn't think about anything but her and the feelings rushing between them. Because he didn't have a choice, he gave himself over to it all. Gave himself over to Isa.

How could he not when the kiss, when *she*, was a strange mix of soft and sharp, poignant and desperate.

The familiar and the exotic. He wanted her—and whatever she would give him—more than he wanted air.

His head was spinning by the time she pulled away. She didn't go far, just broke off the kiss and stood there panting, her forehead resting against his. He let her catch her breath, and dragged precious oxygen into his own overworked lungs, giving his overheated body a chance to calm down. Then he claimed her mouth again.

It was even better the second time.

Her lips were warm and swollen and she tasted so good—like fizzy wine and the sweetest summer blackberries. And the sea. Cool and clean and so, so wild. But then, she always had.

So much about her had changed since he'd last been with her, he'd been afraid that her taste had, too. To find out that it hadn't—it nearly brought him to his knees. Instead of letting it, he kissed her again. And again. And again. Until her skin was hot and flushed against his palms. Until he was rock hard and aching against her. Until their lips were bruised and swollen and tender, so tender..

And then he kissed her some more.

And she let him. She let him kiss her, let him touch her, let him in when he'd spent so long thinking that it would never happen again. That she would never open herself to him and that, if she did, he would never trust her enough to let her.

But this wasn't about trust, he told himself as he continued to take everything she had to offer and push for more. This wasn't about love. It was about need. About chemistry. About a past that burned hotter between them than any jewelry forge ever could.

His mouth was nearly numb by the time she finally broke the kiss. This time she didn't stay in his arms, resting against him. Instead, she shoved him away, hard, then turned to face the ocean. He gave her space, and just watched, fascinated, as her shoulders trembled, as she struggled desperately to get herself under control.

He wished her luck. God knew, he had absolutely no control when it came to her. He never had.

"Don't ever do that again."

It was an order, delivered in a voice that still shook from pent-up desire.

"Never do what?" he asked, turning her around so he could see her face in the shadowy darkness. Her eyes were huge; her pupils wide with passion and seeing her like that sent another shock wave of need through him.

"Never do this?" he asked, stepping so close that every breath she took pressed her breasts against his chest. "Never touch you?" He brushed his knuckles against her jaw, then slid them down, until his open hand rested on her collarbone, his fingers splayed gently against her neck. "Never kiss you?" Her skin was soft and warm against his lips as he kissed a line from her temple to her cheek to the corner of her mouth.

Then he pressed his mouth to hers, pulled her lower lip between his teeth and bit down gently.

Isa's hands slid up his back to tangle in his hair as she made low, urgent sounds deep in her throat. Her lips parted on a shallow exhale as her body arched against him. It was all he could do not to groan. Not to take her right there against the iron railing of the balcony.

"Never want you?" His hand was on her waist, and he slid it down to mold her behind, to press her hips against his while his other hand slid down to cup her breast through the thin, silky fabric of her dress. "Because, I have to say, I think the ship has sailed on that. For both of us."

"Marc." His name was a broken breath on her lips—a prayer, a curse, an absolution, a condemnation. He didn't know which—nor did he care, he assured himself. All that mattered was having her again. He'd spent the past six years thinking about touching her, dreaming about taking her over and over until his mind was calm and his body was finally sated.

Maybe then he could find some peace.

"Let me have you," he whispered in her ear even as he rolled her nipple between his thumb and forefinger. "I'll take care of you, make you feel so good—"

Isa shoved against him, hard. She was a little thing, slender, with tiny bones—but she was a lot stronger than she looked.

"Marc, no!" She twisted her face to the side and shoved again. "Stop."

No. Stop. He hated those two words, almost as much as he hated being told what to do. But they were nonnegotiable, the words and the sentiment behind them not open for discussion when they fell from a woman's lips. And so he stepped back, letting his hands fall away from her lush, inviting curves.

"I know what you're doing," she said. Her eyes were wild, her voice shaky.

"Do you?" he murmured. "Do you really?"

"You're trying to embarrass me at work. You're trying to ruin everything and I'm not going to have it."

He didn't even try to hide his insult. "Embarrass you? Kissing me embarrasses you?"

She must have sensed the danger in his voice, because she ran a nervous hand over her hair while the fingers of her other hand played with her locket. "Don't get all macho and insulted on me," she told him, exasperated.

"I don't do macho," he said, disdain in every syllable.

She snorted. "You don't have to 'do' it. Every cell in your body is alpha and controlling and if you don't know that, you're even more deluded than I thought you were. But, be that as it may, I'm not going to stand out here and be your toy for one second longer. This is a work function for me and, unlike you, I don't have a trust fund and a diamond company to fall back on if I lose my job for inappropriate conduct. This career is all I have and I'm not going to let you ruin it, the way you ruined—"

She broke off before she finished the sentence, moving around him in a quick and desperate attempt to get to the door.

He grabbed her elbow, but it was his will much more than his gentle grip that kept her in place. "The way I ruined our relationship?" he asked silkily. "Because the way I remember it, you did that all on your own."

"I have no doubt that's exactly how you remember it." She glanced pointedly at his hold on her, then pulled her elbow out of his grasp before he could say another word. "Which is how I know you're doing this just to mess with me, to get me in trouble. But I'm not having it. I don't ever want you to touch me again. Go back to whatever you were doing before you decided that humiliating me was your best bet. Or better yet, go to hell."

She moved past him then, disappearing back into the party in a swirl of purple silk, Chanel No. 5 and righteous indignation.

He wasn't sure what it said about him that it was the latter that turned him on the most.

She was insane. Or in the middle of a psychotic break. Or having a stroke. She didn't know which of the three she was suffering from, but it was definitely one of them. There was no other explanation for what had happened on that balcony. No other explanation for why she had fallen into Marc's arms—and onto his lips—as if it had been six minutes since they'd last been together and not six years. Or as if he hadn't sent her packing in the cruelest manner possible.

She understood sexual attraction—when they'd been together, she and Marc could barely keep their hands off each other. But shouldn't that attraction be grounded in respect or love or something other than the intense dislike and distrust they now had for each other?

And still she'd let him kiss her. She'd let him touch her and stroke her and bring her way too close to orgasm. It was ridiculous. Worse, it was self-destructive. She was ashamed of herself. Ashamed of her body for responding so readily to him after everything he'd done to hurt her. After everything she'd done to hurt him, too.

As she walked through the party back to Gideon, Isa could feel Marc's eyes following her. She didn't need to look to know he was running his gaze over her back, her backside, her legs—and then up again. The weight of his stare was a physical touch—like an electric shock all over her body.

By the time she got to Gideon, she was shaking with re-action and self-recrimination. Though she knew the smart thing for her career was to stay at the party, drinking champagne and waiting for her turn to chat up the president of the Gem Institute, the truth was she didn't have it in her to be in this room for one more minute. She had to escape, now, before she freaked out in front of all these people. Or before she threw herself at Marc and begged him to take her right here, in the middle of the crowded gallery.

Just the thought that such a thing was possible had her all but running the last few feet to Gideon. Had her putting her hand on his arm and leaning in so that her lips were only inches from his, so he could hear her in the loud, crowded room. Had her begging off the rest of the night, telling him she'd catch a cab home because she wasn't feeling well. She was pretty sure her sickly pallor and trembling hands lent credence to the assertion.

Gideon, bless him, immediately put his drink on the nearest table and said, "Poor Isa. Let's get you home, then." He slid his arm around her waist to lend extra support and—after making his excuses—steered her toward the door.

"You don't have to come with me," she told him a little frantically. "It's just a headache. I can get myself home."

"Don't be ridiculous! I brought you, I'll escort you home. Besides—" he shot her a goofy grin "—that place was getting damn stuffy, damn fast. In fact, we could say you're rescuing me instead of the other way around."

"I think we both know that's not true," she said, pressing a kiss to his cheek. "But I appreciate the sentiment... and the ride home."

As soon as her lips left Gideon's cheek, she knew the kiss had been the wrong thing to do. She couldn't see Marc, but she could feel the crackling fury of his disapproval all the way across the room. With her back turned. And her attention determinedly fixed somewhere else.

She stiffened her shoulders and tried not to let his reaction bother her. After all, it wasn't as though she was using Gideon to try to make him jealous—it wasn't as though it had even occurred to her that he would *be* jealous. But now that she could feel him seething from across the room, she couldn't help but wonder what this whole thing looked like to Marc. One minute, she was letting him violate her on the balcony and the next minute she was snuggling up to Gideon.

Not that it mattered what Marc thought, she promised herself as she allowed Gideon to propel her toward the exit with a proprietary hand on her lower back. She'd told Marc that what had happened on that balcony wouldn't happen again, and she'd meant it. She'd let him destroy her once. No way would it happen again. It didn't matter if she was still attracted to him, didn't matter if there was unfinished business between them. She was no longer the love-struck girl she'd been six years ago, willing to risk anything and everything for a chance to be with him.

No, life had taught her a lot of hard lessons in the intervening years and she'd ended up building an entirely new life for herself. One she was proud of. One that meant something to her. One that Marc would be only too happy to ruin as completely as he'd ruined her old one.

She couldn't let that happen. Not when her job—and her reputation—were all she had.

Five

The ride home with Gideon was easy. But then, everything was easy with him. There was no smolder. No dark past that tainted every interaction, no love or hate to color the way they looked at each other. The way they were with each other. No, she and Gideon had a comfortable friendship, one built on shared interests, lively conversations and similar senses of humor.

And never had she been more grateful for that than she was right now, as he pulled up in front of the small house she'd bought for herself when she'd moved here four years ago.

Gideon walked her to the door, but he didn't linger. Didn't expect an invite inside or even a good-night kiss. Instead, he hugged her and dropped a quick kiss on her forehead. Then, with a murmured, "Feel better," he was gone. And she was alone.

Thank God.

Ignoring the way memories of Marc simmered right under the surface, she changed out of her dinner clothes into yoga pants and a black tank top. Then she poured herself one more glass of wine and settled on the couch to watch television and try to forget her disaster of a day.

Except she'd barely streamed the opening credits to her current favorite TV show before there was a knock on her door. Figuring Gideon had come back because she'd left something in his car, she opened the front door with a grin. "What did I forget this time? If you want to come in, we can share a bottle of—"

Her voice cut off as it registered just who was standing on her front porch—and he definitely wasn't Gideon.

"What are you doing here?" she demanded. "And how did you even find out where I live?"

"I followed you."

"You followed—Jesus. Stalk much?" She started to close the door in his face.

His hand flashed out, holding the door before she could get it more than halfway closed. "I've spent the last six years looking for you."

For a second, she was sure she had heard him wrong. After all, the last thing Marc had said to her was that if he ever saw her again, he'd make sure she and her father both ended up in prison.

But the look on his face—a little guilty, all annoyed—told her she had heard correctly. And that he hadn't meant to blurt out the truth like that. But now that he had, she wanted to know—"Why? Why would you do that?"

"It was a shitty thing to do."

"I believe we've already covered how you feel about what I did—"

"No. I mean what I did. Tossing you out on the street like that, having security escort you from the building with nothing… I regretted it almost as soon as it happened. I went outside the building, tried to find you. Went to your apartment, but you never went back there. I was worried that something had happened to you because of me."

It was the last thing she'd expected him to say, the last thing she'd ever expected to hear from Marc Durand. For long seconds she could do nothing but stare at him as she tried to absorb the words. She didn't want them to matter, didn't want anything to get in the way of her ability to tell him to go to hell once and for all. After all, the words—and the sentiment behind them—were six years too late.

And still she felt something melt inside her. For six long years she'd carried a twisted mess of betrayal and pain, regret and rage. Every bit of it had his name on it and no matter how many times she'd tried to let it go, no matter how many times she'd tried to move on, it had been there, choking her. But now, somehow, with just a few words, Marc had loosened its stranglehold on her. She could take what felt like her first deep breath in forever.

"I'm sorry," he continued, and it sounded like he was swallowing razor blades. Not that she was surprised. In her experience, men like Marc didn't apologize often.

And now that he had…she had a choice. She could tell him to go to hell and slam the door in his face or she could accept his apology. Since she'd always understood why he'd done what he had—her father *had* stolen from him, and in begging Marc to spare him, she had chosen her father over Marc—there really was only one choice she could make.

Opening the door a little wider, she stepped back. "I just opened a bottle of Pinot Noir. If you're interested."

"I'm very interested." His voice was dark, wicked. She felt the heat of it in her stomach and her sex.

It made her nervous. Made her sweat, despite the chill

of the air-conditioning. "It's probably not as fancy as the wines you're used to," she told him as she entered the kitchen and poured him a glass of her favorite Pinot. "But I like it."

He took the glass, drained it in one long sip. Put it on the counter behind him.

"Okay, then. Do you want m—"

He moved to cage her against the cabinet, an arm on either side of her and his long, lithe body pressed against her own. "I didn't come for the wine, Isa."

"Obv—" Her voice cracked, so she cleared her throat. "Obviously."

"I didn't come to apologize, either. I'm glad I did, but that's not why I'm here."

"Marc." The word was low, broken. "I don't think—"

"Don't think," he said, cupping her face in his big, worn hand. "Just listen." He leaned down until his lips brushed, soft as butterfly wings, against her jaw.

"I wasn't messing with you on the balcony earlier." His breath was hot against her ear. "I wasn't trying to humiliate you at work."

Her nipples beaded despite her earlier resolve to never let him make her feel like this again. "It felt like that to me."

"I know. And that's my fault, too." His mouth skimmed across her jaw, his tongue darting out to taste the corner of her mouth. "Wrong time, wrong place."

He licked his way across her lips, soft and delicate and oh so coaxing. She gasped at the first touch of his tongue on her lower lip and he took instant advantage, licking inside to stroke her.

"My only excuse," he said, in between each dark and wicked kiss, "is that even after all this time, you make me crazy. You make me forget where." His other hand cupped her breast through the thin cotton of her shirt. "You make me forget when." He stroked his thumb around her areola.

Her heart was beating too fast, her chest heaving with each ragged breath she sucked past her too-tight throat. Still, she managed to force out the question she was desperate for an answer to. "Do I make you forget who, as well?"

"I've never been able to forget you, Isa. And believe me, I've tried."

The words stung, of course they did. But there was an honesty to them that echoed her own experience, that had her weakened defenses crumbling into dust.

She could blame her surrender on the wine or the loneliness or the shock of seeing him after all this time. But the truth was, she wanted him. She'd always wanted him. And if this night, this moment, was all she'd ever have of Marc Durand…well, it was a more fitting goodbye than the last one they'd shared.

And so she didn't fight him when he moved to trail kisses down her throat. Instead she let her fingers tangle in his dark, silky hair even as she tilted her head back to give him better access.

"Your heart is beating so fast," he murmured against her skin.

"It's been a long time since—" She forced herself to stop before she revealed too much.

But he wouldn't let her off the hook that easily. "Since what?" he asked between pressing kisses across the upper slope of first one breast and then the other.

She couldn't tell him the truth, didn't want him to know just how much she'd once loved him—or just how long it had been since she'd made love to someone. "Since you've touched me. Our chemistry was never in question."

Then, to keep him from digging any deeper into what was a very sore subject, she ran her hands over his chest.

He'd discarded his jacket and tie before coming to her door, so all that was between her fingers and his hot skin was a thin piece of dark blue silk the same color as his eyes.

He was as powerfully built as ever—maybe more so— and she'd be lying if she said she didn't want to see him naked. Didn't want to feel the heat of his skin, the resilience of his muscles, under her tongue.

But sanity finally intruded—in the form of his long-ago rejection that was still fresh in her mind. She didn't think she'd be able to go through that a second time. At least not if she wanted to come out anywhere close to whole. So instead of unbuttoning his shirt as she longed to do, instead of slipping her hands inside the midnight-blue silk and stroking his pecs, his six-pack, the V-cut that had always made her mouth water, she forced herself to pull back. "What are we doing, Marc?"

He lifted his head from where he was licking a warm strip just below her neckline. "I would have thought that was obvious, Isa."

She blushed then, her face turning hot at the sardonic amusement in his tone and the powerful look in his eye. "I just mean…" She turned away, refusing to look at him. "I don't know what you want from me."

"Yes, you do." He straightened up then and looked her straight in the eye. Meeting his gaze when she felt so vulnerable, so uncertain, was one of the hardest things she'd ever done. But she forced herself to do it. Forced herself not to flinch or blink or look away. She had a right to know what she was getting into. With their history, this could be anything from revenge sex to reunion sex or a bunch of things in between.

Before she gave herself to him, she needed to know just what it was.

Except Marc had always been better at bedroom games

than she. More experienced, more able to control his responses. More able to articulate his thoughts and wishes. Tonight was no different.

"I want you, Isa," he told her, his hands stroking up and down her back in a rhythm that was at once soothing and arousing. "I want to kiss your breasts, to take your nipples into my mouth and see if you can still come from just the feel of me rolling them against my tongue and teeth."

She gasped then, didn't even try to hide the flush of arousal his words sent ricocheting through her.

"I want to be on my knees in front of you. I want to lick along your sex and feel you come on my tongue."

His words were so powerful, the need in his voice so seductive, that she grew wet from them alone.

"I want to pick you up and press you against the nearest wall. Want to feel your gorgeous legs wrap around my waist as I slide into you, nice and slow. I want to feel you clench around me, want to hear you call my name."

"Marc." She cried out his name and it was as much a demand as a plea. "I need—"

"I want you to come again and again and again. On my fingers, on my dick, on my tongue. Until all you know is pleasure. Until—"

He broke off as she threaded her hands into his hair and pulled his mouth to hers in a kiss so hard she knew her lips would be bruised. Not that she cared. Right now, all she cared about was Marc and this moment and the feel of him inside her. She wanted to hold him, wanted him to empty himself inside her until she finally felt full.

Until she finally felt whole.

And then she wanted him to do it all again.

"Yes." She breathed the word into his mouth even as she ripped at the fine silk of his shirt, desperate to get it off him. Desperate to feel his skin—hot and smooth—against her own.

Marc growled low in his throat—whether at her acquiescence or the feel of her nails scratching against his chest, she didn't know. Buttons flew and he shrugged out of his ruined shirt even as he whipped her tank top over her head.

"You're so goddamn beautiful," he growled. And then he was cupping her breasts in his calloused hands. She jerked, arching into the sensation that was somehow familiar and brand-new at the same time.

It was a double shot of sensation, to both watch and feel as he touched her. Need—hot and powerful—skyrocketed inside her with each swirl of his fingers around her nipples. It raced through her blood, slid from nerve ending to nerve ending until she burned with it, consumed by it. Until all she could think or feel, all she could smell or taste or see, was him.

Finally—finally—his thumbs brushed fully over her nipples and she cried out at the streak of pleasure that shot through her. She clutched at his shoulders. Arched her back. And offered herself to him in a way she'd offered herself to no other man.

In answer, he dropped to his knees in front of her. Pulled her yoga pants and panties down her legs. Pressed wet, openmouthed kisses to her belly, her rib cage, her breasts. And then, when she was whimpering—when her hands were clutching at his hair and her body was trembling with the need to feel him—he took her nipple in his mouth and sucked hard enough to make her scream.

He did it again and again, lashing his tongue back and forth over the hard bud until she trembled on the brink of orgasm. She fought it, not wanting to give in to him so easily. And not, she admitted in the deepest parts of herself, wanting it to end so quickly. It had been too long since Marc had held her, kissed her, made love to her, and if this was her one shot to have him again, she wasn't going to rush it.

But then he pinched her other nipple between his thumb and middle finger—all while he continued to suck and lick and bite at her other nipple. Her knees went weak and she clutched onto his shoulders for support, her hips moving restlessly against his chest as she drew closer and closer to the edge.

As if sensing her dilemma, Marc pulled his mouth away from her breast. She whimpered—actually whimpered—until he fiercely whispered, "Let go, Isa. It's okay. I've got you. I promise, I've got you, baby."

And then his mouth was back on her breast and she lost it completely. Dark and broken sounds fell from her lips as she spiraled up, up, up, up.

"Yes, baby," Marc encouraged, his fingers pinching her nipple a little more tightly. She cried out, scratching her nails down his back.

She was right there, her body poised to fly over the edge. Right there, right there, right—Marc bit her, gently, and with a scream that she was sure her neighbors could hear, she hurtled straight into ecstasy, her body convulsing again and again.

He held her, using his mouth and hands to draw out her pleasure until she was an incoherent mess. Then he pulled her close, wrapped his arms around her and murmured sweet love words against her damp skin.

She didn't understand what was happening here, didn't know what had transformed the angry man from earlier into the tender lover she remembered, but she wasn't going to worry about it. Not now, when her body was still singing with the most powerful orgasm she'd had in six years. Not now, when she was wrapped up in his arms so tightly that she could feel his heart beating against her skin. Not now, when she felt whole for the first time since Marc had kicked her out.

She'd do well to remember that—he'd kicked her out with nothing but the clothes on her back. And she would remember it. She *would*. Later. Right now, when she was naked and vulnerable and sated, she wanted to hold him and be held by him.

Wanted to love him and be loved by him—even if it was only her body she dared to give him. Even if it was only his body she was getting in return. Well, his body and long moments of completely unimaginable pleasure.

It wasn't enough, wasn't close to enough, but if it was all she would ever have of him, she would take it.

Six years ago, she'd learned that the future would come whether she worried about it or not. So here, now, she wouldn't worry about what came next. She would have this night, have Marc, and for once, let the future take care of itself.

Six

God, he'd missed her. Missed the taste of her skin. Missed the feel of her body against his. Missed the sound of her cries—broken and breathless—as she came for him. Even as he held her, even as he throbbed with the need for relief, he wanted to hear those sounds again. It wasn't an admission that came easy to him, not with everything that lay between them. But it was the truth, one he'd tried to ignore for six long years.

One—like her—he was desperate to get out of his system, once and for all.

Pushing to his feet, he picked Isa up and held her against his chest. "Which way is your bedroom?"

She stared up at him with passion-dazed eyes, and even though he felt as though he would die if he didn't get inside her in the next two minutes, he couldn't help lowering his head and, once again, taking her mouth with his.

She responded to him like she always did—with warmth

and fire and sweet, sweet surrender. He continued to kiss her as he headed down the hall, continued to kiss her as he lay her across the queen-size bed with the sexy red comforter. Continued to kiss her as he stripped down to the skin. And then he climbed onto the bed next to her and worshipped her the way he used to. The way he'd longed to for so, so long—with his hands and mouth and body touching, teasing, tasting every inch of her soft, sweet-smelling skin.

Isa moaned, her hands clutching at his hair, her body arching beneath him. His own need was sharp and violent inside him, but he wanted to see her come again. Wanted to steep himself in the sound and scent and feel of her as he gave her as much pleasure as she could take.

Fastening his mouth on her neck, he sucked a bruise into the sensitive skin. She shuddered, crying out his name as her fingernails raked down his back.

The quick, sharp pain loosed some wild thing in him he didn't even know was buried there. His control slipped the iron grip he'd kept on it from the moment she'd let him kiss her on that balcony.

And then his lips and tongue skimmed over her torso, her breasts, her stomach, her hips, her sex. He wanted to explore all of her, needed to find each and every change to her body that the past six years had wrought. The extra-fullness of her breasts, the new freckles on the soft insides of her elbows, the three small scars near her belly button that weren't there the last time he'd made love to her.

He traced his fingers over them, started to ask what had happened. But it wasn't his business—*she* wasn't his business—anymore, and he'd do well to remember that.

Except the words escaped of their own volition. "What happened here?"

"What? Where?" Her voice was husky, dazed with pleasure. Pleasure he had given her, he thought with grim satisfaction. Not that pansy-ass professor who couldn't keep his hands off her at the cocktail party.

"Here." He ran a finger over the scars again.

"Oh." She sighed, her fingers sliding down his chest to toy with his nipples as she answered, "Emergency appendectomy."

Her answer floated past him and pleasure coursed through him as she played with him. Her fingers squeezed and stroked and pinched as she pressed hot kisses to his neck and shoulders and chest.

"Isa." It was a warning, more a growl than an actual word.

She didn't pay any attention, though. Instead, she slid slowly down the bed as her mouth worked its way over his pecs, his stomach, his abdomen. He was still above her, but that fact wasn't hampering her at all as her mouth trailed hot kisses over the sparse trail of hair that led from his belly button.

And then she took him in her mouth, sucking him deep even as her tongue licked hotly against the length of him. He bit off a curse, taking her ministrations for several long seconds, his arms trembling as they supported his weight above her.

But when she pulled him deep and he felt his release gathering at the base of his spine, he pulled away with a groan.

"What?" she asked, eyes dazed and mouth swollen as she reached for him. "I want to—"

"I want to be inside you when I come," he told her. He didn't know why it mattered—pleasure was pleasure, after all—but it did. He wanted the first time he came with Isa after their long separation to be when he was inside her.

Ignoring her moan of protest, he shifted off her for several long seconds as he retrieved his pants from the floor. He grabbed his wallet, pulled out a condom. Seconds later, he was back on the bed, his body covering hers.

Sliding a hand between her thighs to make sure she was ready for him, he relished the wet heat that told him she was as affected by him as he was by her.

"Marc, please," she gasped, her hands sliding around to pull him more firmly against her.

"I'm right here, baby." The endearment slipped out, as did the soft kisses he pressed to her flushed cheeks.

And then he was sliding inside her, sliding *home*, after far too long. Isa gasped, moaned, her body arching beneath his. Her arms wrapping around his shoulders. Her legs twining around his hips.

God, she felt good. Warm, wet, willing. *Amazing.*

He plunged into her again and again, relishing the way her body rose to meet his.

The way she whimpered.

The way her beautiful, dark eyes turned hazy as she got closer and closer to orgasm.

He was close, too—so close that it was an agony not to come. But he wanted—needed—her to come first. He wanted to see her face as pleasure took her, wanted to feel her body clutching him, holding him deep inside.

Sweat rolled down his muscles, pulled at the small of his back as he continued to build the pleasure—and the tension—between them. Isa moaned, her voice low and broken as she pleaded with him to send her over. Pleaded with him to let her come.

And while there was nothing he wanted more than to give her release—and take his own—he also wasn't ready to let her go. Wasn't ready for this to end. It had been so long since he'd held Isa like this, that he wanted to make every second last forever. Who knew when—or if—they'd ever have this chance again.

Except Isa wouldn't let him wait. Clutching at him with her arms and legs and body, she pulled him close. Pressed hot kisses to his mouth and jaw and neck. Sucked a bruise of her own right above his collarbone.

It was that mark, that brand, that sent him over the edge. Slipping a hand between them, he stroked her once, twice.

That was all it took to have her crying out his name as her body clenched rhythmically around him. And then he let go, too, coming deep inside her as pleasure roared through him like a freight train. Coming until he couldn't figure out where she left off and he began…or how he was going to live without this, without her.

He woke up feeling better than he had in years. Six years to be exact. His body was sated, his mind at peace. It was a strange feeling—so strange that it sent Marc hurtling from sleep into wakefulness with a speed that was practically painful.

His eyes flew open, and as he glimpsed Isa's bright red hair fanned out next to him on the pillow, the events of the previous night came flooding back in graphic, and arousing, detail. As his body responded to the private slide show in his head he thought about rolling over. About pulling her on top of him. About sliding into her as those gorgeous brown eyes of hers blinked open.

He wanted that, wanted her—even after all the times he'd had her the night before—with an intensity that bordered on desperation. Which was why he did exactly the opposite.

Rolling out of bed, he grabbed his pants and padded quietly down the hall to her kitchen, which was the last place he remembered having his shirt. Sure enough, it was crumpled on the ground, along with his shoes.

As he pulled his clothes back on, he tried not to think about the night before. Tried not to think about how good it had felt to have Isa back in his arms.

He'd never felt with another woman what he felt when he was with her. When they'd been together—when he'd loved and trusted her—making love to her had been an amazing high. He had lost himself in her day after day, night after night. It probably should have been scary to a guy like him—who had trouble trusting anyone—but it hadn't been. He'd been so crazy about her that he had never imagined she might betray him.

But she had and now they were here. The only problem was, he didn't know where here was any more than he knew where he wanted it to be. Yes, last night the sex had been fantastic. More than fantastic, it had been hot and exciting.

But it wasn't the pleasure that had him awake as dawn slowly streaked its rainbow fingers across the ocean outside her window. No, it wasn't the pleasure that was freaking him out. It was the way his body and mind felt balanced and rested and replete for the first time in a very long time.

He didn't like the fact that Isa was responsible for the feeling. It had been less than twenty-four hours since he'd walked into the back of her classroom and seen her teaching and already they were back in bed. Already he was thinking about taking her again. Already, he was thinking of taking her back.

And that was where the trouble lay. Because there was no way he could do that. No way he could forget that she'd betrayed him six years ago. No way he could forget that she had chosen her father—a man who had stolen from Marc, who had destroyed years of his work, who had nearly ruined everything he'd worked for—over him.

Because if she could do it once, in the middle of the most intense and powerful love affair he'd ever had, then she could do it again. And if that was the case, then he needed to walk away right now. Before he fell victim to all the little things he'd once loved about her.

Like her smile and her scent.

Like her wicked sense of humor and her even more wicked intellect.

Like how sleepy she was in the morning, when she wrapped herself around him and begged for kisses.

"You're still here." Her voice was husky with sleep, but when he turned to face her, her eyes were wide-awake. "I thought you'd left."

"Not yet. But I do need to get going. I've got to get to the office."

"It's Saturday."

"I'm aware of that. But I work on Saturdays." He pretty much worked every day. "Especially now that I've taken on the class at the institute."

He thought about crossing to her, about dropping a kiss on her still-swollen lips. But if he was honest with himself, he was as uneasy as she obviously was. More unsure of what he wanted to do and how he wanted to do it than he'd ever been in his life. It was an uncomfortable feeling, one he didn't like at all.

"You never used to work on Saturdays." Her voice was even, but still it sounded like an accusation. Which, in turn, made him feel guilty, even though he had nothing to feel guilty for.

He lashed out before he could think better of it. "Yeah, well, six years ago I thought I was safe. I thought I'd built the company up to a place where I could breathe a little, where I could take an occasional day off and trust things would be okay. If you remember correctly, that didn't work out too well for me." He didn't even try to keep the temper out of his voice. How dare she accuse him of running out on her when she'd been the one to betray him? The one to disappear off the face of the earth for more than half a decade?

She winced, but kept her gaze steady on his as she said, "How long are you going to keep throwing that in my face?"

The small licks of anger grew into wilder flames. "I've mentioned it twice in the last twenty-four hours," he told her, forcing his voice to remain steady. "And before that, I hadn't talked to you in six damn years. So tell me, please, how is it, exactly, that I'm throwing the past in your face?"

"I don't know. But it feels like you are." She wrapped her arms around her waist, hugging herself in a gesture that screamed discomfort and defensiveness.

It should have given him pause, *would* have given him pause if he wasn't so uncomfortable and defensive himself. "Maybe that's your guilty conscience talking. Maybe there's a part of you that feels like you deserve whatever you think I'm doing to you."

"Maybe I do. But that doesn't mean I'm reading the situation wrong." She paused and took a deep breath as if she was gathering her courage.

All of a sudden, he felt ashamed. He hadn't come here to berate her, to make her nervous in her own home. "Say it, Isa. Whatever it is you want to say, just get it off your chest."

"All right." She licked her lips in a gesture that was as familiar to him as her skin sliding against his own. "It's just, I can't figure out what last night was about."

"I'm not sure what you mean." A sick feeling stirred

deep inside him. He didn't want to think too closely about his rationale for last night. At least not beyond scratching an itch that had been six long years in the making.

"I mean, what was the point of it? Was it your way of getting revenge after all this time? Of trying to hurt me?" Despite her earlier nervousness, she said the words as if they were no big deal. As if she'd anticipated he'd do something like that all along.

It got to him, in a huge way. Because last night had been about a lot of things—lust, confusion, jealousy, need—but he could honestly say that revenge had never entered into it. Not when he went out to speak with her on the balcony. Not when he made the decision to follow her home. And definitely not when he showed up at her door. Not once had he been thinking of revenge. Maybe he should have been, but he hadn't. Instead, he'd been thinking about her. Just her.

The fact that she obviously hadn't felt the same way… that she had been analyzing his motives—and him—from the moment she opened her door, wounded him. No, that wasn't true. It didn't hurt him. It made him feel like a fool, and that made him furious. She'd already played him once, and he'd be damned if he ever let her do that to him again. He wasn't that stupid.

"I wouldn't call it revenge so much as closure," he finally told her after several long seconds of silence. "Our relationship ended so abruptly that it always felt…unfinished. I didn't like it."

"And now?" she asked, face calm and brow raised inquiringly.

"Now? It feels done."

It was a lie, but she didn't have to know that. And it wasn't as if it would be a lie forever. This was exactly the closure he'd needed, he assured himself as he bent over and retrieved his keys from where they'd fallen on the floor. He knew she was okay, knew she hadn't been harmed by the cruel way he'd had her removed from his apartment all those years ago. And he'd been able to touch her after all this time, to slake a thirst he hadn't known was there until he'd seen her yesterday. That was enough. More than enough.

Or, at least, it would be.

His will was iron strong and he would make it the truth if it killed him. He'd spent too many years of his life thinking, worrying, *caring* about a woman who would never do the same for him.

That ended here. Now. He knew Isa was safe. He'd even had one last night with her. It was more than enough. It was time for him to close this chapter of his life and move on, once and for all. And he would start by walking out Isa's door.

"Thanks for last night," he told her, dropping a kiss on her cheek as he headed for the entryway. "It was fun."

She nodded, but didn't say anything as he opened the door, stepped onto her porch and took her front steps two at a time. She still didn't say anything, even as he made his way down the walkway to his car.

He didn't know what he wanted her to say—didn't know what he wanted from her at all. But as the front door closed quietly behind him, he knew that silence wasn't it. He knew he wanted more from her than that.

But then, he always had. She'd just never been able to give it.

She was an idiot.

After closing—and locking—the front door after Marc, Isa turned and marched straight back to the master bedroom. Though there was a part of her that wanted nothing more than to fling herself onto the mattress and pull the covers over her head, she knew that wasn't going to work. Partly because her problems would still be there, waiting for her, when she finally managed to resurface. And partly because the sheets still smelled like Marc and she wasn't masochistic enough to climb into them again. Not when she could barely breathe without memories of what had happened last night slicing through her like broken glass.

She'd known while she was doing it that she was making a mistake. After all, Marc wasn't one to forgive betrayal easily. And yet she'd done it anyway. She'd fallen into bed with him. Had given herself to him over and over again without worrying about consequences. Or what would happen in the morning. Or whether or not he was just using her. Instead, for a little while, she'd allowed herself to believe that miracles could happen. She'd allowed herself to believe that it could be like it was six years ago, before her father had ruined everything. Before she'd let him.

Suddenly, she couldn't stand the sight of the rumpled bed for one second more. She threw herself at it in a frenzy, stripping the sheets, the blankets, even the mattress pad. When she was done—when the bed was completely empty—she carried it all into her doll-sized laundry room and shoved as much as she could fit into her washing machine. It would take two loads, but she didn't care. All that mattered was getting rid of every last reminder of Marc and the mistake she had made.

Then, once the bed was taken care of, she started on herself. And realized erasing Marc from her body's memory was going to be a million times more difficult. After all, memories of his existence, his touch, his smell, had lived right under her skin for six long years, just waiting to spring back to life. And now that they had, she wasn't sure she had the strength to banish them—to banish him—again.

Stripping off her nightgown, which had somehow absorbed the scent of him despite the fact that they'd slept naked, she dropped it into the pile of bedding that was still waiting to be washed. And then she walked, naked, down the hall and into the bedroom to take a shower.

As she waited for the water to get warm, she made the mistake of looking in the mirror. What she saw there nearly brought her to her knees.

She looked…like she'd spent the night getting ravaged. Her hair was wild; her skin flushed a rosy pink wherever his stubble had touched her. Her mouth was swollen; her eyes dreamy and a little unfocused. And there were bruises. On her throat. On the outer side of her left breast. On her right hip. On the delicate skin of her inner thigh. They were love bites. Hickeys. Small reminders of him sucked into her skin.

As if she needed the reminders. As if she could forget what he'd done to her—what they'd done to each other.

But she *needed* to forget, she told herself fiercely. She needed to bury the memories of last night somewhere deep inside so she wouldn't have to think about them every time she walked into her bedroom. Or every time she saw him at the institute. She'd spent six long years hearing his name—her specialty was conflict diamonds, after all, and his company was the biggest conflict-free diamond source in North America—which meant his name came up a lot in her research, her lectures, her papers.

She'd managed to ignore it for a long time, to put distance between what had happened between them and the businessman who was making so many important and exciting decisions in the field. Now that she'd slept with him again, she would have to go back to how it had been in the old days. Ignoring every mention of him, writing her way around him, pretending he didn't exist. Not forever, mind you, but for a little while. Just until she could get her head on straight. Just until she could breathe again without bleeding inside.

Fake it until you make it, she told herself grimly as she stepped into the shower and scrubbed herself raw in an attempt to erase the memory of his touch from her skin. Wasn't that the phrase? She'd spent a long time pretending that year in Manhattan had never happened and had finally gotten to a place where she was happy. Healthy. And now, here he was, back again, shaking everything up. Shaking her up. And she was just supposed to go along for the ride.

Cold, hot, cold, hot. Cold.

No. Not this time. And never again. He was too dominant, his moods too mercurial, and she wasn't going to take the ride with him again. It had been fun once, but that was before she'd had anything to lose but him. She'd been drifting when she met him at that gala all those years ago. Stealing had lost its thrill and she'd had nothing to replace it until him.

That wasn't the case anymore. Now she had a career. She had friendships. She had a *life*. And she'd worked too damn hard for that life to let him come in and turn it topsy-turvy because of old mistakes. And even older chemistry.

No, from now on she would ignore Marc whenever she saw him. A quick nod of acknowledgment if she couldn't get around it, but that was it. No interaction, no arguing, and for God's sake, definitely no sex.

Because any interaction with Marc would lead to questions from her peers that she couldn't answer. Questions that would bring up a past she couldn't talk about.

Because one of the world's leading experts on diamonds—a woman who was allowed into and left alone in vaults all over the world—couldn't also be the daughter of the most successful jewel thief who'd ever lived. It didn't work that way.

And since all she'd had was her work from the moment Marc cast her out on that dirty New York sidewalk, since it was what had saved her when the rest of her world had imploded, there was no way she was risking her career for him. Not now. Not ever again. No matter how powerful the chemistry or how good the sex.

Some things just weren't meant to be. And her relationship with Marc was obviously one of those things.

Now all she had to do was remember that.

Seven

"We have a problem."

Marc looked up as Nic blew right past Marc's assistant and entered his office without so much as a knock—or a hello. "What's going on?"

His brother slammed his hand down on the desk hard enough to rattle everything resting on top of it—including Marc's laptop and cup of coffee. For expediency's sake—and to give him a second to settle the alarm raking through his stomach—Marc grabbed the coffee and put it on the credenza behind him.

When he turned back to face Nic, Marc was completely composed. He had a feeling he would need it, since Nic was not one to fly off the handle over every small thing. He was volatile, sure—the flip side of the charm that made him such a perfect fit for the public side of the company—but he never panicked. But Marc was pretty sure that panic was what he saw in Nic's eyes right now. And he'd be lying if he said it didn't make him more than a little nervous.

"Tell me."

"I just got off the phone with a reporter from the *LA Times*. She's doing an exposé on Bijoux and wanted a comment before the article goes to print."

"An exposé? What the hell does she have to expose?" Marc stood up then, walked around the desk. "Between you and me, we're in charge of every aspect of this company. Nothing happens here that we don't know about."

"That's exactly what I told her."

"And?" He ground out the words. "What's she exposing?"

"According to her, the fact that we're pulling diamonds from conflict areas, certifying them as conflict free, and then passing them onto the consumer at the higher rate in order to maximize our profits."

"That's ridiculous."

"I know it's ridiculous! I told her as much. She says she has an unimpeachable source."

"Who's the source?"

Nic thrust a frustrated hand through his hair. "She wouldn't tell me that."

"Of course she wouldn't tell you that, because the source is bullshit. The whole story is bullshit. I know where every single shipment of diamonds comes from. I personally inspect every mine on a regular basis. The certification numbers come straight to me and only our in-house diamond experts—experts that I have handpicked and trust implicitly—ever get near those numbers."

"I told her all of that. I invited her to come in and take a tour of our new facilities and see exactly how things work here at Bijoux."

"And what did she say?"

"She said she had tried to come for a tour, but PR had put her off. It's too late now. The story is slotted to run on

Friday and that she really would like a comment from us before it goes to print."

"That's in six days."

"I'm aware of that. It's why I'm here, freaking out."

"Screw that." Marc picked up his phone and dialed an in-house number. Waited impatiently for the line to be picked up.

"Hollister Banks."

"Hollister. This is Marc. I need you in my office now."

"Be there in five."

He didn't bother to say goodbye before hanging up and dialing another number. "Lisa Brown, how may I help you?"

He told his top diamond inspector the same thing he'd just told the head of his legal team.

"But, Marc, I just got in a whole new shipment—"

"So put it in the vault and then get up here." He must have sounded as impatient as he felt, because she didn't argue with him again. She just agreed before quietly hanging up the phone.

It took Lisa and Hollister less than three minutes to get to Marc's office, and soon the four of them were gathered in the small sitting area to the left of his desk, listening as Nic once again recounted his discussion with the reporter.

"Who's the source?" Marc demanded of Lisa as soon as Nic finished up.

"Why are you asking me? I have no idea who would make up a false story like this and feed it to the *LA Times*. I'm sure it's none of our people."

"The reporter seemed pretty adamant that it was an insider. Someone who had the position and the access to prove what he or she is saying."

"But that's impossible. Because what the person is saying isn't *true*. The claims are preposterous," Lisa asserted.

"Marc and I are the first and last in the chain of command when it comes to accepting and certifying the conflict-free diamonds. There's no way one of us would make a mistake like that—and we sure as hell wouldn't lie about the gems being conflict-free to make extra money. So even if someone messed with the diamonds between when I see them and when Marc does, he would catch it."

"Not to mention the fact that there are cameras everywhere, manned twenty-four seven by security guards who get paid very well to make sure no one tampers with our stones," Nic added.

"What this person is saying just isn't possible," Lisa continued. "That's why Marc insists on being the last point of contact for the stones before we ship them out. He verifies the geology and the ID numbers associated with them."

"There is a way it would work," Marc interrupted, his stomach churning sickly. "If I were involved in the duplicity, it would explain everything."

"But you're not!" Nic said at the same time Lisa exclaimed, "That's absurd!"

Their faith in him was the only bright point in a day that was rapidly going from awful to worse.

"It's what they'll argue," Hollister said, and though it was obvious by his tone that he disagreed, the thought still stung. This was more than a company to Marc, more than cold stones and colder cash. His great-grandfather had started the company nearly a hundred years before and it had been run by a Durand ever since. He'd put his life into continuing that tradition and building Bijoux into the second largest diamond distributor in the world. He'd brought it into the twenty-first century and created a business model that didn't exploit the people who most needed protection. Not dealing in blood diamonds was a matter of honor for him. To be accused of doing that which he most abhorred…it made him furious—and determined.

"I don't care what you have to do," he told Hollister. "I want that story stopped. We've worked too hard to build this company into what it is to have another setback—especially one like this. The jewel theft six years ago hurt our reputation and nearly bankrupted us. This will destroy everything Nic and I have been trying to do. You know as well as I, even if we prove the accusations false in court, the stigma will still be attached. Even if we get the *LA Times* to print a retraction, it won't matter. The damage will have already been done. I'm not having it. Not this time. Not about something like this."

It took every ounce of his self-control not to plow his fist into the wall. Goddamn it. He wasn't doing this again. "Call the editor of the *LA Times*. Tell him the story is blatant bullshit and if he runs it I will sue their asses and tie them up in court for years to come. By the time I'm done, they won't have a computer to their name let alone a press to run the paper on."

"I'll do my best, but—"

"Do better than your best. Do whatever it takes to make it happen. If you have to, remind them that they can't afford to go against Bijoux in today's precarious print media market. If they think they're going to do billions of dollars of damage to this company with a blatantly false story based on a source they won't reveal, and that I won't retaliate, then they are bigger fools than I'm already giving them credit for. You can assure them that if they don't provide me with definitive proof as to the truth of their claims, then I will make it my life's work to destroy everyone and everything involved in this story. And when you tell them that, make sure they understand I don't make idle threats."

"I'll lay it out for them. But, Marc," Hollister cautioned,

"if you're wrong and you've antagonized the largest newspaper on the West Coast—"

"I'm not wrong. We don't deal in blood diamonds. We will never deal in blood diamonds and anyone who says differently is a goddamn liar."

"We need to do more than threaten them," Nic said into the silence that followed his pronouncements. "We need to prove to them that they're wrong."

"And how exactly are we going to do that?" Lisa asked. "If we don't know who they're getting information from, or even what that information is, how can we contradict them?"

"By hiring an expert in conflict diamonds," Hollister chimed in. "By taking him up to Canada where we get our stock, letting him examine the mines we pull from. And then bringing him back here and giving him access to anything and everything he wants. We don't have any secrets—at least not of the blood diamond variety. So let's prove that."

"Yes, but getting an expert of that caliber on board could take weeks," Lisa protested. "There are barely a dozen people in the world with the credentials to sign off unquestioningly on our diamonds. Even if we pay twice the going rate, there's no guarantee that one of them will be available."

"But one is available," Nic told her even as he cast a wary look at Marc. "She lives right here in San Diego and teaches at GIA. She could totally do it."

Hell. He couldn't say he was surprised—from the moment Hollister had suggested hiring an expert, Marc had known they would end up here. But that didn't make it any easier to take.

"Dude, you look like you swallowed a bug," his brother told him.

Yeah, that was pretty much how he felt, too, except worse. Because, no. He wasn't calling her. He *couldn't* call her. Not with their distant past and definitely not with what had just happened between them the night before. She'd laugh in his face. And if she didn't…if she didn't, she'd probably deliberately sabotage them. No, he wouldn't put the future of his company in her hands.

He said as much to Nic, who rolled his eyes in exasperation. "Weren't you the one saying we can't afford to screw around with this? Isa's here, she has the experience, and if you pay her well and get a sub to carry her classes, she's probably available. It doesn't get much better than that."

"You should give her a call," Hollister urged.

"Yeah, absolutely," agreed Lisa. "I'd forgotten about Isabella Moreno being here in San Diego. I've met her a few times and she's really lovely—we should totally get her. I can try to talk to her, if you'd like."

Marc almost said yes, almost passed the buck onto Lisa to deal with. But he couldn't. It would be a slap in the face to Isa—an even bigger one than he'd already delivered to her this morning—and he couldn't afford that. Couldn't afford to antagonize her when she might very well be the only thing standing between Bijoux and total ruin.

The irony of the situation was not lost on him.

"No," he told Lisa harshly, after a few uncomfortable seconds passed. "I'll take care of getting her on board."

He sounded more confident than he felt. Then again, it wasn't as if he had a choice. He couldn't fail. Not now, not on this. His family's business depended on it.

He would do whatever it took to convince Isa to take on Bijoux—and him.

Eight

Isa was in the middle of a cleaning frenzy, one that involved scrubbing down every surface in her house that Marc might have touched. She knew it was ridiculous, knew it had to be her mind playing tricks on her, but that didn't matter. Not when she could smell him everywhere.

Inconsiderate bastard, leaving his dark honey and pine scent all over her house. She refused to acknowledge the little voice that whispered it wasn't her house he'd left his scent on. It was her.

She'd made it through the entire space and was on her knees scrubbing the bottom shelf of her refrigerator when the doorbell rang. She nearly ignored it—it wasn't like she was in the mood to talk to anyone. But when the ringing gave way to a loud and urgent pounding, she rushed to the front door and pulled it open. She lived in a good neighborhood, but that didn't mean someone wasn't in trouble. Maybe they needed—

She froze as she looked straight up and into Marc's narrowed eyes.

So not an emergency, then.

She slammed the door shut in his face before she could worry about what she was giving away by doing so. Then she sagged against it and forced herself to pull air into lungs that had forgotten how to breathe.

What was he doing here? When he'd walked out this morning, she'd been certain she'd never have to see him again—maybe only from a distance on the GIA campus. Had counted on it, in fact. No matter what she'd told herself, her feelings for him, for what had happened last night, were still too raw for her to face him again.

Not yet, she told herself as she worked to get her ragged heartbeat under control. Preferably not ever, but definitely not yet.

Except Marc hadn't gotten the message. The pounding on her door started again, along with his voice, low and urgent, ordering her to "Open up, Isabelle."

It was his use of her formal first name that got her brain functioning again.

She thought about ignoring him. About walking into her bedroom at the back of the house and turning on music, the TV, the shower—anything to drown out the sound of his voice. But doing so would make her look even more ridiculous, more pathetic, than she already did. And that was saying something.

It was that thought—along with her smarting pride—that finally made the decision for her. She rubbed her suddenly sweaty palms down the front of her jean-clad thighs and turned to open the door.

"Hi, Marc," she said as she once again peered up at him, a fake—but bright—smile curving her lips upward. "Sorry about that. You caught me in the middle of something…" She tried to ignore the way her voice trailed off uncertainly, prayed that he would be gentleman enough to do the same. She didn't know what it was about Marc Durand that turned her into a babbling schoolgirl with a crush on the most popular boy in school, but she didn't like it.

Marc must have been feeling merciful, because he didn't call her on her blatant lie. Nor did he try to put his hands on her. Instead, he raised a brow and asked, "Can I come in?"

No. She had spent the past two hours eradicating his presence from her house and now he wanted back in? With his gorgeous scent and his larger-than-life personality and his big hands, which he had used to drive her to orgasm again and again?

No, he couldn't come in. He shouldn't come in.

But, big surprise, knowing the danger was very different from acting on it. Instead of sending him away with another slammed door in his face, she pulled the door open wider and stepped back so he could get inside without his body brushing against her traitorous one. "Of course, yes. I assume you're here for your socks?"

Both brows went up this time. "My socks?"

"Yes." She cleared her throat, awkwardly. "They're very nice socks. I found them when I was straightening up. You must have forgotten them when you left this morning."

Very nice socks? Was she suddenly twelve? she asked herself fiercely. Socks were socks, for God's sake.

Judging by the strange look he shot her, Marc definitely seemed to think so, too. "Oh, um, thanks? I hadn't really noticed."

"How do you not notice that you're not wearing socks with your dress shoes?" She glanced down at his bare ankles doubtfully, even as she told herself to forget about the damn socks. "I can't believe your shoes are all that comfortable, even if they are Hugo Boss."

Then she bit her lip because, really, could she sound more obsessed? She kept harping about his "nice socks" *and* she knew what kind of dress shoes the man wore. He was probably counting himself lucky for the narrow escape he'd made this morning.

But he didn't seem to be inching away in alarm, any more than he seemed concerned by her intimate knowledge of his footwear. Instead he simply said, "I've had other, more important things on my mind today."

For one heart-stopping moment, she thought he was talking about her. About *them*. Her stomach jumped with excitement, even as her brain quelled the reaction. Despite her rather asinine reactions since he'd come to the door, she didn't want him, she reminded herself firmly. And he couldn't possibly want her. Not after all the ugliness that had passed between them—both six years ago and again this morning.

With that thought front and foremost in her mind, she cleared the last of the weirdness away and demanded, "So what are you doing here, then? I don't have much time to stand around and talk—I've got a date in a couple hours and I have to get ready."

"You have a *date*." He said the words in a flat, emotionless tone that she might have mistaken for disbelief, and lack of concern, if she hadn't seen the spark of anger in the depths of his eyes.

"I do." It was really more of an afternoon cocktail party to celebrate the opening of a prestigious jewelry collection by one of her former students at a local gallery, but she wasn't going to tell Marc that. Not when that event was the only thing standing between her and the utter humiliation that came with reliving the morning, when Marc had walked away from her without a backward glance.

"I do."

"With that professor from yesterday?" His voice was a growl now, his eyes a few shades darker than normal. And suddenly he was walking deeper into the house, each step causing her to retreat a little more until her back was, literally, against the wall and he was standing right there, his powerful body pressing into her as he looked down at her, his eyes hot and his mouth twisted in a displeased snarl.

There was a part of her that wanted to give in to his obvious dominance, but that part didn't get to be in control. So she tilted her chin up and met him glare for glare. "How is who I go out with any of your business?"

"Oh, it's my business," he growled as his hand came up to bracket her throat, his fingers resting on her collarbone while his thumb rubbed gently against the love bite he'd sucked into her throat sometime last night. His hold wasn't painful, wasn't even threatening. Instead, it was possessive, arousing as hell, though she fought to keep from acknowledging that fact.

"It isn't," she assured him.

"It is." His fingers massaged her collarbone before sliding slowly up her neck to her cheek. "I was the one inside you just a few hours ago. The one making you come. The one making you *scream*."

She melted at his words, her lower body going hot and wet at the snarly, desire-filled sound of his voice. But still she held her ground, refusing to let him know how much he affected her. "Maybe. But you were also the one babbling about closure and hightailing it out the door this morning as fast as your feet could carry you."

He wrapped his other hand around her waist. "I don't babble."

"And I don't beg," she told him firmly.

"You begged me last night." He stepped even closer,

dropping his head so that his lips were barely an inch from hers.

She felt her muscles go weak, felt herself sag against him for one precious second. Then two. Then three. His hand curved around the back of her head, his fingers tangling in her hair, and she almost gave in. Almost gave herself up to him again. It's what her body wanted—more of the insidious pleasure he could bring her with just a touch of his fingers, his lips, his skin.

But then memories of what it had felt like when he'd kicked her out of his apartment all those years ago rose up inside her, mingled with the hurt from this morning that she'd tried so hard to deny all day.

She wasn't giving in, wasn't yielding to the sexual magnetism he wielded like a sorcerer.

Shoving at his chest, she squeezed out from between his body and the wall. "I'm pretty sure I'm not the only one who begged," she called over her shoulder as she walked down the hall to her kitchen, away from him.

She figured her comment would anger him—she had counted on it, as a matter of fact. But after a second of disgruntled silence, Marc tossed his head back and laughed. His reaction was a million times more disconcerting than what she'd expected. Partly because it was the first time she'd heard him laugh since he'd walked into her classroom the afternoon before and partly because it was a good laugh. A really good laugh, low and smoky and filled with a joy that told her it was genuine, despite the circumstances.

"Touché," he said as she got herself a glass of ice water and then drained it in two long gulps.

When the water was done—when she felt as if she had herself under control, at last—Isa turned back to him and demanded, "Why are you here, Marc? I'm pretty sure we said everything we needed to say to each other this morning before you left."

He winced slightly. "I know I was a little harsh—"

"Don't pull that smarmy rich boy routine on me!" she snapped. "You weren't harsh. You were definite. Sleeping with me was closure and once you'd done it you were finished, ready to move on." She tore her eyes away from his too-beautiful face to glance at the clock on the wall behind his head. "So try again. What do you really want?"

He stared at her for long seconds, until the heat between them grew intolerable. "You," he finally said. "I want you."

"Try again," she replied with a snort that in no way betrayed the riot of emotions exploding inside. "You've had me, twice. And both times it's ended with you kicking me to the curb."

"I didn't kick you to the curb this morning—"

"Maybe not literally, since this is my house," she told him with a shrug she hoped looked negligent. "But you definitely did it metaphorically. Which is fine, I get it. Closure, revenge, whatever. But that still doesn't explain why you're here now. What do you want from me?"

He paused, seeming to weigh his words as carefully as she'd been weighing hers.

Finally, just when she'd given up hope on him telling her anything, he ground out, "I need your help."

Nine

"My help?" She stared at him incredulously.

"Yes." He pulled back, putting some distance between them for the first time since he'd walked back into her house. Damn it. There was no way she would help him, not after what he'd just pulled.

He hadn't meant to go all possessive on her, hadn't meant to give in to the sensual need that throbbed between them with each breath they took. He was there because he needed her help professionally, not because he wanted to get her into bed again. Or at least, that was the lie he was telling himself.

Now that he'd given her some breathing room, she spun around. Pulled another glass out of the cabinet behind her. She filled it with ice and water before handing it to him and demanding, "Explain."

So he did, telling her about the article, about the damage it could do to Bijoux if it ran. About how they needed a conflict diamond expert to sign off on the fact that their stock was completely conflict free.

When he was done, she looked at him over the rim of her cup. "There are other experts out there. You could have gone to any of a dozen people and asked them to work for you."

"I could have, yes."

"But you came to me instead. Because you figured you could use our past to sway my results?"

Fury shot through him. "I don't need to sway your results. When you investigate Bijoux, you'll find that we use only responsibly sourced diamonds. I can assure you, there is not one blood diamond among our stock."

"That's a pretty big assurance," she told him. "How can you be sure?"

"Because I look at each and every diamond that comes through our place. I make sure that, geologically, they come from where we say they do."

"Every diamond?" she asked, skeptical. "You must clear ten thousand of them a month."

"More. And yes," he said before she could ask again, "I look at every single one."

"How do you have that kind of time? Don't you have a company to run?"

"I make time. I know that makes me a control freak, but I don't give a damn. My business almost died once because I took my eye off the ball. I can guarantee you that won't happen again."

She winced. Because of what he'd said or the angry way he'd said it, he didn't know. He should stop throwing that in her face, considering he needed her help, but she'd asked why he was the way he was about his business. What happened six years ago was a huge part of that.

She didn't say anything, didn't fire back like she normally would. That didn't reassure him, though. Not when she was looking at him with something akin to regret in her eyes. He wanted to believe it was for the past they shared, but his gut told him it was about his request.

Sure enough, after a long silence, she told him, "I can't do it."

"You mean you won't do it."

"No, I mean I *can't*. I've got a full load of classes this semester as well as a side project of my own going on—"

"This won't take long," he said. "A day and a half, two at the most for travel to Canada, then a couple days at my headquarters, comparing the mineral composition of my diamonds with those from the Canadian mines. Even if you wanted to trace a random sampling of serial numbers, shipments and documentation, it shouldn't take much longer than that."

"That's best-case scenario, if I don't find any irregularities."

"You won't," he assured her with total confidence. He knew his business inside out. There was no way conflict stones were going through Bijoux. No way. Not when he and Nic worked too damn hard to ensure that they always sourced responsibly.

"You can't guarantee that," she reiterated.

"I damn well can. My business is clean. My stones come from Canada and Australia and each and every one of them can be traced from the mine to me. There are no irregularities."

"You don't source from Africa at all? Or Russia?"

"No."

"There are a number of mines in both places that certify their diamonds as conflict free by Kimberley Process standards—"

"But I can't guarantee that no child labor went into

mining them. I can't know for sure where the profits are going. Most of the mines I use in Canada and Australia have shareholders that they answer to, and those that don't have very rigorous—and open—bookkeeping. My diamonds are as clean as I can possibly make them, Isa. Trust me on that."

She snorted a little, muttered something under her breath that sounded an awful lot like "Yeah, right."

He couldn't help stiffening at her response. She had no reason not to trust him—he'd never lied to her. He'd never betrayed her. He was the first to admit he'd acted like an ass when he'd had her removed from his building, but he hadn't schemed behind her back, hadn't lied over and over again because of misplaced loyalty. No, that had been her modus operandi.

He wanted to call her on it—any other time he *would* have called her on it—but right now, he needed her more than she needed him. The knowledge grated like hell. He'd sworn a long time ago never to give a woman power over him again and yet here he was, giving that power to not just any woman but to the one who had nearly destroyed him.

So instead of picking a fight he couldn't afford to lose, he swallowed back his bitterness and growled, "It's a short-term assignment but that doesn't mean it can't be very profitable for you. I know it's short notice, but I'm more than willing to double—or triple—your regular fee."

She reeled back as if he'd slapped her. "Are you trying to bribe me to certify your diamonds as conflict free?"

"*Bribe* you?" He went from annoyed to furious in two seconds flat. "I already explained that I have no reason to worry. The last thing I need to do is bribe someone to lie about my business."

"Then why the extra money? My regular fee is steep enough to make most companies wince."

"Jesus, you're suspicious."

"You have to admit, I have reason to be."

No, damn it, she didn't. He had never been anything but straight with her. "Bijoux isn't most companies. And I don't have the luxury of time. This ridiculous exposé is supposed to run on Friday and if I don't kill it, it's going to destroy my business. Why the hell wouldn't I pay double your regular fee if it meant you'd take the job?" This time he didn't bother to keep the bite out of his voice. Her lack of trust was getting to him, big-time, and he had no problem letting her know it.

Except Isa didn't seem to care. She narrowed her eyes at his tone, watching him for several long seconds. "You know this isn't going to work, right?" she finally said.

"It will. I've worked too hard to lose my company now."

"I don't mean the certification. I mean us working together. You need to find someone else."

"There is no one else, not with this short notice."

"Have you called around, tried to check it out?"

"No."

"Then how do you know that no one else is available? Stephen Vardeaux operates out of New York now and Byron M—"

"I don't want someone else," he snapped. "I want you."

"Why?" she asked suspiciously, her voice louder than usual with the same frustration that was rushing through him. "Because you think you can use our past to influence—"

"Goddamn it!" He roared as he finally lost his grip on his temper. "What have I ever done to make you think I would use you like that? What have I ever done to give you these kind of qualms about me?"

"Oh, I don't know. Made me fall in love with you and then tossed me out like I was garbage?"

He froze as her words registered, and so did she. "That's not what happened."

"I know." The look on her face said otherwise, though.

"You never loved me."

"You don't get to tell me how I felt."

"You never loved me," he insisted again, a little shocked at how shaky his voice was. How shaky he felt inside. "You betrayed me."

"I didn't betray you. I was caught between two untenable positions—"

"Being with me was an untenable position?"

"Don't put words in my mouth!"

"I'm not. Maybe you should think before you speak."

"God!" She made a sound of total exasperation as she headed out of the kitchen and back toward the front door. "I told you this wouldn't work. You need to leave."

He grabbed her arm, spun her around to face him. "I'm not going anywhere."

"Well, you're not staying here."

He raised a brow at her. "Wanna bet?"

"You need to go!"

"I'll go when you come with me."

"I'm not going anywhere with you. Not now, not ever again!" She was breathing fast, skin flushed and chest heaving. Tendrils of hair had escaped from the wild updo she'd pulled it into and burned like flames around her face.

They were in the middle of a fight and never had she looked so beautiful, so enticing, so delectable. A part of him wanted to shake her but a much bigger part wanted to take her. To shove her against the nearest wall and plunge himself inside her until she forgot every objection she had about him and he forgot every problem he had with her.

Until the past didn't matter anymore.

Until nothing mattered but the fire burning so brightly between them.

He reached for her before he could stop himself, pulled her body flush against his. She cried out, her hands going to his shoulders—to cling, to push him away? He couldn't tell. And by the way she arched against him, he didn't think she could, either.

Her breathing was harsh, her nipples peaked against his chest, and all he wanted to do was slip a hand between her thighs and find out if she was as turned on as he was. If she was as wet and hot for him as she'd been last night.

Overwhelmed with desire—with lust for her that just wouldn't go away—he lowered his head to take her mouth with his. And she almost let him...right up until she shoved at his shoulders hard and ripped her body away from his.

She stumbled back a few steps, staring at him with wide, bruised eyes.

He didn't follow, no matter how much he wanted to. Didn't grab hold of her and pull her back into his arms where a part of him was convinced she belonged. No, when it came to sex—to intimacy—between them, there was no way he would take that choice away from her. No matter how much he wanted her. No matter how certain he was that she wanted him, too.

"Get out," she told him, her voice low and broken.

"I can't. I need—" You, he almost said. *I need you.* Which would have been a disaster on so many levels. He could barely admit to himself how wrapped up in her he still was. There was no way he would admit it to her.

"Find somebody else to lie for you." She threw the words at him. "I won't do it."

Her words snapped him out of the sensual haze that had enveloped him the moment he'd touched her. He had a problem he needed a solution for.

Except, he'd already found a solution, hadn't he? His solution was her. Not just because she was one of the best in the world at what she did, but because—despite everything—he trusted her not to screw him over with this. It was a startling revelation after everything that had passed between them, but that didn't make it any less true. He knew she'd screwed him over once, knew that she'd stood by and watched first as he'd struggled to find out who was responsible for the diamond theft that had nearly ruined his business, and then again as he'd struggled to cover up for her father and keep him safe despite the industry's cries for his head.

But this felt different, and though he'd argued against it at first, now that he was here, staring into her eyes, he knew she wouldn't screw him over. Not on this and, hopefully, never again.

"You owe me," he told her, standing his ground even as she attempted to shove him toward the door.

She froze. "That's not fair."

"Do you think I give a damn about fair right now? My business is on the line. You owe me," he reiterated. "This is how I want to collect."

She turned pale, pressed her lips together so tightly that they turned nearly white. She shook her head, stepped back, but the look in her eyes told him he almost had her. "I can't just drop everything. I have plans—"

At the mention of her date, his patience abruptly ran out. He'd be damned if she turned her back on him because of some other man. Not after last night. And not when he was standing here, almost begging her for her help.

"Break your damn plans," he growled. "Or—"

"Or what?" she demanded, chin raised in obvious challenge.

He'd been about to suggest taking her straight to the

airport after her date, but her obvious belief that he was
threatening her pushed him over the edge. If that was what
she expected of him, then that was what he'd give her. "Or
I'll break them for you. I'll break this new identity you've
assumed wide-open, tell the school, the press, anyone who
will listen who you really are. Then where would you be?"

"You wouldn't dare."

"You'd be surprised what I'd dare."

"If you did that, you wouldn't get your expert testi-
mony."

"Yes, well, according to you, I'm not getting that testi-
mony anyway. So, tell me, what have I got to lose?"

"You're a real bastard, you know that?" Her eyes were
fiery hot as they glared up at him, but that only made the
wet sheen of them stand out more. The knowledge that he'd
brought this strong woman to tears made him feel like the
bastard she'd called him, and for the first time since she'd
pissed him off, he wondered if he'd had more to lose than
he'd imagined.

"Look, Isa—"

"I'll do it," she interrupted, brushing past him. "But
then, you already knew that, didn't you?"

He didn't know whether to be relieved by her acquiescence or upset by it. His father had taught him from an
early age to go after what he wanted—no holds barred—
but Marc had always tempered that ambition with care.
Until now.

There was a part of him that wanted to tell her to forget the whole thing, to pretend he hadn't come here and
threatened her. But then where would Bijoux be? This
article would hit them hard. It wasn't just about what he
wanted or needed. Bijoux employed thousands of people—
where would they be if he let the *LA Times* deal such a
crippling blow?

It was that thought that kept him quiet as Isa swept down the hall. "Where are you going?" he asked.

"To pack a bag. If that's all right with you?" He winced at the tone—and the look on her face. How she managed to look imperious dressed in sweats and a ragged tank top, he would never know.

He didn't answer her question—he knew a minefield when he heard one. Instead, he settled on a simple "Thank you."

"Oh, don't thank me yet. You may think you have the upper hand here, but if so much as one of your diamonds is the wrong composition, I'll crucify you in the press myself. And to hell with the consequences."

He watched her go and couldn't help smiling, despite her very deliberate threat. The fire was back—and he was glad. Despite their past, despite everything stretching between them, he never wanted to be the one to make Isa cry.

Ten

"Which mine are we going to first?" Isa asked as the pilot of Bijoux's private jet came over the intercom to announce that they would be landing in Kugluktuk in approximately twenty minutes. They were the first words she'd spoken to him since they'd gotten on the plane in San Diego, seven hours before.

"We'll go to Ekaori today and then tomorrow I'll take you to Vine Lake and Snow River."

She nodded, because that was pretty much what she'd been expecting. Ekaori sourced diamonds for numerous jewel companies, as did Vine Lake. But Snow River sourced exclusively to Bijoux. It was the newest diamond mine in the Northwest Territories—had only been operational since 2012—and was owned and operated by Bijoux Corporation itself. If anything suspicious was going on, that was where she would expect it to come from. So much easier to pull off a con—or a heist—when you were the one in control of the source material.

As they descended, they hit pretty impressive turbulence. She tried not to let it bother her—she'd flown into Kugluktuk to tour the mines numerous times in the past few years and it was always the same. They were only a hundred or so miles from the Arctic Circle, and the weather up there, even in the middle of summer, was always unpredictable.

Marc, she noticed, was making a valiant effort not to notice the turbulence, either. He kept working, one hand scrolling through the touch screen on his laptop while he glared at the screen. But his other hand was clenched around the armrest as if his will alone was the only thing keeping the plane in the air.

It didn't surprise her that the turbulence made him nervous. He was such a control freak that putting his fate in the hands of someone else had to grate, even at the best of times. Doing it now, as the plane dropped and bucked, had to be awful for him.

Before she could think twice about it—and about all the reasons she was still angry at him—she leaned forward as far as her seat belt would allow and placed her hand over his tense one. Then she squeezed gently.

He was sitting directly across from her, so when his eyes jerked up at the contact, they clashed immediately with her own. She didn't say anything and neither did he, but she felt him relaxing a little more with each swipe of her thumb across the back of his hand.

"We'll be down soon," he said, his voice a little deeper, huskier, than usual. As if she was the one who was nervous.

"I'm not worried." Which was a big, gigantic lie—she was totally worried. Not about the turbulence or landing safely, but about being here, with Marc. About how her hand was still resting on his and how good it felt to touch him. About the fact that, despite everything he'd done—

and everything she'd done—there was a part of her that still wanted him. That would always want him.

The thought stung, had her stomach clenching and nerves skittering up her back. Because the only thing stupider than letting Marc Durand into her bed last night would be letting him back in again tonight. He didn't trust her, didn't want her—hell, he wasn't above blackmailing her when the situation called for it. So why on earth did her body still respond to him? Why on earth did she want to comfort him when he had *never* done anything to comfort her?

Feeling like an idiot—or worse, a dupe—she started to pull back. But Marc's other hand covered hers, trapping her fingers. "Please," he said. "Don't."

Again their eyes met, and though she didn't see nervousness in his gaze any longer—he wasn't a man who tolerated weakness, in others or himself—she did see something that had her breath catching in her throat. That had her errant nerves turning from ice to a dark and sensual kind of heat.

That should have had her sitting back, getting as far away from him as she possibly could. When things had gone bad with them last time—when she'd begged him not to prosecute her ailing father even knowing the request meant he'd lose so much of what he'd worked for—it had nearly killed her. Not the icy walk in the winter rain after he'd kicked her out, though that had been no fun. No, what had nearly destroyed her had been the knowledge that she had hurt Marc irreparably.

Because of his parents, who had always cared more for money and status than they ever had for him and his brother, Marc trusted few people. But he'd trusted her, had believed in her, and in the end she had torn that trust to pieces by picking her jewel thief father over him.

It wasn't her proudest moment—was, in fact, one that still kept her up some nights. But what else could she have done? Her father was old, frail, dying. How could she have turned on him? How could she have let him spend the last year of his life in prison when he'd dedicated his life to giving her the world? To showing her wondrous places and things and teaching her that money wasn't important. Adventure was. People were. Yes, he'd turned her into a thief at an early age, but that wasn't all he'd been. And though she'd rejected that lifestyle when she'd met Marc, that didn't mean she could reject her father. He'd been a great father and she'd loved him very much.

And so she'd turned on Marc—or, at least, that's how he saw it. She'd begged him to understand, begged him to love her as she'd loved him, but that hadn't been possible. Not when all he'd seen was her betrayal.

Outside the plane window, the ground grew closer, lush with greenery as far as the eye could see. The first time she'd flown to Kugluktuk had also been summer, and she'd been astonished at the lack of snow and ice, had figured that this far north the ice would never melt.

But that wasn't the case. Though the mountains in the distance were still covered with white—and pretty much always were—the land down here was verdant and alive. And would be until the end of August, beginning of September, when temperatures dropped significantly.

Not that it was exactly warm here, even in mid-July, she admitted after the plane had landed and they took the stairs down to the tarmac. The temperature was about fifty—or so her phone said—but the fiercely blowing wind made it feel a lot colder.

She shuddered and pulled her jacket more tightly around herself as she thought longingly of the woolen scarf she'd left on her bed. Since it had been in the high sixties the last time she'd been here in July, she'd figured she wouldn't need it. Big mistake—and one she probably wouldn't have made if she hadn't been so annoyed at Marc while she was packing. After all, it didn't take a brain surgeon to remember that weather near the Arctic Circle was bound to be unpredictable.

Something warm brushed against her neck and she jolted, glancing behind her.

"Here, take mine," Marc said as he wrapped a black cashmere scarf around her neck.

"It's okay. I'm—"

"Freezing. You're freezing. And since I'm the reason you're here to begin with, the least I can do is try to keep you warm. Now, come on." He took her overnight bag from her and, with a hand in the center of her back, guided her toward the waiting helicopter.

She should pull away—she knew she should. After all, she was still furious with him for forcing her to come up here when she was still reeling from the way he'd made love to her and then walked out on her. He'd all but admitted that he'd had sex with her in an effort to get her out of his system. And then he'd blackmailed her into coming here to look at his diamond mines.

She should be telling him to go to hell, should be running as far and fast as she could in the opposite direction. What she shouldn't be doing is taking his scarf—and melting into his touch.

With that thought firmly in her mind, she pulled away. Started walking faster. And did her best to ignore the way she could still feel the imprint of his hand burning against her back.

The helicopter ride to the first mine was short—and a lot less windy than any she had ever been on before. Of course, that was because Marc had access to the best of everything—including a top-of–the-line helicopter that felt about as luxurious as a limousine.

They came into Ekaori from the north. She saw the huge, circular pit mine from quite a ways out. Her first glimpse of the mines from the air always startled her and today was no different. It looked much more like a whirlpool carved into granite than it did a functioning mine. But the huge opening in the land was because of the surface mining that had been done for years, before the diamonds had been exhausted and they'd been forced to expand underground.

They landed on the helipad right next to the main building and Marc climbed out first, before extending a hand to help her. She didn't need his help, but she took his hand anyway. Out of politeness, she told herself as she moved past him. Not because she wanted to feel the brush of his warm skin against her own.

The general manager of the mine was obviously expecting them—he was waiting right next to the helipad, with a huge smile on his face as he greeted Marc. She'd been to this mine no less than five times and had never seen Kevin Hartford up close, let alone had him meet her helicopter. But then, she'd never traveled with the head of the largest responsibly sourced diamond corporation in the world, either.

Marc had obviously told Kevin what she would need, because after a few minutes of polite chitchat in the outer office, he took her directly into the lab, where technicians laser cut a serial number and the lab's symbol—a small polar bear cub—directly onto each and every jewelry grade stone. It was the first step in a long series that enabled regulators, and consumers, to track a diamond from the mine through production all the way to the store where it was sold.

Kevin also handed her a large binder with printouts of every serial number given to every diamond that had gone from the Ekaori mine to Bijoux in the past three years.

There were a lot of numbers.

He then led them to the screening plant, where they watched as thousands of pounds of rock were screened by machines and then by people for kimberlite deposits, the substance that created most diamonds. After the kimberlite was separated out, a second, more involved screening took place to find the actual diamonds.

She took samples from the rock and the kimberlite so that she could map the mineral content when she got back to GIA. Part of her wondered if the sampling was super-fluous—after all, she had mapped the mineral content of this mine, and all the mines up here, numerous times, as had any number of other diamond experts. But Marc's business was depending on her doing this completely by the book, and so she would do just that. After nearly cost-ing him his business once, she would be as careful as pos-sible during this trip.

Though she would never admit it to him, especially after he'd blackmailed her into helping him, she did owe him for what he'd done for her father—and for the hit Marc had taken. The least she could do was make sure that her in-vestigation of his diamond sourcing was beyond reproach.

By the time they were done with their tour of the lab and business facilities, it was too late to go down into the mine. Which was fine with her—she'd been in this dia-mond mine before and there was nothing new she needed to see. Besides, all the important documentation and iden-tification work began once the stones were pulled from the rubble and tagged as either industrial or jewelry grade.

Marc hadn't said much during their time at the lab, tak-ing a backseat as she asked questions. But once they were back in the helicopter, he turned to her and said, "I know you didn't want to do this, but I really appreciate you coming up here with me. I knew you were the right choice from the very beginning, but after watching you today, I'm so appreciative that you agreed to help me."

He looked and sounded completely sincere, and though there was a part of her that couldn't help wondering about his motives, she couldn't help responding to the warmth in his voice—and his eyes.

"I'm just doing my job, Marc."

"I know. With the way I coerced you into coming, a lot of people would consider you justified in using the opportunity to retaliate. You could destroy me if you wanted to and it would be no less than I deserved for how I've treated you."

"I would never do that!" She was shocked that he'd even think it. "I don't lie, especially not about something like this—"

"I know," he said again. This time, he was the one who covered her hand with his own. "What I'm trying to say, and obviously doing a crappy job of it, is thank you. I'm grateful for your help."

She stared at him for several seconds, completely non-plussed. This Marc, humble and open and kind, was the Marc she'd fallen in love with all those years ago. The Marc who'd held her and laughed with her and made plans for a future with her. And though she'd promised herself just that morning that she would never let her guard down around him again, Isa could feel herself wavering. Could feel her resolve crumbling as quickly as her defenses.

Which was why, when the helicopter landed in the back parking lot of one of the two hotels in Kugluktuk, she quickly gathered her things and stepped outside. While Marc spoke with the pilot about picking them up in the morning, she made her way into the hotel and registered for their rooms.

By the time he made it in, she had the keys to both rooms in one hand and her overnight bag in the other. She held one key out to him. "I guess I'll see you in the morning," she told him with a forced brightness she was far from feeling.

He raised a brow and for a second, she forgot how to breathe. Why did he keep doing that? she asked herself furiously. He was always gorgeous, usually able to curl her toes with only a look or a touch. But from the very beginning, whenever he had raised that damn brow of his, looking half questioning and half amused, it had made her heart beat too fast and her breath catch in her throat. The fact that it was still doing that, even after all this time and everything that had happened between them, made her take a step back in a futile effort to put enough distance between them.

"I thought I'd buy you dinner," he said. "The hotel has a pretty good restaurant, and the Coppermine Café across the street has great fried chicken."

"Actually, I'm kind of tired. I didn't get much sleep last—" She broke off in the middle of the familiar excuse as a wicked grin split his face. Of course he knew she hadn't gotten much sleep the night before—he'd been the one who'd kept waking her up to make love, over and over again, until now, hours later and thousands of miles away from her small beach cottage, she still couldn't get the scent of him off her skin.

"We can make it quick," he suggested. "We'll put our bags in the room and then—"

"No!" The word came out more forcefully—and more panicked—than she'd intended. But she wasn't stupid. She knew her weaknesses, knew that if Marc kept smiling at her, kept touching her, she'd end up in bed with him despite her resolution to keep her distance. And no matter how good he was in bed, no matter how much she enjoyed making love to him, she just couldn't go there again. Not if she wanted to come out of this situation with some semblance of her heart, and her life, intact.

Six years ago, she'd loved Marc desperately. She'd been caught between him and her father—between a rock and the hardest place possible—and she'd made the only choice she could make. But that didn't mean she hadn't loved Marc, didn't mean she hadn't grieved for him even after he'd ripped her out of his life without a backward glance.

She understood what last night was for him—a chance to exorcise her once and for all—and she needed to remember that. More, she needed to let the way he'd touched her and kissed her—the way he'd loved her—last night be enough.

It *was* enough, she told herself as she took another stumbling step backward. It had to be. She would pay her debt and then she would walk away, conscience clear and heart whole.

Or at least, that was the plan. A plan that would be totally derailed if she had dinner with him, followed by a glass of wine in his room and another night of the most amazing lovemaking a woman could imagine. Oh, he'd only asked her for dinner, but she knew him. She knew the look in his eyes, knew the way his mind worked, and she had no doubt that if she didn't run now, she'd find herself flat on her back under him before the night was out.

"I think I'll just get a snack from room service and then turn in," she told him. "I'm beat."

He didn't look happy now, his eyes clouded with obvious displeasure. But short of wrestling her into the restaurant, there was nothing he could do.

Except, it seemed, drive her absolutely crazy in the few minutes he had left with her tonight.

"All right," he said. "I guess I'll have to settle for taking you to breakfast in the morning." He reached past her to press the up button on the elevator, and though there was plenty of room, he made sure that his hand brushed against her side as he did so.

She bit back a gasp, telling herself the sudden shock of heat radiating from his touch was only because he was hot and not because he heated her up. She didn't believe it, but then, she didn't have to. She just had to pretend.

Fake it till you make it.

That was the motto she'd learned growing up. She might not be much of a liar, but she was a hell of an actress. Growing up the daughter—and accomplice—of the most renowned jewel thief in the world, she'd had to be.

Fake it till you make it.

And that was the same motto she'd lived by when Marc had kicked her out six years ago. For weeks, months, she'd been so morose that most days it had taken every ounce of energy she had just to climb out of bed. But her father was dying and she'd needed to be there for him even if she couldn't be there for herself. Which was why she'd pasted on a smile and pretended that everything was okay even as she was shattering into so many pieces she didn't think she'd ever put them back together again.

But she *had* put the pieces back together, she reminded herself as she stepped onto the elevator. And gorgeous smile or not, sexy eyebrow raise or not, she wasn't going to give Marc Durand the chance to change that. He'd broken her once—or, more accurately, they'd broken each other.

This time around, she'd forego the pleasure. And in doing so also forego the pain. In her mind, it was more than an equal trade-off.

Eleven

He didn't know what was going on with Isa, but whatever it was, he didn't like it. Marc glanced around the Snow River Diamond Mine, owned and operated exclusively by and for Bijoux, and did his best not to scowl with displeasure. Not at the mine, or at the questions Isa was asking, but at the way she had spent the entire day barely acknowledging that he existed. After yesterday, he'd hoped things would be different between them.

Oh, he was the first to admit that yesterday had not gotten off to a good start—how could it have when he'd rolled out of bed with Isa only to tell her that he'd slept with her to banish the ghosts of their shared past? And then he'd blackmailed her into helping him. Definitely not a good move in anyone's book. She'd been furious and had every right to her anger.

But on the plane, she'd seemed to soften. She'd remembered the fact that he was a nervous flyer and had tried to comfort him through the turbulence. She'd even smiled at him, let him touch her as they'd gotten off the plane. As the day had worn on, he'd seen her move from being an angry ex-lover to a consummate professional determined to do her job—even if doing that job meant helping the man causing her anger.

Her kindness had made him feel terrible, had made him determined to apologize for the way he'd treated her—and to make it up to her. She'd let him apologize, had even seemed to take it in the spirit he'd intended it. But then, when he'd wanted to take her to dinner as a kind of peace offering—and to continue the conversation they'd started earlier in the day—she'd frozen him out. Had, in fact, gone so far as to all but slam the door of her hotel room in his face. And since he'd made it a policy never to lie to himself, he had to admit that the rejection had stung.

Which was absurd. He was okay with her rejection piquing his pride, okay with it annoying him. But to actually be hurt by it? That he didn't understand. Because he didn't love Isa anymore, hadn't loved her in a long time. He'd made certain of that.

Sure, he wanted her, but what red-blooded man wouldn't? She was gorgeous, smart, kind, with a killer body and a wicked sense of humor. But just because he desired her, just because he respected the professional life she'd built for herself, didn't mean he was falling for her again. And it sure as hell didn't mean that he *loved* her.

She was doing him a huge favor and being absolutely incredible about it, but that didn't mean he would ever be stupid enough to fully trust her again. And he sure as hell wouldn't be stupid enough to fall for her, no matter how much his body craved hers.

He watched as she charmed his general manager, a grizzly old man by the name of Pete Jenkins. Until now, Marc had pretty much considered Pete completely uncharmable, but somehow Isa had managed it within an hour of meeting him. A couple smiles, a few well-placed questions and she had the diamond industry veteran eating out of her hand.

Marc would be lying if he said the knowledge didn't make him wary—especially since it hadn't taken much more effort on her part to have Marc wrapped around her finger all those years ago. But his wariness wasn't enough to make him keep his distance, especially when she once again gave him a wide berth as she said her goodbyes and made her way back to the helicopter that would take them to the airport, where his plane waited.

He almost hurried to catch up with her, almost grabbed her hand and spun her around so they could have it out right there, and to hell with who was around to witness it. He probably would have done just that—had actually started up the path to the helipad after her—when Pete called his name.

Tamping down the annoyance that was quickly turning to fury, Marc turned back to his GM with the closest thing to a smile he could muster. "What's up, Pete?"

"I was wondering if you'd had time to look at the expansion plans yet? We've got about eighteen months before the surface dries up, but we've got to get started building the underground tunnels if we don't want the mine to come to a screeching halt in the not so distant future."

"I have looked at the plans," Marc told him. "And there are a few things I'm not happy with, so I sent the architects back to take a second try. They're supposed to have them ready for me in a couple weeks—I figured we'd talk about it then."

Pete scratched his chin, nodding thoughtfully. "It's the block caving measurements, right?"

Marc nodded, not the least bit surprised that Pete had

picked up on the same problem he had. "The spacing is way off for this mine. It would work over at Ekaori or some of the other mines, but the veins of kimberlite are very different in this part of the Northwest Territory."

"The pattern they wanted to dig for those tunnels was going to end up costing a lot more than it needed to."

"It was. My geologist and I were also concerned about the maze of them based on the mineral composite of the land. Things are different up here than they are at Ekaori. The last thing I want is a cave-in—you know worker safety is the most important thing to me."

"I do. It's why I wanted to speak with you. I figured we'd be on the same page, but it never hurts to check."

"No," Marc agreed. "It never hurts to check."

He bid goodbye to Pete and headed back to the helicopter, even as he ran the GM's parting words around in his head. No, it never hurt to make sure both parties were on the same page. Especially when one of those parties was a stubborn redhead with a sharp mind and a curvy-as-hell body.

Isa continued to give him the cold shoulder on the helicopter ride to the airport, and though it grated, he took it. It was a short ride and not very private, considering they were in the same cabin as the pilot. He would wait until they were on the plane, where he'd have plenty of privacy and plenty of time to ferret out why she'd started avoiding him when he thought they'd been making progress.

He figured he'd start subtly, ask her questions that would force her to talk to him. After all, if it was business related, she couldn't very well refuse to share her thoughts. This was a business trip, after all.

Except…best laid plans and all that. By the time they were onboard his plane, luggage stowed and seat belts fastened for takeoff, he was seething. And when she took the seat farthest away from him and refused to so much as glance his way, his temper exploded.

"What the hell is wrong with you?" he demanded, unfastening his seat belt and stalking toward her just as the plane hurtled into the air.

"What are you doing? You need to sit down!"

"What I need is for you to stop treating me like I'm a cross between Jack the Ripper and Attila the Hun."

At that moment the plane hit some turbulence and it was sheer will alone that kept him standing, legs locked and arms crossed over his chest as he stared her down. They hit another bump a few seconds later, and he ignored that one, too—refusing to give in to the turbulence, or his uneasiness with flying, now that he had Isa cornered.

"I'm serious, Marc. You're going to get hurt—"

"I'm serious, too, Isa. And I find it rich that you're concerned with me getting hurt when you've spent the last day doing your best to pretend I don't exist."

"That's not true—"

"It's absolutely true and I want to know why. If you're mad at me, I get that. You have every right to be. But don't freeze me out. Yell at me. Call me a bastard again if that's what you want to do. But don't ignore me."

"I'm not mad at you."

"Oh, yeah?" He lifted a brow. "Because it sure feels like that from where I'm sitting."

"You're not sitting. That's the whole point."

They hit more turbulence on their way up and the plane bounced a little, shimmied. At the same time, the pilot came over the intercom reminding them to stay seated with their seat belts fastened until they reached cruising altitude.

"Do you hear that?" Isa demanded. "You need to sit down!"

He moved closer, bending over so that he rested a hand

on the armrests on either side of her and his face was in hers. "You need to talk to me."

"Damn it, Marc." She reached out a hand, splayed it over his chest, as if she planned to push him into a seat if she had to. But the moment she touched him, heat shot through him. Covering her hand with his own, he tried to ignore the fact that he'd gotten hard from just the warmth of her hand on his chest.

It might have been harder to ignore if Isa's breath hadn't hitched in her own chest—and if her pupils hadn't been completely blown out. Add to that the fact that her skin was flushed. Her hand trembled where it rested against his heart, and it didn't take a genius to figure out that she was as turned on by the contact as he was.

"Isa." Her name was ripped from him as he threaded his fingers through hers. "Talk to me."

She turned her head away, looked out the window at the blue sky where they were breaking through the clouds. It was late, nearly ten o'clock at night, but here, near the Arctic Circle, it was as bright as if it was the middle of the day.

She contemplated the sky for long seconds and though he wanted to push for an answer, wanted to push her in general, he waited for her to find the words she needed. It had always been like this when they fought—him shoving at her verbally and her responding by pulling into herself until she had the perfect argument figured out in her mind.

This time, it didn't seem to work, though, because when she spoke it was in little more than a whisper. "I don't want to do this."

"Don't want to do what? Talk to me?" He should probably move back, but he moved closer instead, until his face was only inches from her. "I thought we were getting somewhere yesterday, thought we could be—"

"What? Friends? After everything that's happened between us, you thought you'd just apologize and then we could be friends?"

The virulence in her voice had him rearing back. Maybe he'd read her wrong—maybe the signs he'd taken for arousal had really been nothing more than anger. That didn't make sense, though. Not when she gasped at his touch. And not when she responded so beautifully when they were in bed together.

"Friends might be a stretch," he admitted after several long seconds passed in silence. "But I thought, maybe—"

The pilot chose that moment to interrupt, announcing that they had reached their cruising altitude and that they were now free to move to the more comfortable sofas at the back of the plane.

Isa sprang out of her chair like a jack-in-the-box, nearly knocking into him in her haste to get away.

Except he wasn't letting her go that easily, not when he was so close to getting answers. And not, he admitted, when he was so hard that walking was going to be a problem.

"Where do you think you're going?" he demanded, grabbing her wrist and spinning her around.

"Away from you," she muttered.

"It's a little late for that, isn't it?" He started walking, bumping her breasts with his chest, her abdomen with his erection, her thighs with his.

She backed up a step for each one he advanced, through the narrow row of seats and across the aisle, until her back was pressed against the plane wall and her front was pressed tightly against his own.

"Why are you doing this?" she asked, her voice broken, breathless.

He might have felt bad, might have retreated, if his leg

wasn't between her thighs and if her hips weren't moving restlessly against the thigh he had pressed against her sex.

"Because I've never stopped wanting you." The answer slipped out of his lust-clouded brain. "Because I don't think I ever will."

"It's not enough," she said, even as she arched her back and pressed her breasts more firmly against his chest.

He could feel her nipples, peaked and diamond hard, through the thin fabric of her blouse and his T-shirt. He groaned, rubbed his chest against her breasts once, twice, then again and again as her breathing turned from shallow to ragged in the space between one heartbeat and the next.

"It's more than enough," he told her, bending his head so his mouth was right against hers. Each one of her trembling exhales left her mouth and entered his. "It always has been. Always will be."

"Marc." This time when she said his name it was more plea than protest.

"I've got you, Isa. I've got you, baby," he muttered right before he took her mouth in a kiss it felt like he'd been waiting years for instead of mere hours.

Twelve

She shouldn't be doing this, shouldn't be letting Marc do this. But as his lips took hers, his tongue stroking, slowly, languidly, luxuriously against her own, Isa didn't care about shouldn't. She didn't care about the past and she didn't care about the future, didn't care about how much this would hurt when the plane landed and she was once again alone. All she cared about—all that mattered—was the way Marc felt. The way he made her feel, as if her whole body was electrified. As if she could do anything, everything.

Her arms crept up of their own volition, wrapping around his neck and pulling him closer, closer, closer, until every inch of her was pressed up against some part of him. Mouth to mouth, chest to chest, sex to sex.

It felt so good.

He felt so good.

"Isa, baby," he murmured against her lips. "I want—"

"Yes." She ripped her mouth from his, pressed hot kisses against his jaw, his throat, the sensitive spot behind his ear. "Whatever you want, yes."

It must have been the affirmation he was waiting for, because with one last kiss, he pulled away from her. She made a low, confused sound in the back of her throat, but he just grinned wickedly as he wrapped his hands around her hips, cupped her bottom in his palms and lifted her against him.

"Marc." It was a moan, a plea, a desperate cry for more even as she wrapped her legs around his waist, pressing her sex firmly against his own.

He took her mouth again, his lips hot and firm and desperate. Then he was shifting her weight a little, turning, walking through a door toward the back of the plane. When she'd first come aboard, she'd wondered what was back here. Now she knew—it was a small bedroom, complete with a large bed with a black comforter and gray silk sheets.

He never faltered as he walked her backward across the room, never so much as shifted what she considered her pretty substantial weight. Instead, he kept kissing her, skimming his mouth over every part of her he could reach—every inch of exposed skin—and she marveled at his strength, at the feel of all those hard muscles against her own softness.

And then they were at the bed and he was dropping her into the center of it with no warning and a wicked, wicked grin. She gasped at the short fall—and at the sudden lack of contact with this man she should know better than to fall for again.

She did know better, she told herself as she reached for him, her fingers tangling in the soft cotton of his T-shirt.

She just didn't care, not now when Marc was here, hot and hard and as desperate for her as she was for him.

She pulled him down on top of her, then rolled the both of them until she was the one on top, her thighs straddling his hips as she looked down at him. "It's my turn," she told him a little breathlessly.

He just smiled, lifting that damn eyebrow of his that was responsible for so much of the trouble she'd found herself in. "You look like you expect me to protest."

"Aren't you?"

He smirked then, a small twist of his lips that sent heat streaking through her. "I have you on top of me, warm and willing and—" his fingers skimmed between her legs, rubbed at her sex "—wet. What in the hell is there for me to protest about?"

He looked as though he wanted to say more, but she leaned forward, stopped him with a kiss that had her hands trembling and her brain melting within seconds. Then she was pulling, tugging, yanking at his shirt, desperate to get it off so that she could touch the warmth of his skin, the hard press of his muscles.

He laughed darkly, even as he half sat up in an effort to help her divest him of the garment. And then she was touching him everywhere—his shoulders, his heavily muscled pecs, his too-perfect abs—licking her way across and down his beautiful, glorious body.

He gasped when she got to his belt, arched against her, shuddering, as her fingers—and her tongue—dipped below the waistband of his jeans.

"Isa, baby—"

"I've got you," she said, mimicking his words from earlier as she unbuckled his belt, unbuttoned his jeans. She slid to the floor beside the bed, tugging at his shoes, his pants, his boxer briefs, until Marc was spread out before her, gloriously, perfectly naked.

He muttered a curse, reached for her, but she shook her head, pushed his hands away. "It's my turn," she said again, right before she took him in her mouth.

He groaned, low and long and tortured, his hands tangling in her hair as she pulled off in order to press long, lingering kisses along his length. He shifted, arched his hips, tangled his fingers in her hair. She knew what he wanted, what his body was all but begging for, but she wasn't ready to give it to him, not yet. Not when he'd spent so much of their last night together tormenting her.

But then he cupped her jaw in his big, calloused hand, tilting his head so he could look down at her with his dark, dazed eyes and she lost the last of her willpower. Leaning forward, she took him deep.

Her name was a hoarse cry on his lips as he arched and moved and shuddered against her. It had been a long time since she'd done this to a man—over six years, to be exact—but she still remembered what Marc liked and how he liked it. Still remembered the taste of him as he spilled on her tongue.

She wanted that again.

He was close, so close, and she stroked her fingers across his taut stomach as she prepared to take him over the edge. But Marc was having no part of it. Grabbing her hand in one of his, he held it tight as he used his other hand to coax her mouth back up to his.

"I want to feel you," she protested against his lips. It was a halfhearted protest, though, because he was stroking her breast, pinching her nipple between his thumb and middle finger even as his index finger stroked back and forth against the hardened tip.

She gasped, arching against him. It was all the encouragement he needed. Dropping to his knees beside her, he kissed her slowly, thoroughly, passionately. For long seconds she couldn't move, couldn't think, could barely breathe. She was completely enthralled, completely under his spell and she wanted this moment to go on forever.

Then he was lifting her, spreading her out on the bed before him like a feast. "Marc," she gasped, her fingers clutching at his shoulders as she tried desperately to pull him over her.

Pleasuring him had driven her own need to the breaking point and she wanted—needed—to feel him inside her. But Marc had other ideas. Leaning forward, he pressed hot, wet, openmouthed kisses against her sex.

She lost it then, her fingers twisting in his hair as she arched against his mouth. His wicked, wonderful mouth. He slipped his hands beneath her, cupped her bottom and lifted her hips so there was no escape, no surcease, no moment to catch her breath. There was only him, only Marc, and the crazy pleasure he gave her.

Again and again, he brought her right to the edge of madness, of desire. Again and again, he refused to let her go over. By the time he pulled away to slip on a condom, she was an incoherent mess. Begging, pleading, promising him anything and everything if only he would—

He slid inside her then, his mouth pressed to hers even as he moved a hand between them and stroked her. That was all it took. She went off like a rocket, her body exploding with pleasure that went on and on and on.

Marc rode her through it, his hand and mouth and body taking her higher and higher until she was lost. Lost in pleasure, lost in him, lost in what could be between them if they let it. She gasped out his name, pulled him closer, closer, closer. When he thrust against her one final time, when he took her mouth in a kiss so deep, so passionate, so all-consuming that she could do nothing but surrender to it—to him—she went over the edge again. This time she took him with her, and nothing had ever felt so good.

Thirteen

"Just an FYI, Marc," the pilot's voice came over the loud-speaker in the plane's small bedroom. "We'll be landing in half an hour."

Beside him, Isa stirred, but didn't wake. Pushing up on an elbow, he stared at her, mesmerized, for long seconds that turned into longer minutes. She was beautiful like this.

Actually, she was always beautiful, with her pale skin, dark eyes, luscious hair and even more luscious body. But there was something about her when she was sleeping that made her even more appealing. Maybe it was the fact that this was the only time he'd seen her truly relaxed since he'd walked into her classroom the other day. The only time she'd allowed him to see the real Isa behind Isabella, the woman with the tight braid, quiet demeanor and impressive credentials.

Or maybe it was the vulnerable curve of her full lower lip that made her so enticing. Or the soft pink flush to her normally ivory cheeks. Or the way her hand curled around his biceps, as if, even in sleep, she was trying to hold him. God knew, he hadn't slept for that very same reason. He'd been afraid of falling asleep while holding her only to wake up and find out that the tenderness and the passion had been a dream. Or that somehow, when he loosed his grip, she would slip through his fingers like kimberlite silt.

He didn't want that to happen this time. He didn't know what he *did* want to happen—didn't know, really, how he felt for her outside the need that continued to claw at him. No matter how many times he had her, he continued to want her. Wanted her still, right now. He wasn't ready to let her go.

Maybe that made him a fool. Hell, it probably did considering everything she'd put him through—and everything he'd put her through in return. But as he lay there, watching her, touching her, the past didn't seem to matter nearly as much as it once had. Nothing mattered but Isa and the way she made him feel.

"Fifteen minutes until landing, Marc. You guys need to take your seats if you haven't already."

He leaned over, pressed the button on the nightstand that allowed him to talk to the cockpit. "We'll be out in five, Justin."

Then he woke Isa, forcing himself to gently shake her shoulder until her chocolate-brown eyes looked up at him in confusion. "I'm sorry, baby. We've got to get dressed. We're about to land and we need to take our seats."

She blinked, rubbed her eyes. Then shoved her thick mass of red hair away from her face as she sat up slowly. He froze, watching as the sheet slipped down her torso to pool around her hips.

She looked like a goddess.

Like a vision.

Like the sexiest wet dream he'd ever had.

Eyes sleepy, lips swollen, cheeks warm and flushed. Yes, she looked like every fantasy he'd ever had—*would* ever have. Her hair was long and wild out of its braid, tumbling down around her shoulders and over her soft, full breasts. But he could still see the strawberry pink of her nipples, the pale curves of her breasts. He wanted to taste, wanted to bend his head and pull her nipple between his lips just to hear her make those broken, breathless sounds one more time.

He was actually leaning forward, mouth parted and eyes focused on the prize, when she slapped a hand on the center of his chest. "How long until we land?"

Her voice was low, husky. He grinned and grew hard yet again. The sound of her voice reminded him of what it had felt like to be in her mouth, in her throat. Of what it had felt like to slide between her wet, swollen lips as she took him deep.

"Oh, no," she continued, scrambling out the other side of the bed. "Judging by the time, I'm pretty sure we can't go another round."

She was right, they didn't have time. But that didn't seem to matter to his insistent hard-on. If he was being honest, it didn't matter much to the rest of him, either. Not when he ached to once again feel her skin, her softness— her sweetness—against every part of himself.

But there was something incredibly sexy about watching a well-satisfied woman shimmy into her clothes, her movements slow and languid as she stepped into her jeans or pulled her sweater over her head. He loved how pale her skin was, loved that her breasts and stomach and thighs bore small love bites and patches of whisker burn. Loved that she looked like she'd spent the past several hours being made love to by him. Loved even more that she looked like she belonged to him.

The thought pulled him up short, had him reaching for his own jeans and yanking them on a little harder than necessary. Because wanting Isa, enjoying making love to her, was one thing. Hell, he'd probably still want her when he was dead. But thinking about her belonging to him again—that was dangerous. Really dangerous, considering how much he liked the sound, the look, the feel of it.

"Here." Isa's voice pulled him back from his minor freak-out, and he realized she was holding his shirt out to him. She was also looking at him a little strangely, but he refused to let himself dwell on it. Not when his head was already filled with so many conflicting thoughts.

They finished dressing in silence, but when Isa opened the door and started back to their seats, he grabbed onto her waist, pulling her back to him. He didn't know what to say—he couldn't tell her that he loved her, but he didn't want to leave her with a "wow, that was fun," either. And so he let his actions speak for him, nuzzling his way up her neck and along her jaw.

She relaxed then, a tension he hadn't even recognized leeching slowly out as she melted against him. The moment was broken when Justin's voice came over the intercom, reminding them to take their seats.

They did just that, and this time when Isa reached for his hand it wasn't because of turbulence. And for now, for this moment, that was enough.

An hour later, Isa waved as Marc pulled out of her driveway. She watched him go, hands shaky and with a lump in her throat as big as the entire Ekaori diamond mine.

What had she done? she asked herself as she closed her front door. What was she *doing*? More, what was she *thinking*?—if you could even call the choices she'd made the past few hours "thinking." Which she wasn't sure she could. Committing emotional suicide, probably. Being stupid, absolutely. But thinking? No, she hadn't been thinking—was desperately afraid, in fact, that she'd left her brain somewhere over Northern Canada.

What else could it be? She'd left her house a little more than twenty-four hours ago, determined that Marc would never touch her again. Yet here she was, back home in the early hours of the morning, what was left of her mind preoccupied with Marc and her body pleasantly sore and well used.

So well used. She closed her eyes as images of Marc bombarded her. On top of her, beneath her, on his knees at her feet. His hands on her hips, on her breasts. His mouth skimming over her stomach, over her sex. Kissing her, taking her, loving her… No!

She slammed a mental door on those thoughts. Whatever crazy chemistry was between her and Marc, whatever disaster she was courting by being with him, she wouldn't go that far. She wouldn't call it love, not on his side and definitely not on hers. She didn't know yet what she would call it, but she would not call it that.

Love was too painful—she'd learned that six years ago. She'd loved him then and all it had gotten her was heartbreak. This time she would be smarter. This time she wouldn't let herself care, not like that. Not like her whole heart, her whole soul, depended on him.

Deep inside, a little voice whispered that it was too late. That she was already in way over her head. But she shut it down, refusing to listen. Not right now when she could still feel Marc moving over her, inside her. Not right now when she was too exhausted, too vulnerable, to know what the truth was, let alone face it.

Deciding to let it go for now so that she could maintain some semblance of sanity, Isa carried her overnight bag into her bedroom. She dropped it next to her dresser and then flopped face-first onto the bed.

She could barely breathe with her face buried in the mountain of pillows, but she didn't have the energy to so much as turn her head. It was five thirty in the morning and she had an early lecture at eight—the first of two back-to-back classes that she normally loved since it meant getting done early on Mondays and Wednesdays. At the moment, though, it seemed like torture to expect her to be showered, dressed and out of the house by seven. Not when she had barely slept in the past three days.

She could lay that at Marc's door, too, she told herself. Along with the soreness that came with using muscles long neglected and the love bites that kept popping up in new places, he was also responsible for Saturday's sleepless night, staring at the cracked and stained hotel ceiling. And God knew, Friday and Sunday nights were definitely his fault. The forty-five minute nap she'd gotten after he'd made love to her for hours didn't count as a good night's sleep.

Her phone buzzed in her back pocket and, against her better judgment and the protests of her screaming muscles, she reached for it. Glanced at the text that had just come in. It was from him. Of course it was—who else would be texting her at five thirty on a Monday morning? On this very particular Monday morning.

Marc: Just wanted to say thank you again for making the trip to Canada.

That was it? Thank you for coming to Canada? She waited a few seconds, staring at the screen expectantly, hoping for another text to come in. Because surely that couldn't be it, right? Surely, he hadn't spent the better part of a six-hour plane trip taking her apart, orgasm by orgasm, only to send such a ridiculous text as follow-up?

Seriously, why even bother?

She waited another minute, her stomach clenching despite the fact that she told herself that it didn't matter. Over and over again. Until she almost believed it.

After all, what was he supposed to say? If she'd tried to text him, she wouldn't have a clue what to say—or how to refer to what had happened between them.

Not when there were no established parameters.

Not when the closest thing they had to a relationship had ended six years before.

She'd just put the phone down on the bed next to her—and reburied her face in the pillows—when the damn thing buzzed three more times in quick succession.

Marc: I'll see you at Bijoux headquarters at noon today.

Marc: That is, if we're still on?

Marc: Also, I had a really nice time. Hope you did, too.

A nice time? He'd had *a nice time*? What the hell was that supposed to mean? A trip to the park was a nice time. Going to a movie with a friend was *a nice time*. Totally fabulous, completely toe-curling, absolutely mind-blowing sex was *not* a nice time. It wasn't close to being a nice time. And while she'd already established that she didn't know what it *was*, she definitely knew what it wasn't. And it simply was not a nice time.

Shouldn't Marc know better than to call it that? Especially if he wanted more fabulous, toe-curling, mind-blowing sex in the near future. Which, judging by the way he'd kissed her goodbye, he absolutely did. Although why he'd want sex with her when it was merely "nice," Isa didn't know.

She debated answering him, debated sending him a text that was as innocuous and insipid and soul-crushing as the ones he'd just sent her. She could tell him what a "nice time" she'd had, as well. Might even mention how much she'd enjoyed the seven orgasms—not that she'd been counting—that he'd given her. She could even say that she looked forward to running into him sometime at GIA. That would certainly get her point across.

But in the end, she did none of those things, because the truth was, she didn't have it in her to play games with him. She never had—she just wasn't the kind of person who enjoyed dangling a guy on a line simply to watch him squirm. It was why she and Marc had done so well together in the time they'd been a couple. He'd never been interested in artifice, either, had always been a straight shooter. Or at least until now. Until he'd sent her a text that said he hoped she'd had a nice time.

As if.

Though she'd originally flopped into bed with the hopes of catching an hour of sleep before going to work, she was now way too wound up to even think about sleeping. Her brain whirred at a hundred miles a minute as she tried to figure out just how big a mistake she'd made in sleeping with Marc, not just for one night, but two.

So instead of taking a nap, or sending him a return text, or relaxing after what had been a mentally and physically grueling thirty-six hours, she forced herself to get up and go into the bathroom for a quick shower.

After drying her hair and putting on a quick swipe of mascara and lipstick, which was all the fuss and muss she had the energy for today, Isa settled herself at her kitchen table with her laptop and a cup of coffee. Once there, she pulled up all the known data she had on the diamonds coming out of Canada—including the composition of impurities from the different mines. And then she got to work.

Besides serial number and mine symbol, the impurities were the best way for a gemologist to determine where a diamond actually came from. For example, African diamonds had impurities that were made of certain kinds of sulfides while Russian diamonds had impurities made largely of nitrogen. Unfortunately, or fortunately depending on how you looked at it, Canadian diamonds had neither—and very few impurities in general when compared to other diamonds in the world. This was good for the Canadian mine owners, because while the diamonds coming out of Canada only accounted for about three percent of the bulk sales of diamonds worldwide, they also accounted for over eleven percent of the revenue. This was due to their exceptionally high quality and low level of inclusions.

Which was very nice for Bijoux and all of the other companies with mines in Canada, but it certainly was a pain for gemologists trying to prove definitively that a diamond came from any of those mines. Which wasn't to say that it couldn't be done. It could. Just not in the normal way used to identify most diamonds.

The first thing she had to do was check the serial numbers on a wide range of the diamonds in Bijoux's vault, making sure that they matched up exactly to the ones from the Canadian mines. She had the binder, but she also had a USB stick with each of the serial numbers on it—she inserted it into her computer and downloaded the information into a program on her hard drive that would allow her to easily match up the numbers from the mine with the numbers on the diamonds in the Bijoux vault.

Next, she pulled up all the documentation on which levels were mined at which times, including the exact dates each level was declared extinct. As she did this, she checked to make sure that she had the exact mineral makeup of the soil found at each level. In most cases the soil compositions were similar or identical, but every once in a while one of the lower levels differed significantly from what was above it. Tomorrow, when she was in the lab, she would compare the silt samples she'd taken with her previous documentation—and then she'd look at the makeup of the Bijoux diamonds and ensure the probability that they came from these mines.

It was an important step in the process—both were—but the fact of the matter was neither would give her, or Marc, the definitive answer they were looking for. Diamond sourcing was a tricky business, made so by the nearly identical mineral composites of the stones no matter where in the world they were found, and by the less than up-front business dealings so many of the world's diamond traders engaged in.

Which left her with one final thing she was looking for—one final thing to try. It couldn't be forged, couldn't be erased and was, quite often, overlooked by people trying to pass off blood diamonds as conflict free: hydrogen atoms or isotopes on the surface of the diamond. These atoms were deposited on the stone by rainwater that sank into the ground around the stones before they were mined. They clung to the surface of the diamonds. Once there, they were notoriously hard to remove.

While the presence of isotopes wasn't enough to prove that a stone came from a certain region, the chemical makeup of the individual isotopes definitely could. The exact makeup of rainwater differed from place to place around the globe and because of this, the hydrogen isotopes deposited on the diamonds also differed so that each region had very different isotopes attached to its diamonds.

Years of research—from her and other gemologists who specialized in diamonds—had provided a pretty decent mapping of these isotopes. On her computer, she stored a breakdown of rainwater composition in all the major diamond mining areas—including Canada's Northwest Territories. So while she would, of course, scrutinize Bijoux's records, serial numbers and the impurities of their diamonds, it was these isotopes that she was counting on to prove Marc's case. Or disprove it.

She really hoped it wasn't the latter.

Not because she was sleeping with him and not because she had a past with him, but because—despite how things had ended between her and Marc—she had always thought of Bijoux as one of the good guys. In an industry that was both highly dangerous and highly monopolized by companies that didn't mind trading in blood, terrorism and child labor, Bijoux had always been clean. Or, it had been for at least as long as Marc and Nic had been in control. From the very beginning, the brothers had run the company differently from most other gem companies, ensuring that they did as little harm, and as much good, as they possibly could.

Both men had a strong environmental conscience and an even stronger social conscience, both of which leant themselves to making sure the Bijoux mines were the safest in the world, both ecologically and for their workers. For years, she'd held up Bijoux in her classes as examples to strive for in a business that far too often lacked heroes. After all, gems were pretty but for most companies, the mining—and trading—of them was anything but.

To find out that the Durand brothers had given up on the beliefs they'd always espoused—simply to line their already too-full pockets—would destroy the last of her already flagging idealism.

With that thought uppermost in her mind, Isa spent the next hour and a half poring over every piece of recorded data she had, or could find, about the diamond mines that Bijoux did business with.

She looked at hydrogen isotopes until her eyes crossed.

Memorized the mineral makeup of silt at all the mine levels Bijoux had bought stones from in the past eighteen months.

And she prayed, entirely too hard for a woman who shouldn't care one way or another, that when she started combing through Bijoux's vaults, everything would match up.

Because if it didn't... If it didn't, she would end up breaking a lot more than just Marc's company. She was going to break his heart. And no matter what lies she fed herself to get through the day, if that happened she was very, very afraid that she would break her own heart, as well.

Fourteen

"Has Isa found anything yet?" Nic asked the second he hit Marc's office on Monday afternoon.

"She's only been here three hours," he told his brother without looking up from his computer screen, where he was going through what felt like a never-ending string of emails that had accumulated in the day and a half he'd been in Canada. "Give the woman a chance to do her job."

"I'm giving her a chance. But we're getting down to the wire here. We only have a few days before the *LA Times* runs that article and I want to debunk them well before their Thursday night deadline hits."

"Believe me, you can't possibly want that any more than I do. But that doesn't mean we need to stick our noses in the vaults every five minutes and pressure Isa. She's already working overtime—we only got back from Canada this morning and she has to be exhausted." God knew, he was. "But she's here and she's doing her best to find the truth."

"Wow." Nic stopped pacing long enough to glance at his brother with raised eyebrows. "Since when did you start defending Isa Moreno?"

Since…since… He didn't know when. "What does that matter? We should be worrying about finding whatever traitor planted a false story with the *LA Times*."

"Believe me, I am worrying about that. But despite my seemingly carefree disposition, I'm actually quite good at worrying about more than one thing at a time." Nic grinned. "So hit me, big brother. What's going on with you and Isa?"

"Nothing's going on between us!" Marc barked, suddenly uncomfortable with the turn the conversation had taken. He'd barely wrapped his head around the fact that he was back to sleeping with Isa. He sure as hell didn't need anyone else—especially his smart-ass little brother—poking at their relationship right now.

"You sure about that? Because you seem awfully touchy for a man who's got nothing going on. Then again, maybe that's *why* you're touchy—"

"I am not touchy! And if I were, it would be because I'm waiting, just like you, to hear something from the vault. I know three hours is nothing when it comes to the job Isa has to do, but that doesn't mean I like the wait. And it sure as hell doesn't mean I like the silence."

"Amen to that, brother," Nic said, plopping himself down in one of the chairs opposite Marc's desk. Before Marc could blink, his brother had kicked his feet up onto the polished wood of his desk and leaned his very expensive antique chair back on its hind two legs.

"Could we say amen to you not killing yourself? And you not breaking my chair into fifty ridiculously small pieces?"

Nic just rolled his eyes. "You worry too much."

"I'm CEO. It's my job to worry too much." Marc glanced at the clock for what had to be the tenth time in as many minutes. He was trying to keep his calm for his brother, but the truth was, he was a wreck inside. He knew that none of his stones were conflict diamonds. He knew that they all came from the Canadian diamond mines that were ecologically sound and paid high wages. But that didn't keep him from wondering, or from worrying. Not when there was some traitor in their midst, slipping ridiculous stories to the *LA Times*. If they could make up a story about Bijoux dealing in conflict diamonds, what would stop them from bringing in a few of the blood-soaked diamonds to cement their case?

Just the thought made him sick. And had him pacing the same route back and forth across his office that his brother had just vacated.

"It's going to be fine," Nic said, sounding as if he was trying to convince himself as much as he was trying to convince Marc. "Besides, no news is good news. Right?"

"Right." Marc forced himself to think through the worry. "Lisa is with Isa in the vault and I'm sure she'll let us know the second Isa finds something that proves—or disproves—the article."

"She isn't going to find anything that proves the article," Nic told him confidently. "Because there's nothing to find. So what are we worried about?"

"Absolutely nothing," Marc told him, even as he contemplated pacing another lap around his office.

Except Lisa chose that moment to stick her head in. "Any news?" she asked as both brothers came to attention.

"Why are you asking us?" Marc said in disbelief. "You're the one who's been hanging out in the vault with our expert for the last three hours."

"Actually, I left her a couple hours ago. I had a meeting

to go to and she was pretty much lost in her own world anyway."

"A meeting? You left Isa alone in the diamond vault because you had a meeting to go to?"

"I left Dr. Moreno alone in the diamond vault." She looked uncertain for the first time. "Is that a problem? It's standard protocol with experts from the GIA—if anyone can be trusted, it's them. Besides, what's she going to do? There are fifty cameras in that vault, plus high-resolution imaging machines that record every single thing on your person as you enter and exit. Even if she wanted to steal something—which I'm sure she doesn't—she couldn't."

Marc knew Lisa was right, knew he'd set up the best security for his vault that an unlimited budget and years of expertise in the business could provide. Not to mention the fact that Isa had never stolen from him. Her father had, but she hadn't. Not six years ago when they were together and not anytime since.

Still, he exchanged an uneasy look with Nic. His brother had been her greatest champion, in the past and the present, and yet even he looked uneasy at the idea of Isa being alone in the vault. Marc moved swiftly for his office door.

"What's wrong?" Lisa asked. "Where are you going?"

"Don't worry about him," Nic said as Marc walked out the door, obviously covering—for him or for Isa, he didn't know. Nor did he care. "He's just uptight about this whole thing."

"We all are. I know you think it's just your reputations on the line, but it's all of ours. I stand behind every single diamond in that vault and the idea that some jerk has the nerve to lie about it—lie about us—makes me crazy. Especially when he's too much of a coward to accuse us to our faces. He has to go behind our backs, to some sleazy journalist, and try to discredit us that way."

Marc missed Nic's response to her diatribe as he was already halfway to the elevator. He told himself that everything was fine, told himself that he was paying Isa an exorbitant amount of money to certify his diamonds—money that she would be a fool to risk for the one or two diamonds she might actually be able to sneak out of the vault unseen.

And still he couldn't help cursing the elevator for taking as long as it did to arrive. He believed in Isa's integrity, believed she would never steal from him. Hell, he even believed that she hadn't stolen anything from anyone since she'd first met him; she had access to gems at GIA all the time. And still the little voice in his head urged him to hurry. Still he wanted to be up there in that vault with her. Not because he really thought she'd steal from him, but because he wanted to avoid having her face the temptation.

Most jewel thieves were like junkies—they couldn't stop even after they'd amassed enough money to retire. Isa's father had been like that. The man was a millionaire many times over, and dying of cancer to boot, but still he hadn't been able to resist the big score. Still, he'd stolen from his daughter's fiancé without remorse or concern. Hell, for a long time, Isa had been like that, too. When she'd begged him to keep her father out of jail, she'd told him about the thrill she'd always felt when stealing. Had told him how much she loved the adrenaline rush but how she'd given it up because the rush she got from being with him was so much bigger, so much more than she could ever get from stealing.

Now, after all these years, he knew she'd meant that. Knew she wasn't like that anymore. But what if the temptation was too much? What if she wanted to take one little stone, just to see if she could do it? Just because she wanted to?

Sometime in the past few days—probably right around the time she'd agreed to help him despite his over-the-top behavior—he'd forgiven her for what had happened all those years ago. Had forgiven her for choosing her father over him and leaving him, and his company, to flounder in the wake of it all. The man was her father, after all, and he'd needed her more than Marc had. But just because he understood, didn't mean he fully trusted her. Forgiven her, yes. But trust…he was still working on that.

If she did this, though, if she stole from him after everything they'd gone through, he knew he would never be able to forgive her. Hell, he wasn't sure he'd even be able to look at her again.

Maybe he should be grateful for this opportunity, he thought, as the elevator doors finally opened. It would show him what she was made of before he risked anything else on her. But the fact of the matter was, he wasn't grateful. He was scared. Not because he was worried about losing inventory, he realized as he swiped the badge that would take him to the top floor of the building where the vault was housed. But because he was worried about losing Isa. He'd already lost her once. He didn't want to go through that again, no matter what lies he'd told himself about his feelings for her when they were in Canada.

The elevator dinged to announce its arrival at his destination, and Marc waited impatiently as the doors slid open. They seemed to be taking three times longer than usual to do so, and though he knew that wasn't actually the case, it didn't make the wait any easier.

Finally, the doors opened and he all but launched himself out of the elevator and down the hall toward the main vault, where Isa was supposed to be working. In his haste, he nearly ran over Victor, one of their most accomplished diamond techs and a man who had worked his way up from stone polisher to management in a very short amount of time.

Victor smiled, called hello, but Marc was in too big of a hurry to do much more than nod at the man. And then he was around the corner, staring at the blinking lights that meant the vault was occupied but that its security—sans motion detectors—was fully engaged. He didn't know whether to be grateful or concerned.

In the end, he was neither. He kept his mind blank, open, as he swiped his badge and his fingerprints. Then he entered his personal code for the vault and waited for the thick steel door to unlock. It only took a couple of seconds, but it felt like an eternity.

Then he flung the door open and rushed inside like a crazy person. And all but bumped into the makeshift desk Isa had set up near the opening of the vault, a desk that held a laptop, a microscope and a small drawer of diamonds. She had one of the diamonds under the microscope, had obviously been studying it intensely when he'd barged in. Now she was studying him intensely.

"You okay?" she asked, putting the diamond down and pushing back from the table.

"Yeah, of course. I'm fine," he said because, really, what else could he say? *I freaked out because I thought you were going to steal from me*? Or how about, *I'm still freaking out because you've been alone in this vault for two hours and I don't know if you've pocketed anything*? Yeah, right, because either of those would go over so well. "I just wanted to check on your progress, to see if you'd found anything one way or another."

She laughed, even as she reached a casual hand out and rubbed his shoulder. "I know it's nerve-wracking, especially with that article hanging over your head, but nothing of any value can be done in an afternoon, especially in a vault of this size, with this many diamonds. If you're lucky, I'll be able to discuss my findings on Wednesday, but more likely it's going to be Thursday. And that's only if I spend every working hour here while my substitute teaches at the GIA."

She didn't sound bothered by that fact, but he was suddenly—overwhelmingly—swamped by guilt. Guilt for thinking, even for a second, that she was a thief. And guilt that she was working so hard to reassure him when he'd been suspecting terrible things about her. It didn't seem fair. Not when he'd been the one to almost beg her to take this assignment. Of course, that was before he'd known she'd be left alone in the vault.

Searching for something to say to diffuse the awkwardness he felt he glanced at the diamonds spread out on the table in front of her. Then stiffened because, well, honestly, they were small diamonds. Easy to lose, easy to fence. Easy to pretend away if things weren't going her way.

"Is there anything you need?" he asked as casually as he could. "Anything I can get for you?"

"Not right now. Tomorrow I'll need access to your labs, but for now I'm okay here if you have other stuff you want to do. You know, like run a company." She smiled as she teased him.

"Actually, I thought I'd hang out here for a while, if that's okay with you. Just in case something comes up. You're doing Bijoux a huge favor and I'd hate for you to have to wait for something you need."

"I'm actually good. I'm doing the serial number check right now and will probably be on that for the rest of the day so I really won't have anything to report unless I find a stone with a mismatched number." She put a hand on his shoulder, squeezing gently in what he assumed she thought of as support. "It's *nice* of you to offer, but there's nothing for you to do right now."

He didn't like the way she stressed the word *nice*, as if he was missing something. Considering that was exactly what he was afraid of, it ratcheted up his suspicion, had him walking toward the end of the vault and retrieving a chair from the small display there. He carried it back to her, set it down a few feet from her desk. Then slid into it with an easy smile he was far from feeling.

"Even so," he said, pulling out his phone and pretending to be busy. "I've cleared the rest of my afternoon, so I'm at your service."

She shot him an odd look. "You're seriously going to stay here the whole afternoon?"

"The whole afternoon," he agreed. And though he felt guilty for his suspicions, he still wasn't moving. Not when she was trying so hard to get rid of him. And not when she was currently concentrating on some of the smallest diamonds in the vault. He didn't like the looks of it and while he wasn't stupid enough to tell her that, he also wasn't stupid enough to leave her alone in here like a kid in an unsupervised candy store.

Isa gave him a strange look as she settled back down at her desk and returned to work, but he pretended not to notice. Which was so much better than letting her see how nervous she made him…and on how many different levels.

Fifteen

Marc was acting weird. Not crazy, need-a-straitjacket weird or anything like that, but he was definitely a little off. She glanced at him out of the corner of her eye as she finally finished checking the last diamond in the current batch and placed it back in the blue velvet–lined drawer.

He wasn't looking at her, wasn't paying attention to her at all. Which was fine—he was CEO of Bijoux, after all, and she was sure he had a lot of work to do, especially considering the allegations leveled at the company—but it still made her feel funny. As if she wasn't important enough for him to pay attention to. Or, as he hadn't made any move to touch her since he came into the vault, as if what had passed between them over the weekend had never happened.

He hadn't even risen to the bait when she'd used the word *nice*...which made her feel even more as though he wanted to forget making love to her.

Having sex, she reminded herself a little bitterly as she carried the drawer back to its place and slid it into the long, slender opening in a wall that was covered with row after row, column after column, of just such drawers.

The Bijoux vault was organized by size, color and clarity—pretty much like any vault she'd ever been in. Sticking with the smaller stones of lesser quality she moved to her right two columns and pulled out a drawer that was second from the top, then carried it back to her makeshift desk.

Marc had yet to say anything, or even look up from his smartphone, where he was currently scrolling away like the weight of the world depended on how fast he moved his index finger. It annoyed her all over again—she didn't need much attention, but *something* would be nice. A smile. A few careless sentences. An acknowledgment that they'd spent the entire weekend together, working and making love.

She ended up slamming down the drawer on the desk a lot harder than she'd intended to.

The sharp crack echoed through the room and for the first time since he'd settled in the chair next to her, Marc looked up with a frown. "Everything okay?" he asked.

"Yes. Everything's *nice*." She stressed the word a second time, even knowing she was being something of a brat. But he was getting under her skin and though she knew it was her fault for letting him, she couldn't help it. If all he'd wanted was a two-night stand, he could have said so, right? He'd had no problem saying it after the first time he'd crawled out of bed with her on Saturday morning. Why hadn't he said something to the same effect this morning when he'd dropped her off? Something like, "I had a nice time, but with the work you're doing for Bijoux, I really think we should keep it professional from here on out."

She probably would have snarled at him, would definitely have thought he was a douche. But then, she'd decided sometime in the past hour that he was a douche anyway, so it's not as if he'd gained anything by playing his games. Whatever those games might be and whatever purpose he thought they might serve.

She didn't say anything as she got back to work, opening the drawer and pulling out a selection of diamonds in the quarter carat, slightly included range. As with the drawer she had just examined, these were some of the cheapest diamonds in the vault. While the drawer of them was worth hundreds of thousands of dollars, individually each was only worth a hundred or so.

"Can I ask a question?" Marc asked, and she looked up to find him studying her intently.

"Of course. That'd be nice," she answered.

His eyes narrowed to slits and she knew she'd pushed the nice thing as far as she would get away with. Which was fine, because the longer he went without calling her on it, the more like a spoiled brat she felt.

"Why are you dealing with only the small diamonds? Shouldn't you be looking at the bigger ones? If someone at Bijoux is playing fast and loose with serial numbers and countries of origin, they'd be more likely to make a significant amount of money by passing off a large diamond as conflict free rather than a small one."

"You'd think so, but my colleagues' and my experience has borne out the exact opposite to be true. Big diamonds are flashy, they draw more attention and so it's harder to keep a fraud going for any length of time. There's just too much scrutiny on stones over a carat, especially when they're VVS1 or VVS2. Everyone wants a look at stones that are only very, very slightly included.

"Whereas, with these stones, nobody pays much attention. They aren't very glamorous and they aren't worth very much money in the grand scheme of things, so people—jewelers, conflict-free experts, consumers—have a tendency to not pay as much attention to them. After all, who would go through the trouble of forging papers on a stone that's barely worth a hundred bucks? Especially if they only stand to gain a couple extra dollars on it?"

"Someone who's faking it on thousands of stones," he offered.

"Yes. Or, more likely, hundreds of thousands. Then the money suddenly becomes a lot more worth it."

"Yeah, I guess. If you don't mind selling your soul for a little profit."

He looked so disgusted that she couldn't help laughing. "I think you've forgotten the basics of Human Greed 101," she told him. "Not to mention the very foundations on which the diamond market functions."

"I wish." He flashed her his first real smile of the afternoon. "So that's why you're concentrating on the small diamonds. Because it's easier for someone to flip in a few fakes there than in the stones of significant size."

"Absolutely." She looked at him curiously. "Why else would I be spending all my time with these stones when the right side of the vault is filled with so many more beautiful ones? Which, incidentally, I will be getting to. But not until after I deal with these."

He shrugged, grinned at her. "No rush. I want both of us to be completely satisfied as to the validity of my stones' origins."

She nodded hesitantly, feeling a little like Alice tumbling down the rabbit hole as he shot her another blinding smile. Because this time when she settled back down to work, Marc didn't ignore her. Instead, he lifted his head often and smiled at her. Offered to refill the water bottle that rested, forgotten, on the corner of her desk. It was as if he was a different man than the one she'd spent the past hour with and she couldn't help wondering at the schizophrenic behavior. Especially when she'd convinced herself that his previous behavior had been because he wanted to make sure she got the hint about his intentions—or lack of intentions—about their relationship.

She still wasn't sure what was going on. After all, who wanted to waste their time on "nice" when they could be aiming for spectacular?

She didn't say anything to him, though, and he didn't bring it up with her—at least not until it was well after dark and the rest of the company had closed around them.

She was working to finish a drawer of half-carat stones and was hoping to get one more drawer done after that before calling it quits. But as she put the last VVS1 stone back into its drawer, Marc's hand covered hers. For the first time she realized he'd put his phone away and his chair back and was pretty much just hovering over her.

"I'll put this bunch back," he told her. "Why don't you get your stuff together?"

She glanced at her watch, surprised to find it was after nine. "Actually, I was hoping to do one more drawer before heading home. It shouldn't take me long—"

"Maybe not, but you look dead on your feet," he said. "Whatever you still have to do will be here tomorrow."

She thought about protesting—she had a limited amount of time and a lot of ground to cover—but she wasn't the only one who looked exhausted. He was hiding it well, but Marc looked like he, too, was feeling the effects of three nights without sleep.

"Yes, all right," she agreed. It only took her a couple of minutes to put her laptop away and gather the rest of her stuff. Then they walked out together, Marc making sure the vault was sealed behind them, the alarms and motion sensors all activated.

They were out of the building and almost to her car in the parking lot before he spoke again. "What kind of take-out do you like?"

"Takeout?" she parroted, the words so far from where her brain was that it took her a minute to process them.

"Food?" he said, his voice deep and amused. "I figured we'd grab something to eat on the way back to your place."

"My place?" she echoed.

He looked at her strangely, the warmth in his smile fading as he took in her total surprise at the suggestion. "Unless you'd rather not have a meal together?" he said, and she knew he was thinking about Saturday night, when she'd refused every overture he'd made to get her to eat with him.

"No, no. Takeout would be nice." This time, the word slipped out without her permission or attention.

But he picked up on it—of course he did—his eyes narrowing as he asked, "What is it with you and your preoccupation with the word *nice* today?"

She flushed a bright red, ducking her head as she tried to either avoid the question or figure out a way to answer him that didn't make her sound like a complete crazy person. But he wasn't having any of it, his fingers going to her chin and tilting her face up until her eyes met his.

She didn't say anything and neither did he and, of course, she cracked first. She always had when it came to him—how had she not remembered that until this moment? The way Marc noticed every small detail about her? The way he'd wait her out whenever he asked her uncomfortable questions, never getting bored or anxious, but rather pausing patiently for her to wrap her mind—and her courage—around whatever it was she wanted to say.

"I just—" She broke off, shook her head. "Any chance we can just leave that alone for now?"

He quirked a brow in that way that made her insane—with affection, with envy, with *lust*. "Pretty much no chance at all."

"Yeah, that's what I figured." She sighed heavily, shifting her weight. She shoved her free hand in her pocket. Anything and everything to kill time as she tried to figure out what she wanted to say. But in the end, though Marc hadn't grown impatient, she certainly had and she just blurted out the truth. "You said last night was 'nice.'"

He looked baffled. "When did I do that?"

"In your text message to me this morning. You said you'd had 'a nice time.'"

"And there's something wrong with that?"

Her embarrassment faded as annoyance took its place. "I don't know, Marc. Why don't we test it out? You take me home, make love to me, and then—on your way out the door—I'll tell you how nice it was."

He didn't say anything for long seconds, just stared at her as if she'd lost her mind. And maybe she had. At this point, she really couldn't tell. All she knew was that she didn't want him to drop his hand from her face, didn't want him to stop touching her. Ever. And that was a huge problem considering the fact that she'd been promising herself all along that she wouldn't fall for him again. That she wouldn't let herself love him.

"Seriously, sweetheart?" he said after a minute. He dropped his hand and she made some kind of noise at the loss of contact—half protest, half plea. He responded by wrapping her in his arms, pressing her body against his from shoulders to shins. "I was half-asleep and barely coherent and that's what you've been holding against me all day? Do you think maybe you could cut a guy some slack?"

When he said it like that, he made his words seem completely reasonable. But, still, before she got in any deeper, she needed to know. "You weren't trying to blow me off? To distance yourself from me?"

He lowered his head, pressed kisses to her forehead, her cheeks, her mouth. "Does this feel like I'm trying to distance myself?"

"No." She shook her head. It felt kind of wonderful, actually. Familiar, but not. Safe, but not—in the best possible way.

"Okay, then. Since that's settled, why don't you tell me what kind of takeout you want and I'll swing by and get it on my way to your place. If I'm invited, that is?" He was grinning, his eyes bright with mischief as he teased her. But she could see the uncertainty there, too, lurking behind the easy facade. Almost as if he was as weirded out and nervous about this thing between them as she was. Almost as if he had as much to lose as she did.

Just the thought had her breath catching in her throat, had her searching his face for signs of the same overwhelming feelings she was having. She found them in the crinkle of his eyes, in the soft corners of his smile, in the hand that wasn't quite steady on her arm.

And somehow the knowledge that she wasn't alone made everything better. She'd loved Marc Durand once, with every beat of her heart, with every ounce of her being. Losing him had nearly killed her, which was why she'd sworn never to repeat the mistake. And yet, here she was, after several strong warnings to herself, in the middle of the fall all over again. It wasn't a comfortable place to be, not by a long shot. But when he looked at her like that—all soft and sweet and *involved*—it wasn't a bad place, either. It was actually a little wonderful.

"I choose Greek," she told him. "There's a little place

two blocks over from my house. It's a hole-in-the-wall but the food is amazing."

"Greek it is, then. Text me the name and I'll find it," he replied, dropping one last, lingering kiss on her lips before pulling open her car door for her. "Drive safely."

She laughed. "Same old Marc."

"Hey. You used to like the old Marc."

He was right. She had. Right up until he'd tossed her out on her butt without so much as her apartment key. Unbidden, the memory of that long-ago night crept in—along with an uneasiness she refused to feel.

Not now, when Marc was looking at her with such warmth.

Not now, when she could feel herself melting into a puddle of warm goo at the look in his eyes.

And so she settled for a half-truth, as she wrapped her arms around his neck and pressed her mouth against the dark stubble on his jaw. "I still do like him."

This time she was sure it was his breath that caught in his throat, his heart that was beating way too fast. "Go," he said, after taking her mouth in a swift, hard kiss that set her nerves jangling and her sex pulsing. "Before I decide to take you right here in the parking lot with my security guards looking on."

She wasn't sure what it said about her that right then, at that moment, that didn't sound like such a bad proposition.

Still, she climbed in her car, let him close the door after her. And, as she drove home, she refused to think about the future. For the first time in her adult life, she refused to think about the consequences of what she was doing. Instead, she decided that, just this once, she would look before she leaped.

And pray that she landed on her feet.

Sixteen

Two days later, she was still leaping. And still falling, with no hint of the ground in sight.

It was wonderful and awful, exhilarating and terrifying, all at the same time. Especially since Marc seemed to feel exactly the same way.

Last night he'd invited Nic to come to dinner with them and she'd spent the two-hour meal laughing until her sides hurt. Even with the threat of the newspaper article hanging over their heads, Nic was just that kind of guy. He always had been, but she'd forgotten that in the years since she'd seen him last. Just as she had blocked out so much of her time with Marc because it was too painful to remember.

She was remembering it now, remembering all the fun they'd had together. The million ways Marc had to make her smile. The million and one ways she'd had to make him relax, no matter how stressful his day had been.

And now, as she walked up to his office, she couldn't

keep the triumphant smile from her face. She'd completed the last of her tests, had spent the entire day looking at hydrogen isotopes until her eyes crossed and her brain felt as if it would bleed out of her ears.

She'd crashed what was normally a ten-day certification process into five days and she was exhausted, completely wiped out. But none of that mattered because she had good news for Marc. It was news he already knew, of course, but it would still be a relief to him and Nic to know that she concurred. And that none of their employees had snuck something shady in under the radar.

Marc's assistant, a really nice guy named Thomas, waved her toward Marc's door as soon as he spotted her. "Go right in. He's been waiting for you for the last two hours."

Of course he had. He was that kind of guy. She'd told him she thought she'd be finished around four and her phone had buzzed with a text at exactly 4:01, checking to see if she was finished for the day.

She'd put him off for two hours as she ran more isotope tests than she ever had before—many more than the industry considered necessary. But she wanted this certification to be beyond reproach, wanted Marc to have the peace of mind of knowing there was no truth to the *LA Times* article at all.

After the debacle of their past, she owed it to him. More, she wanted it for him. He deserved it.

He and Nic and Harrison, one of the attorneys working on their end of the situation, were all gathered around Marc's desk when she walked in. And though they were chatting amiably enough, the tension in the air was thick enough to scoop with an ice cream spoon.

All eyes turned to her and she smiled, holding out to Marc the folder of documents she'd put together—and signed—certifying Bijoux as carrying only conflict-free diamonds. She would send him electronic copies of the same papers, but for now, handing him a folder felt more official. More real. She supposed she was old-school like that.

It must have felt official to him, too, because the moment he opened the folder and saw the first page, her lover grinned like a crazy man.

"We got it?" he asked, his voice slightly hushed despite the excitement on his face.

"You absolutely got it," she said.

Nic jumped out of his chair, pumped a fist in the air. "I knew it, baby! I knew that reporter had a bad source." He gave Marc a second to look over the documentation she'd provided, then ripped the folder out of his hands and headed for the door.

"Where are you going?" Marc demanded.

"To make a copy of this file. And then I'm going down to the *LA Times* myself and force-feed every single page of this to that jackal of a reporter. I hope she chokes on it."

"I feel obliged to warn you of the illegality of such actions," Hollister said. But he was grinning, and Nic just rolled his eyes and flipped him off, so she figured it was a long-standing joke between them. Which didn't surprise her at all—Nic was totally the kind of guy to skirt the rules just enough to make a lawyer like Hollister absolutely insane.

She started to sit down in the chair vacated by Nic, but Marc grabbed her and pulled her into his arms. Then he picked her up and actually spun her around his office, laughing the entire time.

"Yes, well, I guess I'll leave you to your celebrating," Hollister said. "Send me a copy of the report when you get it back from Nic. I'll make sure to have it messengered over to the editor of the *LA Times* before I go home tonight."

"I thought Nic was already doing that?" she asked as Marc finally set her back on her feet. "He looked like a publicity director on a mission to me."

"Oh, he is," Hollister assured her. "But I just want to cover all the bases. Make sure no one has a chance to say the verification—and our comment on it—slipped through the cracks."

He left the office after that, leaving her and Marc alone to grin stupidly at each other.

"I want to celebrate," he said, grabbing her hand and bringing it to his mouth. "I want to take you out somewhere fancy and ply you with champagne and chocolate and moonlight." He pressed several kisses to her fingers, before turning her hand over and doing the same to her palm and wrist.

Shivers of excitement went through her at the whisper soft contact, and she leaned into Marc. Let him hear the hitch in her breathing and let him see the way her hands were suddenly a little unsteady.

His eyes darkened and then he was kissing her, his lips and tongue and mouth devouring her own as need—hot and dark and overwhelming—flowed between them.

"Hold that thought," he growled when he finally ripped his mouth from hers. Then, grabbing a small remote from his desk drawer, he darkened the privacy shades on the windows until no one could see in. Then he strode over to the door, starting to close and lock it. But before he'd done much more than swing it shut, Lisa appeared, pale and disheveled.

"I need to talk to you," she said. She looked absolutely panicked, her face drained of color and her hands shaking as she made her way into his office without an invitation.

"What's wrong?" Marc asked, leading her to a chair. "Are you okay?"

"I'm fine," she told him, placing the tablet she held on the desk. "But the vault isn't."

Isa felt her stomach plummet to the floor, felt her heart stick in her throat. "What does that mean?"

Lisa pulled up a spreadsheet on the computer, gestured to it wildly. "It means we're missing several of the large, two-carat and above VVS1 diamonds. It means," she said, choking on tears, "that Bijoux has been robbed."

"That's not possible," Marc said, keeping his voice—and himself—as calm as possible.

"That's what I said when I went in to pack up several of the jewels for shipment this morning. But they're missing. I've checked and double-checked the logs. I've searched every drawer within five rows in both directions, just in case they were put back in the wrong place for the first time *ever*. I've even pulled up the security tapes and nothing suspicious popped at all. No one has been in that vault in the last three days who doesn't belong there."

"Three days? Is that the last time you saw those diamonds?"

"I saw them Saturday. I had just secured them in the vault when you called me into your office. I haven't checked them since—have had no reason to until today. No one except Isa has."

He could barely think around the suspicion—around the rage—that was seeping into him from all directions. This couldn't be happening again. It simply couldn't. It wasn't possible. Isa wouldn't do this to him a second time, not when they were finally starting to get somewhere. Not when he was finally beginning to move past her betrayal of six years ago.

Yes, he'd been suspicious enough to stay in the vault with her. But they'd moved past that. No way would she do this. And no way would he be so stupid that he didn't see it. Not when he'd been so careful. Not when he'd worked so hard to make sure she wouldn't fall victim to temptation while she was here.

While she was in his vaults.

He told himself not to jump to conclusions, not to let his suspicions run away with him. But still he couldn't look at Isa as he called up security and ordered the video for the past five days to be emailed to him.

"What can I do to help?" Isa asked from where she was standing, frozen, next to his desk.

He didn't answer. Didn't trust his voice, or the words that would spew out of his mouth.

Picking up his phone, he called his head of security. Demanded that the man meet Marc at the vault in the next five minutes. Then he grabbed his cell phone and the tablet Lisa had brought with her and made a beeline for the door and the elevator.

As if the machine understood the rage coursing through him—and the fact that Marc was one breath away from jumping out of his goddamn skin—the elevator came right away. He got on, waited for Lisa to do the same. But when Isa went to join them, he told her, "Don't."

She froze, eyes wide and cheeks pale. It was the last visual he had before the elevator doors slid shut.

He pulled up the video, had it running on the tablet before he even hit the vault floor. He kept it running as he did the usual security routine to open the vault, his eyes never leaving the footage as it ran through Saturday afternoon.

He paused it when Bob, his head of security, showed up. "Seven of the nearly flawless one-point-five-carat diamonds are missing," he told Bob, as he thrust the tablet at him. "Find out what the hell happened."

Before entering the vault, he called up the IDs of everyone who had entered in the past ninety-six hours. Lisa was right—there was no one suspicious on the list. Nobody suspicious but the woman who had spent the past three nights in his bed.

He blocked out the thought, along with the fresh wave of rage that threatened to swamp him, to pull him under. He concentrated on the job at hand.

"I want three pairs of eyes on the footage from every camera in this vault," he barked at Bob. "I want to know what happened in this room every second of the last ninety-six hours and then I want to know what happened in every other room on this floor. In the bathroom down the hall. In the only two damn elevators that actually reach this floor. And I want to know these things in the next four hours.

"I also," he continued, gritting his teeth and doing his damnedest not to bellow like a wounded bear, "want to know where the bloody damn hell my diamonds are. I want to know how they got out of the vault, I want to know how they got out of the building and I want to know where the hell they are right now!"

"Yes, Marc." Bob looked as pale as Isa had right before the elevator doors closed on her. Good. It was his damn job to make sure this didn't happen and now that it had… he damn well better figure out how to fix it.

Except it wasn't fair to blame Bob, the little voice in the back of Marc's head whispered. Not when Marc had knowingly, wittingly, brought an ex-thief into his building. Into his vault. Not when he'd trusted her despite her track record—and despite his misgivings. No, this wasn't Bob's fault so much as it was his. He was the one who had trusted Isa. He was the one who—after that first day in the vault—had given her more and more freedom at Bijoux. He had given her the run of the place because he'd begun to trust her again.

Because he'd wanted to believe in her, no matter who her father was. No matter what she'd done in her past.

Jesus Christ. Six years and he hadn't learned a damn thing. He was still a sucker for red hair, a sweet smile and a pair of chocolate-brown eyes. Still a sucker for Isa.

No, not a sucker, he told himself viciously as more of his security team swarmed into the vault. He wasn't a sucker. He was a goddamn fool. An idiot. A moron who deserved every bit of this. He hadn't learned the first time, hadn't been smart enough to keep from repeating his mistakes, so fate had stepped in to teach him a lesson once and for all.

Well, he'd learned it this time. Christ, had he ever. No way would Isa ever pull one over on him again.

Jesus, he thought even as he barked orders to start inventorying the drawers. They would have to eat the loss of those diamonds. He wasn't going to some insurance investigator with this story. They'd laugh him out of the building. After they crucified him, that is.

Provided nothing else was missing but those seven stones, it wasn't a big deal. They were nice stones, but they weren't anything spectacular. They sure as hell weren't worth enough that they would disrupt anything important, not even his profit and loss margins.

Three hundred grand retail, maybe. A hundred grand sold to a fence on the streets. That was it. A hundred thousand dollars. Is that what his love was worth to Isa? A hundred grand? Silly girl. If she'd stuck with him she could have had a lot more than that. She could have had everything that was his. He'd been so close to loving her again, so close to giving her anything and everything she could ever want.

And instead of loving him back, instead of caring about him at all, she'd done this. Stabbed him in the back even while she continued to make love to him.

His stomach clenched at the thought and for a minute he thought he was going to embarrass himself all to hell by getting sick. But he swallowed down the nausea, forced his body to take it just as he forced himself to take the pain of Isa's betrayal. Better to deal with it now than to sublimate it and give it the power to bring him to his knees later.

He did everything he could in the vault, issued all the orders that needed to be given at this first stage of the investigation. He supposed he could thank Isa for that, too. Isa and her father. If it hadn't been for the robbery six years ago, Marc wouldn't be as well versed in what needed to be done.

It took him nearly three hours to make his way back down to his office. Three hours in which he watched time-lapse video of every single person who had been in the vault since Saturday afternoon. Three hours in which he had to tell his brother that they'd been robbed, again. Three hours in which he stewed and brooded and grew angrier and angrier as the truth became clear. No one had been in this vault in the past four days who hadn't been in it hundreds of times before. No one had been in this vault who hadn't worked for his company for at least five years. Nobody, that is, except the woman who insisted on making a fool of him over and over again.

He didn't know what he'd find in his office, didn't have a clue if Isa had fled the premises or if she would be stupid enough to be waiting for him. Nor was he sure what it said about him that he didn't know which option he would prefer.

The choice was taken out of his hands, however, when

he pushed the door to his office open and found Isa curled up on his sofa, eyes wide and feet tucked under her.

She jumped up as soon as she saw him, crossed the room at close to a dead run. "Did you find out what happened? Does Security know where the diamonds went? Or how they were smuggled out? Or—"

She broke off when he held up a hand. "I'm going to ask you once, Isa, and then I'm never going to ask you again. Did you take those diamonds?"

"No, Marc. No! Of course I didn't. I would never do that to you. I would never do that to us."

He stared at her for long seconds, searched her face for sincerity. Then nodded. "You need to leave."

"Leave? But—"

"You need to leave now. I'll have accounting cut you a check for the work you did for me and then you need to get whatever things you have here and you need to leave the premises. Forever."

"You don't mean that."

"Oh, I mean it, Isa. I mean it more than you could possible imagine."

"Seriously?" she demanded. "It's been six years and we're right back here again?"

"Don't act offended. After all, you're the one who put us here."

"No, Marc. You're the one at fault this time. Because I didn't steal those diamonds."

"Stop talking!" he ordered her as fury threatened to swallow him whole. "Stop lying to me. I can take anything but that. I can take knowing you stole from me, but I can't take you looking me in the eye and lying to me."

"I'm not—"

"Get out!" he yelled. "Before I have you escorted from

the premises. Get out now and I'll have your check mailed to you tonight. Just get out."

"Marc, please—"

He whirled on her then, the rage breaking wide-open inside him. "Get the hell out, Isa, or this time, I really will call the police."

He walked over to the bar in the corner, poured himself a tall Scotch, and drained it in one long swallow. Then he poured another one and did the same thing.

When he turned around again, prepared to face Isa one last time, he found that she'd finally given him what he'd asked for. She was gone and he was alone. Again.

Seventeen

She didn't know what to do, didn't know where to go. Didn't know how to deal with the fact that her heart had just split open and broken into a million pieces. Again.

After she'd fled Marc's office, his words ringing in her ears, she'd run through the halls, down the stairs and out onto the grounds that stretched along the ocean.

And now, here she was, staring out at that ocean and wondering how, how, *how*, she could be in this position again. How, after everything that had happened six years ago, that the *two* of them could be in this position? Again.

She told herself to just leave.

Told herself to walk to the parking lot, climb in her car and drive away.

Told herself that this time, she wouldn't look back. Ever.

Marc had turned on her again. The thought slammed into her over and over. With each step she took on the sand, with each wave that rolled in, the knowledge that he didn't trust her ripped at her.

He thought she was a thief, thought that after everything that had happened these past few days—after everything that had happened six years ago—she had actually turned around and stolen from him.

As if she would do that. As if it was even possible for her to hurt him that way.

Then again, maybe it wasn't so far-fetched that he believed it. After all, he had no problem hurting her. Had no problem turning his back on her six years ago and no problem turning his back on her now—despite all the sweet words he'd spent the past few days, and nights, whispering in her ear.

Just the memory of these few stolen days had her feeling like her whole body would break apart. Like her skin would crack under the weight of her sorrow and her limbs, her organs, her *heart* would fly right out of her in a million different directions.

Isa wrapped her arms around herself at the thought, tight around her middle, her hands clutching her sides. And she walked along the shore, right where the water met the sand. Right where the infinite waves swamped the crumbling shore.

She walked and walked and walked.

And as she did, she lambasted herself for all the things she'd done wrong. For all the hope she'd let herself feel even when it was idiotic and dangerous...and painful. So painful.

She'd known better, even as she was doing it. Had known better than to trust Marc after what had happened between them six years ago. More, she'd known that *he* would never be able to fully trust *her*.

Which was the real problem, wasn't it? The fact that

no matter what she did, no matter how she'd changed her
life or how she'd tried to help him, he was never going to
get past who she'd been. Never going to see her for who
she really was.

It was a hard truth to swallow, one made harder by the
fact that she had never stolen from him. Not then, and
not now.

No, she hadn't stolen from him, she forced herself to
acknowledge as she kept walking, her shoulders hunched
against the wind blowing in off the water. But she'd certainly thought about it six years ago. It would be a lie to
pretend otherwise.

That was who she'd been then, what she'd done. Not because she needed the money—her father had stolen enough
through the years that her children's children would probably never need for money—but because she'd wanted
the thrill.

The old Isa had been an adrenaline junkie, raised by her
jewel thief father after her mother passed away. She had
loved the game, the con, the robbery more than anything
else in the world. Except her father…and eventually, Marc.

She'd met him at a big society party she'd been casing, had fallen for him hard the moment he'd handed her
a glass of champagne with a smile and a quip. And that
damn raised eyebrow of his. She still remembered what
he'd said to her at that moment—would probably remember it until she died. Because even as it was happening,
she'd known that it was one of those life defining moments.

She'd looked up into his shining sapphire eyes, ripe with
amusement and desire, and she'd realized that she wanted
to know more. Realized that she wanted to know *him*.

And so she'd ditched the friends she'd been with,
ditched her plans to steal the big, fat Poinsettia Ruby that
had drawn her to the party in the first place. She wasn't

going to lie—it had hurt a little to walk away from the huge, thirty-five-carat stone surrounded by ten carats of flawless diamonds—but she'd done it. Despite the fact that it had been right there, just waiting for her to pluck.

Okay, so maybe it had hurt more than a little. Maybe it still did.

But that night she'd wanted Marc more than she'd wanted the stone. More than she'd wanted to please her father. More than she'd wanted the life she had. And during the six months they'd had together, she'd continued to want him more than anything.

She'd given it all up, cold turkey. She'd missed it—of course she had. For most of her life, stealing big, flashy jewels and pretty paintings had been as natural to her as breathing. But she'd wanted what she saw in Marc's eyes, what she felt in his arms, more than she wanted the dark, shiny, illicit thrill that came every time she'd pulled a heist.

Her father hadn't understood—he'd never wanted anything more than he'd wanted the rush of the next job. Had, for the longest time, thought she'd been casing Marc, trying to find his weakness. Trying to get inside Bijoux's vault, where—at the time—two of the most perfect diamonds ever found were being housed. The Midnight Sun, a colorless and flawless forty-carat Russian diamond valued in the tens of millions and Hope's Fire, a twenty-seven-carat nearly flawless diamond whose value came as much from its rich and violent history as it did its quality.

Marc had been preparing to auction off both of them—at the time, he'd spent the first few years of his career moving Bijoux away from blood diamonds and firmly into the conflict-free arena. A huge event was planned—a huge gala that she had contributed time and expertise to helping him pull off—with the proceeds going to a char-

ity that helped children in areas where blood diamonds
were mined.

Her father had been thrilled when he'd found out, had
been convinced that she was just using Marc to find an
in with the diamonds. When he found out that wasn't the
case, found out that she was with Marc because she loved
him and wanted to spend the rest of her nonthieving life
with him—he'd been furious. He'd accused her of turning her back on him.

And she hadn't been able to argue, had she? Because
she *had* turned her back, not on her father, but definitely
on the life he'd given her. The life he'd raised her to want,
to expect, to relish.

She should have known then what would happen, what
he would do. In many ways, her father was a child, as
thrilled by the chase, by the hunt, as he was by the shiny
baubles he stole. And once he was focused on a score, nothing short of the apocalypse could tear him away.

What she hadn't realized—what she'd been too naive at
the time to understand—was that in falling for Marc, she
might as well have painted a target on him and his business. In giving him her attention, her love, her *loyalty*,
she'd made him and his diamonds the focus of her father's
attention. In fact, when she'd told her father that she wasn't
going to steal anymore, that she was going straight and
building a life for herself as a normal person, she'd pretty
much put a giant red *X* over Marc.

When the diamonds turned up stolen and Marc's whole
business—his whole life—had gone to hell, she'd known
who had done it. Of course she'd known. She'd stolen with
her father since she was nine years old, had recognized the
earmarks of a Salvatore job as easily as she recognized her
own face in the mirror.

That was where she'd made her second mistake. Because she hadn't told Marc then what she knew. Hadn't gone to him and explained who she was and who her father was and offered to help him get the stones back. Instead she'd gone to her father, and tried to convince him to return the stones. He'd refused—of course, he'd refused. It was, in its own way, a matter of honor to him. Marc Durand had stolen something precious from him and he had returned the favor.

Even after that encounter, she still hadn't told Marc the truth. How could she when doing so would not only send her dying father to prison but would also make Marc look at her with scorn, hate, disgust. She hadn't been able to do it then. Hadn't been able to ruin all of her dreams, all of her happily-ever-after fantasies, in one fell swoop. Even though in keeping her own dreams alive, she'd destroyed Marc's.

And perhaps she would have gone on living a lie forever if things hadn't gotten so bad for Marc. She liked to think the guilt would have made her confess eventually, but after everything that had happened these past few years, she was honest enough to admit that very well might not have been the case.

As it was, she'd stood by for weeks as Marc's life became a nightmare. As the insurance company hounded him, refusing to pay because they were convinced the entire thing was an inside job. That he was guilty of fraud and a myriad other crimes. That he'd done the entire thing for the money, and as some sick kind of publicity stunt.

He'd kept most of it from her, but she'd seen. How could she not when he was growing more haggard, more worried with every day that passed. And when the cops, at the insurance agency's behest, started looking at him and Nic, she'd known she couldn't keep quiet any longer.

She'd talked her father into returning the jewels—largely because he'd known she would steal them back if she had to—and then brought them to Bijoux headquarters in the most complicated reverse heist that—she was sure—had ever been pulled off.

The insurance company, the cops, Marc's board of directors—none of them had known what had hit them. And they still didn't—except for Marc, who she had confessed everything to.

And who had returned her grand gesture by kicking her out of his life without a backward glance.

She'd known it could happen before she told him—she had been lying to him for weeks, after all, while he went through hell. While the company he'd worked so hard to build had begun falling apart piece by piece. But there was a part of her that still hadn't expected it, still hadn't been ready for it. How could she have been when her love for him was so absolute, so boundless, that there was nothing he could have done that would have made her turn her back on him?

And now he'd turned his back on her again. Even after everything she'd done to create a new, legitimate life for herself. As she'd wandered the streets six years ago, she'd promised herself that she would turn her life around. That she would become someone better, someone that no one could ever accuse, ever toss aside like that, again.

She'd done it, too. She'd given up being a jewel thief when she met Marc, and once her father had died she'd given up all connections to that life—her friendships, her apartment, even her name. She'd built a new life instead, one where she could use her expertise to help, to teach, instead of to harm.

She'd done it for herself, because it had been important to her to make amends for everything she'd done. And, she realized as she walked the lonely stretch of beach watching the sky slowly turn the inky purple of twilight, she'd done it to impress Marc, too. Though she'd never sought him out, never told him who she had become, there was a part of her that had always believed that if he knew—if he found her—he'd accept the new Isa and forget the pain and the disloyalty and damage of the past.

She hadn't let herself acknowledge any of those hidden hopes until this moment, however, and now that she had, all they brought was more of the crippling pain she'd sworn she'd leave behind.

Because he didn't believe in the new her.

He didn't believe that she had changed at all.

The magnitude of the pain made her want to whimper, to cry. Why, she wanted to shout to the unsympathetic sea, why was there always more pain?

She kept walking, head bowed against the cold rolling in as darkness descended over the roiling sea. The wind picked up, blew her hair around her face, snuck inside the thin blouse that was no protection at all. It creeped inside, bringing the cold under her skin. Bringing it all the way to her bones.

And still she walked. And still, as she looked out at the waves crashing against the shore, all she could see was him.

Eyes shadowed.

Skin pale.

Jaw tight.

Fists clenched.

He'd been all but seething with rage, with betrayal, with the past that lay between them like a wasteland.

She'd known better. Had known not to take this job, not to do him this favor. Everything inside her had screamed that it was a bad idea. And yet, she'd done it anyway. How could she not have, when he'd needed her? When—despite how it had ended six years ago—she'd once loved him with everything inside her? With her heart, her soul, her entire being.

When—and she hated to admit it almost as much as she hated that it was true, that it would always be true—she loved him still.

It was because she loved him that the pain was so catastrophic.

Oh, the trip she'd just taken down memory lane had been a bitter one, filled with all the mistakes she couldn't change. But the pain of that didn't come close to the pain she'd felt seeing the look on Marc's face as he'd demanded to know if she had stolen from him again. As he'd ordered her, voice blank and eyes dead, to get out of his office. Out of his building.

Out of his life.

Just the memory had her breath hiccupping in her throat and tears blooming in her eyes. She told herself she wasn't crying, that it was just the sharpness of the wind that had her eyes stinging and her chest aching.

She didn't buy it, though.

She wasn't much of a crier—could count on one hand the number of times she'd cried in her adult life—but right here, right now, she couldn't *not* feel the agony and the defeat of what could have been.

She couldn't not cry.

She didn't know how long she stood staring out at the vast and endless ocean.

Long enough for the tide to roll in and over her toes, across her feet, up her calves.

Long enough for stars to twinkle against the darkness of the night sky.

More than long enough for her tears to dry and her heart to crack wide-open as the truth settled over her like a mantle. Like a weight she couldn't bear.

Marc would never believe in her. Even if he found proof that she hadn't stolen those diamonds, he still wouldn't trust her. No matter what she did, no matter how much she'd changed her life, no matter how much she tried to convince him that she wasn't the person she'd once been, it wouldn't matter. He would see only what he wanted to see, believe only what he'd always believed.

It was a bitter pill to swallow, one that shattered the last vestiges of hope she hadn't even realized she'd been holding on to. But it was also the catalyst she needed to get moving again, the impetus that got her started on the long walk back to Bijoux's headquarters—and her car.

And if she cried the whole way back, well then, nobody needed to know but her...

Eighteen

Marc kept his staff working well into the night, trying to find out what had happened to the diamonds. Or, more accurately, trying to find proof that Isa had stolen them. Not because he planned to press charges but because he wanted to know.

No, not wanted. Needed. He *needed* to know. Needed the vindication that came with being proven right. He needed to know that the look on her face—in her eyes—as he'd gone off on her had been as fake as the tender words she'd whispered to him while they made love.

Because if that look wasn't fake— He shut the thought down fast. No, he wasn't going there. Wasn't going to think, even for a second, that he had made a mistake. Because if he let that idea in now, he'd never get it out of his head again. And he wanted to believe it so badly, wanted so much for Isa to be innocent, that he was afraid he would convince himself she was, even if she wasn't.

Or worse, he would convince himself that the theft didn't matter at all.

It hadn't been big diamonds, wouldn't cost his company much of anything, really, except the annoyance and manpower that came with trying to figure out how the theft had been accomplished.

He'd been over the tapes himself. He'd had Nic and Lisa and his most trusted security people go over them, too. He'd examined every second Isa had been in the vault, had studied every drawer she'd opened, every diamond she'd looked at. And he couldn't see it. Couldn't find where— or how—she'd done it.

And he needed to know how because he was never going to know why. They'd spent the past three nights making love and it had felt so good, so right. They'd fallen into old routines, old patterns of conversation, so easily. As if the six years he'd spent without her hadn't happened. As if the whole debacle back in New York was just a nightmare and not the sad, awful truth that had woken him up in the middle of the night for years.

When he thought about going back to that loneliness, thought about the fact that he would never hold Isa in his arms again, it made him crazy. Made him want to grab her and shake her all over again.

How could she do this?

Why would she do this?

How could the money from fencing the diamonds be more important to her than what they had between them?

Maybe that was the problem. Maybe he was only imagining that there were feelings under the heat. Maybe, when he'd been falling for her all over again, she'd only been using him. Only been looking for a way to get back at him for the way he'd kicked her out all those years ago.

It made sense—it really did. As long as he didn't take

into account how hard she'd worked these past few days to help him debunk that ridiculous *LA Times* article. Or how her arms had felt around him after they'd made love, so warm and sexy and perfect.

But if all that mattered to her was the thrill of the boost, why had she held him so tenderly? Why had she gone so high, so deep, when he made love to her? Why had she given herself to him so completely?

The questions were driving him crazy, the lack of understanding made him hurt in a way he hadn't let himself experience in six long years.

Furious, frustrated, completely fed up with himself and the entire situation, he turned back to his computer. Pulled up the video footage for the third time that night. And once again, watched every second of film showing Isa in the vault.

Every single second.

Most of it was boring, with nothing happening except Isa studying the diamonds under a microscope and triple-checking the serial numbers. But the times she moved, the times she crossed the vault to get a new drawer or to put one away or, ostensibly, only to stretch, he watched those the most intently.

Because he was looking for the theft, he told himself. He wanted to know when she'd dropped the diamonds into her pocket and how she'd gotten them out of the vault, out of the building. But the sad truth was, even with everything that had happened, for most of the video he just found himself watching her.

The fluid way she walked.

The way her hips swayed with each step.

The way her hair curled over her shoulders, caressed her breasts.

And damn, this so wasn't helping. It wasn't helping

him find whatever he'd missed and it sure as hell wasn't helping him forget what it felt like to touch Isa's beautiful body, to hold her in his arms as he slipped inside her.

He reached for his mouse, scrolled the video back several minutes and promised himself that this time he would pay attention. This time he wouldn't be distracted by thoughts of what she looked like and smelled like and tasted like.

Except he was only a minute into the video when a knock sounded on his office door. He froze the screen, and even though it was ridiculous, he couldn't help feeling like a kid who'd been caught watching porn. The fact that Isa had all her clothes on and was doing nothing more than counting diamonds didn't make him any less guilty.

Shoving his chair back from his desk, he walked to the door. Pulled it open. And found Bob standing there, looking as close to frantic as he'd ever seen his security chief look.

Marc's stomach sank even as he stepped aside so Bob could enter. "What's wrong now?"

"There's a problem with the video," he responded, walking around Marc's desk so that he was stationed in front of his laptop. "Can you pull up your email?"

"What kind of problem?" he demanded, already logging in and opening the first email on the list.

"There's a time lapse." Bob clicked on the attachment, then waited impatiently for the footage to download.

"A time lapse?"

"The feed in the vault was cut for a period of approximately seven minutes."

"From which camera?" Marc demanded, impatience thrumming through him.

"From all of them."

"Excuse me?"

Bob paled at his tone. "That's what it looks like, at least. Every camera in and outside the vault has a seven-minute time lapse."

"And no one noticed that the feed had been cut? Where the hell was Security?"

"That's the thing. I don't think those seven minutes were cut out until after the theft—the footage was recorded, then deleted."

"So, again, I'm asking you. Where the hell was Security?" Marc demanded with a glare. "People are paid to do nothing but watch those monitors twenty-four hours a day."

"That's what I'm trying to figure out. We don't yet know if they fed other footage into the digital stream, but that's what I'm surmising. At this point, there's no other explanation that makes sense."

"Someone hacked into my system—my specially designed, one-of-a-kind, cover-all-the-bases system—and took control of every camera in or around the vault. That's what you're telling me?"

"Essentially, yes."

"And no one noticed."

"That's not totally true. We noticed."

"Not until after the theft!" he snapped, then bent down to look at the dates at the bottom of the footage. "This happened on Monday?"

"Yes."

"How did they hack in?"

"We're still working on that."

"Work harder. And get Geoffrey and Max on it. I want an answer—tonight."

"I get that you're upset, Marc, but we're doing the best we can. The work was so good that it's damn impressive one of my guys even caught—"

"It will be damn impressive when you find the weakness he exploited and eliminate it. Until then, it's only sloppy." He stared at the screen grimly. "On every single one of our parts."

Bob didn't have much more to say after that—not that Marc blamed him. He was furious, absolutely seething now that he knew some thief had hacked into his computer system. He had two of the best internet security guys in the world on his payroll and some jackass had managed to completely hijack his security feed?

Enraged didn't begin to cover what Marc was feeling.

He spent the next few hours snapping at his employees as every single one of them—including him—searched for the weakness. For how it had been done. By the time midnight rolled around, they still hadn't found the weakness in the operating system that had allowed this to happen. Which made him—and his computer security guys—even more suspicious.

Usually, hackers and thieves didn't care if you knew how they got in. They'd already gotten what they wanted, after all, so why should it matter to them if you closed the hole after they'd left? But this person had made sure to cover their tracks so well that Marc couldn't help wondering if this was the first time it had happened—or if it was merely the first time the thief had gotten caught? Maybe the person had been stealing from them for quite some time, taking only a couple small, inconsequential stones every few months, all in an effort to stay off the radar.

They only inventoried the vault fully twice a year. So if this hadn't been going on very long—if they'd only caught it because of the internal audit they were running—

He finally let himself acknowledge what had been racing around his mind for hours. He finally let himself admit how thoroughly he'd screwed up.

The thought had him sweating, had his stomach clenching and his heart beating too fast. Because if this was an inside job, which he and his security guys thought it was, and it had been going on for a while, then...then there was no way Isa was responsible for it.

He'd blamed her, cut her out, and she hadn't done it.

The thought made him sick, especially if he let himself think about what she'd looked like after he'd confronted her. How shocked, how hurt...how devastated.

She'd looked like he'd felt, as if her whole world had been yanked out from under her. Again.

And he'd done it to her. Just like he'd done it to her six years ago. He'd let his anger and his pride and his distrust get the better of him, again. The fact that he'd actually let her collect her things this time didn't make him feel any better about himself as a human being—or as a boyfriend.

With a curse, he shoved back from the conference room table they'd been using as command central.

Nic, Bob, Geoffrey—and all the others gathered there—stared at him in trepidation. It made him realize just how angry, and vile, he'd been to all of them since the theft was discovered.

"Go home," he told them gruffly. "We'll pick this up tomorrow."

"Home?" Geoffrey repeated, as if it was a concept utterly foreign to him.

"We've been at this for days, pretty much nonstop. Go home, get some sleep, relax a little. We'll pick it up in the morning."

"Who are you?" Nic demanded. But Marc noticed that his brother shoved away from the table pretty damn quickly.

"The damage has already been done, right? I want two extra guards stationed on the vault floor—one right outside the vault and an extra guard running patrol and—weakness or not—the vault should be okay for another night, right?"

They nearly tripped over themselves agreeing with him.

"Okay, then. Go home and I'll see you back here at 7 a.m."

Before they could say anything else, he turned on his heel and strode out. He had something important to do and it was already days—years—overdue.

Nineteen

Isa woke up from a fitful sleep at the first round of violent pounding on her front door. Fumbling for her phone—just in case she had to call 9-1-1—she glanced at the time. One o'clock. Who on earth was at her door at one in the morning?

Snatching her robe from the chair by her bed, she shrugged it on as she made her way cautiously to her front door. A look through the window told her Marc was her middle-of-the-night visitor. He looked better than he had any right to, especially considering how haggard and exhausted she knew she must look.

Their gazes met through the glass and for a second she was mesmerized by the look in his eyes. But then her sense of self-preservation kicked in and she yanked her gaze away—at the same time she took a couple steps back. She didn't want to see him, didn't want to talk to him or even look at him. Not now, when the wounds were still so fresh. Not now, when it still hurt to breathe.

Marc must have read her intention on her face, though, because the pounding doubled. And then he started to call to her. "Open the door, Isa. Please. I just want to talk to you."

She shook her head even though he couldn't see her anymore, backed away a few more steps. She didn't want to see him—couldn't see him. It hurt too much. Even knowing that she was responsible for his distrust, that she'd brought all of this on herself with how she'd behaved six years ago, didn't make the pain any easier to bear.

"Damn it, Isa, please! I just want to talk to you."

But she didn't want to talk to him. She couldn't handle any more accusations, couldn't handle him looking at her as if she was trash. Or worse, as if she'd ripped out his heart. She hadn't done it, hadn't stolen the jewels, but that didn't make her feel any less guilty. Not when she'd been responsible for so much of what had happened to him, and Bijoux, six years ago.

"Isa! Please! I'm sorry." For the first time, his voice cracked. "I'm so sorry. Please let me in."

It hurt her to hear him sound so broken. Before she could think better of it, she cleared her throat, told him, "Go away, Marc. This isn't helping anyone."

"Isa, please. You have every right to hate me, every right to be angry with me. But please, I'm begging of you, don't send me away."

She didn't know how to respond to that. He sounded so different from the man she'd spoken to on Wednesday that it broke her heart all over again. She couldn't stand to hear the pain in his voice, couldn't stand to hear him beg when she'd been the one to hurt him so badly that he'd never be able to trust her again.

Her body moved before her mind made a conscious decision, sliding the dead bolt back and taking the chain off and opening the door to him. To Marc. The only man she'd ever loved.

The only man she'd ever hurt.

"I'm sorry," he told her the moment they were face-to-face. "I'm so sorry."

"It's okay," she told him, stepping back to let him in the house. "I assume you've found the thief?"

"No." He shook his head. "Not yet."

His words didn't make any sense. "I don't understand. If you don't know who did it, why are you here?"

"Because I know it wasn't you. Because I'm an asshole who let the pain of the past blind him to the woman you've become, the woman you are now."

She stared at him stupidly. She could hear what he was saying, but she couldn't comprehend it. Not when it was so far from what she'd expected. So far from anything in their experience so far.

"How do you know it wasn't me?"

"I know because I know you."

"You knew me three days ago. That didn't seem to matter."

"Three days ago, I was a blind, bullheaded ass who was too busy trying to hide his wounds to think things through."

"What things?"

"Everything. The idea that you would steal from Bijoux is ridiculous. And if you did, I'd like to think you'd have better taste than to take a few mundane diamonds that don't matter much to anyone."

"Seriously?" she demanded, feeling as if she'd fallen down some kind of rabbit hole. For the first time, anger cut through the grief. "That's why you're here? Because the thief's taste wasn't good enough, therefore it couldn't be me who did it?"

"No," he said, grabbing her elbows in his big hands and pulling her close. She wanted to shrug him off, wanted to back away, but her body yearned for his touch, his warmth. "I'm here because I made a mistake. Because I know you wouldn't steal from me, wouldn't hurt me that way. And because I want—need—to tell you how sorry I am for hurting you the way I did. Three days ago and six years ago.

"I've been an ass, more concerned with protecting myself than with protecting you, and that's inexcusable."

"It's not your job to protect me   "

"That's bullshit. I love you, Isa. I love you more than I can ever tell you, more than you'll ever believe considering my actions. And it is absolutely my job to protect you and take care of you and make you understand just how precious you are. And I've totally screwed all that up."

He shook his head, looking so disgusted with himself that she nearly cried at the injustice of it. "I did terrible things—"

"No, you didn't. You were young, and torn between two men you loved—neither of whom deserved you. I'm sorry, Isa. I'm so sorry."

He pulled her even closer then and rested his forehead against hers. "I don't deserve you. Don't deserve your forgiveness and I sure as hell don't deserve your love. But I want it, Isa. I want it so bad."

His words turned her brain to mush, and her heart into a ray of light. She threw her arms around him, pulled him close even as harsh sobs ripped through her.

"Don't cry, baby," he said, holding her tightly. "Please don't cry. I'll make it up to you if you let me. I'll—"

She kissed him then, with all the pent-up passion and love and fear and forgiveness she had inside herself. She kissed him and kissed him and kissed him.

And he kissed her back.

Minutes, hours—days—passed before they finally came up for air. His hands on her cheeks, her arms around his neck. Their gazes locked together. "I'm sorry," Marc said again. "I'm so sorry."

"So am I."

"You don't have anything—"

"I do," she told him, pressing kisses along his strong and stubbled jawline. "You aren't the only one who made mistakes. I messed up six years ago, badly, and I don't blame you for thinking I messed up again."

"You didn't, though. I know that even if we never find the thief—"

"Oh, we'll find him," she declared adamantly. "No way is some jerk getting away with stealing from the man I love."

Marc laughed even as he hugged her closer. "You sound so fierce."

"I feel fierce," she said, tugging him down the hall toward her bedroom.

"Do you?" He crooked that brow that always made her crazy.

"I do. And as soon as it's morning, we're going back to Bijoux and we're going to start figuring who did this to you. To us. Together."

"Together." He bent, pressed his own kisses against her lips, her cheek, her forehead, her eyes. "I like the sound of that."

"So do I." She held him tight. "I love you, Marc. I love you so much."

"I love you, too. I always have and I always will."

His words reached inside, thawing out the last of the cold that had lingered there since that long-ago night in Manhattan. And as she pulled him into her room—into her bed—she couldn't help thinking that it had all been worth it. To get here, to this moment, she'd trade a million diamonds, go through whatever pain it took.

Because Marc was worth it. And so was the life they would build together.

* * * * *

Don't miss Nic's story
PURSUED

Coming October 2015
only from
New York Times *bestselling author Tracy Wolff*

"Listen, you want to talk about that kiss? We kissed. It was nothing we hadn't done before."

Of course this kiss was so, so much more than she was letting on. *Damn it.*

"But I'm not the same girl you used to know," she continued, propping her hand on her hip. "I'm not looking for a relationship. I'm not looking for love. I'm not even interested in you anymore, Will."

Cat nearly choked on that lie, but mentally applauded herself for the firmness in her delivery and for stating all she needed to. She wasn't about to start playing whatever game Will had in mind because she knew one thing for certain…she'd lose.

Will stepped closer, took hold of her wrist and pulled her arm gently behind her back. Her body arched into his as she gripped her feather duster and tried to concentrate on the bite of the handle into her palm and not the way those mesmerizing eyes were full of passion and want.

"Not interested?" he asked with a smirk. "You may be able to lie to yourself, Cat, but you can never lie to me. I know you too well."

* * *

Maid for a Magnate
is part of the series Dynasties: The Montoros—
One royal family must choose between
love and destiny!

MAID FOR
A MAGNATE

BY
JULES BENNETT

Published in Great Britain 2015
by Mills & Boon, an imprint of Harlequin (UK) Limited,
Eton House, 18-24 Paradise Road, Richmond, Surrey, TW9 1SR

© 2015 Harlequin Books S.A.

Special thanks and acknowledgement are given to Jules Bennett for her contribution to the Dynasties: The Montoros series.

ISBN: 978-0-263-25276-7

51-0915

Harlequin (UK) Limited's policy is to use papers that are natural, renewable and recyclable products and made from wood grown in sustainable forests. The logging and manufacturing processes conform to the legal environmental regulations of the country of origin.

Printed and bound in Spain
by CPI, Barcelona

Award-winning author **Jules Bennett** is no stranger to romance—she met her husband when she was only fourteen. After dating through high school, the two married. He encouraged her to chase her dream of becoming an author. Jules has now published nearly thirty novels. She and her husband are living their own happily-ever-after while raising two girls. Jules loves to hear from readers through her website, www.julesbennett.com, her Facebook fan page or on Twitter.

A huge thanks to the Harlequin Desire team
for including me in this amazing continuity.
And a special thanks to Janice, Kat,
Katherine, Andrea and Charlene.
I loved working with you all on this project.

<u>One</u>

JUAN CARLOS SALAZAR II TRUE HEIR
TO THRONE

Will Rowling stared at the blaring headline as he
sipped his coffee and thanked every star in the sky that
he'd dodged marrying into the royal family of Alma.
Between the Montoro siblings and their cousin Juan
Carlos, that was one seriously messed up group.

Of course his brother, James, had wedded the beautiful Bella Montoro. Will's father may have had hopes of
Will and Bella joining forces, but those devious plans
obviously had fallen through when James fell in love
with Bella instead.

Love. Such a fickle thing that botched up nearly
every best laid plan. Not that Will had ever been on
board with the idea of marrying Bella. He'd rather re-

main single than marry just to advance his family's business interests.

The Montoros were a force to be reckoned with in Alma, now that the powerful royal family was being restored to the throne after more than seventy years in exile. And Patrick Rowling was all too eager to have his son marry into such prestige, but thankfully that son was not to be Will.

Bella's brother had been heading toward the throne, until shocking letters were discovered in an abandoned family farmhouse, calling into question the lineage of the Montoros and diverting the crown into the hands of their cousin.

Secrets, scandal, lies... Will was more than happy to turn the reins over to his twin.

And since Will was officially single, he could carry out his own devious plan in great detail—his plot didn't involve love but a whole lot of seduction.

First, though, he had to get through this meeting with his father. Fortunately, Will's main goal of taking back control of his life involved one very intriguing employee of his father's household so having this little meeting at the Rowling home in Playa del Onda instead of the Rowling Energy offices was perfectly fine with him. Now that James had married and moved out and Patrick was backing away from working as much, Patrick used his weekend home more often.

"Rather shocking news, isn't it?"

Still clutching the paper in one hand and the coffee mug in the other, Will turned to see his father breeze into the den. While Patrick leaned more toward the heavier side, Will prided himself on keeping fit. It was just another way he and his father were different though some around them felt Will was a chip off the old block.

At one time Will would've agreed with those people, but he was more than ready to show everyone, including his father, he was his own man and he was taking charge.

"This bombshell will certainly shake things up for Alma." Will tossed the newspaper onto the glossy mahogany desktop. "Think parliament will ratify his coronation?"

Patrick grunted as he sank into his leather desk chair. "It's just a different branch of the Montoro family that will be taking the throne, so it really doesn't matter."

Will clutched his coffee cup and shook his head. Anything to do with the Montoros was not his problem. He had his own battles to face, starting with his father right now.

"What did you need to see me so early about?" his father asked, leaning back so far in the chair it squeaked.

Will remained standing; he needed to keep the upper hand here, needed to stay in control. Even though he was going up against his father's wishes, Will had to take back control of his own life. Enough with worrying about what his father would say or do if Will made the wrong move.

James had never bowed to their father's wishes and Will always wondered why his twin was so against the grain. It may have taken a few years to come around, but Will was more than ready to prove himself as a formidable businessman.

Will was a master at multitasking and getting what he wanted. And since he'd kissed Cat a few weeks ago, he'd thought of little else. He wanted her...and he would have her. Their intense encounter would allow for nothing less.

But for right this moment, Will was focusing on his

new role with Rowling Energy and this meeting with his father. Conquering one milestone at a time.

"Up till now, you've had me dealing with the company's oil interests," Will stated. "I'm ready to take total control of the real estate division, too."

His father's chest puffed out as he took in a deep breath. "I've been waiting for you to come to me with this," Patrick said with a smile. "You're the obvious choice to take over. You've done a remarkable job increasing the oil profits. They're up twelve percent since you put your mark on the company."

Will intended to produce financial gains for all of the company's divisions. For years, he'd wanted to get out from under his father's thumb and take control, and now was his chance. And that was just the beginning of his plans where Rowling Energy was concerned.

Finally, now that Will was seeing clearly and standing on his own two feet, nothing would stand in his way. His father's semiretirement would just help ease the path to a beautiful life full of power and wealth... and a certain maid he'd set in his sights.

"I've already taken the liberty of contacting our main real estate clients in London," Will went on, sliding his hands into his pockets and shifting his weight. "I informed them they would be dealing with me."

Will held his father's gaze. He'd taken a risk contacting the other players, but Will figured his father would be proud and not question the move. Patrick had wanted Will to slide into the lead role of the family business for years. Slowly Will had taken over. Now he was ready to seal every deal and hold all the reins.

"Another man would think you're trying to sneak behind his back." Patrick leaned forward and laced his fingers together on the desktop. "I know better. You're taking charge and that's what I want. I'll make sure my assistant knows you will be handling the accounts from here on out. But I'm here anytime, Will. You've been focused on this for so long, your work has paid off."

Will nodded. Part one of his plan was done and had gone just as smoothly as he'd envisioned. Now he needed to start working on the second part of his plan. And both aspects involved the same tactic…trust. He needed to gain and keep the trust of both his father and Cat or everything would blow up in his face.

Will refused to tolerate failure on any level.

Especially where Cat was concerned. That kiss had spawned an onslaught of emotions he couldn't, wouldn't, ignore. Cat with her petite, curvy body that fit perfectly against his. She'd leaned into that kiss like a woman starved and he'd been all too happy to give her what she wanted.

Unfortunately, she'd dodged him ever since. He didn't take that as a sign of disinterest. Quite the opposite. If she wasn't interested, she'd act as if nothing had happened. But the way she kept avoiding him when he came to visit his father at the Playa del Onda estate only proved to Will that she was just as shaken as he was. There was no way she didn't feel something.

Just one kiss and he had her trembling. He'd use that to his advantage.

Seeing Cat was another reason he opted to come to his father's second home this morning. She couldn't avoid him if he cornered her at her workplace. She'd been the maid for his twin brother, James, but James had often been away playing football—or as the Yanks called it, soccer—so Cat hadn't been a temptation thrust right in Will's face. But now she worked directly under Patrick. Her parents had also worked for Patrick, so

Cat had grown up around Will and James. It wasn't that long ago that Will had set his sights on Cat. Just a few years ago, in fact, he'd made his move, and they'd even dated surreptitiously for a while. That had ended tragically when he'd backed down from a fight in a moment of weakness. Since their recent kiss had brought back their scorching chemistry, Will knew it was time for some action.

Will may have walked out on her four years ago, but she was about to meet the new Will…the one who fought for what he wanted. And he wanted Cat in his bed and this time he wouldn't walk away.

Will focused back on his father. "I'll let myself out," he stated, more than ready to be finished with this part of his day. "I'll be in touch once I hear back from the investors and companies I contacted."

Heading for the open double doors, Will stopped when his father called his name.

"You know, I really wanted the thing with you and Bella to work," Patrick stated, as he stared at the blaring, boldface headline.

"She found love with my brother. She and I never had any type of connection. You'd best get used to them together."

Patrick focused his attention back on Will. "Just keep your head on your shoulders and don't follow the path your brother has. Getting sidetracked isn't the way to make Rowling Energy grow and prosper. Just do what you've been doing."

Oh, he intended to do just that.

Will gave his father a brief nod before heading out into the hallway. Little did his father know, Will was fully capable of going after more than one goal at a time. He had no intention of letting the oil or real estate businesses slide. If anything, Will fully intended to expand both aspects of the business into new territory within the next year.

Will also intended to seduce Cat even sooner. Much sooner. And he would stop at nothing to see all of his desires fulfilled.

That familiar woodsy scent assaulted her...much like the man himself had when he'd kissed her a few weeks ago.

Could such a full-on assault of the senses be called something so simple as a kiss? He'd consumed her from the inside out. He'd had her body responding within seconds and left her aching and wanting more than she should.

Catalina kept her back turned, knowing full well who stood behind her. She'd managed to avoid running into him, though he visited his father more and more lately. At this point, a run-in was inevitable.

She much preferred working for James instead of Patrick, but now that James was married, he didn't stay here anymore and Patrick did. Catalina had zero tolerance for Patrick and the fact that she worked directly for him now only motivated her more to finish saving up to get out of Alma once and for all. And the only reason she was working for Patrick was because she needed the money. She knew she was well on her way to leaving, so going to work for another family for only a few months didn't seem fair.

Years ago her mother had moved on and still worked for a prestigious family in Alma. Cat prayed her time here with Patrick was coming to an end, too.

But for now, she was stuck here and she hadn't been able to stop thinking about that kiss. Will had silently taken control of her body and mind in the span of just a few heated moments, and he'd managed to thrust her directly into their past to the time when they'd dated.

Unfortunately, when he'd broken things off with her, he'd hurt her more than she cared to admit. Beyond leaving her when she hadn't even seen it coming, he'd gone so far as to say it had all been a mistake. His exact words, which had shocked her and left her wondering how she'd been so clueless. Catalina wouldn't be played for a fool and she would never be his "mistake" again. She had more pride than that…even if her heart was still bruised from the harsh rejection.

Even if her lips still tingled at the memory of their recent kiss.

Catalina continued to pick up random antique trinkets on the built-in bookshelves as she dusted. She couldn't face Will, not just yet. This was the first encounter since that night three weeks ago. She'd seen him, he'd purposely caught her eye a few times since then, but he'd not approached her until now. It was as if the man enjoyed the torture he inflicted upon her senses.

"You work too hard."

That voice. Will's low, sultry tone dripped with sex appeal. She didn't turn around. No doubt the sight of him would still give her that swift punch of lust to the gut, but she was stronger now than she used to be…or she'd been stronger before he'd weakened her defenses with one simple yet toe-curling kiss.

"Would that make you the pot or the kettle?" she asked, giving extra attention to one specific shelf because focusing on anything other than this man was all that was holding her sanity together.

His rich laughter washed over her, penetrating any

defense she'd surrounded herself with. Why did her body have to betray her? Why did she find herself drawn to the one man she shouldn't want? Because she hadn't forgotten that he'd recently been the chosen one to wed Bella Montoro. Bella's father had put out a false press release announcing their engagement, but of course Bella fell for James instead and Will ended up single. James had informed Cat that Bella and Will were never actually engaged, but still. With Will single now, and after that toe-curling kiss, Cat had to be on her guard. She had too much pride in herself to be anybody's Plan B.

"That spot is clean." His warm, solid hand slid easily onto her shoulder. "Turn around."

Pulling in a deep breath, Catalina turned, keeping her shoulders back and her chin high. She would not be intimidated by sexy good looks, flawless charm and that knowing twinkle in Will's eye. Chemistry wouldn't get her what she wanted out of life…all she'd end up with was another broken heart.

"I have a lot on my list today." She stared at his ear, trying to avoid those piercing aqua eyes. "Your dad should be in his den if you're looking for him."

"Our business is already taken care of." Will's hand dropped, but he didn't step back; if anything, he shifted closer. "Now you and I are going to talk."

"Which is just another area where we differ," she retorted, skirting around him to cross in front of the mantel and head to the other wall of built-in bookcases. "We have nothing to discuss."

Of course he was right behind her. The man had dropped her so easily four years ago yet in the past few weeks, he'd been relentless. Perhaps she just needed to be more firm, to let him know exactly where she stood.

"Listen." She spun back around, brandishing her feather duster at him. Maybe he'd start sneezing and she could make a run for it. "I've no doubt you want to talk about that kiss. We kissed. Nothing we hadn't done before."

Of course this kiss was so, so much more; it had penetrated to her very soul. Dammit.

"But I'm not the same girl you used to know," she continued, propping her hand on her hip. "I'm not looking for a relationship, I'm not looking for love. I'm not even interested in you anymore, Will."

Catalina nearly choked on that lie, but she mentally applauded herself for the firmness in her delivery and for stating all she needed to. She wasn't about to start playing whatever game Will had in mind because she knew one thing for certain...she'd lose.

Will stepped closer, took hold of her wrist and pulled her arm gently behind her back. Her body arched into his as she gripped her feather duster and tried to concentrate on the bite of the handle into her palm and not the way those mesmerizing eyes were full of passion and want.

"Not interested?" he asked with a smirk. "You may be able to lie to yourself, Cat, but you can never lie to me. I know you too well."

She swallowed. "You don't know me at all if you think I still like to be called Cat."

Will leaned in until his lips caressed the side of her ear. "I want to stand out in your mind," he whispered. "I won't call you what everyone else does because our relationship is different."

"We have nothing but a past that was a mistake." She purposely threw his words back in his face and she didn't care if that was childish or not.

Struggling against his hold only caused her body to respond even more as she rubbed against that hard, powerful build.

"You can fight this all you want," he said as he eased back just enough to look into her eyes. "You can deny you want me and you can even try to tell yourself you hate me. But know this. I'm also not the same man I used to be. I'm not going to let you get away this time."

Catalina narrowed her gaze. "I have goals, Will, and you're not on my list."

A sultry grin spread across his face an instant before he captured her lips. His body shifted so that she could feel just how much he wanted her. Catalina couldn't stop herself from opening her mouth for him and if her hands had been free, she probably would've fully embarrassed herself by gripping his hair and holding him even tighter.

Damn this man she wanted to hate, but couldn't.

He demanded her affection, demanded desire from her and she gave it. Mercy, she had no choice.

He nipped at her, their tongues tangling, before he finally, finally lifted his head and ran a thumb across her moist bottom lip.

"I have goals, too, Cat," he murmured against her mouth. "And you're on the top of *my* list."

The second he released her, she had to hurry to steady herself. By the time she'd processed that full-on arousing attack, Will was gone.

Typical of the man to get her ready for more and leave her hanging. She just wished she still wasn't tingling and aching all over for more of his touch.

Two

William sat on his patio, staring down at his boat and contemplating another plan of action. Unfortunately his cell phone rang before he could fully appreciate the brilliant idea he'd just had.

His father's name popped up on the screen and Will knew without answering what this would be about. It looked as if Patrick Rowling had just got wind of Will's latest business actions.

"Afternoon," he greeted, purposely being more cheerful than he assumed his father was.

"What the hell are you doing with the Cortes Real Estate company?"

Will stared out onto the sparkling water and crossed his ankles as he leaned back in his cushioned patio chair. "I dropped them."

"I'm well aware of that seeing as how Dominic called me to raise hell. What were you thinking?" his father demanded. "When you steamrolled into the head position, I thought you'd make wise moves to further the family business and make it even more profitable into the next generation. I never expected you to sever ties with companies we've dealt with for decades."

"I'm not hanging on to business relationships based on tradition or some sense of loyalty," Will stated, refusing to back down. "We've not gained a thing in the past five years from the Corteses and it was time to cut our losses. If you and Dom want to be friends, then go play golf or something, but his family will no longer do business with mine. The bottom line here is money, not hurt feelings."

"You should've run this by me, Will. I won't tolerate you going behind my back."

Will came to his feet, pulled in a deep breath of ocean air and smiled because he was in charge now and his father was going to start seeing that the "good" twin wasn't always going to bend and bow to Patrick's wishes. Will was still doing the "right thing," it just so happened the decisions made were Will's version of right and not his father's.

"I'm not sneaking at all," Will replied, leaning against the scrolling wrought iron rail surrounding his deck. "I'll tell you anything you want to know, but since I'm in charge now, I'm not asking for permission, either."

"How many more phone calls can I expect like the one I got from Cortes?"

His father's sarcasm wasn't lost on Will.

"None for the time being. I only let one go, but that doesn't mean I won't cut more ties in the future if I see we aren't pulling any revenue in after a period of time."

"You run your decisions by me first."

Giving a shrug even though his father couldn't see him, Will replied, "You wanted the golden son to take over. That's exactly what I'm doing. Don't second-guess me and my decisions. I stand to gain or lose like you do and I don't intend to see our name tarnished. We'll come out on top if you stop questioning me and let me do this job the way it's meant to be done."

Patrick sighed. "I never thought you'd argue with me."

"I'm not arguing. I'm telling you how it is."

Will disconnected the call. He wasn't going to get into a verbal sparring match with his father. He didn't have time for such things and nothing would change Will's mind. He'd gone over the numbers and cross-referenced them for the past years. Though that was a job his assistant could easily do, Will wanted his eyes on every report since he was taking over. He needed to know exactly what he was dealing with and how to plan accordingly.

His gaze traveled back to his yacht nestled against his private dock. Speaking of planning accordingly, he had more personal issues to deal with right now. Issues that involved one very sexy maid.

It had taken a lifeless, arranged relationship with Bella to really wake Will up to the fact his father had his clutches so tight, Will had basically been a marionette his entire life. Now Will was severing those strings, starting with the ridiculous notion of his marrying Bella.

Will was more than ready to move forward and take all the things he'd been craving: money and Cat. A beautiful combo to start this second stage of his life.

And it would be soon, he vowed to himself as he stalked around his outdoor seating area and headed inside. Very soon he would add to his millions, secure his place as head of the family business by cementing its leading position in the oil and real estate industries and have Cat right where he wanted her…begging.

Catalina couldn't wait to finish this day. So many things had come up that hadn't been on her regular schedule…just another perk of working for the Rowling patriarch. She had her sights set on getting home, taking off her ugly, sensible work shoes and digging into another sewing project that would give her hope, get her one step closer to her ultimate goal.

This next piece she'd designed late last night would be a brilliant, classy, yet fun outfit to add to her private collection. A collection she fully intended to take with her when she left Alma very soon.

Her own secret goal of becoming a fashion designer had her smiling. Maybe one day she could wear her own stylish clothes to work instead of boring black cotton pants and button-down shirt with hideous shoes. Other than her mother, nobody knew of Catalina's real dream, and she had every intention of keeping things that way. The last thing she needed was anyone trying to dissuade her from pursuing her ambitions or telling her that the odds were against her. She was fully aware of the odds and she intended to leap over them and claim her dream no matter how long it took. Determination was a hell of a motivator.

She came to work for the Rowlings and did her job— and that was about all the human contact she had lately. She'd been too wrapped up in materials, designs and fantasies of runway shows with her clothing draped on models who could fully do her stylish fashions justice.

Not that Catalina hated how she looked, but she

wasn't blind. She knew her curvy yet petite frame wasn't going to get her clothing noticed. She merely wanted to be behind the scenes. She didn't need all the limelight on her because she just wanted to design, no more.

As opposed to the Rowling men who seemed to crave the attention and thrive on the publicity and hoopla.

Adjusting the fresh arrangement of lilacs and white calla lilies in the tall, slender crystal vase, Catalina placed the beautiful display on the foyer table in the center of the open entryway. There were certain areas where Patrick didn't mind her doing her own thing, such as choosing the flowers for all the arrangements. She tended to lean toward the classy and elegant...which was the total opposite of the man she worked for.

James on the other hand had more fun with her working here and he actually acknowledged her presence. Patrick only summoned her when he wanted to demand something. She hated thinking how much Will was turning into his father, how business was ruling him and consuming his entire life.

Will wasn't in her personal life anymore, no matter how much she still daydreamed about their kisses. And Patrick would only be her employer for a short time longer. She was hoping to be able to leave Alma soon, leave behind this life of being a maid for a man she didn't care for. At least James was pleasant and a joy to work for. Granted, James hadn't betrayed Cat's mother the way Patrick had. And that was just another reason she wanted out of here, away from Patrick and the secret Cat knew about him.

Catalina shoved those thoughts aside. Thinking of all the sins from Patrick's past wouldn't help her mood.

Patrick had been deceitful many years ago and Catalina couldn't ignore her mother's warning about the Rowling men. Even if Will had no clue how his father had behaved, it was something Catalina would never forget. She was only glad she'd found out before she did something foolish like fall completely in love with Will.

Apparently the womanizing started with Patrick and trickled down to his sons. James had been a notorious player before Bella entered his life. After all, there was nothing like stealing your twin brother's girl, which is what James had done to Will. But all had worked out in the end because Bella and James truly did love each other even if the way they got there was hardly normal. Leave it to the Rowlings and the Montoros to keep life in Alma interesting.

Catalina just wished those recent kisses from Will weren't overriding her mother's sound advice and obvious common sense.

Once the arrangement was to her liking—because perfection was everything whether you were a maid or a CEO—Catalina made her way up the wide, curved staircase to the second floor. The arrangements upstairs most likely needed to be changed out. At the very least, she'd freshen them up with water and remove the wilting stems.

As she neared the closed door of the library, she heard the distinct sound of a woman sobbing. Catalina had no clue who was visiting. No women lived here, and she'd been in the back of the house most of the morning and hadn't seen anyone come in.

The nosy side of her wanted to know what was going on, but the employee side of her said she needed to mind her own business. She'd been around the Rowling family enough to know to keep her head down, do her job and remember she was only the help.

Inwardly she groaned. She hated that term. Yes, she was a maid, but she was damn good at her job. She took pride in what she did. No, cleaning toilets and washing sheets wasn't the most glam of jobs, but she knew what she did was important. Besides, the structure and discipline of her work was only training her for the dream job she hoped to have someday.

The rumble of male voices blended in with the female's weeping. Whatever was going on, it was something major. Catalina approached the circular table in the middle of the wide hall. As she plucked out wilted buds here and there, the door to the library creaked open. Catalina focused on the task at hand, though she was dying to turn to see who came from the room.

"Cat."

She cringed at the familiar voice. Well, part of her curiosity was answered, but suddenly she didn't care what was going on in that room. She didn't care who Will had in there, though Catalina already felt sorry for the poor woman. She herself had shed many tears over Will when he'd played her for a fool, getting her to think they could ignore their class differences and have a relationship. "I need to see you for a minute."

Of course he hadn't asked. Will Rowling didn't ask… he demanded.

Stiffening her back, she expected to see him standing close, but when she turned to face him, she noted he was holding onto the library door, with only the top half of his body peeking out of the room.

"I'm working," she informed him, making no move to go see whatever lover's spat he was having with the unknown woman.

"You need to talk to Bella."

Bella? Suddenly Catalina found herself moving down

the hall, but Will stepped out, blocking her entry into the library. Catalina glanced down to his hand gripping her bicep.

"Her aunt Isabella passed away in the middle of the night," he whispered.

Isabella Montoro was the grand matriarch of the entire Montoro clan. The woman had been around forever. Between Juan Carlos being named the true heir to the throne and now Isabella's death, the poor family was being dealt one blow after another.

Will rubbed his thumb back and forth over Catalina's arm. "You know Bella enough through James and I figured she'd want another woman to talk to. Plus, I thought she could relate to you because…"

Swallowing, she nodded. When she and Will had dated briefly, Catalina had just lost her grandmother, a woman who had been like a second mother to her. Will had seen her struggle with the loss…maybe the timing of the loss explained why she'd been so naïve to think she and Will could have a future together. For that moment in time, Catalina had clung to any hope of happiness and Will had shown her so much…but it had all been built on lies.

Catalina started to move by him, but his grip tightened. "I don't want to bring up bad memories for you." Those aqua eyes held her in place. "As much as Bella is hurting, I won't sacrifice you, so tell me if you can't go in there."

Catalina swallowed as she looked back into those eyes that held something other than lust. For once he wasn't staring at her as if he wanted to rip her clothes off. He genuinely cared or at least he was playing the part rather well. Then again, he'd played a rather im-

pressive role four years ago pretending to be the doting boyfriend.

Catalina couldn't afford to let her guard down. Not
again with this man who still had the power to cripple
her. That kiss weeks ago only proved the control he still
had and she'd never, ever let him in on that fact. She
could never allow Will to know just how much she still
ached for his touch.

"I'll be fine," she replied, pulling her arm back. "I'd
like to be alone with her, though."

Will opened his mouth as if to argue, but finally
closed it and nodded.

As soon as Catalina stepped inside, her heart broke.
Bella sat in a wingback chair. James rested his hip on
the arm and Bella was curled into his side sobbing.

"James." Will motioned for his twin to follow him
out.

Leaning down, James muttered something to Bella.
Dabbing her eyes with a tissue, Bella looked up and
saw she had company.

Catalina crossed to the beautiful woman who had
always been known for her wild side. Right now she
was hurting over losing a woman who was as close as
a mother to her.

The fact that Will thought Catalina could offer
comfort, the fact that he cared enough to seek her out,
shouldn't warm her heart. She couldn't let his moment
of sweetness hinder her judgment of the man. Bella
was the woman he'd been in a relationship with only a
month ago. How could Catalina forget that? No matter
the reasons behind the relationship, Catalina couldn't
let go of the fact that Will would've said *I do* to Bella
had James not come along.

Will had an agenda, he always did. Catalina had no

clue what he was up to now, but she had a feeling his newfound plans included her. After all this time, was he seriously going to pursue her? Did he honestly think they'd start over or pick up where they'd left off?

Catalina knew deep down he was only after one thing…and she truly feared if she wasn't careful, she'd end up giving in.

Three

William lifted the bottle of scotch from the bar in the living room, waving it back and forth slightly in a silent invitation to his brother.

James blew out a breath. "Yeah. I could use a drink."

Neither mentioned the early time. Sometimes life's crises called for an emergency drink to take the edge off. And since they'd recently started building their relationship back up, Will wanted to be here for his brother because even though Bella was the one who'd suffered the loss, James was no doubt feeling helpless.

"Smart thinking asking Catalina to help." James took the tumbler with the amber liquid and eased back on the leather sofa. "Something going on there you want to talk about?"

Will remained standing, leaning an elbow back against the bar. "Nothing going on at all."

Not to say there wouldn't be something going on very

soon if he had his way about it. Those heated kisses only motivated him even more...not to mention the fact that his father would hate knowing "the good twin" had gone after what he wanted, which was the total opposite of Patrick's wishes.

James swirled the drink as he stared down into the glass. "I know Isabella has been sick for a while, but still, her death came as a shock. Knowing how strong-willed she was, I'd say she hung on until Juan Carlos was announced the rightful heir to the throne."

Will nodded, thankful they were off the topic of Cat. She was his and he wasn't willing to share her with anyone right now. Only a month ago, Bella had caught Will and Cat kissing, but at the time she'd thought it was James locking lips with the maid. The slight misunderstanding had nearly cost James the love of his life. "How is Bella dealing with the fact her brother was knocked off the throne before he could fully take control?"

The Montoro family was being restored to the Alma monarchy after decades of harsh dictatorship. First Rafael Montoro IV and then, when he abdicated, his brother Gabriel were thought to be the rightful heirs. However, their sister, Bella, had then uncovered damning letters in an old family farmhouse, indicating that because of a paternity secret going back to before World War II, Juan Carlos's line of the family were the only legitimate heirs.

"I don't think that title ever appealed to Gabriel or Bella, to be honest." James crossed his ankle over his knee and held onto his glass as he rested it on the arm of the sofa. "Personally, I'm glad the focus is on Juan Carlos right now. Bella and I have enough media attention as it is."

In addition to the fact that James had married a member of Alma's royal family, he was also a star football player who drew a lot of scrutiny from the tabloids. The newlyweds no doubt wanted some privacy to start building their life together, especially since James had also recently taken custody of his infant baby, Maisey—a child from a previous relationship.

"Isabella's passing will have the media all over the Montoros and Juan Carlos. I'm probably going to take Bella and Maisey back to the farmhouse to avoid the spotlight. The renovations aren't done yet, but we need the break."

"What can I do to help?" Will asked.

James tipped back the last of the scotch, and then leaned forward and set the empty tumbler on the coffee table. "Give me back that watch," he said with a half smile and a nod toward Will's wrist.

"Nah, I won this fair and square," Will joked. "I told you that you wouldn't be able to resist putting a ring on Bella's finger."

James had inherited the coveted watch from their English grandfather and wore it all the time. It was the way people told the twins apart. But Will had wanted the piece and had finally won it in a bet that James would fall for Bella and propose. Ironically, it had almost ended James and Bella's relationship because Will had been wearing the watch that night he'd kissed Cat in the gazebo. Bella had mistaken him for James and jumped to conclusions.

"Besides the watch, what else can I do?" Will asked.

"I have no idea." James shook his head and blew out a sigh. "Right now keeping Dad out of my business would be great."

Will laughed. "I don't think that will be a problem.

He's up in arms about some business decisions I've made, so the heat is off you for now."

"Are you saying the good twin is taking charge?"

"I'm saying I'm controlling my own life and this is only the first step in my plan."

Leaning forward, James placed his elbows on his knees. "Sounds like you may need my help. I am the black sheep, after all. Let me fill you in on all the ways to defy our father."

"I'm pretty sure I'm defying him all on my own." Will pushed off the bar and shoved his hands in his pockets. "I'll let you know if I need any tips."

James leveled his gaze at Will. "Why do I have a feeling this new plan of yours has something to do with the beautiful maid?"

Will shrugged, refusing to rise to the bait.

"You were kissing her a few weeks ago," James reminded him. "That little escapade nearly cost me Bella."

The entire night had been a mess, but thankfully things ultimately worked out the way they should have.

"So Catalina…"

Will sighed. "You won't drop it, will you?"

"We practically grew up together with her, you dated before, you were kissing a few weeks ago. I'm sure dear old Dad is about to explode if you are making business decisions that he isn't on board with and if you're seducing his maid."

"I'm not seducing anyone." Yet. "And what I do with my personal life is none of his concern."

"He'll say different once he knows you're after the maid. He'll not see her as an appropriate match for you," James countered, coming to his feet and glancing toward the ceiling as if he could figure out what was going on upstairs between the women. "What's taking them so long? Think it's safe to go back?"

Will nodded. "Let's go see. Hopefully Cat was able to calm Bella down."

"Cat, huh?" James smiled as he headed toward the foyer and the staircase. "You called her that years ago and she hated it. You still going with that?"

Will patted his brother on the shoulder. "I am going for whatever the hell I want lately."

And he was. From this point on, if he wanted it, he was taking it...that went for his business and his bedroom.

The fact that the maid was consoling a member of the royal family probably looked strange from the outside, and honestly it felt a bit weird. But Catalina had been around Bella enough to know how down-to-earth James's wife was. Bella never treated Catalina like a member of the staff. Not that they were friends by any means, but Catalina was comfortable with Bella and part of her was glad Will had asked her to come console Bella over the loss of her aunt.

"You're so sweet to come in here," Bella said with a sniff.

Catalina fought to keep her own emotions inside as she hugged Bella. Even though years had passed, Catalina still missed her grandmother every single day. Some days were just more of a struggle than others.

"I'm here anytime." Catalina squeezed the petite woman, knowing what just a simple touch could do to help ease a bit of the pain, to know you weren't alone in your grief. "There will be times memories sneak up on you and crush you all over again and there will be days you are just fine. Don't try to hide your emotions.

Everyone grieves differently so whatever your outlet is, it's normal."

Bella shifted back and patted her damp cheeks. "Thank you. I didn't mean to cry all over you and bring up a bad time in your life."

Pushing her own memories aside, Catalina offered a smile. "You didn't do anything but need a shoulder to cry on. I just hope I helped in some small way to ease the hurt and I'm glad I was here."

"Bella."

The sound of James's voice had Catalina stepping back as he came in to stand beside his wife. Tucking her short hair behind her ears, Catalina offered the couple a brief smile. James hugged Bella to his side and glanced at Catalina.

"I didn't want to interrupt, but I know you need to work, too," James said. "We really appreciate you."

Those striking Rowling eyes held hers. This man was a star athlete, wanted by women all over the world. Yet Catalina felt nothing. He looked exactly like Will, but in Catalina's heart…

No. Her heart wasn't involved. Her hormones were a jumbled mess, but her heart was sealed off and impenetrable…at least where Will was concerned. Maybe when she left Alma she'd settle somewhere new and find the man she was meant to be with, the man who wouldn't consider her a mistake.

Those damning words always seemed to be in the forefront of her mind.

"I'm here all day through the week," Catalina told Bella. "You can always call me, too. I'm happy to help any way I can."

"Thank you." Bella sniffed. She dabbed her eyes again and turned into James's embrace.

Catalina left the couple alone and pulled the door shut behind her. She leaned against the panel, closed her eyes and tipped her head back. Even though Catalina still had her mother, she missed her grandmother. There was just something special about a woman who enters your life in such a bold way that leaves a lasting impression.

Catalina knew Bella was hurting over the loss of her aunt, there was no way to avoid the pain. But Bella had a great support team and James would stay by her side.

A stab of remorse hit her. Bella's and Catalina's situations were so similar, yet so different. Will had comforted her over her loss when they'd first started dating and Catalina had taken his concern as a sign of pure interest. Unfortunately, her moments of weakness had led her to her first broken heart.

The only good thing to come out of it was that she hadn't given him her innocence. But she'd certainly been tempted on more than one occasion. The man still tempted her, but she was smarter now, less naïve, and she had her eyes wide open.

Pushing off the door, she shoved aside the thoughts of Will and their past relationship. She'd jumped from one mistake to another after he broke things off with her. Two unfortunate relationships were more than enough for her. Focusing on turning her hobby and passion for making clothes into a possible career had kept her head on straight and her life pointed in the right direction. She didn't have time for obstacles...no matter how sexy.

She made her way down the hall toward the main bathroom on the second floor. This bathroom was nearly the size of her little flat across town. She could afford something bigger, but she'd opted to keep her place small because she lived alone and she'd rather save her money for fabrics, new sewing machines, investing in her future and ultimately her move. One day that nest egg she'd set aside would come in handy and she couldn't wait to leave Alma and see how far her dreams could take her. Another couple months and she truly believed she would be ready. She still couldn't pinpoint her exact destination, though. Milan was by far the hot spot for fashion and she could head there and aim straight for the top. New York was also an option, or Paris.

Catalina smiled at the possibilities as she reached beneath the sink and pulled out fresh white hand towels. Just as she turned, she collided with a very hard, very familiar chest.

Will gripped her arms to steady her, but she wasn't going anywhere, not when she was wedged between his solid frame and the vanity biting into her back.

"Excuse me," she said, gripping the terrycloth next to her chest and tipping her chin up. "I'm running behind."

"Then a few more minutes won't matter." He didn't let up on his hold, but instead leaned back and kicked the door shut with his foot. "You're avoiding me."

Hadn't she thought this bathroom was spacious just moments ago? Because now it seemed even smaller than the closet in her bedroom.

"Your ego is getting in the way of common sense," she countered. "I'm working. Why are you always here lately anyway? Don't you have an office to run on the other side of town?"

The edge of his mouth kicked up in a cocky half smile. "You've noticed. I was beginning to think you were immune."

"I've been vaccinated."

Will's rich laugh washed over her and she cursed the goose bumps that covered her skin. Between his touch, his masculine scent and feeling his warm breath on her, her defenses were slipping. She couldn't get sucked back into his spell, not when she was so close to breaking free once and for all.

"Come to dinner with me," he told her, smile still in place as if he truly thought she'd jump at the chance. "Your choice of places."

Now Catalina laughed. "You're delusional. I'm not going anywhere with you."

His eyes darkened as they slid to her lips. "You will."

Catalina pushed against him, surprised when he released her and stepped back. She busied herself with changing out the hand towels on the heated rack. Why wouldn't he leave? Did he not take a hint? Why suddenly was he so interested in her when a few years ago she'd been "a mistake"? Plus, a month ago he'd almost been engaged to another woman.

Being a backup plan for anybody was never an option. She'd rather be alone.

Taking more care than normal, Catalina focused on making sure the edges of the towels were perfectly lined up. She needed to keep her shaking hands busy.

"You can't avoid this forever." Will's bold words sliced through the tension. "I want you, Cat. I think you know me well enough to realize I get what I want."

Anger rolled through her as she spun around to face him. "For once in your life, you're not going to be able to have something just because you say so. I'm not just a possession, Will. You can't buy me or even work your charm on me. I've told you I'm not the same naïve girl I used to be."

In two swift steps, he'd closed the gap between them

and had her backed against the wall. His hands settled on her hips, gripping them and pulling them flush with his. This time she didn't have the towels to form a barrier and his chest molded with hers. Catalina forced herself to look up into his eyes, gritted her teeth and prayed for strength.

Leaning in close, Will whispered, "I'm not the man I used to be, either."

A shiver rippled through her. No, no he wasn't. Now he was all take-charge and demanding. He hadn't been like this before. He also hadn't been as broad, as hard. He'd definitely bulked up in all the right ways...not that she cared.

"What would your father say if he knew you were hiding in the bathroom with the maid?" she asked, hoping the words would penetrate through his hormones. He'd always been yanked around by Daddy's wishes... hence their breakup, she had no doubt.

Will shifted his face so his lips were a breath away from hers as his hands slid up to her waist, his thumbs barely brushing the underside of her breasts. "My father is smart enough to know what I'd be doing behind a closed door with a sexy woman."

Oh, man. Why did she have to find his arrogance so appealing? Hadn't she learned her lesson the first time? Wanting Will was a mistake, one she may never recover from if she jumped in again.

"Are you saying you're not bowing down to your father's commands anymore? How very grown up of you."

Why was she goading him? She needed to get out of here because the more he leaned against her, the longer he spoke with that kissable mouth so close to hers, the harder he was making her life. Taunting her, making her ache for things she could never have.

"I told you, I'm a different man." His lips grazed hers as he murmured, "But I still want you and nobody is going to stand in my way."

Why did her hormones and need for his touch override common sense? Letting Will kiss her again was a bad, bad idea. But she couldn't stop herself and she'd nearly arched her body into his just as he stepped back. The heat in his eyes did nothing to suppress the tremors racing through her, but he was easing backward toward the closed door.

"You're leaving?" she asked. "What is this, Will? A game? Corner the staff and see how far she'll let me take things?"

He froze. "This isn't a game, Cat. I'm aching for you, to strip you down and show you exactly what I want. But I need you to literally hurt for wanting me and I want you to be ready. Because the second I think we're on the same level, you're mine."

And with that, he turned and walked out, leaving the door open.

Catalina released a breath she hadn't realized she'd been holding. How dare he disrupt her work and get her all hot and bothered? Did he truly think she'd run to him begging to whisk her off to bed?

As much as her body craved his touch, she wouldn't fall into his bed simply because he turned on the sex appeal. If he wanted her, then that was his problem.

Unfortunately, he'd just made his wants her problem as well because now she couldn't think of anything else but how amazing he felt pressed against her.

Catalina cursed herself as she gathered the dirty towels. If he was set on playing games, he'd chosen the wrong opponent.

Four

Catalina lived for her weekends. Two full days for her to devote to her true love of designing and sewing. There was nothing like creating your own masterpieces from scratch. Her thick portfolio binder overflowed with ideas from the past four years. She'd sketched designs for every season, some sexy, some conservative, but everything was timeless and classy in her opinion.

She supposed something more than just heartache and angst had come from Will's exiting her life so harshly. She'd woken up, finally figured out what she truly wanted and opted to put herself, her dreams as top priority. And once she started achieving her career goals, she'd work on her personal dreams of a family. All of those were things she couldn't find in Alma. This place had nothing for her anymore other than her mother, who worked for another family. But her mother had already said she'd follow Catalina wherever she decided to go.

Glancing around, Catalina couldn't remember where she put that lacy fabric she'd picked up in town a few weeks ago. She'd seen it on the clearance table and had nothing in mind for it at the time, but she couldn't pass up the bargain.

Now she knew exactly what she'd use the material for. She had the perfect wrap-style dress in mind. Something light and comfortable, yet sexy and alluring with a lace overlay. The time would come when Catalina would be able to wear things like that every single day. She could ditch her drab black button-down shirt and plain black pants. When she dressed for work every morning, she always felt she was preparing for a funeral.

And those shoes? She couldn't wait to burn those hideous things.

Catalina moved around the edge of the small sofa and thumbed through the stack of folded materials on the makeshift shelving against the wall. She'd transformed this spare room into her sewing room just last year and since then she'd spent nearly all of her spare time in the cramped space. One day, though… One day she'd have a glorious sewing room with all the top-notch equipment and she would bask in the happiness of her creations.

As she scanned the colorful materials folded neatly on the shelves, her cell rang. Catalina glanced at the arm of the sofa where her phone lay. Her mother's name lit up the screen.

Lunging across the mess of fabrics on the cushions, Catalina grabbed her phone and came back to her feet as she answered.

"Hey, Mum."

"Sweetheart. I'm sorry I didn't call earlier. I went out to breakfast with a friend."

Catalina stepped from her bedroom and into the cozy

living area. "No problem. I've been sewing all morning and lost track of time."

"New designs?" her mother asked.

"Of course." Catalina sank down onto her cushy sofa and curled her feet beneath her. "I actually have a new summery beach theme I'm working on. Trying to stay tropical and classy at the same time has proven to be more challenging than I thought."

"Well, I know you can do it," her mother said. "I wore that navy-and-gray-print skirt you made for me to breakfast this morning and my friend absolutely loved it. I was so proud to be wearing your design, darling."

Catalina sat up straighter. "You didn't tell her—"

"I did not," her mother confirmed. "But I may have said it was from a new up-and-coming designer. I couldn't help it, honey. I'm just so proud of you and I know you'll take the fashion world by storm once you leave Alma."

Just the thought of venturing out on her own, taking her secret designs and her life dream and putting herself out there had a smile spreading across her face as nerves danced in her belly. The thought of someone looking over her designs with a critical eye nearly crippled her, but she wouldn't be wielding toilet wands for the rest of her life.

"I really think I'll be ready in a couple of months," Catalina stated, crossing back to survey her inventory on the shelves. "Saying a timeframe out loud makes this seem so real."

Her mother laughed. "This is your dream, baby girl. You go after it and I'll support you all the way. You know I want you out from under the Rowlings' thumb."

Catalina swallowed as she zeroed in on the lace and

pulled it from the pile. "I know. Don't dwell on that, though. I'm closer to leaving every day."

"Not soon enough for me," her mother muttered.

Catalina knew her mother hated Patrick Rowling. Their affair years ago was still a secret and the only reason Catalina knew was because when she'd been dumped by Will and was sobbing like an adolescent schoolgirl, her mother had confessed. Maria Iberra was a proud woman and Catalina knew it had taken courage to disclose the affair, but Maria was dead set on her daughter truly understanding that the Rowling men were only after one thing and they were ruthless heartbreakers. Feelings didn't exist for those men, save for James, who seemed to be truly in love and determined to make Bella happy.

But Patrick was ruthless in everything and Will had followed suit. So why was he still pursuing her? She just wanted a straight answer. If he just wanted sex, she'd almost wish he'd just come out and say it. She'd take honesty over adult games any day.

Before she could respond to her mother, Catalina's doorbell rang. "Mum, I'll call you back. Someone is at my door."

She disconnected the call and pocketed her cell in her smock pocket. She'd taken to wearing a smock around her waist to keep pins, thread, tiny scissors and random sewing items easily accessible. Peeking through the peephole, Catalina only saw a vibrant display of flowers.

Flicking the deadbolt, she eased the door open slightly. "Yes?"

"Catalina Iberra?"

"That's me."

The young boy held onto the crystal vase with two hands and extended it toward her. "Delivery for you."

Opening the door fully, she took the bouquet and soon realized why this boy had two hands on it. This thing was massive and heavy.

"Hold on," she called around the obscene arrangement. "Let me give you a tip."

"Thank you, ma'am, but that was already taken care of. You have a nice day."

Catalina stepped back into her apartment, kicked the door shut with her foot and crossed the space to put the vase on her coffee table. She stood back and checked out various shades and types of flowers. Every color seemed to be represented in the beautiful arrangement. Catalina couldn't even imagine what this cost. The vase alone, made of thick, etched glass, appeared to be rather precious.

A white envelope hung from a perfectly tied ribbon around the top of the vase. She tugged on the ribbon until it fell free and then slid the small envelope off. Pulling the card out and reading it, her heart literally leapt up into her throat. *Think of me. W.*

Catalina stared at the card, and then back at the flowers. Suddenly they weren't as pretty as they'd been two minutes ago. Did he seriously think she'd fall for something as cliché as flowers? Please. And that arrogant message on the card was utterly ridiculous.

Think of him? Lately she'd done little else, but she'd certainly never tell him that. What an ego he'd grown since they were last together. And she thought it had been inflated then.

But because no one was around to see her, she bent down and buried her face in the fresh lilacs. They smelled so wonderful and in two days they would still look amazing.

A smile spread across her face as her plan took shape. Will had no idea who he was up against if he thought an expensive floral arrangement was going to get her to drop her panties or common sense.

As much as she was confused and a bit hurt by his newfound interest in her now that he wasn't involved with Bella, she had to admit, toying with him was going to be fun. Only one person could win this battle...she just prayed her strength held out and she didn't go down in the first round.

Will slid his cell back into his pocket and leaned against the window seat in his father's office at his Playa del Onda home. "We've got them."

Patrick blinked once, twice, and then a wide smile spread across his face. "I didn't think you could do it."

Will shrugged. "I didn't have a doubt."

"I've been trying to sign with the Cherringtons for over a year." Patrick shook his head and pushed off the top of his desk to come to his feet. "You're really making a mark here, Will. I wondered how things would fair after Bella, but business is definitely your area of expertise."

Will didn't tell his father that Mrs. Cherrington had tried to make a pass at Will at a charity event a few months back. Blackmail in business was sometimes not a bad thing. It seemed that Mrs. Cherrington would do anything to keep her husband from learning she'd had too much to drink and gotten a little frisky. She apparently went so far as to talk him into doing business with the Rowlings, but considering both families would prosper, Will would keep her little secret.

In Will's defense, he didn't let her advances go far. Even if she weren't old enough to be his mother and if she hadn't smelled as if she bathed in a distillery, she was married. He may not want any part of marriage for himself, but that didn't mean he was going to home in on anybody else's, either.

Before he could say anything further, Cat appeared in the doorway with an enormous bouquet. The arrangement reminded him of the gift he'd sent her. He'd wondered all weekend what she'd thought of the arrangement. Had she smiled? Had she thought about calling him?

He'd end this meeting with his father and make sure to track her down before he headed back to the Rowling Energy offices for an afternoon meeting. He had an ache that wasn't going away anytime soon and he was starting to schedule his work around opportunities to see Cat. His control and priorities were becoming skewed.

"I'm sorry to interrupt," she stated, not glancing Will's way even for a second. "I thought I'd freshen up your office."

Patrick glanced down at some papers on his desk and motioned her in without a word. Will kept his eyes on Cat, on her petite, curvy frame tucked so neatly into her black button-down shirt and hip-hugging dress pants. His hands ached to run over her, *sans* clothing.

She was sporting quite a smirk, though. She was up to something, which only put him on full alert.

"I don't always keep flowers in here, but I thought this bouquet was lovely." She set it on the accent table nestled between two leather wingback chairs against the far wall. "I received these the other day and they just did a number on my allergies. I thought about trashing them, but then realized that you may want something fresh for your office, Mr. Rowling."

Will stood straight up. She'd received those the other day? She'd brought his bouquet into his father's office and was giving it away?

Apparently his little Cat had gotten feisty.

"I didn't realize you had allergies," Will stated, drawing her attention to him.

She tucked her short black hair behind her ears and smiled. "And why should you?" she countered with a bit more sass than he was used to from her. "I'll leave you two to talk."

As she breezed out just as quickly as she'd come, Will looked at his father, who was staring right back at him with a narrowed gaze. Why did Will feel as if he'd been caught doing something wrong?

"Keep your hands off my staff," his father warned. "You already tried that once. I hesitated keeping her on, but James swore she was the best worker he'd ever had. Her mother had been a hard worker, too, so don't make me regret that decision."

No way in hell was he letting his father, or anybody else for that matter, dictate what he could and couldn't do with Cat. Listening to his father's instructions about his personal life was what got Will into this mess in the first place.

"Once we've officially signed with the Cherringtons, I'll be sure to send them a nice vintage wine with a personalized note."

Patrick came to his feet, rested his hands on his desk and leaned forward. "You're changing the subject."

"The subject of your staff or my personal life has no relevance in this meeting," Will countered. "I'll be sure to keep you updated if anything changes, but my assistant should have all the proper paperwork emailed by the end of the day."

Will started to head out the door, but turned to glance over his shoulder. "Oh, and the next time Cat talks to you, I suggest you are polite in return and at least look her in the eye."

Leaving his father with his mouth wide open, Will turned and left the office. Perhaps he shouldn't have added that last bit, but Will wasn't going to stand by and watch his father dismiss Cat like that. She was a person, too—just because she cleaned for Patrick and he signed her checks didn't mean he was more important than she. Will had no doubt that when Cat worked for James, he at least treated her with respect.

Dammit. Why was he getting so defensive? He should be pissed she'd dumped his flowers onto his father. There was a twisted irony in there somewhere, but Will was too keyed up to figure it out. What was it about her blatantly throwing his gift back in his face that had him so turned on?

Will searched the entire first and second floors, but Cat was nowhere to be found. Granted, the house was twelve thousand square feet, but there weren't that many people on staff. How could one petite woman go missing?

Will went back to the first floor and into the back of the house where the utility room was. The door was closed and when he tried to turn the knob, he found it locked. That was odd. Why lock a door to the laundry? He heard movement, so someone was in there.

He tapped his knuckles on the thick wood door and waited. Finally the click of a lock sounded and the door eased open. Cat's dark eyes met his.

"What do you want?" she asked.

"Can I come in?"

"This isn't a good time."

He didn't care if this was good or bad. He was here and she was going to talk to him. He had to get to another meeting and wasn't wasting time playing games.

Will pushed the door, causing her to step back. Squeezing in, he shut the door behind him and flicked the lock into place.

Cat had her back to him, her shoulders hunched. "What do you want, Will?"

"You didn't like the flowers?" he asked, crossing his arms over his chest and leaning against the door.

"I love flowers. I don't like your clichéd way of getting my attention or trying to buy me."

He reached out, grabbed her shoulder and spun her around. "Look at me, dammit."

In an instant he realized why she'd been turned away. She was clutching her shirt together, but the swell of her breasts and the hint of a red lacy bra had him stunned speechless.

"I was trying to carry a small shelf into the storage area and it got caught on my shirt," she explained, looking anywhere but at his face as she continued to hold her shirt. "I ran in here because I knew there was a sewing kit or maybe even another shirt."

Everything he'd wanted to say to her vanished from his mind. He couldn't form a coherent thought at this point, not when she was failing at keeping her creamy skin covered.

"I'd appreciate it if you'd stop staring," she told him, her eyes narrowing. "I don't have time for games or a pep talk or whatever else you came to confront me about. I have work to do and boobs to cover."

Her snarky joke was most likely meant to lighten the mood, but he'd wanted her for too long to let anything deter him. He took a step forward, then another, until he'd backed her up against the opposite wall. With her hands holding tight onto her shirt, her eyes wide and her cheeks flushed, there was something so wanton yet innocent about her.

"What do you like?" he asked.

Cat licked her lips. "What?" she whispered.

Will placed a hand on the wall, just beside her head, and leaned in slightly. "You don't like flowers. What do you like?"

"Actually, I love flowers. I just took you for someone who didn't fall into clichés." She offered a slight smile, overriding the fear he'd seen flash through her eyes moments ago. "But you're trying to seduce the maid, so maybe a cliché is all we are."

Will slid his other hand across her cheek and into her hair as he brought his mouth closer. "I don't care if you're the queen or the maid or the homeless person on the corner. I know what I want and I want you, Cat."

She turned her palms to his chest, pushing slightly, but not enough for him to think she really meant for him to step back…not when she was breathless and her eyes were on his mouth.

"I'm not for sale," she argued with little heat behind her words.

He rubbed his lips across hers in a featherlight touch that instantly caused her to tremble. That had to be her body, no way would he admit those tremors were from him.

"Maybe I'll just sample, then."

Fully covering her mouth, Will kept his hand fisted in her hair as he angled her head just where he wanted it. If she didn't want him at all, why did she instantly open for him?

The sweetest taste he'd ever had was Cat. No woman compared to this one. As much as he wanted to strip her naked right here, he wanted to savor this moment and simply savor her. He wanted that familiar taste only Cat could provide, he wanted to reacquaint himself with every minute sexy detail.

Delicate hands slid up his chest and gripped his shoulders, which meant she had to have released her hold on her shirt. Will removed his hand from the wall and gripped her waist as he slid his hand beneath the hem of her shirt and encountered smooth, warm skin. His thumb caressed back and forth beneath the lacy bra.

Cat arched into him with a slight moan. Her words may have told him she wasn't interested, but her body had something else in mind…something much more in tune with what he wanted.

Will shifted his body back just enough to finish unbuttoning her shirt. He parted the material with both hands and took hold of her breasts. The lace slid beneath his palm and set something off in him. His Cat may be sweet, somewhat innocent, but she loved the sexy lingerie. Good to know.

Reluctantly breaking the kiss, Will ached to explore other areas. He moved down the column of her throat and continued to the swell of her breasts. Her hands slid into his hair as if she were holding him in place. He sure as hell wasn't going anywhere.

Will had wanted this, wanted her, four years ago. He'd wanted her with a need that had only grown over the years. She'd been a virgin then; he'd known it and respected her for her decisions. He would've waited for her because she'd been so special to him.

Then his father had issued an ultimatum and Will had made the wrong choice. He didn't fight for what he wanted and he'd damn well never make that mistake again.

Now Cat was in his arms again and he'd let absolutely nothing stand in the way of his claiming her.

"Tell me you want this," he muttered against her heated skin. "Tell me."

His hands encircled her waist as he tugged her harder against his body. Will lifted his head long enough to catch the heat in her eyes, the passion.

A jiggling of the door handle broke the spell. Will stepped back as Cat blinked, glanced down and yanked her shirt together.

"Is someone in there?" a male voice called.

Cat cleared her throat. "I got something on my shirt," she called back. "Just changing. I'll be out shortly, Raul."

Will stared down at her. "Raul?" he whispered.

Cat jerked her shirt off and stalked across the room. Yanking open a floor-to-ceiling cabinet, she snagged another black shirt and slid into it. As she secured the buttons, she spun back around.

"He's a new employee, not that it's any of your business." When she was done with the last button, she crossed her arms over her chest. "What just happened here, as well as in the bathroom the other day, will not happen again. You can't come in to where I work and manhandle me. I don't care if I work for your family. That just makes this even more wrong."

Will couldn't suppress the grin. "From the moaning, I'd say you liked being manhandled."

He started to take a step forward but she held up her hand. "Don't come closer. You can't just toy with me, Will. I am not interested in a replay of four years ago. I have no idea what your agenda is, but I won't be part of it."

"Who says I have an agenda?"

Her eyes narrowed. "You're a Rowling. You all have agendas."

So she was a bit feistier than before. He always loved a challenge—it was impossible to resist.

"Are you still a virgin?"

Cat gasped, her face flushed. "How dare you. You have no right to ask."

"Considering I'm going to take you to bed, I have every right."

Cat moved around him, flicked the lock and jerked the door open. "Get the hell out. I don't care if this is your father's house. I'm working and we are finished. For good."

Will glanced out the door at a wide-eyed Raul. Before he passed, he stopped directly in front of Cat. "We're not finished. We've barely gotten started."

Crossing into the hall, Will met Raul's questioning stare. "You saw and heard nothing. Are we clear?"

Will waited until the other man silently nodded before walking away. No way in hell did he need his father knowing he'd been caught making out in the damn laundry room with the maid.

Next time, and there would be a next time, Will vowed she'd be in his bed. She was a willing participant every time he'd kissed her. Hell, if the knock hadn't interrupted them, they'd probably both be a lot happier right now.

Regardless of what Cat had just said, he knew full well she wanted him. Her body wasn't lying. What kind of man would he be if he ignored her needs? Because he sure as hell wasn't going to sit back and wait for another man to come along and explore that sexual side.

She was his.

Five

Alma was a beautiful country. Catalina was going to miss the island's beautiful water and white sandy beaches when she left. Swimming was her first love. Being one with the water, letting loose and not caring about anything was the best source of therapy.

And tonight she needed the release.

For three days she'd managed to dodge Will. He had come to Patrick's house every morning, holed himself up in the office with his father and then left, assumedly to head into the Rowling Energy offices.

Will may say he'd changed, but to her he still looked as if he was playing the perfect son, dead set on taking over the family business. Apparently he thought he could take her over as well. But she wasn't a business deal to close and she certainly wouldn't lose her mind again and let him devour her so thoroughly no matter how much she enjoyed it.

Lust was something that would only get her into trouble. The repercussions of lust would last a lifetime; a few moments of pleasure wouldn't be worth the inevitable heartache in the end.

Catalina sliced her arms through the water, cursing herself for allowing thoughts of Will to infringe on her downtime when she only wanted to relax. The man wanted to control her and she was letting him because she had no clue how to stop this emotional roller coaster he'd strapped her into.

Heading toward the shoreline, Catalina pushed herself the last few feet until she could stand. Shoving her short hair back from her face, she took deep breaths as she sloshed through the water. With the sun starting to sink behind her, she crossed the sand and scooped up her towel to mop her face.

He'd seriously crossed the line when he'd asked about her virginity. Yes, she'd gotten carried away with him, even if she did enjoy those stolen moments, but her sexual past was none of his concern because she had no intention of letting him have any more power over her. And she sure as hell didn't want to know about all of his trysts since they'd been together.

Cat wrapped the towel around her body and tucked the edge in to secure the cloth in place. This small stretch of beach wasn't far from her apartment, only a five-minute walk, and rarely had many visitors in the evening. Most people came during the day or on weekends. On occasion, Catalina would see families playing together. Her heart would always seize up a bit then. She longed for the day when she could have a family of her own, but for now, she had her sights set on fashion.

Giving up one dream for another wasn't an option. Who said she couldn't have it all? She could have her ideal career and then her family. She was still young. At twenty-four some women were already married and had children, but she wasn't like most women.

And if Will Rowling thought he could deter her from going after what she wanted, he was delusional. And sexy. Mercy, was the man ever sexy.

No, no, no.

Will and his sexiness had no room in her life, especially her bed, which he'd work his way into if she wasn't on guard constantly.

Catalina pulled out her tank-style sundress and exchanged the towel for the modest coverup. After shoving the towel into her bag, she slid into her sandals and started her walk home. The soft ocean breeze always made her smile. Wherever she moved, she was going to need to be close to water or at least close enough that she could make weekend trips.

This was the only form of exercise she enjoyed, and being so short, every pound really showed. Not that she worried about her weight, but she wanted to feel good about herself and she felt her best when she'd been swimming and her muscles were burning from the strain. She wanted to be able to throw on anything in her closet and have confidence. For her, confidence came with a healthy body.

Catalina crossed the street to her apartment building and smiled at a little girl clutching her mother's hand. Once she reached the stoop leading up to her flat, she dug into her bag for her keys. A movement from the corner of her eye caught her attention. She knew who was there before she fully turned, though.

"What are you doing here, Will?"

She didn't look over her shoulder, but she knew he

followed her. Arguing that he wasn't invited was a moot point; the man did whatever he wanted anyway.

"I came to see you."

When she got to the second floor, she stopped outside her door and slid her key into the lock. "I figured you'd given up."

His rich laughter washed over her chilled skin. Between the warm water and the breezy air, she was going to have to get some clothes on to get warm.

"When have you known me to give up?" he asked.

Throwing a glance over her shoulder, she raised a brow. "Four years ago. You chose your career over a relationship. Seeing me was the big mistake. Ring any bells?"

Will's bright aqua-blue eyes narrowed. "I didn't give up. I'm here now, aren't I?"

"Oh, so I was just put on hold until you were ready," she mocked. "How silly of me not to realize."

"Can I come in?" he asked. "I promise I'll only be a couple minutes."

"You can do a lot of damage in a couple minutes," she muttered, but figured the sooner she let him in, the sooner he'd leave…she hoped.

Catalina pushed the door open and started toward her bedroom. Thankfully the door to the spare room was closed. The last thing she needed was for Will to see everything she'd been working on. Her personal life was none of his concern.

"I'm changing and you're staying out here."

She slammed her bedroom door, hoping he'd get the hint he wasn't welcome. What was he doing here? Did he think she'd love how he came to her turf? Did he think she'd be more comfortable and melt into a puddle at his feet, and then invite him into her bed?

Oh, that man was infuriating. Catalina jerked off

her wet clothes and draped them over her shower rod in her bathroom. Quickly she threw on a bra, panties and another sundress, one of her own designs she liked to wear out. It was simple, but it was hers, and her confidence was always lifted when she wore her own pieces.

Her damp hair wasn't an issue right now. All she wanted to know was why he was here. If he only came for another make-out scene that was going to leave her frustrated and angry, she wanted no part of it. She smoothed back a headband to keep her hair from her face. It was so short it would be air-dried in less than an hour.

Padding barefoot back into her living room, she found Will standing near the door where she'd left him. He held a small package in his hands that she hadn't noticed before. Granted she'd had her back to him most of the time because she didn't want to face him.

"Come bearing gifts?" she asked. "Didn't you learn your lesson after the flowers?"

Will's smile spread across his face. "Thought I'd try a different tactic."

On a sigh, Catalina crossed the room and sank into her favorite cushy chair. "Why try at all? Honestly. Is this just a game to see if you can get the one who got away? Are you trying to prove to yourself that you can conquer me? Is it a slumming thing? What is it, Will? I'm trying to understand this."

He set the box on the coffee table next to a stack of the latest fashion magazines. After taking a seat on her couch, Will rested his elbows on his knees and leaned forward.

Silence enveloped them and the longer he sat there, the more Catalina wondered what was going through his mind. Was he planning on lying? Was he trying to figure out how to tell her the truth? Or perhaps he was second-guessing himself.

She studied him—his strong jawline, his broad frame taking up so much space in her tiny apartment. She'd never brought a man here. Not that she'd purposely brought Will here, but having such a powerful man in her living room was a new experience for her.

Maybe she was out of her league. Maybe she couldn't fight a force like Will Rowling. But she was sure as hell going to try because she couldn't stand to have her heart crushed so easily again.

Catalina curled her feet beside her in the spacious chair as Will met her gaze. Those piercing aqua eyes forced her to go still.

"What if I'm here because I've never gotten over you?"

Dammit. Why did he let that out? He wasn't here to make some grand declaration. He was here to soften her, to get her to let down that guard a little more because he was not giving up. He'd jump through whatever hoop she threw in front of him, but Cat would be his for a while. A steamy affair that no one knew about was exactly what they needed whether she wanted to admit it or not.

When he'd been given the ultimatum by his father to give up Cat or lose his place in Rowling Energy, Will hadn't had much choice. Oh, and his father had also stated that he'd make sure Catalina Iberra would never work anywhere in Alma again if Will didn't let her go.

He'd had to protect her, even though she hated him at the time. He'd do it all over again. But he didn't want to tell her what had happened. He didn't want her to feel guilty or to pity him. Will would win her back just as he'd won her the first time. He'd be charming and wouldn't take no for an answer.

His quiet, almost vulnerable question still hung heavy in the space between them as he waited for her response. She hadn't kicked him out of her flat, so he was making progress. Granted, he'd been making progress since that spur-of-the-moment kiss a month ago, but he'd rather speed things along. A man only had so much control over his emotions.

"You can have any woman you want." Catalina toyed with the edge of the hem on her dress, not making eye contact. "You let me go, you called me a mistake."

He'd regret those words until he died. To know he'd made Cat feel less than valuable to him was not what he'd wanted to leave her with, but once the damning words were out, he couldn't take them back. Anything he said after that point would have been moot. The damage had been done and he'd moved on…or tried to. He'd said hurtful things to get her to back away from him; he'd needed her to stay away at the time because he couldn't afford to let her in, not when his father had such a heavy hand.

Will had been devastated when she'd started dating another man. What had he expected? Did he think a beautiful, vibrant woman was just going to sit at home and sulk about being single? Obviously she had taken the breakup better than he had. And how sick was that, that he wished she'd been more upset? He wanted her to be happy…he just wanted it to be with him.

"I can't have any woman," he countered. "You're still avoiding me."

She lifted her dark eyes, framed by even darker lashes, and focused on him. Every time she looked at him, Will felt that punch to the gut. Lust. It had to be lust because he wouldn't even contemplate anything else. They'd been apart too long for any other emotion to have settled in. They were two different people now and he just wanted to get to know her all over again, to prove himself to her. She deserved everything he had to give.

Will came to his feet. He couldn't stay here because the longer he was around her, the more he wanted her. Cat was going to be a tough opponent and he knew all too well that the best things came from patience and outlasting your opponent. Hadn't it taken him four years to best his father? And he was still in the process of doing that.

"Where are you going?" she asked, looking up at him.

"You want me to stay?" He stepped forward, easing closer to the chair she sat in. "Because if I stay, I'm going to want more than just talking."

"Did you just come to see where I lived? Did you need this reminder of how opposite we are? How I'm just—"

Will put his hand over her mouth. Leaning down, he gripped the arm of her chair and rested his weight there. He eased in closer until he could see the black rim around her dark eyes.

"We've been over this. I don't care what you are. I know what I want, what I need, and that's you."

Her eyes remained locked on his. Slowly he drew his hand away and trailed his fingertips along the thin tan line coming down from behind her neck.

"You're getting red here," he murmured, watching her shiver beneath his touch. "I haven't seen you out of work clothes in years. You need to take better care of your skin."

Cat reached up, grabbed his hand and halted his movements. "Don't do this, Will. There's nothing for you here and I have nothing to give. Even if I gave you my body, I'd regret it because you wouldn't give me any more and I deserve so much. I see that now and I won't lose sight of my goals just because we have amazing chemistry."

Her pleading tone had him easing back. She wanted him. He'd broken her down enough for her to fully admit it.

What goals was she referring to? He wanted to know what her plans were because he wouldn't let this go. He'd waited too long for this second chance and to finally have her, to finally show his father he was in control now, was his ultimate goal.

"I'm not about to give up, Cat." Will stood straight up and kept his eyes on hers. "You have your goals, I have mine."

As he turned and started walking toward the door, he glanced back and nodded toward the package on the table. "You didn't like flowers. This may be more practical for you."

Before she could say a word, he let himself out. Leaving her flat was one of the hardest things he'd done. He knew if he'd hung around a bit longer she would give in to his advances, but he wanted her to come to him. He wanted her to be aching for him, not reluctant.

Cat would come around. They had too much of a history and a physical connection now for her to ignore her body. He had plenty to keep him occupied until she decided to come to him.

Starting with dropping another bomb on his father where their investments and loyalties lay.

Six

Damn that man.

Catalina resisted the urge to march into the Rowling Energy offices and throw Will's gift back in his face.

But she'd used the thing all weekend. Now she was back at the Playa del Onda estate cleaning for his father. Same old thing, different day.

Still, the fact that Will had brought her a sewing kit, a really nice, really expensive sewing kit, had her smiling. She didn't want to smile at his gestures. She wanted to be grouchy and hate them. The flowers had been easy to cast aside, but something as personal as the sewing kit was much harder to ignore.

Will had no idea about her love of sewing, he'd merely gotten the present because of the shirt she'd ripped the other day. Even though he had no clue of her true passion, he thought outside the proverbial box and took the time to find something to catch her attention... as if he hadn't been on her radar already.

Catalina shoved a curtain rod through the grommets and slid it back into place on the hook. She'd long put off laundering the curtains in the glass-enclosed patio room. She'd been too distracted since that initial kiss nearly a month ago.

Why, after four years, why did Will have to reawaken those feelings? Why did he have to be so bold, so powerful, making her face those desires that had never fully disappeared?

The cell in her pocket vibrated. Pulling the phone out, she glanced down to see Patrick's name on the screen. She wasn't afraid of her boss, but she never liked getting a call from him. Either she'd done something wrong or he was about to unload a project on her. He'd been so much more demanding than James had. Granted James had traveled all over the world for football and had rarely been home, but even when he was, he treated Catalina with respect.

Patrick acted as if the dirt on his shoe had a higher position in the social order than she did.

But she needed every dime she could save so that she could leave once she'd finished all her designs. She made a good income for a maid, but she had no idea how much she'd need to start over in a new country and get by until she got her big break.

"Hello?" she answered.

"Come to my office."

She stared at the phone as he hung up. So demanding, so controlling…much like his son.

Catalina made her way through the house and down the wide hall toward Patrick's office. Was Will here today? She didn't want to pry or ask, but she had a feeling Patrick was handing over the reins to the twin he'd groomed for the position.

The office door stood slightly ajar, so Catalina tapped her knuckles against the thick wood before entering.

"Sir," she said, coming to stand in front of Patrick's wide mahogany desk.

The floral arrangement she'd brought a few days ago still sat on the edge. Catalina had to suppress her grin at the fact that the gift a billionaire purchased for a maid now sat on said billionaire's father's desk.

When Patrick glanced up at her, she swallowed. Why did he always make her feel as if she was in the principal's office? She'd done nothing wrong and had no reason to worry.

Oh, wait. She'd made out with his son in the laundry room and there had been a witness outside the door. There was that minor hiccup in her performance.

"I'm going to have the Montoro family over for a dinner," Patrick stated without preamble. "With the passing of Isabella, it's fitting we extend our condolences and reach out to them during this difficult time."

Catalina nodded. "Of course. Tell me what we need."

"The funeral will be Wednesday and I know they will have their own gathering. I'd like to have the dinner Friday night."

Catalina pulled out her cell and started typing in the notes as he rattled off the details. Only the Montoros and the Rowlings would be in attendance. Patrick expected her to work that day preparing the house and that evening cleaning up after the party... Long days like that were a killer for her back and feet. But the double time pay more than made up for the aches and pains.

"Is that all?" she asked when he stopped talking.

He nodded. "There is one more thing."

Catalina swallowed, slid her phone into her pocket and clasped her hands in front of her body. "Yes, sir?"

"If you have a notion of vying for my son's attention, it's best you stop." Patrick eased back in his chair as if he had all the power and not a worry in the world. "He may not be marrying Bella as I'd hoped, but that doesn't mean he's on the market for you. Will is a billionaire. He's handling multimillion dollar deals on a daily basis and the last thing he has time for is to get tangled up in the charms of my maid."

The threat hung between them. Patrick wasn't stupid; he knew exactly what was going on with his own son. Catalina wasn't going to be a pawn in their little family feud. She had a job to do. She'd do it and be on her way in just a few months. Patrick and Will would still be bringing in money and she'd be long forgotten.

"I have no claim on your son, Mr. Rowling," she stated, thankful her voice was calm and not shaky. "I apologize if you think I do. We dated years ago but that's over."

Patrick nodded. "Let's make sure it stays that way. You have a place here and it's not in Will's life."

Even though he spoke the truth, a piece of her heart cracked a bit more over the fact.

"I'll get to work on these arrangements right away," she told Patrick, purposely dropping the topic of his son.

Catalina escaped the office, making it out to the hall before she leaned back against the wall and closed her eyes. Deep breaths in and out. She forced herself to remain calm.

If Patrick had known what happened in the laundry room days ago, he would've outright said so. He wasn't a man known for mincing words. But he knew something was up, which was all the more reason for her to stay clear of Will and his potent touch, his hypnotizing kisses and his spellbinding aqua eyes.

Pushing off the wall, Catalina made her way to the kitchen to speak to the head chef. They had a dinner to discuss and Catalina needed to focus on work, not the man who had the ability to destroy her heart for a second time.

He'd watched her bustle around for the past hour. She moved like a woman on a mission and she hadn't given him one passing glance.

Will wouldn't tolerate being ignored, especially by a woman he was so wrapped up in.

Slipping from the open living area where Cat was rearranging seating and helping the florist with new arrangements, Will snuck into the hallway and pulled his phone from his pocket. Shooting off a quick text, he stood in a doorway to the library and waited for a reply.

And waited. And waited.

Finally after nearly ten minutes, his phone vibrated in his hand. Cat hadn't dismissed him completely, but she wasn't accepting his offer of a private talk. What the hell? She was just outright saying no?

Unacceptable.

He sent another message.

Meet me once the guests arrive. You'll have a few minutes to spare once you're done setting up.

Will read over his message and quickly typed another. I'll be in the library.

Since he hadn't seen his father yet, Will shot his dad a message stating he may be a few minutes late. There was no way he could let another opportunity pass him by to be alone with Cat.

He'd worked like a madman these past few days and

hadn't even had a chance to stop by for a brief glimpse of her. He knew his desires ran deep, but he hadn't realized how deep until he had to go this long without seeing her, touching her, kissing her.

In the past two days Will had severed longstanding ties with another company that wasn't producing the results he wanted. Again he'd faced the wrath of his father, but yet again, Will didn't care. This was his time to reign over Rowling Energy and he was doing so by pushing forward, hard and fast. He wasn't tied to these companies the way his father was and Will intended to see the real estate division double its revenues in the next year.

But right now, he didn't want to think about finances, investments, real estate or oil. He wanted to focus on how fast he could get Cat in his arms once she entered the room. His body responded to the thought.

She wasn't even in the same room and he was aching for her.

Will had plans for the weekend, plans that involved her. He wanted to take her away somewhere she wouldn't expect, somewhere they could be alone and stop tiptoeing around the chemistry. Stolen kisses here and there were getting old. He felt like a horny teenager sneaking around his father's house copping a feel of his girl.

Will took a seat on the leather sofa near the floor-to-ceiling windows. He kept the lights off, save for a small lamp on the table near the entryway. That soft glow was enough; he didn't want to alert anyone who might be wandering outside that there was a rendez-vous going on in here.

Finally after he felt as if he'd waited for an hour,

the door clicked softly and Cat appeared. She shut the door at her back, but didn't step farther into the room.

"I don't have much time," she told him.

He didn't need much...yet. Right now all he needed was one touch, just something to last until he could execute his weekend plans.

Will stood and crossed the spacious room, keeping his eyes locked on hers the entire time. With her back to the door, he placed a hand on either side of her face and leaned in.

His lips grazed over hers softly. "I've missed kissing you."

Cat's body trembled. When her hands came up to his chest, he thought she'd take the initiative and kiss him, but she pushed him away.

"I know I've given mixed signals," she whispered. "But this has to end. No matter how much I enjoy kissing you, no matter how I want you, I don't have the energy for this and I can't lose my j—"

Cat put a hand over her mouth, shook her head and glanced away.

"Your job?" he asked, taking hold of her wrist and prying her hand from her lips. "You think you're going to lose your job over what we have going?"

Her deep eyes jerked back to his. "We have nothing going, Will. Don't you get that? You can afford to mess around. You have nothing at stake here."

He had more than she realized.

"I need to get back to the guests. Bella and James just arrived."

He gripped her elbow before she could turn from him. "Stop. Give me two minutes."

Tucking her hair behind her ears, she nodded. "No more."

Will slid his thumb beneath her eyes. "You're exhausted. I don't like you working so hard, Cat."

"Some of us don't have a choice."

If she were his woman, she'd never work a day in her life.

Wait. What was he saying? She wasn't his woman and he wasn't looking to make her his lifelong partner, either. Marriage or any type of committed relationship was sure as hell not something he was ready to get into. Yes, he wanted her and wanted to spend time with her, but anything beyond that wasn't on his radar just yet.

Gliding his hands over her shoulders, he started to massage the tense muscles. His thumbs grazed the sides of her neck. Cat let out a soft moan as she let her head fall back against the door.

"What are you doing to me?" she groaned.

"Giving you the break you've needed."

Will couldn't tear his gaze from her parted lips, couldn't stop himself from fantasizing how she would look when he made love to her...when, not if.

"I really need to get back." Cat lifted her head and her lids fluttered open. "But this feels so good."

Will kept massaging. "I want to make you feel better," he muttered against her lips. "Let me take you home tonight, Cat."

On a sigh, she shook her head and reached up to squeeze his hands, halting his movements. "You have to know your father thinks something is going on with us."

Will stilled. "Did he say something to you?"

Her eyes darted away. "It doesn't matter. What matters is I'm a maid. You're a billionaire ready to take on the world. We have different goals, Will."

Yeah, and the object of his main goal was plastered against his body.

Will gripped her face between his palms and forced her to look straight at him. "What did he say?"

"I'm just fully aware of my role in this family and it's not as your mistress."

Fury bubbled through Will. "Patrick Rowling does not dictate my sex life and he sure as hell doesn't have a clue what's going on with us."

The sheen in her eyes only made Will that much angrier. How dare his father say anything? He'd done that years ago when Will had let him steamroll over his happiness before. Not again.

"There's nothing going on between us," she whispered.

Will lightened his touch, stroked her bottom lip with the pads of his thumbs. "Not yet, but there will be."

Capturing her lips beneath his, Will relaxed when Cat sighed into his mouth. Will pulled back because if he kept kissing her, he was going to want more and he'd be damned if he had Cat for the first time in his father's library.

When he took Cat to bed, it would be nowhere near Patrick Rowling or his house.

"Get back to work," he muttered against her lips. "We'll talk later."

"Will—"

"Later," he promised with another kiss. "I'm not done with you, Cat. I told you once, I've barely started."

He released her and let her leave while he stayed behind.

If he walked out now, people would know he'd been hiding with Cat. The last thing he ever intended was to get her in trouble or risk her job. He knew she took pride in what she did and the fact she was a perfectionist only made Will respect her more. She was so much more, though. She was loyal and determined. Qualities he admired.

Well, he was just as determined and his father would never interfere with his personal life again. They'd gone that round once before and Patrick had won. This time, Will intended to come out, not only on top, but with Rowling Energy and Cat both belonging to him.

Seven

Will stared over the rim of his tumbler as he sipped his scotch. The way Cat worked the room was something he'd seen in the past, but he hadn't fully appreciated the charm she portrayed toward others during such a difficult time.

There were moments where she'd been stealthy as she slipped in and out of the room, removing empty glasses and keeping the hors d'oeuvre trays filled. Will was positive others hadn't even noticed her, but he did. He noticed every single thing about her.

The dinner was due to be served in thirty minutes and the guests had mostly arrived. Bella stood off to the side with her brother Gabriel, his arm wrapped around her shoulders.

"Your maid is going to get a complex if you keep drilling holes into her."

Will stiffened at James's words. His brother came to stand beside him, holding his own tumbler of scotch.

"I'm not drilling holes," Will replied, tossing back the last of his drink. He welcomed the burn and turned to set the glass on the accent table. "I'm making sure she's okay."

James's brief laugh had Will gritting his teeth to remain quiet and to prevent himself from spewing more defensive reasons as to why he'd been staring at Cat.

"She's used to working, Will. I'd say she's just fine."

Will turned to face his twin. "Did you come over here to hassle me or did you actually want to say something important?"

James's smile spread across his face. Will knew that smile, dammit. He'd thrown it James's way when he'd been in knots over Bella.

"Shut up," Will said as he turned back to watch Cat.

If his brother already had that knowing grin, then Will's watching Cat wouldn't matter at this point. She was working too damn hard. She'd been here all day to make sure the house was perfect for the Montoros and she was still busting her butt to make everyone happy. The chef was really busting it, too, behind the scenes. Cat was definitely due for a much needed relaxing day away from all of this.

"You appear to be plotting," James commented. "But right now I want to discuss what Dad is in such a mood about."

Will threw his brother a glance. "He's Patrick Rowling. Does he need a reason?"

"Not necessarily, but he was a bit gruffer than usual when I spoke with him earlier."

Will watched his father across the room as the man approached Bella and Gabriel. As they all spoke, Will knew his father was diplomatic enough to put on a front of being compassionate. He wouldn't be his stiff, grouchy self with those two.

"I may have made some business decisions he wasn't happy with," Will stated simply.

"Business? Yeah, that will do it." James sighed and finished his scotch. "He put you in charge, so he can't expect you to run every decision by him."

"That's what I told him. I'm not one of his employees, I'm his son and I'm the CEO of Rowling Energy now."

"Plus you're trying to seduce his maid," James added with a chuckle. "You're going to get grounded."

Will couldn't help but smile. "You're such an ass."

"It's fun to see the tables turned and you squirming over a woman for once."

"I'm not squirming, dammit," Will muttered.

But he wouldn't deny he was using Cat as another jab at his father. Yes, he wanted Cat and always had, but if being with her still irritated the old man, so much the better.

Part of him felt guilty for the lack of respect for his father, but that went both ways and the moment Patrick had issued his ultimatum years ago, Will had vowed then and there to gain back everything he deserved, no matter what the cost to his relationship with his father.

Bella's oldest brother, Rafe, and his very pregnant wife, Emily, crossed the room, heading for Will and James. Since he'd abdicated, Rafe and Emily had lived in Key West. But they'd traveled back to be with the family during this difficult time.

"This was a really nice thing for Patrick to do," Rafe stated as he wrapped an arm around his wife's waist. "Losing Isabella has been hard."

"I'm sorry for your loss," Will said. "She was definitely a fighter and Alma is a better place because of her."

"She was quite stubborn," Emily chimed in with a smile. "But we'll get through this because the Montoros are strong."

Will didn't think this was the appropriate time to bring up the subject of Rafe resigning from his duties before his coronation. It was the proverbial elephant in the room.

"I'm going to save my wife from my father," James told them. "Excuse me."

Rafe and Emily were talking about the funeral—how many people had turned out and how supportive the country was in respecting their time of mourning. But Will was only half listening. Cat glanced his way once and that's all it took for his heart to kick up and his body to respond. She didn't smile, she merely locked those dark eyes on him as if she knew his every thought.

Tension crackled between them and everyone else in the room disappeared from his world. Nobody existed but Cat and he knew without a doubt she would agree to his proposal.

He wouldn't accept no for an answer.

Her feet were absolutely screaming. Her back wasn't faring much better. The Montoros lingered longer than she'd expected and Catalina had stuck around an hour after the guests had left.

This fourteen-hour workday would certainly yield a nice chunk of change, but right now all Catalina could think of was her bed, which she hoped to fall into the moment she got home. She may not even take the time to peel out of her clothes.

Catalina nearly wept as she walked toward her car.

She'd parked in the back of the estate near the detached garage where Patrick kept his sporty cars that he only brought out on special occasions. The motion light popped on as she approached her vehicle.

Instantly she spotted Will sitting on a decorative bench along the garage wall. Catalina stopped and couldn't help but smile.

"Are you hiding?" she asked as she started forward again.

"Waiting." He unfolded that tall, broad frame and started coming toward her. "I know you're exhausted, but I just wanted to ask something."

Catalina crossed her arms and stared up at him. "You could've called or texted me your question."

"I could've," he agreed with a slight nod. "But you could say no too easily. I figure if you're looking me in the eye—"

"You think I can't resist you?" she laughed.

Exhaustion might have been consuming her and clouding her judgment, but there was still something so irresistible and charming about this overbearing man...and something calculating as well. He'd purposely waited for her, to catch her at a weak moment. He must really want something major.

"I'm hoping." He reached out, tucking her hair behind her ears before his fingertips trailed down her jawline. "I want to take you somewhere tomorrow afternoon. Just us, on my yacht for a day out."

Catalina wanted to give in to him, she wanted to forget all the reasons they shouldn't be together in any way. She wished her head and her heart would get on the same page where Will Rowling was concerned. She had goals, she had a job she needed to keep in order to reach those goals...yet everything about Will made her want to entertain the idea of letting him in, even if just for one night.

"I even have the perfect spot chosen for a swim," he added, resting his hands on her shoulders. Squeezing her tense muscles, Will smiled. "I'll be a total gentleman."

"A total gentleman?" Catalina couldn't help but laugh. "Then why are you so eager to go?"

"Maybe I think it's time someone gives back to you." His hands stilled as he held her gaze and she realized he wasn't joking at all. "And maybe it's time you see that I'm a changed man."

Her heart tumbled in her chest. "I'm so tired, Will. I'm pretty sure I'm going to spend the next two days sleeping."

"You won't have to do a thing," he promised. "I'll bring the food. All you have to do is wear a swimsuit. I promise this will be a day of total relaxation and pampering."

Catalina sighed. "Will, your father—"

"He's not invited."

She laughed again. "I'm serious."

"I am, too."

Will backed her up to her car and towered over her with such an intense gaze, Catalina knew she was fighting a losing battle.

"This has nothing to do with my father, your job or our differences." His strong jaw set firm, he pressed his gloriously hard body against hers as he stared into her eyes. "I want to spend time with you, Cat. I've finally got my sights set on what is important to me and I'm not letting you get away again. Not without a fight."

"That's what scares me." She whispered the confession.

"There's nothing to be afraid of."

"Said the big bad wolf."

Will smiled, dropped his hands and eased back. "No pressure, Cat. I want to spend time with you, but if you're not ready, I understand. I'm not going anywhere."

The man knew exactly what to say and his delivery was flawless. In his line of work, Will was a master at getting people to see things his way, to ensure he got what he wanted at the end of the day.

No matter what common sense tried to tell her, Catalina wasn't about to start in on a battle she had no chance of winning.

"I'll go," she told him.

The smile that spread across his face was half shadowed by the slant of the motion lights, but she knew all too well how beautiful and sexy the gesture was.

"I'll pick you up at your apartment around noon," he told her. "Now, go home. I'm going to follow you to make sure you get there safely since you're so tired."

"That's not necessary."

Will shrugged. "Maybe not, but I wasn't kidding when I said someone needed to take care of you and pamper you for a change. I'm not coming in. I'll just follow, and then be on my way home."

"I live in the opposite direction from your house," she argued.

"We could've been halfway to your flat by now." He slid his arm around her and tugged on her door handle. "Get in, stop fighting me and let's just save time. You know I'll win in the end anyway."

That's precisely what she feared the most. Will having a win over her could prove more damaging than the last time she'd let him in, but she wanted to see this new side of him. She wanted to take a day and do absolutely nothing but be catered to.

Catalina eased behind the wheel and let Will shut her door. Tomorrow would tell her one of two things: either she was ready to move on and just be his friend or she wanted more with him than stolen kisses behind closed doors.

Worry and panic flooded Catalina as she realized she already knew what tomorrow would bring.

Will had been meaning to see his niece, Maisey, and this morning he was making her his top priority. Before he went to pick up Cat for their outing, he wanted to surprise his adorable niece with a gift…the first of many. He had a feeling this little girl was going to be spoiled, which was better than a child being ignored.

Maisey Rowling would want for nothing. Will's brother had given up being a playboy and was growing into his family-man role rather nicely, and Bella was the perfect stepmother to the infant. Will figured since he and his twin were growing closer, he'd stop in and offer support to James. This complete one-eighty in lifestyles had to be a rough transition for James, but he had Bella and the two were completely in love. And they both loved sweet Maisey.

A slight twinge of jealousy speared through Will, but not over the fact that his brother had married Bella. There had been no chemistry between Will and Bella. She was sweet and stunning, but Will only had eyes for one woman.

The jealousy stemmed from the thought of his brother settling down with his own family. Will hadn't given much thought to family before. He'd been raised to focus solely on taking over Rowling Energy one day.

Will tapped on the etched glass front door to James and Bella's temporary home. They were living here until they knew for sure where they wanted to be permanently. They were in the middle of renovating the old farmhouse that belonged to the Montoros and James had mentioned that they'd probably end up there.

But for now, this house was ideal. It was near the beach, near the park and near Bella's family. Family was important to the Montoros…and yet Will was still thrilled he'd dodged that clan.

The door swung open and Bella greeted him with a smile. "Will, this is a surprise. Come on in."

Clutching the doll he'd brought as a present, Will stepped over the threshold. "I should've called, but I really thought of this last-minute."

Bella smoothed her blond hair behind her shoulders. "This is fine. Maisey and James are in the living room. They just finished breakfast and they're watching a movie."

Her blue eyes darted down to his hands. "I'm assuming that's for Maisey?"

Will nodded. "I haven't played the good uncle yet. Figured it was time I started spoiling her."

Bella's smile lit up her face. "She's going to love it."

The thought of being married to this woman did nothing for Will. Yes, she was stunning, but he'd never felt the stirrings of lust or need when he'd been around her. Their fathers never should have attempted to arrange their engagement, but thankfully everything had worked out for the best…at least where Bella and James were concerned. They were a unified family now.

The thought of his black sheep, playboy brother snuggling up with a baby girl and watching some kid flick was nearly laughable. But Will also knew that once James had learned he had a child, his entire life had changed and his priorities had taken on a whole new order, Maisey being at the top.

Bella led Will through a wide, open-arched doorway to a spacious living room. Two pale yellow sofas sat facing each other with a squat, oversized table between them. An array of coloring books and crayons were scattered over the top of the glossy surface.

James sat on one of the sofas, legs sprawled out before him with Maisey on his lap. James's short hair was all in disarray. He still wore his pajama bottoms and no shirt, and Maisey had a little pink nightgown on; it was obvious they were enjoying a morning of laziness.

As Will stepped farther into the room, James glanced over and smiled. "Hey, brother. What brings you out?"

Bella sat at the end of the couch at her husband's feet. Maisey crawled over her father's legs and settled herself onto Bella's lap. Will looked at his niece and found himself staring into those signature Rowling aqua eyes. No denying who this baby's father was.

"I brought something for Maisey." Will crossed the room and sat on the edge of the coffee table. "Hey, sweetheart. Do you like dolls?"

What if she didn't like it? What if she didn't like him? Dammit. He should've planned better and called to see what Maisey actually played with. He'd just assumed a little girl would like a tiny stuffed doll.

"Her dress matches your nightgown," Bella said softly to the little girl.

Maisey kept her eyes on him as she reached for the toy. Instantly the blond hair went into Maisey's mouth.

"She likes it." James laughed. "Everything goes into her mouth these days."

Will continued to stare at his niece. Children were

one area where he had no clue, but if James said Maisey liked it, then Will had to assume she did.

James swung his legs to the floor and leaned forward. "You hungry?" he asked. "We still have some pancakes and bacon in the kitchen."

"No, I'm good. I'm getting ready to pick up Cat, so I can't stay anyway."

James's brows lifted as he shot Bella a look. "Is this a date?"

Will hadn't intended on telling anyone, but in growing closer with James over the past couple months, he realized he wanted this bond with his twin. Besides, after their conversation last night, James pretty much knew exactly where Will stood in regards to Cat.

He trusted James, that had never been an issue. The issue they'd had wedged between them stemmed from their father always doting on one brother, molding him into a disciple, while ostracizing the other one.

"I'm taking her out on my yacht," Will told him. "We're headed to one of the islands for the day. I'm hoping for total seclusion. Most tourists don't know about them."

There was a small cluster of islands off the coast of Alma. He planned on taking her to Isla de Descanso. The island's name literally meant Island of Relaxation. Cat deserved to be properly pampered and he was going to be the man to give her all of her needs…every single one.

"Sounds romantic." Bella shifted Maisey on her lap as she stared at Will. "I wasn't aware you and Catalina were getting more serious."

James laughed. "I think they've been sneaking."

"We're not serious and we're not sneaking," Will

defended himself. "Okay, fine. We were sneaking, but she's private and she's still leery of me."

"You can't blame her," James added.

Will nodded. "I don't, which is why we need this time away from everything. Plus she's working like crazy for Dad and she's never appreciated."

James snorted. "He barely appreciates his sons. You think he appreciates a maid? I was worried when he moved into my old house. I tried to warn her, but she said she could handle it and she needed the job."

Will hated the thought of her having to work. Hated how much she pushed herself for little to no praise and recognition.

"Well, I appreciate her," Bella chimed in. "I saw how hard she worked the dinner last night. I can't imagine the prep that she and the cooks went through, plus the cleanup after. Catalina is a dedicated, hard worker."

"She won't stay forever," James stated as he leaned over and ruffled Maisey's hair.

Will sat up straighter. "What do you mean?"

His brother's eyes came back to meet his. "I'm just saying someone who is such a perfectionist and self-disciplined surely has a long-term goal in mind. I can't imagine she'll want to play maid until she's old and gray. She hinted a few times when she worked for me that she hoped to one day leave Alma."

Leave Alma? The thought hadn't even crossed Will's mind. Would Cat really go somewhere else? Surely not. Her mother still worked here. She used to work for Patrick, but years ago she had suddenly quit and gone to work for another prominent family. Cat had been with the Rowlings for five years, but James was right. Someone as vibrant as Cat wouldn't want to dust and wash

sheets her entire life. He'd already seen the toll her endless hours were taking on her.

Will came to his feet, suddenly more eager than ever
to see her, to be alone with her. "I better get going. I just
wanted to stop by and see Maisey before I headed out."

James stood as well. "I'll walk you to the door."

Bidding a goodbye to Bella and Maisey, Will followed his brother to the foyer.

"Don't say a word about Cat and me," Will said.

Gripping the doorknob, James nodded. "I'm not saying a word. I already know Dad would hate the idea and
he's interfered enough in our personal lives lately. And
I'm not judging you and Catalina. I actually think you
two are a good match."

"Thanks, man, but don't let this happily-ever-
after stuff you have going on filter into my world. I'm
just spending time with Cat. That's all." Will gave his
brother a one-armed man hug. "I'll talk to you next
week."

Will headed toward his car, more than ready to pick
up Cat and get this afternoon started. He planned to
be in complete control, but he'd let her set the tone. As
much as he wanted her, he wasn't going to pressure her
and he wasn't going to deceive her.

Yes, there was the obvious appeal of the fact that
his father would hate Will bedding the maid, but he
wouldn't risk her job that way even to get petty revenge
on his domineering father.

Besides, Cat was so much more than a romp. He
couldn't figure out exactly what she was…and that irritated him.

But now he had another worry. What was Cat's ultimate goal in life? Would she leave Alma and pursue
something more meaningful? And why did he care? He

wasn't looking for a ring on his finger and he wasn't about to place one on hers, either.

Still, the fact that she could leave bothered him more than he cared to admit.

Will pushed those thoughts aside. Right now, for today, all he was concerned with was Cat and being alone with her. All other world problems would have to wait.

Eight

Nerves kicked around in Catalina's belly as she boarded the yacht. Which seemed like such a simple word for this pristine, massive floating vessel. The fact that the Rowlings had money was an understatement, but to think that Will could own something this amazing…it boggled her mind. She knew he would make a name for himself, knew he'd climb to the top of Rowling Energy. There was never any doubt which twin Patrick was grooming for the position.

But she wasn't focusing on or even thinking of Patrick today. Will wanted her to relax, wanted her to enjoy her day off, and she was going to take full advantage.

Turning toward Will, Catalina laughed as he stepped on board. "I'm pretty sure my entire flat would fit on this deck."

Near the bow, she surveyed the wide, curved outdoor seating complete with plush white pillows. There was even a hot tub off to the side. Catalina couldn't even imagine soaking in that warm water out under the stars. This yacht screamed money, relaxation...and seduction.

She'd voluntarily walked right into the lion's den.

"Let me show you around." Will took hold of her elbow and led her to the set of steps that went below deck. "The living quarters are even more impressive."

Catalina clutched her bag and stepped down as Will gestured for her to go first. The amount of space in the open floor plan below was shocking. It was even grander than she'd envisioned. A large king-sized bed sat in the distance and faced a wall of curved windows that overlooked the sparkling water. Waking up to a sunrise every morning would be heavenly. Waking up with your lover beside you would simply be the proverbial icing on the cake.

No. She couldn't think of Will as her lover or icing on her cake. She was here for a restful day and nothing else. Nookie could not play a part in this because she had no doubt the second he got her out of her clothes, she'd have no defense against him. She needed to stay on guard.

A deep, glossy mahogany bar with high stools separated the kitchen from a living area. The living area had a mounted flat-screen television and leather chairs that looked wide enough for at least two people.

The glossy fixtures and lighting only added to the perfection of the yacht. It all screamed bachelor and money...perfect for Will Rowling.

"You've done well for yourself," she told him as she placed her tote bag on a barstool. "I'm impressed."

Will's sidelong smile kicked up her heart rate. They hadn't even pulled away from the dock and he was already getting to her. This was going to be a day full of her willpower battling her emotions and she didn't know if she'd have the strength to fight off Will's advances.

Who was she kidding? Catalina already knew that if Will tried anything she would succumb to his charms. She'd known this the moment she'd accepted his invitation. But that didn't mean she'd drop her wall of defenses so easily. He'd seriously hurt her before and if he wanted to show her what a changed man he was now, she was going to make him work for it.

"Did you think I was taking you out in a canoe for the day?"

"I guess I hadn't given much thought to the actual boat," she replied, resting her arm on the smooth, curved edge of the bar. "I was too worried about your actions."

"Worried you'd enjoy them too much?" he asked with a naughty grin.

"More like concerned I'd have to deflate your ego," she countered with a matching smile. "You're not seriously going to start putting the moves on me now, are you?"

Will placed a hand over his heart. "You wound me, Cat. I'm at least going to get this boat on course before I rip your clothes off."

Catalina's breath caught in her throat.

Will turned and mounted the steps to go above deck, and then froze and threw a sexy grin over his shoulder. "Relax, Cat. I won't do anything you don't want."

The playful banter had just taken a turn, a sharp turn that sent shivers racing through her entire body. Was she prepared for sex with this man? That's what everything leading up to this moment boiled down to.

Cat would be lying to herself if she tried to say she

didn't want Will physically. That had been proven each time he'd kissed her recently.

I won't do anything you don't want, he'd said.

And that was precisely what scared her the most.

With the ocean breeze sliding across his face, Will welcomed the spittle of spray, the taste of salt on his lips. He needed to get a damn grip. He hadn't meant to be so teasing with Cat.

Okay, he had, but he hadn't meant for her to get that panicked look on her face. He knew full well she was battling with herself where he was concerned. There wasn't a doubt in his mind she wanted him physically and that was easy to obtain. But there was part of Will that wanted her to see that he wasn't at all the same man he used to be.

She would get to see that side of him today. He intended to do everything for her, to prove to her just how appreciated she was and how valued. Will had fully stocked the yacht when he'd had this idea a couple days ago. He'd known he would take her out at some point, but it wasn't until he saw her working the crowd, with circles under her eyes and a smile on her face at the dinner last night, that he decided to invite her right away.

With all of the recent upheaval in Alma—the Montoro monarchy drama and Isabella's passing, not to mention Will's taking the reins of Rowling Energy—there was just too much life getting in the way of what he wanted. Too many distractions interfering with his main goal...and his goal was to have Cat.

He may be the good son, the twin who was raised to follow the rules and not question authority. But Will wasn't about to make the same mistake with Cat as he had in the past. The moment he'd let her walk away years ago, he'd already started plotting to get her back. Then the whole debacle with Bella had happened and Will knew more than ever that it was time to make his move with Rowling Energy and Cat.

Spending the day together on his yacht, however, was something totally unrelated to everything else that had happened in their past. Today was all about them and nothing or nobody else. Everything that happened with Cat from here on out was going to be her call…he may just silently nudge and steer her in the right direction. Those initial kisses had reignited the spark they'd left burning long ago and he knew without a doubt that she felt just as passionate as he did.

He didn't blame her one bit for being leery. He'd done some major damage before and she wouldn't let him forget it anytime soon. Not that he could. He'd never forget that look on her face when he'd told her they'd been a mistake and then walked away. That moment had played over and over in his mind for the past several years. Knowing he'd purposely hurt Cat wasn't something he was likely to ever forget.

Still, if she ever discovered the truth, would she see that he'd done it for her? He'd best keep that secret to himself and just stay on course with his plan now. At least she was here, she was talking and she was coming around. The last thing Will wanted to do was rehash the past when they could be spending their time concentrating on the here and now.

Will steered the yacht toward the private island not too far from Alma. In just under an hour he'd have Cat on a beach with a picnic. He wondered when the last time was that she'd had someone do something like that for her, but quickly dismissed the thought. If another man had pampered her, Will sure as hell didn't want to know.

Of course, there was no man in her life now. Will was the one kissing her, touching her. She was his for at least today so he needed to make the most of every moment they were alone. He truly hoped the tiny island was deserted. He'd come here a few times to think, to get away from all the pressure and stress. Only once had he run into other people.

Cat stayed below for the duration of the trip. Perhaps she was trying to gather her own thoughts as well. Maybe she was avoiding him because she thought that taking her out to a private island for sex was so cliché, so easy to read into.

But for reasons Will didn't want to admit or even think about, this day was so much more than sex. *Cat* was more than sex. Yes, he wanted her in the fiercest way imaginable, but he also wanted more from her… he just didn't know what.

No, that was wrong. The first thing he wanted was for her to see him in a different light. He wanted her to see the good in him she'd seen when they'd grown up together, when they'd laughed and shared secrets with each other. He wanted her to see that he wasn't the monster who had ripped her heart out and diminished their relationship into ashes with just a few damning words.

Perhaps this outing wasn't just about him proving to her what a changed man he was, but for him to try to figure out what the hell to do next and how far he wanted to take things with her once they got back to reality.

When he finally pulled up to the dock and secured the yacht, he went below deck. He hoped the last forty-five minutes had given Cat enough time to see that he

wasn't going to literally jump her. The playful banter
had taken a sexual turn, but he wasn't sorry. He was
only sorry Cat hadn't come up once to see him. This initial space was probably for the best. After all, today was
the first time they'd been fully alone and not sneaking
into the bathroom or laundry area of his father's home
for a make-out session.

Yeah, his seduction techniques needed a bit of work
to say the least. But he'd had four years to get control
over just how he wanted to approach things once he finally got his Cat alone. And now he was ready.

As he stepped below, Will braced his hands on the
trim overhead and froze on the last step. Cat lay side-
ways, curled into a ball on his bed. The innocent pose
shouldn't have his body responding, but...well, he was a
guy and this woman had had him tied in knots for years.

Will had wanted Cat in his bed for too long. All his
fantasies involved the bed in his house, but the yacht
would do. At this point he sure as hell wasn't going to
be picky. He'd waited too damn long for this and he
was going to take each moment he could get, no matter the surroundings.

And the fact that she was comfortable enough to
rest here spoke volumes for how far they'd come. Just
a few weeks ago he'd kissed her as if she was his next
breath and she'd run away angry. Though Will was
smart enough to know her anger stemmed from arousal.

Passion and hate...there was such a fine line between the two.

Slowly, Will crossed the open area and pulled a small
throw from the narrow linen closet. Gently placing the
thin blanket over her bare legs and settling it around her
waist, Will watched the calm rise and fall of her chest.
She was so peaceful, so relaxed and not on her guard.

For the first time in a long time, Will was finally seeing the woman he knew years ago, the woman who was more trusting, less cautious.

Of course, he'd helped shape her into the vigilant person she was today. Had he not made such bad choices when they'd been together the first time, perhaps she wouldn't have to feel so guarded all the time. Perhaps she'd smile more and laugh the way she used to.

Cat shifted, let out a throaty moan and blinked up at Will. Then her eyes widened as she sat straight up.

"Oh my. Was I asleep?"

Will laughed, crossing his arms over his chest. "Or you were playing dead."

Cat smoothed her short hair away from her face and glanced toward the wall of windows. "I was watching the water. I was so tired, so I thought I'd just lie here and enjoy the scenery."

"That was the whole point in having my bed right there. It's a breathtaking view."

When she turned her attention back to him, she gasped. That's right, he hadn't been discussing the water. The view of the woman was much more enticing.

"Why don't you use the restroom to freshen up and change into your suit?" he suggested. "I'll get our lunch set up."

The bright smile spreading across her face had something unfamiliar tugging on his heart. He may not be able to label what was going on between them, but he couldn't afford to be emotional about it.

Dammit. He didn't even know what to feel, how to act anymore. He wanted her, but he wasn't thinking of forever. He wanted now. He needed her to see he was a different man, yet he was more than ready to throw this relationship into his father's face.

Sticking to business would have been best; at least he knew exactly what he was getting into with real estate and oil. With Cat, he had no clue and the fact that she had him so tied in knots without even trying was terrifying.

Once his mission had been clear—to win back Cat to prove he could and to show his father who was in charge. But then, somewhere along the way, Will had shifted into needing Cat to see the true person he'd come to be, the man who still had feelings for her and cared for her on a level even he couldn't understand.

Cat came to her feet and started folding the throw. "I'm sorry I fell asleep on you."

Stepping forward and closing the space between them, Will pulled the blanket from her hands, wadded it up and threw it into the corner. "You aren't cleaning. You aren't folding, dusting, doing dishes. Your only job is to relax. If you want a nap, take a nap. The day is yours. The cleaning is up to me. Got it?"

Her eyes widened as she glanced at the crumpled blanket. "Are you just going to leave that there?"

Will took her chin between his thumb and finger, forcing her to look only at him. "You didn't answer my question."

Her wide, dark eyes drew him in as she merely nodded. "I can't promise, but I'll try."

Unable to help himself, Will smacked a kiss on her lips and pulled back as a grin spread across his face. "Go freshen up and meet me on the top deck."

Will watched as Cat grabbed her bag off the barstool and crossed to the bathroom. Once the door clicked shut, he let out a breath.

He'd sworn nobody would ever control him or hold any power over him again. Yet here was a petite, doe-eyed maid who had more power over him than any business magnate or his father ever could.

Will raked a hand through his hair. He'd promised Cat a day of relaxation and he intended to deliver just that. If she wasn't ready for more, then he'd have to pull all of his self-control to the surface and honor her wishes.

What had he gotten himself into?

Nine

Maybe bringing this particular swimsuit had been a bad idea. When she'd grabbed the two-piece black bikini, Catalina had figured she'd make Will suffer a little. But, by wearing so little and having him so close, she was the one suffering.

Catalina pulled on a simple red wrap dress from her own collection and slipped on her silver flip-flops.

One glance in the mirror and she laughed. The bikini would at least draw attention away from the haggard lines beneath her eyes and the pallor of her skin. Over the past few months, if she wasn't working for James or Patrick, she was working for herself getting her stock ready to showcase when the opportunity presented itself. She believed in being prepared and the moment she saw an opening with any fashion design firm, she was going to be beating down their doors and promoting her unique styles.

Catalina tossed her discarded clothes back into her tote and looked around to make sure she hadn't left anything lying around in the bathroom. Could such a magnificent room be a simple, mundane bathroom?

With the polished silver fixtures, the glass wall shower and sparkling white tile throughout, Catalina had taken a moment to appreciate all the beauty before she'd started changing. The space screamed dominance…male dominance.

Will was pulling out all the stops today. He'd purposely invited her aboard his yacht because he knew that given her love of water she'd never be able to say no. He was right. Anything that got her away from her daily life and into the refreshing ocean was a no-brainer.

Exiting the bathroom, Catalina dropped her bag next to the door and headed up to the top deck. The sun warmed her skin instantly as she turned and spotted Will in a pair of khaki board shorts and a navy shirt he'd left completely unbuttoned. The man wasn't playing fair…which she assumed was his whole plan from the start.

Fine. She had a bikini and boobs. Catalina figured she'd already won this battle before it began. Men were the simplest of creatures.

Will had transformed the seating area into a picnic. A red throw covered the floor, a bucket with ice and wine sat to one side and Will was pulling fruit from a basket.

"Wow. You really know how to set the stage."

He threw her a smile. "Depends on the audience."

"It's just me, so no need to go to all the trouble." She edged around the curving seats and stood just to the side of the blanket. "I'd be happy with a simple salad."

"There is a need to go to all this trouble," he corrected her as he continued to pull more food from the basket. "Have a seat. The strawberries are fresh, the wine is chilled and I have some amazing dishes for us."

Catalina couldn't turn down an invitation like that. She eased down onto the thick blanket and reached for a strawberry. She'd eaten three by the time Will came to sit beside her.

With his back resting against the sofa, he lifted his knee and wrapped his arm around it. "I have a variety of cheese, salmon, baguettes, a tangy salad my chef makes that will make you weep and for dessert..."

He reached over and pulled the silver lid from the dish. "Your favorite."

Catalina gasped as she stared at the pineapple upside-down cheesecake. "You remembered?"

"Of course I did." He set the lid back down. "There's not a detail about you that I've forgotten, Cat."

When she glanced over at him, she found his eyes locked on hers and a small smile dancing around his lips. "I remembered how much you love strawberries and that you will always pick a fruity dessert over a chocolate one. I also recall how much you love salmon, so I tried to incorporate all of your favorites into this lunch."

Strawberry in hand, she froze. "But you just asked me last night. How did you get all of this together?"

Will shrugged and made up a plate for her. "I knew I wanted to take you out on my yacht at some point. I was hoping for soon, but it wasn't until yesterday that I realized how hard you've been working."

He passed her the plate with a napkin. "You need this break and I want to be the one to give it to you. Besides, there's a lot I can do with a few hours and the right connections."

Catalina smiled as she picked up a cube of cheese.

"I'm sure your chef was making the cheesecake before the crack of dawn this morning."

Will shrugged. "Maybe. He did have nearly everything else done by the time I headed out to James and Bella's house this morning."

"You visited James already, too?"

Will settled back with his own plate and forked up a bite of salmon before answering. "I wanted to see Maisey before James heads back out on the road for football. I haven't really bonded with her much, especially with the strain on my relationship with James. But we're getting there and I wanted to see my niece. I'm sure she and Bella will accompany James on the road when they can."

Something inside Catalina warmed at the image of Will playing the doting, spoiling uncle. A family was definitely in her future plans, but knowing Will was taking an active part in little Maisey's life awakened something in her she hadn't yet uncovered.

But no. Will couldn't be father material. He wasn't even husband material. No matter how much, at one time, she'd wished he was. Will was a career-minded, power-driven man who valued family, but he didn't scream minivan and family portraits.

"How did the bonding go?" she asked, trying to concentrate on her food and not the fact that the image had been placed in her head of Will with a baby. Was there anything sexier than a big, powerful man holding an innocent child?

"She seemed to like the doll I brought her."

Of course he'd brought a doll. Now his "aww" level just exploded. Why did the man have to be so appealing on every single level? She didn't want to find him even more irresistible. She couldn't afford to let her heart get tangled up with him again.

Catalina couldn't handle the struggle within her. "You took her a doll? Did your assistant or someone on your staff go buy it?"

Will glanced at her, brows drawn in. "No, I bought it the other day when I was out and just got the chance to take it to her this morning. Why?"

The man was gaining ground and scaling that wall of defenses she'd so carefully erected. And in unexpected ways. He'd wanted to have a special moment with his niece, which had nothing to do with Catalina. Yet here she sat, on his boat, eating her favorite foods that he'd remembered while listening to him talk of his love for his baby niece.

Why was she keeping him at a distance again?

Oh, yeah. That broken heart four years ago.

They ate the rest of their lunch in silence, except when she groaned like a starved woman as she inhaled her piece of cheesecake. As promised, Will cleaned up the mess and took everything back down to the galley. Once he returned, he extended his hand to her.

"Ready to go for a walk?" he asked.

Catalina placed her hand in his, allowing him to pull her up. "I'm not sure I can walk after that, but I can waddle. I'm pretty stuffed."

Will laughed as he led her from the boat. Once they stepped off the wooden dock, Catalina slipped out of her sandals to walk on the warm, sandy beach. The sand wasn't too hot to burn her feet and as the soft grains shifted beneath her, she found herself smiling. She couldn't remember the last time she'd done absolutely nothing by way of working in one form or another.

"I hope that smile has something to do with me,"

Will stated, again slipping his hand into hers as they walked along the shoreline.

"I'm just happy today. I needed a break and I guess I didn't realize it."

"From one workaholic to another, I recognized the signs."

His confession had her focusing on the words and not how powerful and wonderful his fingers felt laced with hers.

"I never thought you took a break," she replied.

Catalina looked at all the tiny seashells lining the shore and made a mental note to find some beautiful ones to take back with her.

"I've had breaks," he replied. "Not many, mind you, but I know when I need to step back so I don't get burnt out."

Catalina turned her face toward the ocean. She'd been burnt out on cleaning since she started. But sewing and designing, she could never imagine falling out of love with her passion.

They walked along in silence and Catalina let her thoughts run wild. What would've happened between them had Will not succumbed to his father's demands that he drop her? Would they have these romantic moments often? Would he make her take breaks from life and put work on hold for her?

She really couldn't see any of that, to be honest. Will was still under his father's thumb, whether he admitted it or not. He'd been at the house most mornings going over Rowling Energy stuff, which Catalina assumed was really just Will checking in.

"Why did you give up on us before?" she asked before she could think better of it.

Will stopped, causing Catalina to stop as well. She dropped his hand and turned to fully face him.

"Never mind," she said, shaking her head. "It doesn't matter now."

The muscle in Will's jaw ticked as he stared back at her. "It does matter. Our breakup damaged both of us."

Catalina pushed her hair behind her ears, which was useless as the wind kept whipping it out. "I'm pretty sure you weren't damaged, seeing as how ending our relationship was your decision."

When she started to walk on, Will gripped her elbow. "You think seeing you move on and dating another man wasn't crushing to me? You think knowing you were in another man's arms, maybe even in his bed, didn't tear me up?"

She'd tried not to think about Will when she threw herself into another relationship to mask the hurt. From the angst in his tone and the fire in his eyes, though... *had* Will been hurt over the breakup? How could that be when he was the one who had ultimately ended things? Did he not want the split? Was he doing it to appease his father? If that was the case then she was doubly angry that he hadn't fought for them.

"You thought I'd sit around and cry myself to sleep over you?" she retorted, refusing to feel guilt over a decision he'd made for both of them.

And so what if she'd shed tears over him? Many tears, in fact, but there was no way she'd admit such a thing. As far as he knew she was made of steel and stronger than her emotions.

"Besides, you had moved on quite nicely. You ended up in a relationship with a Montoro princess."

Dammit. She hadn't meant for that little green monster to slip out. Catalina knew just how much Bella and

James loved each other, yet there was that sliver of jealousy at the fact that Will had been all ready to put a ring on Bella's finger first.

Will laughed. "That fake engagement was a mistake from all angles. James and Bella have found something she never would've had with me."

"But you would've married her."

And that fact still bothered Catalina. She hated the jealousy she'd experienced when she'd discovered Will was engaged. Not that she ever thought she stood a chance, but how could anyone compete with someone as beautiful and sexy as Bella Montoro? She was not only royalty, she was a humanitarian with a good heart.

On a sigh, Catalina started walking again, concentrating on the shells lining the shore. "It doesn't matter, honestly. I shouldn't have brought it up."

She reached down to pick up an iridescent shell, smoothing her finger over the surface to swipe away the wet sand. Catalina slid the shell into the small hidden pocket on the side of her dress and kept walking, very much aware of Will at her side. He was a smart man not to deny her last statement. They both knew he would've married Bella because that's what his father had wanted. Joining the fortunes of the two dynamic families was Patrick's dream…the wrong son had fallen for the beauty, though.

They walked a good bit down the deserted beach. Catalina had no idea how Will had managed to find such a perfect place with total privacy, but he had no doubt planned this for a while. On occasion he would stop and find a shell for her, wordlessly handing it to her as they walked on. The tension was heavier now that she'd opened up the can of worms. She wished she'd kept her feelings to herself.

What did it matter if he was going to marry Bella? What man wouldn't want to spend his life with her? Not only that, had Catalina truly thought Will would remain single? Had she believed he was so exclusively focused on work that he wouldn't want to settle down and start the next generation of Rowling heirs?

The warm sun disappeared behind a dark cloud as the wind kicked into high gear. Catalina looked up and suppressed a groan. Of course a dark cloud would hover over her. The ominous sky was starting to match her mood.

"Should we head back to the yacht?" she asked, trying to tuck her wayward strands of hair behind her ears as she fought against the wind.

"I don't think it's going to do anything major. The forecast didn't show rain."

That nasty cloud seemed to indicate otherwise, but she wasn't going to argue. They already had enough on their plate.

Catalina glanced through the foliage, squinting as something caught her eye. "What's that?"

Will stopped and looked in the direction she'd indicated. "Looks like a cabin of sorts. I've not come this far inland before. Let's check it out."

Without waiting for her, Will took off toward the small building. Catalina followed, stepping over a piece of driftwood and trailing through the lush plants that had nearly overtaken the property.

"I wonder who had this cabin built," he muttered as he examined the old wood shack. "The island belongs to Alma from what I could tell when I first started coming here."

The covered porch leaned to one side, the old tin roof had certainly seen better days and some of the wood around the door and single window had warped. But the place had charm and someone had once cared enough to put it here. A private getaway for a couple in love? A hideout for someone seeking refuge from life? There was a story behind this place.

Will pushed on the door and eased inside. Catalina couldn't resist following him. The musty smell wasn't as bad as she'd expected, but the place was rather dusty. Only a bit of light from outside crept in through the single window, but even that wasn't bright because of the dark cloud covering.

"Careful," he cautioned when she stepped in. "Some of those boards feel loose."

There was enough dim light coming in the front window for them to see a few tarps, buckets and one old chair sitting against the wall.

"Looks like someone was working on this and it was forgotten," Catalina said as she walked around the room. "It's actually quite cozy."

Will laughed. "If you like the rustic, no-indoor-plumbing feel."

Crossing her arms over her chest, she turned around. "Some of us don't need to be pampered with amenities. I personally enjoy the basics."

"This is basic," he muttered, glancing around.

The sudden sound of rain splattering on the tin roof had Catalina freezing in place. "So much for that forecast."

Will offered her a wide smile. "Looks like you get to enjoy the basics a bit longer unless you want to run back to the yacht in the rain."

Crossing the room, Catalina sank down onto the old, sheet-covered chair. "I'm good right here. Will you be able to handle it?"

His aqua eyes raked over her, heating her skin just as effectively as if he'd touched her with his bare hands. "Oh, baby, I can handle it."

Maybe running back to the yacht was the better option after all. How long would she be stranded in an old shack with Will while waiting out this storm?

Catalina wasn't naïve. She knew full well there were only so many things they could talk about and nearly every topic between them circled back to the sexual tension that had seemed to envelop them and bind them together for the past several weeks.

Her body trembled as she kept her gaze locked onto his.

There was only one way this day would end.

Ten

Will stared out the window at the sheets of rain coming down. He didn't need to look, though; the pounding on the roof told him how intense this storm was.

So much for that flawless forecast.

Still, staying across the room from Cat was best for now. He didn't need another invisible push in her direction. He glanced over his shoulder toward the woman he ached for. She sat as casual as you please with her legs crossed, one foot bouncing to a silent beat as her flip-flop dangled off her toes. Those bare legs mocked him. The strings of her bikini top peeking out of her dress mocked him as well. Every damn thing about this entire situation mocked him.

What had he been thinking, inviting her for a day out? Why purposely resurrect all of those old, unresolved feelings? They'd gone four years without bringing up their past, but Will had reached his breaking point. He needed to know if they had a chance at... what? What exactly did he want from her?

He had no clue, but he did know the need for Cat had never lessened. If anything, the emptiness had grown without her in his life. He'd let her go once to save her, but he should've fought for them, fought for what he wanted and found another way to keep her safe. He'd been a coward. As humiliating as that was to admit, there was no sugarcoating the truth of the boy he used to be.

"You might as well have a seat," she told him, meeting his gaze. "The way you're standing across the room is only making the tension worse. You're making me twitchy."

Will laughed. Leave it to Cat to call him on his actions, though he didn't think the tension could get worse.

He crossed the room and took a seat on the floor in front of the chair.

"This reminds me of that time James, you and I were playing hide-and-seek when it started raining," she said. "You guys were home from school on break and I had come in to work with my mum."

Will smiled as the memory flooded his mind. "We were around eight or nine, weren't we?"

Cat nodded. "James kept trying to hold my hand when we both ran into the garage to hide and get dry."

Will sat up straighter. "You never told me that."

"Seriously?" she asked, quirking a brow. "You're going to get grouchy over the actions of a nine-year-old?"

"I'm not grouchy. Surprised, but not grouchy."

"James was only doing it because he knew I had a thing for you."

The corner of Will's mouth kicked up. "You had a thing for me when you were that young?"

Cat shrugged, toying with the edge of her dress. "You were an older man. Practically worldly in all of your knowledge."

"It was the Spanish, wasn't it?" he asked with a grin.

Cat rolled her eyes and laughed. "James was fluent in Spanish as well. You two both had the same hoity-toity schooling."

Will lifted his knee and rested his arm on it as he returned her smile. "Nah. I was better. We would sometimes swap out in class because the teacher couldn't tell us apart. She just knew a quiet blond boy sat in the back. As long as one of us showed up, she didn't pay much attention to the fact there were really supposed to be two."

"Sneaky boys. But, I bet if I asked James about the Spanish speaking skills he'd say he was better," she countered.

"He'd be wrong."

Cat tipped her head, shifting in her seat, which only brought her bare legs within touching distance. "You tricked your teachers and got away with it. Makes me wonder how many times you two swapped out when it came to women."

Will shook his head. "I'm not answering that."

"Well, I know that watch nearly cost James the love of his life," Cat said, nodding toward the gold timepiece on his wrist.

"It was unfortunate Bella saw you and me kissing. I truly thought we were secluded." Will sighed and shifted on the wood floor. "She had every right to think James was kissing someone else because she had no clue about the bet."

The rain beat against the window as the wind kicked up. Cat tensed and her eyes widened.

"Hope this old place holds up," she said. "Maybe running back to the yacht would have been a better idea."

"Too late now." Will reached over, laying his hand on her knee. "We're fine. It's just a pop-up storm. You know these things pass fast."

With a subtle nod, she settled deeper into the seat and rested her head on the back cushion. Guilt rolled through Will. He'd planned a day for her, and had been hopeful that seduction would be the outcome. Yet here they sat in some abandoned old shack waiting out some freak storm. Even Mother Nature was mocking him.

But there was a reason they were here right now, during this storm, and Will wasn't going to turn this chance away. He planned on taking full advantage and letting Cat know just how much he wanted her.

Shifting closer to her chair, Will took Cat's foot and slid her shoe off. He picked up her other foot and did the same, all while knowing she had those dark, intoxicating eyes focused on his actions. It was her exotic eyes that hypnotized him.

Taking one of her delicate feet between his hands, Will started to massage, stroking his thumb up her arch.

"I'll give you ten minutes to stop that," she told him with a smile.

The radiant smile on her face was something he hadn't realized he'd missed so much. Right now, all relaxed and calm, even with the storm raging outside, Cat looked like the girl he once knew...the girl he'd wanted something more with.

But they were different people now. They had different goals. Well, he did; her goals were still unclear to him. He suddenly found himself wanting to know about those dreams of hers, and the fact that she'd hinted to James that she wouldn't stay in Alma forever.

But all of those questions could come later. Right now, Cat's comfort and happiness were all that mattered. Tomorrow's worries, issues and questions could be dealt with later. He planned on enjoying Cat for as long as she would allow.

Damn. When had this petite woman taken control over him? When had he allowed it? There wasn't one moment he could pinpoint, but there were several tiny instances where he could see in hindsight the stealthy buildup of her power over him.

Cat laughed as she slid down a bit further in the chair and gazed down at him beneath heavy lids. "If your father could see you on the floor rubbing his maid's feet, you'd lose your prestigious position at Rowling Energy."

Will froze, holding her gaze. It may have been a lighthearted joke, but there was so much truth to her statement about how angry this would make his father. But Will had already set in motion his plan to freeze his father out of the company.

Besides, right now, Will didn't care about Patrick or Rowling Energy. What he did care about was the woman who was literally turning to putty in his hands. Finally, he was going to show her exactly what they could be together and anticipation had his heart beating faster than ever.

"Does this feel good?" he asked.

Her reply was a throaty moan, sexy enough to have his body responding.

"Then all of the other stuff outside of this cabin doesn't matter."

Blinking down at him, Cat replied, "Not to me, but I bet if your father made you choose, you'd be singing a different tune."

Just like last time.

The unspoken words were so deafening, they actually drowned out the beating of the rain and the wind against the small shelter.

Will's best option was to keep any answer to himself. He could deny the fact, but he'd be lying. He'd worked too hard to get where he was to just throw it all away because of hormones.

At the same time, he planned on working equally as hard to win over Cat. There was no reason he had to give up anything.

His hand glided up to her ankle, then her calf. She said nothing as her eyes continued to hold his. He purposely watched her face, waiting for a sign of retreat, but all that was staring back at him was desire.

There was a silent message bouncing between them, that things were about to get very intimate, very fast.

The old cabin creaked and groaned against the wind's force. Cat tensed beneath him.

"You're safe," he assured her softly, not wanting to break this moment of trust she'd settled into with him. "This place is so old. I know it has withstood hurricanes. This little storm won't harm the cabin or us."

And there weren't any huge trees around, just thick bushes and flowers, so they weren't at risk for anything falling on them.

Right now, the only thing he needed to be doing was pushing through that line of defense Cat had built up. And from her sultry grin and heavy lids, he'd say he was doing a damn fine job.

Catalina should tell him to stop. Well, the common sense side of her told her she should. But the female side, the side that hadn't been touched or treasured in more time than she cared to admit, told her common sense to shut up.

Will had quite the touch. She had no idea the nerves in your feet could be so tied into all the girly parts. She certainly knew it now. Every part of her was zipping with ache and need. If he commanded her to strip and dance around the room naked, she would. The power he held over her was all-consuming and she was dying to know when he was going to do more.

She'd walked straight into this with her eyes wide open. So if she was having doubts or regrets already, she had no one to blame but herself. Though Catalina wasn't doubting or regretting. She was aching, on the verge of begging him to take this to the next level.

Catalina's head fell back against the chair as his hands moved to her other calf, quickly traveling up to her knee, then her thigh. She wanted to inch down further and part her legs just a tad, but that would be a silent invitation she wasn't quite brave enough for.

Yet.

"I've wanted to touch you for so long," he muttered, barely loud enough for her to hear over the storm. "I've watched you for the past four years, wondering if you ever thought of me. Wondering if you ever fantasized about me the way I did you."

Every. Single. Night.

Which was a confession she wasn't ready to share. The ball was in his court for now and she planned on just waiting to see how this played out.

He massaged her muscles with the tips of his fingers and the room became hotter with each stroke. If the man could have such power over her with something so simple as a foot massage, how would her body react once Will really started showing her affection?

"Do you remember that time your mother caught us making out?" he asked with a half laugh.

At the time, Catalina had been mortified that her mother caught them. But it wasn't until after the breakup that she realized why her mother had been so disappointed.

Patrick Rowling had really done a number on Catalina's mum. And it was those thoughts that could quickly put a bucket of cold water on this encounter, but she refused to allow Patrick to steal one more moment of happiness from her life…he'd already taken enough from her.

Will may not be down on his knees proposing marriage, but he was down on his knees showing her affection. And maybe she hoped that would be a stepping-stone to something more… But right now, that was all she wanted. She'd fought this pull toward him for too long. She hadn't wanted to let herself believe they could be more, but now she couldn't deny herself. She couldn't avoid the inevitable…she was falling for Will all over again.

"She didn't even know we were dating," Catalina murmured, her euphoric state suddenly overtaking her ability to speak coherently.

"Not many people did. That's when I realized I didn't want to keep us a secret anymore."

And that had been the start of their spiral toward the heartbreak she'd barely recovered from.

Once they were an "official" item, Patrick had intervened and put a stop to his good son turning to the maid. Shocking, since turning to the staff for pleasure certainly hadn't been below Patrick at one time. Not that what Catalina and Will shared had been anything like that. But the idea that Patrick could act as if he were so far above people was absolutely absurd.

"Don't tense on me now," Will warned. "You're supposed to be relaxing."

Catalina blew out a breath. "I'm trying. It's just hard when I'm stuck between the past and whatever is happening to us now."

Will came up to his knees, easing his way between her parted legs, his hands resting on the tops of her thighs, his fingertips brushing just beneath the hem of her dress.

"It's two different times. We're two different people. There's nothing to compare. Focus on now."

She stared down at those bright blue eyes, the wide open shirt and something dark against his chest. Was that...

"Do you have a tattoo?" she asked, reaching to pull back the shirt.

He said nothing as she eased the material aside. The glimpse she got wasn't enough. Catalina didn't ask, she merely gripped the shirt and pushed it off his shoulders. Will shifted until it fell to the floor.

Sure enough, black ink swirled over the left side of his chest and over his shoulder. She had no idea what the design was. All she knew was that it was sexy.

Without asking, she reached out and traced a thin line over his heart, then on up. The line thickened as it curled around his shoulder. Taut muscles tensed beneath her featherlight touch.

Catalina brought her gaze up to Will's. The intensity of his stare made her breath catch in her throat and stilled her hand.

"Don't stop," he whispered through clenched teeth. "Will..."

His hand came up to cover hers. "Touch me, Cat."

He'd just handed her the reins.

With just enough pressure, he flattened her hand between his palm and his shoulder. The warmth of his skin penetrated her own, the heat sliding through her entire body.

"I—I want to but—"

She shook her head, killing the rest of her fears before they could be released and never taken back.

"But what?" he muttered, pushing her hair behind her ear, letting his fingertips trail over her cheek, her jawline and down her neck until she trembled.

"I'm not sure I can go any farther than that," she confessed. "I don't want to tease you."

"I've fantasized about you touching me like this for years. You're not teasing, you're fulfilling a fantasy."

Catalina stared into those aqua eyes and knew without a doubt he was serious. The fact that he'd been dreaming of her for this long confused her further, brought on even more questions than answers.

"Don't go there," he warned as if he knew where her thoughts were headed. "Keep touching me, Cat. Whatever happens here is about you and me and right this moment. Don't let past memories rob us of this time together."

Catalina opened her mouth, but Will placed one finger over her lips. "I have no expectations. Close your eyes."

Even though her heart beat out of control from anticipation and a slither of fear of the unknown, she did as he commanded.

"Now touch me. Just feel me, feel this moment and nothing else."

His tone might have been soft, but everything about

his words demanded that she obey. Not that he had to do much convincing. With her eyes closed, she wasn't forced to look at the face of the man who'd broken her heart. She wanted this chance to touch him, to ignore all the reasons why this was such a bad idea. But she couldn't look into those eyes and pretend that this was normal, that they were just two regular people stranded in an old shack.

With her eyes closed she actually felt as if they were regular people. She could pretend this was just a man she ached for, not a man who was a billionaire with more power than she'd ever see.

With her eyes closed she could pretend he wanted her for who she was and not just because she was a challenge.

Catalina brought her other hand up and over his chest. If she was given the green light to explore, she sure as hell wanted both hands doing the job. Just as she smoothed her palms up and over his shoulders, over his thick biceps, she felt the knot on her wrap dress loosen at her side.

Her eyes flew open. "What are you doing?"

"Feeling the moment."

The dress parted, leaving her torso fully exposed. "You don't play fair."

The heat in his eyes was more powerful than any passion she'd ever seen. "I never will when it comes to something I want."

"You said—"

"I'd never force you," he interrupted, gliding his fingertips over the straps of her bikini that stretched from behind her neck to the slopes of her breasts. "But that doesn't mean I won't try to persuade you."

As the rain continued to beat against the side of the

shack, Catalina actually found herself happy that she was stuck here. Perhaps this was the push she needed to follow through with what she truly wanted. No, she wasn't looking for happily-ever-after, she'd never be that naïve again where Will was concerned. But she was older now, was going into this with both eyes wide open.

And within the next couple months, hopefully she'd be out of Alma and starting her new life. So why not take the plunge now with a man she'd always wanted? Because he was right. This was all about them, here and now. Everything else could wait outside that door.

For now, Catalina was taking what she'd wanted for years.

Eleven

Catalina came to her feet. From here on out she was taking charge of what she'd been deprived of and what she wanted...and she wanted Will. Whatever doubts she had about sleeping with him wouldn't be near as consuming as the regret she'd have if she moved away and ignored this opportunity.

The moment she stood before him, Will sank back down on the floor and stared up at her as her dress fell into a puddle around her feet. As she stepped away and kicked the garment aside, his eyes roamed over her, taking in the sight of the bikini and nothing else.

The image of him sitting at her feet was enough to give her a sense of control, a sense of dominance. The one time when it counted most, she didn't feel inferior.

Will could've immediately taken over, he could've stood before her and taken charge, but he'd given her the reins.

"That bikini does some sinful things to your body." He reached out, trailed his fingertips over the sensitive area behind her knee and on up to her thigh. "Your curves are stunning, Cat. Your body was made to be uncovered."

"How long have you wanted me, Will?" she asked, needing to know this much. "Did you want me when we were together before?"

"More than anything," he rasped out, still sliding his fingers up and down the backs of her legs. "But I knew you were a virgin and I respected you."

"What if I were a virgin now?" she asked, getting off track. "Would you still respect me?"

"I've always respected you." He came up to his knees, putting his face level with her stomach. He placed a kiss just above her bikini bottoms before glancing up at her. "And I don't want to discuss if there's been another man in your bed."

With a move she hadn't expected, he tossed her back into the chair and stood over her, his hands resting on either side of her head. "Because I'm the only man you're going to be thinking of right now."

"I've only been with one other, but you're the only man I've ever wanted in my bed," she admitted. "I need you to know that."

Maybe she was naïve for letting him in on that little piece of information she'd kept locked in her heart for so long, but right now, something more than desire was sparking between them. He was too possessive for this to just be something quick and easy.

They weren't just scratching an itch, but she had no clue what label to put on what was about to happen. Which was why she planned on not thinking and just feeling. This bond that was forming here was something she'd have to figure out later...much later.

"All I need to know is that you want this as much as I do," he told her. "That you're ready for anything that happens because I can't promise soft and gentle. I've wanted you too long."

A shiver of arousal speared through her. "I don't need gentle, Will. I just need you."

In an instant his lips crushed hers. She didn't know when things had shifted, but in the span of about two minutes, she'd gone from questioning sex with Will to nearly ripping his shorts off so she could have him.

Will's strong hands gripped her hips as he shifted the angle of his head for a deeper kiss. Cat arched her body, needing to feel as much of him as possible. There still didn't seem to be enough contact. She wanted more... she wanted it all. The need to have everything she'd deprived herself of was now an all-consuming ache.

"Keep moaning like that, sweetheart," he muttered against her lips. "You're all mine."

She hadn't even realized she'd moaned, which just proved how much control this man had over her actions.

Gripping his shoulders, she tried to pull him down further, but he eased back. With his eyes locked onto hers, he hooked his thumbs in the waistband of his board shorts and shoved them to the floor. Stepping out of them he reached down, took her hand and pulled her to her feet.

Keeping her eyes on his, she reached behind her neck and untied her top. It fell forward as she worked on the knot. Soon they'd flung the entire scrap of fabric across the room. Will's eyes widened and his nostrils flared.

Excitement and anticipation roiled through her as she shoved her bottoms down without a care. She had no clue who reached for whom first, but the next second she was in his arms, skin to skin from torso to knees and she'd never felt anything better in her entire life.

Will's arms wrapped around her waist, his hands splaying across her bare back. He spun her around and sank down into the chair, pulling her down with him. Instinctively her legs straddled his hips. Catalina fisted her fingers in his hair as his lips trailed down her throat.

"So sexy," he murmured against her heated skin. "So mine."

Yes. She was his for now…maybe she always had been.

When his mouth found her breast, his hands encircled her hips. She waited, aching with need.

"Will," she panted, not recognizing her own voice. "Protection."

With his hair mussed, his lids heavy, he looked up. "I don't have any with me. Dammit, they're on the yacht. I didn't expect to get caught out here like this." Cursing beneath his breath, he shook his head. "I'm clean. I swear I wouldn't lie about something like that. I haven't been with a woman in…too long, and I recently had a physical."

"I know I'm clean and I'm on birth control."

He gave her a look, silently asking what she wanted to do. Without another word she slowly sank down onto him, so that they were finally, fully joined after years of wanting, years of fantasizing.

Their sighs and groans filled the small room. Wind continued to beat against the window as rain pelted the tin roof. Everything about this scenario was perfect. Even if they were in a rundown shed, she didn't care. The ambiance was amazingly right. The storm that had swept through them over the years only matched Mother

Nature's fury outside the door. This was the moment they were supposed to be together, this was what they'd both waited for so long.

"Look at me," he demanded, his fingertips pressing into her hips.

Catalina hadn't realized she'd closed her eyes, but she opened them and found herself looking into Will's bright, expressive aqua eyes. He may be able to hold back his words, but those eyes told her so much. Like the fact that he cared for her. This was sex, but there was so much more going on…so much more they'd discuss later.

As her hips rocked back and forth against his, Will continued to watch her face. Catalina leaned down, resting her hands on his shoulders. The need inside her built so fast, she dropped her forehead against his.

"No," he stated. "Keep watching me. I want to see your face."

As she looked back into his eyes, her body responded to every touch, every kiss, every heated glance. Tremors raced through her at the same time his body stilled, the cords in his neck tightened and his fingertips dug even further into her hips.

His body stiffened against hers, his lips thinned as his own climax took control. Catalina couldn't look away. She wanted to see him come undone, knowing she caused this powerful man to fall at the mercy of her touch.

Once their bodies eased out of the euphoric state, Catalina leaned down, rested her head on his shoulder and tried to regain some sense of normal breathing. She didn't know what to say now, how to act. They'd taken this awkward, broken relationship and put another speed bump in it. Now all they had to do was figure out how

to maneuver over this new hurdle since they'd moved
to a whole new, unfamiliar level.

Will trailed his hand up and down Cat's back, which
was smooth and damp with sweat. Damn, she was sexier
than he'd ever, *ever* imagined. She'd taken him without
a second thought and with such confidence. Yet she'd
been so tight…had she not slept with anyone? How
had that not happened? Surely she wasn't still a virgin.

Had Cat kept her sexuality penned up all this time?
For completely selfish reasons, this thought pleased
him.

As much as Will wanted to know, he didn't want
to say a word, didn't want to break the silence with
anything that would kill the mood. The storm raged
on outside, the cabin creaked and continued to groan
under the pressure, but Cat was in his arms, her heart
beating against his chest, and nothing could pull him
from this moment.

The fact that he was concentrating on her heartbeat
was a bit disconcerting. He didn't want to be in tune
with her heart, he couldn't get that caught up with her,
no matter how strong this invisible force was that was
tugging him to her. Having her in his arms, finally making love to her was enough.

So why did he feel as if there was more to be had?

Because when he'd originally been thinking of the
here and now, he'd somehow started falling into the
zone of wanting more than this moment. He wanted
Cat much longer than this day, this week, even. Will
wanted more and now he had to figure out just how the
hell that would work.

"Tell me I wasn't a substitute for Bella."

Will jerked beneath her, forcing her to sit up and meet his gaze. "What?"

Cat shook her head, smoothing her short hair away from her face. "Nothing," she said, coming to her feet. "That was stupid of me to say. We had sex. I'm not expecting you to give me anything more."

As she rummaged around the small space searching for her bikini and dress, Will sat there dumbfounded. So much for not letting words break the beauty of the moment.

What was that about Bella? Seriously? Did Cat honestly think that Will had had a thing for his brother's fiancée?

"Look at me," he demanded, waiting until Cat spun around, gripping her clothing to her chest. "Bella is married to James. I have no claim to her."

"It's none of my business."

Will watched as she tied her top on and slid the bikini bottoms up her toned legs. "It is your business after what we just did. I don't sleep with one woman and think of another."

Cat's dark eyes came up to his. A lock of her inky black hair fell over her forehead and slashed across her cheek.

"You owe me no explanations, Will." Hands on her hips, she blew the rogue strand from her face. "I know this wasn't a declaration of anything to come. I'm grown up now and I have no delusions that things will be any different than what they are. We slept together, it's over."

Okay, that had originally been his mindset when he'd gone into this, but when the cold words came from her mouth, Will suddenly didn't like the sound of it. She wasn't seeing how he'd changed at all and that was his fault. She still believed he was a jerk who had no cares at all for her feelings. But he did care…too damn much.

"I know you saw me as a challenge," she went on as she yanked the ties together to secure her dress. "A conquest, if you will. It's fine, really. I could've stopped you, but I was selfish and wanted you. So, thanks for—"

"Do not say another word." Pushing to his feet, Will jerked his shorts from the floor and tugged them on before crossing to her. "You can't lie to me, Cat. I know you too well. Whatever defense mechanism you're using here with ugly words isn't you. You're afraid of what you just felt, of what just happened. This wasn't just sex and you damn well know it."

Her eyes widened, her lips parted, but she immediately shut down any emotion he'd just seen flash across her face. No doubt about it, she was trying to cut him off before he did anything to hurt her…again. He should have seen this coming.

Guilt slammed into him. Not over sleeping with her just now, but for how she felt she had to handle the situation to avoid any more heartache.

"Will, I'm the maid," she said softly. "While I'm not ashamed of my position, I also know that this was just a onetime thing. A man like you would never think twice about a woman like me for anything more than sex."

Will gripped her arms, giving her a slight shake. "Why are you putting yourself into this demeaning little package and delivering it to me? I've told you more than once I don't care if you're a maid or a damn CEO. What just happened has nothing to do with anything other than us and what we feel."

"There is no us," she corrected him.

"There sure as hell was just a minute ago."

Why was he so dead set on correcting her? Here he

stood arguing with her when she was saying the same exact thing he'd been thinking earlier.

"And I have no clue why you're bringing Bella into this," he added.

Cat lifted her chin in a defiant gesture. "I'm a woman. Sometimes my insecurities come out."

"Why are you insecure about her?"

Cat laughed and broke free from his hold, taking a step back. "You were with one of the most beautiful women I've ever seen. Suddenly when that relationship is severed, you turn to me. You haven't given me any attention in nearly four years, Will. Forgive me if suddenly I feel like leftovers."

"Don't downgrade what just happened between us," he demanded. "Just because I didn't seek you out in the past few years doesn't mean I didn't want you. I wanted the hell out of you. And I was fighting my way back to you, dammit."

He eased closer, watching as her eyes widened when he closed the gap and loomed over her. "Seeing you all the time, being within touching distance but knowing I had no right was hell."

"You put yourself there."

As if he needed the reminder of the fool he'd been.

Will smoothed her hair back from her forehead, allowing his hand to linger on her jawline. "I can admit when I was wrong, stubborn and a jerk. I can also admit that I have no clue what just happened between us because it was much more than just sex. You felt it, I felt it, and if we deny that fact we'd just be lying to ourselves. Let's get past that. Honesty is all we can have here. We deserve more than something cheap, Cat."

Cat closed her eyes and sighed. When her lids lifted,

she glanced toward the window. "The rain has let up. We should head back to the yacht."

Without another word, without caring that he was standing here more vulnerable than he'd ever been, Cat turned, opened the door and walked out.

Nobody walked out on Will Rowling and he sure as hell wasn't going to let the woman he was so wrapped up in and had just made love to be the first.

Twelve

Catalina had known going into this day that they'd most likely end up naked and finally giving into desires from years ago.

And she hadn't been able to stop herself.

No matter what she felt now, no matter what insecurities crept up, she didn't regret sleeping with Will.

This was a one and done thing—it had to be. She couldn't afford to fall any harder for this man whom she couldn't have. She was planning on leaving Alma anyway, so best to cut ties now and start gearing up for her fresh start. Letting her heart interfere with the dreams she'd had for so long would only have her working backward. She was so close, she'd mentally geared up for the break from Alma, from Will…but that was before she'd given herself to him.

But what had just transpired between them was only closure. Yes, that was the term she'd been looking for.

Closure. Nothing else could come from their intimacy and finally getting each other out of their systems was the right thing to do...wasn't it?

While the rain hadn't fully stopped, Catalina welcomed the refreshing mist hitting her face. She had no clue of the amount of time that had passed while they'd been inside the cabin lost in each other. An hour? Three hours?

The sand shifted beneath her bare feet as she marched down the shore toward the dock. Sandals in her hand, she kept her focus on the yacht in the distance and not the sound of Will running behind her. She should've known he'd come chasing after her, and not just because he wanted to get back to the yacht.

She'd left no room for argument when she'd walked out, and Will Rowling wouldn't put up with that. Too bad. She was done talking. It was time to move on.

Too bad her body was still humming a happy tune and tingling in all the areas he'd touched, tasted.

Figuring he'd grab her when he caught up to her, Catalina turned, ready to face down whatever he threw her way. Will took a few more steps, stopping just in front of her. He was clutching his wadded up shirt at his side. Catalina couldn't help but stare at his bare chest and the mesmerizing tattoo as he pulled in deep breaths.

"You think we're done?" he asked as he stared her down. "Like we're just heading back to the yacht, setting off to Alma and that's it? You think this topic is actually closed? That I would accept this?"

Shrugging, Catalina forced herself to meet his angry gaze. "You brought me here to seduce me. Wasn't that the whole plan for getting me alone? Well, mission accomplished. The storm has passed and it'll start getting dark in a couple hours. Why wait to head back?"

"Maybe because I want to spend more time with you," he shouted. "Maybe because I want more here than something cheap and easy."

As the misty rain continued to hit her face, Catalina wanted to let that sliver of hope into her heart, but she couldn't allow it...not just yet. "And what do you want, Will? An encore performance? Maybe in your bed on the yacht so you can have a more pampered experience?"

His lips thinned, the muscle in his jaw tightened. "What made you so harsh, Cat? You weren't like this before."

Before when she'd been naïve, before when she'd actually thought he may love her and choose her over his career. And before she discovered a secret that he still knew nothing about.

Beyond all of that, she was angry with herself for allowing her emotions to get so caught up in this moment. She should've known better. She'd never been someone to sleep around, but she thought for sure she could let herself go with Will and then walk away. She'd been wrong and now because of her roller coaster of emotions, she was taking her anger out on him.

Shaking her head, Catalina turned. Before she could take a step, she tripped over a piece of driftwood she hadn't seen earlier. Landing hard in the sand, she hated how the instant humiliation took over.

Before she could become too mortified, a spearing pain shot through her ankle. She gasped just as Will crouched down by her side.

"Where are you hurt?" he asked, his eyes raking over her body.

"My ankle," she muttered, sitting up so she could look at her injury.

"Anywhere else?" Will asked.

Catalina shook her head as she tried to wiggle her ankle back and forth. Bad idea. She was positive it wasn't broken—she'd broken her arm as a little girl and that pain had been much worse—but she was also sure she wouldn't be able to apply any pressure on it and walk. The piercing pain shot up her leg and had her wincing. She hoped she didn't burst into tears and look even more pathetic.

So much for her storming off in her dramatic fit of anger.

Will laid his shirt on her stomach.

"What—?"

Before she could finish her question, he'd scooped her up in his arms and set off across the sand. Catalina hated how she instantly melted against his warm, bare chest. Hated how the image of them in her mind seemed way more romantic than what it was, with Will's muscles straining as he carried her in his arms—yeah, they no doubt looked like something straight out of a movie.

"You can't carry me all the way to the yacht," she argued. "This sand is hard enough to walk in without my added weight."

"Your weight is perfect." He threw her a glance, silently leaving her no room for argument. "Relax and we'll see what we're dealing with once I can get you on the bed in the cabin."

Those words sent a shiver of arousal through her that she seriously did not want. Hadn't she learned from the last set of shivers? Hadn't she told herself that after they slept together she'd cut ties? She had no other choice, not if she wanted to maintain any dignity and sanity on her way out of his life for good.

As they neared the dock, Will was breathing hard,

but he didn't say a word as he trudged forward. Her ankle throbbed, which should have helped shift her focus, but being wrapped in Will's strong arms pretty much overrode any other emotion.

Catalina had a sinking feeling that in all her pep talks to herself, she'd overlooked the silent power Will had over her. She may have wanted to have this sexcapade with him and then move on, but she'd seriously underestimated how involved her heart would become.

And this hero routine he was pulling was flat-out sexy…as if she needed another reason to pull her toward him.

Will quickly crossed toward the dock, picking up his pace now that he was on even ground. When he muttered a curse, Catalina lifted her head to see what the problem was. Quickly she noted the damage to the yacht and the dock. Apparently the two had not played nice during the freak storm.

"Oh, Will," she whispered.

He slowed his pace as he carefully tested the weight of the dock. Once his footing was secure, and it was clear that the planks would hold them, he cautiously stepped forward.

"I need to set you down for a second to climb on board, but just keep pressure off that ankle and hold onto my shoulders."

She did as he asked and tried not to consider just what this damage meant for their return trip home. When Will was on deck, he reached out, proceeded to scoop her up again and lifted her onto the yacht.

"I can get down the steps," she told him, really having no clue if she could or not. But there was no way they could both fit through that narrow doorway to get below deck. "Go figure out what happened."

He kept his hold firm. "I'm going to get you settled, assess your ankle and then go see what damage was done to the yacht."

Somehow he managed to get her down the steps and onto the bed without bumping her sore, now swollen ankle along the way. As he adjusted the pillows behind her, she slid back to lean against the fluffy backdrop. Will took a spare pillow and carefully lifted her leg to elevate her injury.

"It's pretty swollen," he muttered as he stalked toward the galley kitchen and returned with a baggie full of ice wrapped in a towel. "Keep this on it and I'll go see if I can find some pain reliever."

"Really, it'll be fine," she lied. The pain was bad, but she wanted him to check on the damage so they could get back to Alma… She prayed they could safely get back. "Go see how bad the destruction is. I'm not going anywhere."

Will's brows drew in. With his hands on his hips, that sexy black ink scrolling over his bare chest and the taut muscles, he personified sex appeal.

"Staring at my ankle won't make it any better," she told him, suddenly feeling uncomfortable.

His unique blue eyes shifted and held her gaze. "I hate that I hurt you," he muttered.

So much could be read from such a simple statement. Was he referring to four years ago? Did he mean the sexual encounter they'd just had or was he referencing her fall?

No matter what he was talking about, Catalina didn't want to get into another discussion that would only take them in circles again. They were truly getting nowhere…well, they'd ended up naked, but other than that, they'd gotten nowhere.

"Go on," she insisted. "Don't worry about me."

He looked as if he wanted to argue, but ended up nodding. "I'll be right back. If you need something, just yell for me. I'll hear you."

Catalina watched as he ascended the steps back up to the deck. Closing her eyes, she dropped her head against the pillows and pulled in a deep breath. If the storm had done too much damage to the yacht, she was stuck. Stuck on a glamorous yacht with an injured ankle with the last person she should be locked down with.

The groan escaped before she could stop it. Then laughter followed. Uncontrollable laughter, because could they be anymore clichéd? The maid and the millionaire, stranded on a desert island. Yeah, they had the makings for a really ridiculous story or some skewed reality show.

Once upon a time she would've loved to have been stranded with Will. To know that nothing would interrupt them. They could be who they wanted to be without pretenses. Just Will and Catalina, two people who l—

No. They didn't love each other. That was absurd to even think. Years ago she had thought they were in love, but they couldn't have been. If they'd truly been in love, wouldn't he have fought for everything they'd discussed and dreamed of?

Maybe he'd been playing her the entire time. A twenty-year-old boy moving up the ladder of success really didn't have much use for a poor staff member. She was a virgin and an easy target. Maybe that's all he'd been after.

But she really didn't think so. She'd grown up around Will and James. James was the player, not Will. Will had always been more on the straight and narrow, the rule follower.

And he'd followed those rules right to the point of breaking her heart. She should have seen it coming, really. After their mother passed away, Will did every single thing he could to please his father, as if overcompensating for the loss of a parent.

Yet there was that little girl fantasy in her that had held out hope that Will would see her as more, that he would fall in love with her and they could live happily ever after.

Catalina sighed. That was long ago; they were different people now and the past couldn't be redone…and all those other stupid sayings that really didn't help in the grand scheme of things.

And it was because she was still so tied up in knots over this man that she needed to escape Alma, fulfill her own dreams and forget her life here. She was damn good at designing and she couldn't wait to burn her uniforms and sensible shoes, roast a marshmallow over them and move on.

"We're not going anywhere for a while."

Catalina jerked her head around. Will was standing on the bottom step, his hands braced above him on the doorframe. The muscles in his biceps flexed, drawing her attention to his raw masculinity. No matter how much the inner turmoil was caused by their rocky relationship, Catalina couldn't deny that the sight of his body turned her on like no other man had ever been able to do.

"There's some major damage to the starboard side. I thought maybe I could get it moving, but the mechanics are fried. I can only assume the boat was hit by lightning as well as banging into the dock repeatedly."

Catalina gripped the plush comforter beneath her palms. "How long will we be stuck here?"

"I have no clue."

He stepped farther into the room and raked a hand over his messy hair. Will always had perfectly placed hair, but something about that rumpled state made her hotter for him.

"The radio isn't working, either," he added as he sank down on the edge of the bed, facing her. "Are you ready for some pain medicine since we're going to be here awhile?"

She was going to need something a lot stronger if she was going to be forced to stick this out with him for too long. Hours? Days? How long would she have to keep her willpower on high alert?

"I probably better," she admitted. "My ankle's throbbing pretty good now."

Will went to the bathroom. She heard him rummaging around in a cabinet, then the faucet. When he strode back across the open room, Catalina couldn't keep her eyes off his bare chest. Why did he have to be so beautiful and enticing? She wanted to be over her attraction for this man. Anything beyond what happened in that cabin would only lead to more heartache because Will would never choose anyone over his father and Rowling Energy and she sure as hell wasn't staying in Alma to clean toilets the rest of her life waiting to gain his attention.

Catalina took the pills and the small paper cup of water he offered. Hoping the medicine kicked in soon, she swallowed it as Will eased back down beside her on the bed.

"Dammit," he muttered, placing his hand on the shin of her good leg. "If we hadn't been arguing—"

"We've argued for weeks," she told him with a half smile. "It was an accident. If anyone is to blame it's me for not watching where I was going and for trying to stomp off in a fit."

"Were you throwing a fit?" he asked. "I don't remember."

Catalina lifted an eyebrow. "You're mocking me now."

Shaking his head, he slid his hand up and down her shin. "Not at all. I just remember thinking how sexy you looked when you were angry. You have this red tint to your cheeks. Or it could've been the great sex. Either way, you looked hot."

"Was that before or after I was sprawled face first in the sand?" she joked, trying to lighten the mood.

"You can't kill sexy, Cat, even if you're eating sand."

The slight grin he offered her eased her worry. Maybe they could spend the day here and actually be civil without worrying about the sexual tension consuming them. Maybe they had taken the edge off and could move on.

Well, they could obviously move on, but would this feeling of want ever go away? Because if anything, since they'd been intimate, Catalina craved him even more.

So now what could she do? There was nowhere to hide and definitely nowhere to run in her current state.

As she looked into Will's mesmerizing eyes, her worry spiked once again because he stared back at her like a man starved...and she was the main course.

Thirteen

Thankfully the kitchen was fully stocked and the electricity that fed the appliances hadn't been fried because right now Will needed to concentrate on something other than how perfect Cat looked in his bed.

He'd come to the kitchen a while ago to figure out what they should do for dinner. Apparently the pain pills had kicked in because Cat was resting peacefully, even letting out soft moans every now and then as she slept.

It was those damn moans that had his shorts growing tighter and his teeth grinding as he attempted to control himself. He'd heard those groans earlier, up close and personal in his ear as she'd wrapped her body around his.

The experience was one he would never forget.

Will put together the chicken and rice casserole that his mother used to make. Yes, they'd had a chef when he was a child, but James and Will had always loved this dish and every now and then, Will threw it together just to remember his mother. He still missed her, but it was the little things that would remind him of her and make him smile.

Setting the timer on the oven, Will glanced back to the sleeping beauty in his bed. His mother would have loved Cat. She wouldn't have cared if she was the maid or—

What the hell? How did that thought sneak right in without his realizing the path his mind was taking? It didn't matter what his mother would have thought of Cat. He wasn't getting down on one knee and asking her into the family.

He needed to get a grip because his hormones and his mind were jumbling up all together and he was damn confused. Sleeping with Cat should have satisfied this urge to claim her, but instead of passing, the longing only grew.

With the casserole baking for a good bit, Will opted to grab a shower. He smelled like sex, sand and sweat. Maybe a cold shower would help wake him up to the reality that he'd let Cat go once. Just because they slept together didn't mean she was ready to give this a go again. And was that what he wanted? In all honesty did he want to try for this once more and risk hurting her, hurting himself, further?

He was making a damn casserole for pity's sake. What type of man had he become? He'd turned into some warped version of a homemaker and, even worse, he was perfectly okay with this feeling.

Before he went to the shower, he wanted to try the radio one more time. There had to be a way to communicate back to the mainland. Unfortunately, no matter which knobs he turned, which buttons he hit, nothing sparked to life. Resigned to the fact they were indeed stuck, Will went to his master suite bathroom.

As he stripped from his shorts and stepped into the spacious, open shower, he wondered if maybe being stranded with Cat wasn't some type of sign. Maybe they were supposed to be together with no outside forces hindering their feelings or judgment.

And honestly, Will wanted to see what happened with Cat. He wanted to give this another chance because they were completely different people than they were before and he was in total control of his life. She was that sliver of happiness that kept him smiling and their verbal sparring never failed to get him worked up.

No other woman matched him the way she did and he was going to take this opportunity of being stranded and use every minute to his advantage. He'd prove to her he was different because just telling her he was really wouldn't convince her. He needed to show her, to let her see for herself that he valued her, that he wanted her. He'd never stopped wanting her.

While he may want to use this private time to seduce the hell out of her, Will knew those hormones were going to have to take a back seat because Cat was worth more and they were long overdue for some relaxing, laid back time. And then maybe they could discuss just what the hell was happening between them.

Whatever that smell was, Catalina really hoped she wasn't just dreaming about it. As soon as she opened her eyes, she was greeted with a beautiful orange glow across the horizon. The sun was setting, and lying in this bed, Will's bed, watching such beauty was a moment she wanted to lock in her mind forever.

She rolled over, wincing as the pain in her ankle reminded her she was injured. The ice bag had melted and slid off the pillow she'd propped it on. As soon as she sat up, she examined her injury, pleased to see the swelling had gone down some.

"Oh, good. Dinner is almost ready."

Catalina smoothed her hair away from her face and smiled as Will scooped up something from a glass pan.

"I tried the radio again," he told her. "It didn't work. The whole system is fried."

Catalina sighed. As much as she wanted to get back home, she couldn't deny the pleasure she'd experienced here, despite the injury. She had a feeling she was seeing the true Will, the man who wasn't all business and power trips, but a man who cared for her whether he was ready to admit it or not.

"Someone will come for us," she told him. "Besides, with you cooking and letting me nap, you're spoiling me. Dinner smells a lot like that chicken dish you made me for our first date."

Will grinned back at her and winked. *Winked*. What had she woken to? Will in the kitchen cooking and actually relaxed enough to wink and smile as if he hadn't a care in the world.

"It is," he confirmed. "I'll bring it to you so don't worry about getting up."

"I actually need to go to the restroom."

In seconds, Will was at her side helping her up. When he went to lift her in his arms, she pushed against him.

"Just let me lean on you, okay? No need to carry me."

Wrapping an arm around her waist, Will helped her stand. "How's the ankle feeling?"

"Really sore, but better than it was." She tested it, pulling back when the sharp throbbing started again.

"Putting weight on it still isn't a smart move, but hopefully it will be much better by tomorrow."

Will assisted her across the room, but when they reached the bathroom doorway, she placed a hand on his chest. "I can take it from here."

No way was he assisting her in the bathroom. She'd like to hold onto some shred of dignity. Besides, she needed a few moments to herself to regain mental footing since she was stuck playing house with the only man she'd ever envisioned spending forever with.

"I'll wait right here in case you need something," he told her. "Don't lock the door."

With a mock salute, Catalina hobbled into the bathroom and closed the door. The scent of some kind of masculine soap assaulted her senses. A damp towel hung over the bar near the shower. He'd made use of the time she'd been asleep. Her eyes darted to the bathtub that looked as if it could seat about four people. What she wouldn't give to crawl into that and relax in some hot water, with maybe a good book or a glass of wine. When was the last time she'd indulged in such utterly selfish desires?

Oh, yeah, when she'd stripped Will naked and had her way with him in the old cabin earlier today.

A tap on the door jerked her from her thoughts. "Are you okay?"

"Yeah. Give me a minute."

A girl couldn't even fantasize in peace around here. She still needed time to process what their intimacy meant and the new, unexpected path their relationship had taken. Will had most likely thought of what happened the entire time she'd been asleep. Of course he was a man, so he probably wasn't giving their encounter the amount of mind space she would.

Minutes later, Catalina opened the door to find Will leaning against the frame. Once again he wrapped an arm around her and steered her toward the bed.

"I can eat at the table." She hated leaning on him, touching him when her nerves were still a jumbled up mess. "I'm already up. That bed is too beautiful to eat on."

In no time he'd placed their plates on the table with two glasses of wine…again, her favorite. A red Riesling.

"If I didn't know better, I'd say you stocked this kitchen just for me," she joked as she took her first sip and knew it wasn't the cheap stuff she kept stocked in her fridge.

"I did buy a lot of things I knew you liked." His fork froze midway to his mouth as he looked up at her. "At least, you liked this stuff four years ago."

For a split second, he seemed unsure. Will was always confident in everything, but when discussing her tastes, he suddenly doubted himself. Why did she find that so adorable?

She felt a shiver travel up her spine. She didn't have time for these adorable moments and couldn't allow them to influence her where this man was concerned. That clean break she wanted couldn't happen if she let herself be charmed like that.

They ate in silence, but Catalina was surprised the strain wasn't there. Everything seemed…normal. Something was up. He wasn't trying to seduce her, he wasn't bringing up the past or any other hot topic.

What had happened while she'd been asleep? Will had suddenly transformed into some sort of caretaker with husbandlike qualities.

But after a while she couldn't take the silence anymore. Catalina dropped her fork to her empty plate.

"That was amazing. Now, tell me what's going through your mind."

Will drained his glass before setting it back down and focusing on her. "Right now I'm thinking I could use dessert."

"I mean why are you so quiet?"

Shrugging, he picked up their plates and put them in the kitchen. When he brought back the wine bottle, she put a hand over hers to stop him from filling her glass back up.

"If I need more pain pills later, it's best I don't have any more even though I only took a half pill."

Nodding, he set the bottle on the table and sat across from her again.

"Don't ignore the question."

A smile kicked up at the corners of his mouth. "I'm plotting."

Catalina eased back in her seat, crossing her arms over her chest. "You're always plotting. I take it I'm still in the crosshairs?"

His eyes narrowed in that sexy, toe-curling way that demanded a woman take notice. "You've never been anywhere else."

Her heart beat faster. When he said those things she wanted to believe him. She wanted to be the object of his every desire and fantasy. And when he looked at her as if nothing else in the world mattered, she wanted to stay in that line of sight forever, though she knew all of that was a very naïve way of thinking.

"I only set out to seduce you," he went on, toying with the stem on his glass. "I wanted you in my bed more than anything. And now that I've had you…"

Catalina wished she'd had that second glass of wine after all. "What are you saying?"

His intense stare locked onto her. "We're different people. Maybe we're at a stage where we can learn from the past and see…"

It took every ounce of her willpower not to lean forward in anticipation as his words trailed off yet again. "And see what?" she finally asked.

"Maybe I want to see where we could go."

Catalina gasped. "You're not serious."

Those heavy-lidded eyes locked onto her. "I can't let you go now that I know how right we are together."

Her eyes shifted away and focused on the posh living space while she tried to process all he was saying.

Her mother's words of warning from years ago echoed in Catalina's mind. How could she fall for this man with his smooth words and irresistible charm? Hadn't her mother done the same thing with Patrick?

No. Will wasn't Patrick and Catalina was not her mother.

To her knowledge, Will, even to this day, had absolutely no idea what had transpired when he'd been a young boy right around the time of his mother's death. That hollow pit in Catalina's stomach deepened. Had the affair been the catalyst in Mrs. Rowling's death?

"Why now?" she asked, turning back to face him. "Why should I let you in now after all this time? Is it because I'm convenient? Because I'm still single or because you're settling?"

Why was fate dangling this right in front of her face when she'd finally decided to move on? It had taken her years to get up the nerve to really move forward with her dream and now that she'd decided to take a chance, Will wanted back in?

"Trust me, you're anything but convenient," he laughed.

"I've busted my butt trying to think of ways to get your attention."

Catalina swallowed. "But why?"

"Because you want this just as much as I do," he whispered.

Catalina stared down at her hands clasped in her lap. "We're at the age now that our wants don't always matter." Letting her attention drift back up, she locked her eyes on him. "We both have different goals, Will. In the end, nothing has really changed."

"On that we can agree." Will came to his feet, crossed to her side of the table and loomed over her. His hands came to rest on the back of her chair on either side of her shoulders. "In the end, I'll still want you and you'll still want me. The rest can be figured out later."

Before she could say anything, he'd scooped her up in his arms. "Don't say a word," he chided. "I want to carry you, so just let me. Enjoy this moment, that's all I'm asking. Don't think about who we are away from here. Let me care for you the way you deserve."

His warm breath washed over her face as she stared back at him. He didn't move, he just waited for her reply.

What could she say? He was right. They both wanted each other, but was that all this boiled down to? There were so many other outside factors driving a wedge between them. Did she honestly believe that just because he said so things would be different?

Catalina stared into those eyes and for once she saw hope; she saw a need that had nothing to do with sex.

Resting her head on his shoulder, Catalina whispered, "One of us is going to get hurt."

Fourteen

Catalina leaned back against Will's chest as they settled onto the oversized plush sofa on the top deck. The full moon provided enough light and just the perfect ambiance; even Will couldn't have planned it better.

Granted he didn't like that the yacht was damaged or that Catalina had been injured, but the feel of her wrapped in his arms, their legs intertwined, even as he was careful of her ankle, was everything he'd wanted since he let her walk away so long ago.

Will laced his hands over her stomach and smiled when she laid her hands atop his.

"It's so quiet and peaceful," she murmured. "The stars are so vibrant here. I guess I never pay much attention in Alma."

"One of these days you're going to have your own maid, your own staff," he stated firmly. "You deserve to be pampered for all the hours you work without asking for anything in return. You work too hard."

"I do," she agreed. "I have so many things I want to do with my life and working is what keeps me motivated."

A strand of her hair danced in the breeze, tickling his cheek, but he didn't mind. Any way he could touch her and be closer was fine with him. She wasn't trying to ignore this pull and she'd actually relaxed fully against him. This is what they needed. The simplicity, the privacy.

"What are your goals, Cat?"

"I'd love a family someday."

The wistfulness in her tone had him wanting to fulfill those wishes. Will knew he'd never be able to sit back and watch her be with someone else, make a life and a family with another man.

"What else?" he urged. "I want to know all of your dreams."

She stiffened in his arms. Will stroked her fingers with his, wanting to keep her relaxed, keep her locked into this euphoric moment.

"It's just me, Cat." He purposely softened his tone. "Once upon a time we shared everything with each other."

"We did. I'm just more cautious now."

Because of him. He knew he'd damaged that innocence in her, he knew full well that she was a totally different woman because of his selfish actions. And that fact was something he'd have to live with for the rest of his life. All he could do was try to make things better now and move forward.

"I shouldn't have let you go," he muttered before he could think.

"Everything happens for a reason."

Will didn't miss the hint of pain in her tone. "Maybe so, but I should've fought for you, for us."

"Family has always been your top priority, Will. You've been that way since your mother passed. You threw yourself into pleasing your father and James ran wild. Everyone grieves differently and it's affected your relationships over the years."

Will shouldn't have been surprised that she'd analyzed him and his brother so well. Cat had always been so in tune with other people's feelings. Had he ever done that for her? Had he ever thought of her feelings if they didn't coincide with his own wants and needs?

"I never wanted you hurt." Yet he'd killed her spirit anyway. "I have no excuse for what I did. Nothing I say can reverse time or knock sense into the man I was four years ago."

"Everything that happened made me a better person." She shifted a bit and lifted her ankle to resettle it over the edge of the sofa. "I poured myself into new things, found out who I really am on my own. I never would've done that had I been with you."

Will squeezed her tighter. "I wouldn't have let you lose yourself, Cat. Had you been with me I would've pushed you to do whatever you wanted."

She tipped her head back and met his gaze. "You wouldn't have let me work. You would've wanted the perfect, doting wife."

There was a ring of truth to her words. He most likely would have tried to push her into doing what he thought was best.

"I wasn't good to you." He swallowed. "You were better off without me, but it killed me to let you go, knowing you'd be fine once you moved on."

Silence settled heavily around them before she finally said, "I wasn't fine."

"You were dating a man two months after we broke up."

Cat turned back around, facing the water. "I needed to date, I needed to move on in any way that I could and try to forget you. When I was alone my mind would wander and I'd start to remember how happy I was with you. I needed to fill that void in any way I possibly could."

Will swallowed. He'd hated seeing her with another man, hated knowing he was the one who drove her into another's arms.

"I slept with him."

Her words cut through the darkness and straight to his heart. "I don't want—"

"I slept with him because I was trying to forget you," she went on as if he hadn't said a word. "I was ready to give myself to you, then you chose to obey your father once again at my expense. When I started dating Bryce, I mistook his affection for love. I knew I was on the rebound, but I wanted so badly to be with someone who valued me, who wanted to be with me and put me first."

Those raw, heartfelt words crippled him. He'd had no idea just how much damage he'd caused. All this time, she'd been searching for anyone to put her at the top of their priority list when he'd shoved her to the bottom of his.

"Afterward I cried," she whispered. "I hated that I'd given away something so precious and I hated even more that I still wished I'd given it to you."

Her honesty gutted him. Will wished more than anything he could go back and make changes, wished he could go back and be the man she needed him to be.

But he could be honest now, he could open up. She'd shared such a deep, personal secret, he knew she deserved to know why he'd let her go so easily.

"I had to let you go."

"I know, your father—"

"No." Will adjusted himself in the seat so he could face her better. "I need you to know this, I need you to listen to what I'm saying. I let you go because of my father, but not for the reasons you think."

The moon cast enough of a glow for Will to see Cat's dark eyes widen. "What?"

"I let you go to save you. My father's threats..." Will shook his head, still angry over the way he'd let his father manipulate him. "As soon as I let you go, I was plotting to get you back, to put my father in his place. I didn't care how long it took, didn't care what I had to do."

Cat stared back at him, and he desperately wanted to know what was swirling around in her head. There was so much hurt between them, so many questions and years of resentment. Will hated his father for putting him in this position, but he hated even more the way Cat had been the victim in all of this.

"Your father threatened me, didn't he?" Cat asked, her voice low, yet firm. "He held me over your head? Is that why you let me go?"

Swallowing the lump of guilt, Will nodded.

Cat sat up, swung her feet over the side and braced her hands on either side of her hips. Will lifted his leg out of her way and brought his knee up to give her enough room to sit. He waited while she stared down at the deck. Silence and moonlight surrounded them, bathing them in a peace that he knew neither of them felt.

"Talk to me." He couldn't handle the uncertainty. "I don't want you going through this alone."

A soft laugh escaped her as she kept her gaze averted. "But you didn't care that I went through this alone four years ago."

"Dammit, Cat. I couldn't let you get hurt. He had the ability to ruin you and I wasn't going to put my needs ahead of yours."

When she threw him a glance over her shoulder, Will's gut tightened at the moisture gathered in her eyes. "You didn't put my needs first at all. You didn't give me a chance to fight for us and you took the easy way out."

Raking a hand over his hair, Will blew out a breath. "I didn't take the easy way," he retorted. "I took the hardest way straight through hell to keep you safe and to work on getting you back."

She continued to stare, saying nothing. Moments later her eyes widened. "Wait," she whispered. "How did Bella come into play?"

"You know I never would've married her. That was all a farce to begin with." Will shifted closer, reaching out to smooth her hair back behind her ear. "And once I kissed you, I knew exactly who I wanted, who I needed."

Cat started to stand, winced and sat back down. Will said nothing as he pushed his leg around her, once again straddling her from behind. He pulled her back against his chest and leaned on the plush cushions. Even though she remained rigid, he knew the only way to get her to soften was for him to be patient. He'd waited four years; he was the epitome of patient.

Wrapping his arms around her, he whispered in her ear. "I messed up," he admitted. "I only wanted to protect you and went about it the wrong way. Don't shut me

out now, Cat. We have too much between us. This goes
so much deeper than either of us realizes and I won't let
my father continue to ruin what we have."

Dammit, somewhere along the way to a heated affair Will had developed stronger feelings, a deeper bond
with Cat than he'd anticipated. And now that he knew
he wanted more from her, he was close to losing it all.

"And what do we have, Will?" Her words came out
on a choked sob.

"What do you want?"

What do you want?

Catalina couldn't hold in the tension another second.
There was only so much one person could handle and
Will's simple question absolutely deflated her. Melting
back against his body once more, she swallowed the
emotion burning her throat.

"I want…" Catalina shut her eyes, trying to figure
out all the thoughts fighting for head space. "I don't
know now. Yesterday I knew exactly what I wanted. I
was ready to leave Alma to get it."

Will's fingertips slid up and down her bare arms,
causing her body to tremble beneath his delicate touch.
"And now? What do you want now, Cat?"

Everything.

"I don't want to make things harder for you," he went
on. "But I'm not backing down. Not this time."

And there was a portion of her heart that didn't
want him to. How could she be so torn? How could
two dreams be pulling her in completely different directions?

Because the harder she'd tried to distance herself
from him, the more she was being pulled back in.

"I'm afraid," she whispered. "I can't make promises and I'm not ready to accept them from you, either."

His hands stilled for the briefest of moments before he kissed the top of her head. Catalina turned her cheek to rest against his chest, relishing the warmth of his body, the strong steady heartbeat beneath her. Part of her wanted to hate him for his actions years ago, the other part of her wanted to cry for the injustice of it all.

But a good portion of her wanted to forgive him, to believe him when he said that he'd sacrificed himself to keep her safe. Why did he have to be so damn noble and why hadn't he told her to begin with? He didn't have to fight that battle all on his own. Maybe she could have saved him, too.

Catalina closed her eyes as the yacht rocked steadily to the soothing rhythm of the waves. She wanted to lock this moment in time and live here forever. Where there were no outside forces trying to throw obstacles in their way and the raw honesty…

No. She still carried a secret that he didn't know and how could she ever tell him? How could she ever reveal the fact that his father had had an affair with her mother? Would he hate her for knowing?

"Will, I need—"

"We're done talking. I just want to hold you. Nothing else matters right now."

Turning a bit more in his arms, Catalina looked up into those vibrant eyes that had haunted her dreams for years. "Make love to me, Will. I don't care about anything else. Not when I can be with you."

In one swift, powerful move, he had her straddling his lap. Catalina hissed a breath when her ankle bumped his thigh.

"Dammit. Sorry, Cat."

She offered him a smile, stroking the pad of her thumb along the worry lines between his brows. "I'm fine," she assured him as she slid the ties at the side of her dress free. "I don't want to think about my injury, why we're stuck here or what's waiting for us when we get back. All I want is to feel you against me."

Will took in the sight of her as she continued to work out of her clothing. When his hands spanned her waist, she arched against his touch.

He leaned forward, resting his forehead against her chest as he whispered, "You're more than I deserve and everything I've ever wanted."

Framing his face with her hands, Catalina lifted his head until she could look him in the eyes. "No more talking," she reminded him with a soft kiss to his lips. "No more talking tonight."

Tomorrow, or whenever they were able to get off this island, she'd tell him about his father. But for now, she'd take this gift she'd been given and worry about the ugly truth, and how they would handle it, later.

Fifteen

By the second day, Catalina still hadn't told Will the truth. How could she reveal such a harsh reality when they'd been living in passionate bliss on a beautiful island in some fantasy?

They'd both fiddled with the radio and tried their cell phones from various spots on the island, but nothing was going through. She wasn't going to panic quite yet. They had plenty of food and for a bit, she could pretend this was a dream vacation with the man she'd fallen in love with.

Will rolled over in bed, wrapping his arm around her and settling against her back. "I'd like to say I can't wait to get off this island, but waking up with you in my arms is something I could get used to."

His husky tone filled her ear. The coarse hair on his chest tickled her back, but she didn't mind. She loved the feel of Will next to her.

"I'm getting pretty spoiled, too." She snuggled deeper into his embrace. "I'm never going to want to leave."

"Maybe that's how I want you to be," he replied, nipping her shoulder.

"We can't stay here forever," she laughed.

"As long as you don't leave Alma, I'm okay with going back."

A sliver of reality crept back in. Catalina shifted so that she could roll over in his arms and face him.

"I don't plan on working as a maid forever," she informed him, staring into his eyes. "And after what you told me about your father, I think it's best if I don't work there anymore. I can't work for a man who completely altered my future. I stayed with James because I adore him and I moved on to Patrick because I needed the job, but now that I know the full truth, I can't stay there."

Will propped himself up on his elbow and peered down at her. "I understand, but stay in Alma. Stay with me."

"And do what?" she asked, already knowing this conversation was going to divide them. "I have goals, Will. Goals that I can't ignore simply because we're... I don't even know what this is between us right now."

"Do you need a label?" he asked.

Part of her wanted to call this something. Maybe then she could justify her feelings for a man who'd let her go so easily before.

She had no idea what she was going to do once she got back to Alma. Working for Patrick was not going to happen. She'd put up with his arrogance for too long. Thankfully she'd only worked for him a short time because up until recently, James had been the one occupying the Playa del Onda home. Catalina had had a hard enough time working for Patrick knowing what she did about her mother, but now knowing he'd manipulated his son and crushed their relationship, Catalina couldn't go back there. Never again.

So where did that leave her? She didn't think she was quite ready to head out with her designs and start pursuing her goal. She had a few more things she'd like to complete before she made that leap.

"What's going through your mind?" Will asked, studying her face.

"You know the sewing set you got me?"

Will nodded.

"You have no idea how much that touched me." Catalina raked her hand through his blond hair and trailed her fingertips down his jaw, his neck. "I've been sewing in my spare time. Making things for myself, for my mother. It's been such a great escape and when I saw what you'd gotten me, I…"

Catalina shook her head and fell back against the bed. She stared up at the ceiling and wished she could find the right words to tell him how much she appreciated the gift.

"So you're saying it was a step up from the flowers?" he joked.

Shifting her gaze to him, her heart tightened at his playful smile. "I may have cried," she confessed. "That was the sweetest gift ever."

Will settled over her, his hands resting on either side of her head. "It was meant more as a joke," he said with a teasing smile. "And maybe I wanted to remind you of what we did in the utility room."

Cat smacked his chest. "As if I could've forgotten. That's all I could think about and you know it."

He gave her a quick kiss before he eased back. "It's all I could think of, too, if that helps."

Catalina wrapped her arms around his neck, threading her fingers through his hair. "What are we going to do when we get back?"

"We're going to take this one day at a time because I'm not screwing this up again."

"We can't seem to function in normal life."

Will's forehead rested against hers as he let out a sigh. "Trust me, Cat. I've fought too hard to get you back. I'm going to fight just as hard to keep you."

Catalina prayed that was true, because all too soon she was going to have to reveal the final secret between them if she wanted a future with this man.

Cat lay on the deck sunbathing in that skimpy bikini, which was positively driving him out of his mind. Right now he didn't give a damn that the radio was beyond repair or that their phones weren't getting a signal. For two days they'd made love, stayed in bed and talked, spending nearly every single moment together.

Perhaps that's why he was in such agony. He knew exactly what that lush body felt like against his own. He knew how amazingly they fit together with no barriers between them.

Will couldn't recall the last time he'd taken this much time away from work. Surprisingly he wasn't getting twitchy. He'd set his plan into motion a couple months ago for Rowling Energy and it shouldn't be too much longer before everything he'd ever wanted clicked into place like a perfectly, methodically plotted puzzle.

Will folded his arms behind his head and relaxed on the seat opposite Cat. But just as he closed his eyes, the soft hum of an engine had him jumping to his feet.

"Do you hear that?" he asked, glancing toward the horizon.

Cat sat up, her hand shielding her eyes as she glanced in the same direction. "Oh, there's another boat."

Will knew that boat and he knew who would be on board. Good thing his brother hadn't left to go back to training for football yet because that meant he could come to their rescue. Which was what he was doing right now.

"Looks like our fairy tale is over," Catalina muttered.

He glanced her way. "It's not over," he corrected. "It's just beginning."

As James's yacht closed the distance between them, Will slid his shoes back on. "Stay here. I'll wave James to the other side of the dock where the damage isn't as bad. And I'll carry you on board once we're secure."

Cat rolled her eyes and reached for her wrap draped across the back of the white sofa. "I can walk, Will. My ankle is sore, but it's much better than it was."

Will wasn't going to argue. He'd win in the end regardless.

As soon as James was near enough, Will hopped up onto the dock and made his way toward the other end. By the time James came to a stop, Bella was at his side, a worried look etched across her face.

"Coast guard has arrived," James said, coming up behind his wife.

"I figured you'd come along sooner or later," Will replied.

James took in the damage to the dock and the yacht. "Damn, you've got a mess. That must've been one hell of a storm. It rained and there was some thunder and wind in Alma, but no damage."

"Let me go get our things," Will told his brother. "I need to carry Cat, too. She's hurt."

"Oh no," Bella cried. "What happened?"

"I fell."

Will turned to see Cat leaning over the side of the yacht. "You're supposed to be sitting down," he called back.

"I'm fine. I will need some help off this thing, but I can walk if I go slow."

Will shook his head. "I'll carry her," he told his brother. "Give me a few minutes to get our personal stuff gathered."

Once they transferred everything Will and Cat needed to his brother's yacht and Will carried a disgruntled Cat on board, they were ready to head out. The trip back to Alma was filled with questions from Bella and James. Their worry was touching and Will actually found himself loving this newfound bond he and his brother shared. This is what he'd been missing for years. This is what their grief had torn apart after their mother had died. But now they were slowly making their way back to each other.

"I wasn't quite sure which island you went to," James said as they drew nearer to Alma's coastline. "I went to two last night and had to start again today when I couldn't find you."

"Did you tell anyone what was going on?" Will asked.

"No." James maneuvered the boat and pulled back on the throttle. "Bella and I are the only ones who know where you were."

Will was relieved nobody else knew. He didn't want to share Cat or their relationship with anyone just yet. He wanted to bask in their privacy for a bit longer.

"Dammit," James muttered as they neared what was supposed to be a private dock where Alma's rich and famous kept their boats. "The damn press is here."

"What for?" Cat asked, her eyes widening.

"There were a few reporters here when I left earlier,"

James stated as he steered the yacht in. "They were speculating because Will's yacht had been missing for a few days and they knew a storm had come through. They asked me where you were and I ignored them."

Will groaned. So much for that privacy he'd been clinging to. "Don't they have anything better to cover? Like the fact Juan Carlos is going to be crowned king in a few weeks? Do they seriously have to focus on me?"

Cat's eyes remained fixed on the throng of reporters and cameras turning in their direction.

Will crouched down before her seat and smoothed her hair back from her face. "Ignore them. No matter what they say, do not make a comment. They'll forget about this by tomorrow and we can move on."

Her eyes sought his and she offered him a smile. "Ignore them. That I can do."

Will stood back up and offered her his hand. "I'm going to at least put my arm around you so you can put some of your weight on me. Anyone looking will just think I'm helping you."

"I'll carry her bag," Bella offered. "I'll go first. Maybe they'll focus on James and me. I can always just start discussing my upcoming fund-raiser for my foundation next weekend. I'm okay with yanking the reporters' chains, too."

Will couldn't help but laugh at Bella's spunk. She was the perfect match for his brother.

As they made their way down the dock, Will kept his arm secured around Cat's waist. James and Bella took the lead, holding hands as they wedged through the sea of nosy people.

The reporters seemed to all start shouting at once.

"Where have you been for three days?"

"Was your yacht damaged by the storm?"

"Were you stranded somewhere?"

"Who is with you, Will?"

The questions kept coming as Will tried to shield Cat from the press. The whispers and murmurs infuriated him. Seriously? Wasn't there other newsworthy stuff happening in Alma right now? Dammit, this was one major drawback to being a wealthy, well-known businessman. And if he thought for a second he could have any privacy with Cat now that they were back, he was living in a fantasy.

When he heard someone say the word "staff" he clenched his jaw. He wouldn't respond. That's what they wanted: some type of reaction. He heard his father's name and for reasons unbeknownst to Will, the gossipmongers were starting to piece things together rather quickly. Where the hell would they have seen Cat? On occasion his father would allow a few press members to attend certain parties thrown by the Rowlings if there was a charity involved. Cat had been James's maid, too, though.

Will groaned as he kept his sights on his brother's back as the foursome pushed through to the waiting car in the distance. They couldn't get there fast enough for Will.

"Is your mistress a member of your family's staff, Mr. Rowling?"

The rude question had Cat stiffening at his side. "Keep going," he murmured. "Almost there."

"Wasn't she working for your brother?"

"Is she on Patrick's staff?"

"How long have you been seeing your father's maid?"

"Weren't you just engaged to your brother's wife?"

"What does your father think about you and his maid?"

Will snapped. "This isn't like that. You're all making a mistake."

Catalina's gasp had him jerking his gaze toward her. "Dammit," he muttered beneath his breath. "You know that's not what I mean."

Those damn words echoed from the last time he'd said them to her. And this time they were just as damaging when taken out of context.

Easing back from his side, Cat kept her eyes on his. "I'm not sure, Will. Because only moments ago you said ignore them and you said we'd take this one day at a time. We've only been back in Alma five minutes and you're already referring to me as a mistake."

Will raked a hand through his hair. From the corner of his eye he spotted James and Bella standing close. For once the reporters weren't saying a word. They waited, no doubt hoping to really get something juicy for their headlines.

"Marry me."

Okay, he hadn't meant to blurt that out there, but now that the words hovered between them, he wasn't sorry. Maybe Cat would see just how serious he was about them.

"Marry you?" she asked, her brows drawn in. "You're not serious."

He stepped forward and took her hand. "We are not a mistake, Cat. You know we're perfect together. Why wouldn't you?"

Cat stared back at him, and then shook her head and let out a soft laugh. "This is ridiculous. You don't mean this proposal so why would you do this to me? Why would you ask that in front of all these people? To prove them wrong? Because you got caught with the maid and you're trying to glamorize it?"

"Dammit, Cat, this has nothing to do with anyone else. We can talk later, in private."

He didn't want to hash this out here in front of the press. And he sure as hell didn't want to sound as if he was backpedaling because he'd chosen the worst possible time to blurt out a proposal.

Crossing her arms over her chest, she tipped her chin up just a notch, but enough for him to know she was good and pissed. "Would you have proposed to me if all of these people hadn't been around? Later tonight when we were alone, would you have asked me to marry you?"

Will gritted his teeth, clenched his fists at his side and honestly had no reply. He had absolutely no idea what to say. He didn't want to have such an intimate talk in front of the whole country, because that's exactly what was happening. The press would no doubt splash this all over the headlines.

"That's what I thought." Cat's soft tone was full of hurt. "I'd say it's officially over between us."

When she turned, she winced, but just as Will reached to help her, Bella stepped forward and slowly ushered Cat to the car. James moved in next to Will and ordered the press away. Will didn't hear much, didn't comprehend what was going on because in the span of just a few minutes, he'd gone from deliriously happy and planning his future, to seeing that future walk away from him after he'd hurt her, called her a mistake, once again.

This time, he knew there would be no winning her back.

Sixteen

"What the hell is this?"

Will turned away from his office view to face his father, who stood on the other side of his desk with a folder in his hand. Will had been waiting for this moment. But he hadn't expected to feel this enormous pit of emptiness inside.

"I see you received the notice regarding your shares in Rowling Energy." Will folded his arms across his chest and leveled his father's gaze. "Your votes in the company are no longer valid. I held an emergency meeting with the other stockholders and we came to the decision."

Patrick's face reddened. "How dare you. What kind of son did I raise that he would turn around and treat his father like this?"

"You raised the son who fought for what he wanted." Will's blood pressure soared as he thought of all he'd lost and all he was still fighting for. "You raised a son who watched his father put business first, above family, and to hell with the rest of the world. I'm taking Rowling Energy into new territory and I need sole control. I'm done being jerked around by you."

Patrick rested his palms on the desk and leaned in. "No, you'd rather be jerked around by my maid. You two made quite a scene yesterday—it made headlines. You're becoming an embarrassment and tarnishing the Rowling name."

Will laughed. "What I do in my personal life is not your concern. You poked your nose in years ago when you threatened to dismiss Catalina if I didn't dump her. I won't be manipulated ever again and you will leave Cat alone. If I even think you've tried to—"

"Knock off the threats," his father shouted as he pushed off the desk. "Your little maid quit on me and has really left me in a bind. If you were smart, you'd stay away from her. You two get cozy and she quits. I don't believe in coincidences. Those Iberra women are nothing but gold diggers."

Will stood up straighter, dropped his arms to his sides. "What did you say?"

Patrick waved a hand in the air, shaking his head. "Forget it."

"No. You said 'those Iberra women.' What did you mean?"

Will knew Cat's mother had worked for Patrick years ago. Maria had been around when James and Will had been young, when their mother was still alive.

"What did Maria do that you would call her a gold digger?" Will asked when his father remained silent.

Still, Patrick said nothing.

Realization dawned on Will. "No. Tell me you didn't have an affair with Maria."

"Every man has a moment of weakness," Patrick stated simply. "I expect this past weekend was yours."

Rage boiled to the surface. Will clenched his fists. "You slept with Cat's mother while my mother was still alive? Did Mum know about the affair?"

The thought of his sweet, caring mother being betrayed tore through Will's heart. Part of him prayed she never knew the ugly acts his father had committed.

"She found out the day she died." Patrick let out a sigh, his eyes darting to the ground. "We were arguing about it when she left that night."

For once the great Patrick Rowling looked defeated. Which was nothing less than he deserved. Will's heart was absolutely crushed. He reached out, gripped the back of his desk chair and tried to think rationally here. Finding out your father had an affair with the mother of a woman you had fallen for was shocking enough. But to add to the intensity, his mother had died as a result of the affair.

Dread settled deep in Will's his gut. Did Cat know of this affair? Surely not. Surely she would have told him or at least hinted at the knowledge. Would this crush her, too?

"Get out," Will said in a low, powerful tone as he kept his eyes on the blotter on his desk. "Get the hell out of my office and be glad my freezing your voting rights in this company is all I'm doing to you."

Patrick didn't move. Will brought his gaze up and glared at the man he'd once trusted.

"You have one minute to be out of this building or I'll call security."

"I never thought you'd turn on me," his father replied.

"I turned on you four years ago when you threatened the woman I love."

Will hadn't meant to declare his love for Cat, but it felt good to finally let the words out. And now more than ever he wasn't giving up. He was going to move heaven and earth to win her back because he did love her. He'd always loved her if he was honest with himself. And he wanted a life with her now more than ever.

Bella was having a fund-raiser this coming weekend and Will knew he was going to need reinforcements. He wasn't letting Cat go. Not this time. Never again.

"I figured you'd be at work today." James sank down onto the chaise longue on his patio as Maisey played in her sandbox. "You look like hell, man."

Will shoved his hands in his pockets and glanced toward the ocean. "I feel like hell. Thanks for pointing it out."

"You still haven't talked to Catalina?"

Maisey squealed, threw her toy shovel and started burying her legs beneath the sand. Will watched his niece and wondered if there could ever be a family for Cat and him. She wanted a family and the more he thought of a life with her, the more he wanted the same thing.

"No, I haven't seen her." Will shifted his focus to his brother and took a seat on the edge of a chair opposite him. "Bella's fund-raiser is going to be at the Playa del Onda house this weekend, right?"

"Yes. Dad will be out of town and that house is perfect for entertaining. Why?"

"I want you to ask Cat to help with the staff there." Will held up a hand before his brother could cut him off. "I have my reasons, but I need your help in order to make this work."

James shook his head and stared down at his daughter for a minute before he looked back at Will. "This could blow up in your face."

Will nodded. "It's a risk I'm willing to take."

"What's in it for me?" James asked with a smirk.

Will laughed. Without even thinking twice, he unfastened the watch on his wrist and held it up. "This."

James's eyes widened. "I was joking."

"I'm not." Will reached out and placed the watch on the arm of his brother's chair. "You deserve it back. This has nothing to do with you helping me with Cat. The watch is rightfully yours."

James picked it up and gripped it in his hand. "We've really come a long way," he muttered.

Will had one more piece of business to take care of and he was not looking forward to this discussion at all. There was no way James knew of the affair or he definitely would've said something. Will really hated to crush his brother with the news, but James deserved to know.

"I need to tell you something." Will glanced at Maisey. "Is your nanny here or is Bella busy?"

James sat up in his seat, slid his watch on and swung his legs around to the deck. "Bella was answering emails, but she can watch Maisey. Is everything okay?"

Will shook his head. "Not really."

Worry and concern crossed James's face as he nodded. After taking Maisey inside, he returned moments later, closing the patio doors behind him.

"This must really be something if it has you this upset." James sat back down on the edge of his chair. "What's going on?"

Will took in a deep breath, blew it out and raked a hand through his hair. "This is harder than I thought," he said on a sigh. "Do you remember the night Mum died? Dad woke us and said she'd been in an accident?"

James nodded. "I heard them arguing earlier that evening. I was heading downstairs to get some water and heard them fighting so I went back upstairs."

Will straightened. "You heard them arguing?"

James nodded. "Dad raised his voice, and then Mum was crying and Dad was saying something else but in a lower tone. I didn't hear what all he said."

Will closed his eyes and wished like hell he could go back and...what? What could he have done differently? He'd been a kid. Even if James had gone downstairs and interrupted the fight, most likely their mother still would've walked out to get away from their father.

"What is it?" James prodded. "What aren't you telling me?"

Will opened his eyes and focused on his brother. "Dad had an affair. They were arguing about that."

"What?" James muttered a curse. "Has that man ever valued his family at all?"

"There's more." Will hesitated a moment, swallowed and pushed forward. "The affair was with Maria. Cat's mum."

Will started to wonder if James had heard him, but suddenly his brother jumped to his feet and let out a chain of curses that even had Will wincing. James kicked the leg of the chair, propped his hands on his hips and dropped his head between his shoulders.

"If I'd have gone downstairs that night..." he muttered.

"Mum still would've left," Will said softly. "We can't go back in time and you're not to blame. Our dad is the one whose selfish needs stole our mother. He crushed her. She would've done anything for him and he threw it all away."

James turned. "Does Cat know this?"

Shaking his head, Will came to his feet. "I doubt it. She's never said a word to me."

"Do you think once she knows the truth she'll take you back?"

Yeah, the odds were more than stacked against him, but he refused to back down. Nobody would steal his life again. And Cat was his entire life.

"I don't even know what to say about this," James said, staring out to the ocean. "I never had much respect for Dad, but right now I hate that man."

"I've made his life hell." Will was actually pleased with the timing. "As CEO of Rowling Energy, I've frozen his shares. He can no longer vote on any company matters that come before the board."

James smiled. "If this action were directed to an enemy, dear old Dad would be proud of your business tactics."

"Yeah," Will agreed, returning the grin. "He's not too proud right now, though. But I have more pressing matters to tend to."

James reached out, patted Will on the back. "I'll do what I can where Cat is concerned. I know what this is like to be so torn over a woman."

Torn wasn't even the word.

"I never thought either of us would fall this hard." Will pulled in a deep breath. "Now we need Bella to convince Cat to work the party. I can take it from there. I just need you guys to get her there."

Seventeen

If Catalina didn't adore Bella and her valiant efforts to raise money for the Alma Wildlife Conservation Society which she'd recently founded, Catalina wouldn't have stepped foot back into this house.

But Patrick was out of town and Bella and James had caught Catalina at a weak moment, offering her an insane amount of money to help set up for the event.

In the past week since she'd last seen Will, she'd not heard one word from him. Apparently she wasn't worth fighting for after all. Not that she would have forgiven him, but a girl likes to at least know she's worth something other than a few amazing sexual encounters.

Catalina hurried through the house, hoping to get everything set up perfectly before the first guests arrived.

Okay, fine. There was only one person on the guest list she was trying like hell to avoid.

She'd spent this past week furiously working on her

final designs. She didn't have the amount of money saved up that she wanted before she left Alma, but it would just have to be enough. Alma had nothing left to offer her. Not anymore.

Catalina took a final walkthrough, adjusting one more floral arrangement on the foyer table before she was satisfied with everything. She'd already double-checked with the kitchen to make sure the food was ready and would be served according to the set schedule. She'd also told Bella she would be back around midnight to clean up. There was just no way she could stay during the party. That had been her only condition for working tonight, and thankfully Bella had agreed.

Catalina checked her watch. Only thirty minutes until guests were due to arrive. Time to head out. She'd opted to park near the side entrance off the utility room. Just as she turned into the room to grab her purse and keys, she ran straight into a very hard, very familiar chest.

Closing her eyes, she tried like hell not to breathe in, but Will's masculine aroma enveloped her just as his strong arms came around to steady her.

"Running away?" he whispered in her ear.

Knowing she'd never get out without talking, Catalina shored up all of her courage and lifted her gaze to his. "I'm not the one who usually runs."

Keeping his aqua eyes on her, Will reached around, slammed the door and flicked the lock. "Neither of us is getting out of here until we talk."

"I don't need you to hold onto me," she told him, refusing to glance away. No way was he keeping the upper hand here just because her heart was in her throat.

"I want to make sure you'll stay put."

He dropped his hands but didn't step back. The

warmth from his body had hers responding. She wished she didn't fall so easily into the memories of their lovemaking, wished she didn't get swept away by such intriguing eyes. Even through their rocky moments, Catalina couldn't deny that all the good trumped the bad…at least in her heart.

"I'll stay." She stepped back until she was flat against the door. "If I don't listen now, I know you'll show up at my apartment. Might as well get this over with."

Why couldn't he be haggard or have dark circles beneath his eyes? Had he not been losing sleep over the fact he'd been a jerk? Why did he have to be so damn sexy all the time and why couldn't she turn off her hormones around this man who constantly hurt her?

"There's so much I want to say," he muttered as he ran a hand over his freshly shaven jaw. "I don't know where to start."

Catalina tapped her watch. "Better hurry. The party starts soon."

"I don't give a damn about that party. I already gave Bella a check for the foundation."

"Of course you did," she muttered. "What do you want from me, Will?"

He stepped forward until her body was firmly trapped between his and the door. Placing a hand on either side of her head, he replied, "Everything."

Oh, mercy. She wasn't going to be able to keep up this courage much longer if he kept looking at her like that, if he touched her or used those charming words.

"You can't have everything." She licked her lips and stared up at him. "You can't treat everything like a business deal, only giving of yourself when it's convenient for you or makes you look good in the public eye."

Will smoothed her hair away from her face and she

simply couldn't take it anymore. She placed her hands on his chest and shoved him back, slipping past him to get some breathing room before she lost her mind and clung to him.

"I'm actually glad you cornered me," she went on, whirling around to face him. "I didn't want to run into you tonight, but we both need closure. I don't want to leave Alma with such awkwardness between us."

"Leave Alma," he repeated. "You're not leaving Alma."

Catalina laughed. "You know you can't control everyone, right? I am leaving. In two weeks, actually. My mother and I have tickets and we're heading to Milan."

"What's in Milan?"

Catalina tucked her hair behind her ears and crossed her arms. "My new life. I've been working for nearly four years and I'm finally ready to take my clothing designs and see what I can do in the world. I may not get far, but I'm going to try."

Will's brows drew in as he listened. Catalina actually liked the fact that she'd caught him off guard. He'd been knocking the air out of her lungs for a good while now and it was only appropriate she return the favor.

"I know you're angry with me for blurting out the proposal in front of such an audience, but you have to listen to me now."

"I'll listen, but you're wasting your time if you're trying to convince me of anything. We're not meant to be, Will. We've tried, and we weren't successful either time. I don't want to keep fighting a losing battle."

"I've never lost a battle in my life," he informed her as he took a step closer. "I don't intend to lose this one."

"You already lost," she whispered. "On the island we were so happy and for that time I really thought we could come back here and build on that. But once again, I was naïve where you were concerned. As soon as we stepped foot back in Alma, you turned into that take-charge man who didn't want to look like a fool in front of the cameras. You were embarrassed to be seen with the maid, and then when you realized just how much of a jerk you were being, you opted to propose? Did you honestly think I'd accept that?"

Will was close enough to touch, but he kept his hands propped on his hips. "I reacted without thinking. Dam-mit, Cat we'd just had the best few days together and I was scared, all right? Everything about us terrifies me to the point I can't think straight. I've never wanted anything or anyone the way I want you and I've never been this afraid of losing what I love forever."

Catalina gasped. He didn't just say... No, he didn't love her. He was using those pretty words to control her, to trick her into...

What? What was his end game here?

"You don't love me, Will." Oh, how she wished he did, but that was still the naïve side of her dreaming. "You love power."

"I won't deny power is important to me. But that also means I can use that power to channel some pretty damn intense emotions." He leaned in, close enough for her to feel his breath on her face, yet he still didn't touch her. "And I love you more than any business deal, more than any merger or sale. I love you, Catalina."

She didn't want to hear this. He'd used her full name so she knew he was serious, or as serious as he could be.

"I don't want this," she murmured, trying to look away, but trapped by the piercing gaze. "I have plans, Will, and I can't hinge my entire life around a man who may or may not put me above his career."

And even if she could give in and let him have her heart, she carried this secret inside of her that would surely drive another sizeable wedge between them.

"Listen to me." He eased back, but reached out and placed his hands on either side of her face. "Hear every single word I'm about to tell you. For the past four years I've fought to get you back. At first I'll admit it was because my father wanted something else for my life and I was being spiteful, but the longer you and I were apart, the more I realized there was an empty ache inside of me that couldn't be filled. I poured myself into work, knowing the day would come when I'd take over Rowling Energy. Even through all of that, I was plotting to get you back."

He stared at her, his thumb stroking back and forth along the length of her jawline as if he was putting her into some type of trance.

"Just the thought of you with another man was crushing, but I knew if I didn't fight for you, for us, then you'd settle down and I'd lose you forever. I've always put you first, Cat. Always. Even when we weren't together, I was working my way back to you."

When she started to glance away, he tipped her head up, forcing her to keep her eyes on his. "You think I was working this long to win you back just to have sex with you? I want the intimacy, I want the verbal sparring matches we get into, I want to help you pick up those little seashells along the beach and I want to wake up with you beside me every day for the rest of my life. Rowling Energy and all I have there mean nothing in the grand scheme of things. I want the money and the power, but I want you more than any of that."

Catalina chewed on her bottom lip, trying to force her chin to stop quivering. She was on the verge of losing it and once the dam burst on her tears, she might never regain control.

"Before you decide, I don't want anything coming between us again," he went on. "I need to tell you something that is quite shocking and I just discovered myself."

Catalina reached up, gripped his wrists and eased his hands away from her face. She kept hold of him, but remained still. "What is it?"

"There's no easy way to tell you this without just saying it."

Fear pumped through her as her heart kicked up the pace. What on earth was he going to reveal? Whatever it was, it was a big deal. And once he told her his shocking news, she had a bombshell of her own to drop because she also couldn't move forward, with or without him, and still keep this secret.

"I found out that my father and your mother had an affair."

When Catalina stared at him for a moment, his eyes widened and he stepped back. She said nothing, but the look on his face told her all she needed to know.

"You already knew?" he asked in a whisper. "Didn't you?"

Cat nodded. Will's heart tightened. How had she known? How could she keep something so important from him?

"You've known awhile," he said, keeping his eyes on her unsurprised face. "How long?"

Cat blinked back the moisture that had gathered in her dark eyes. "Four years."

Rubbing the back of his neck, Will glanced down at

the floor. He couldn't look at her. Couldn't believe she'd keep such a monumental secret from him.

"I didn't know when we were together," she told him. "My mom told me after we broke up. I was so upset and she kept telling me how the Rowling men… Never mind. It's not important."

Everything about this was important, yet the affair really had nothing to do with how he felt for Cat. The sins of their parents didn't have to trickle down to them and ruin their happiness.

"I still can't believe you didn't say anything."

Cat turned, walked to the door and stared out into the backyard. Will took in her narrow shoulders, the exposed nape of her neck. She wasn't wearing her typical black shirt and pants. Right now she had on a pair of flat sandals, a floral skirt and some type of fitted shirt that sat right at the edge of her shoulders. She looked amazing and she was just out of his reach, physically and emotionally.

"I wanted to tell you on the island," she said, keeping her back to him. "I tried once, but we got sidetracked. That's an excuse. I should've made you listen, but we were so happy and there was no such thing as reality during those few days. I just wanted to stay in that euphoric moment."

He couldn't fault her for that because he'd felt the exact same way.

"There's just so much against us, Will." She turned back around and the lone tear on her cheek gutted him. "Sometimes people can love each other and still not be together. Sometimes love isn't enough and people just need to go their own way."

Will heard what she was saying, but how could he not hone in on the one main point to her farewell speech?

"You love me?" He couldn't help but smile as he crossed to her. "Say it, Cat. I want to hear the words."

She shook her head. "It doesn't mean anything."

"Say it." His hands settled around her waist as he pulled her flush against him. "Now."

"I love you, Will, but—"

He crushed his lips to hers. Nothing else mattered after those life-altering words. Nothing she could say would erase the fact that she loved him and he loved her, and he'd be damn it if he would ever let her walk away.

Her body melted against his as her fingers curled around his biceps. Will lifted his mouth from hers, barely.

"Don't leave, Cat," he murmured against her lips. "Don't leave Alma. Don't leave me."

"I can't give up who I am, Will." She closed her eyes and sighed. "No matter how much I love you, I can't give up everything I've worked for and I wouldn't expect you to give up your work for me. We have different goals in different directions."

The fear of losing her, the reality that if he didn't lay it all on the line, then she would be out of his life for good hit him hard.

"I'm coming with you."

Cat's eyes flew open as Will tipped his head back to see her face better. "What?"

"I meant what I said. I won't give you up and you're more to me than any business. But I can work from anywhere and I can fly to Alma when I need to."

"You can't be serious." Panic flooded her face. "This is rushed. You can't expect me to just say okay and we'll be on our way to happily-ever-after. It's too fast."

Will laughed. "I've known you since you were a little girl. I dated you four years ago and last weekend you spent nearly three days in my bed. You said you love me and I love the hell out of you and you think this is too fast? If we move any slower we'll be in a nursing home by the time you wear my ring on your finger."

"I can't think." Once again she pushed him aside and moved past him. "I can't take all this in. I mean, your dad and my mom...all of the things that have kept us apart. And then you corner me in a laundry room of all places to tell me you want me forever."

"So we don't do things the traditional way." He came up behind her, gripped her shoulders and kissed the top of her head. "I'm done with being by the book and boring. I want adventure, I want to be on a deserted island with the only woman in the world who can make me angry, laugh and love the way you do. I want to take care of you, I want to wear out the words *I love you* and I want to have no regrets from here on out where we are concerned."

Cat eased back against him, her head on his shoulder. "I want to believe all of that is possible. I want to hold on to the hope that I can still fulfill my dreams and I can have you. But I won't give up myself, no matter how much I love you, Will."

Wrapping his arms around her waist, he leaned his cheek on her head. "I wouldn't ask you to give up anything. I just didn't want you leaving Alma without me. We can live wherever you want. I have a jet, I have a yacht...well, I'll have a new one soon. I can travel where I need to be for work and I can take you where you need to go in order to fulfill this goal of yours. I want to be with you every step of your journey."

"I want to do it on my own," she stated, sliding her hands over his.

"I wouldn't dream of interfering," he replied. "I'll

support you in any way you need. I'll be the silent financial backer or I'll be the man keeping your bed warm at night and staying out of the business entirely. The choice is yours."

Cat turned in his arms, laced her hands behind his neck and stared up at him. "Tell me this is real. Tell me you don't hate me for keeping the secret and that you will always make me first in your life."

"It's real." He kissed her forehead. "I could never hate you." He kissed her nose. "And you'll never question again whether you're first in my life."

He slid his mouth across hers, gliding his hands down her body to the hem of her shirt. Easing the hem up, he smoothed his palms up over her bare skin, pleased when she shivered beneath his touch.

"Are you seriously trying to seduce me in a laundry room all while your sister-in-law is throwing a party to raise money for her foundation a few feet away?"

Will laughed as his lips traveled down the column of her throat. "I'm not trying. I'm about to succeed."

Cat's body arched back as her fingers threaded through his hair. "I hope no partygoers take a stroll through the backyard and glance in the window of the door," she panted when his hands brushed the underside of her breasts.

"We already made headlines." He jerked the shirt up and over her head, flinging it to the side without a care. "Another one won't matter at this point."

"What will your brother think if you don't show at the party?"

Will shrugged. "James is pretty smart. I'd say he'll know exactly where I am."

Cat started working on the buttons of his shirt and

soon sent the shirt and his jacket to the floor. "We still don't have a solid plan for our future."

Hoisting her up, Will sat her on the counter and settled between her legs. "I know how the next several minutes are going to play out. Beyond that I don't care so long as you're with me."

Will kissed her once more and eased back. "But I already have the perfect wedding present for you."

Cat laughed as her arms draped over his shoulders. "And what's that?"

"A maid. You'll not lift a finger for me ever. I want you to concentrate on your design career and the babies we're going to have in the future."

When Cat's smile widened and she tightened her hold on him, Will knew the four years he'd worked on getting back to her were worth it. Everything he'd sacrificed with his father and personal life was worth this moment, knowing he was building a future with the only woman he'd ever loved.

* * * * *

MILLS & BOON®

Desire™

PASSIONATE AND DRAMATIC LOVE STORIES